AFTER
SHE'D
GONE

Also by Alex Dahl

The Boy at the Door
The Heart Keeper
Playdate
Cabin Fever

AFTER
SHE'D
GONE

Alex Dahl

An Aries Book

First published in the UK in 2022 by Head of Zeus
This paperback edition first published in 2023 by Head of Zeus,
part of Bloomsbury Publishing Plc

9 7 5 3 1 2 4 6 8

A catalogue record for this book is available from
the British Library.

ISBN (PB): 9781801108287
ISBN (E): 9781801108294

Typeset by Divaddict Publishing Solutions

Printed and bound in Great Britain by
CPI Group (UK) Ltd, Croydon CR0 4YY

Head of Zeus
5–8 Hardwick Street
London EC1R 4RG

WWW.HEADOFZEUS.COM

For the fiercest women I've known – Marianne, Fevziye, Emmanuelle, Silje Birgitte and Anastasia

Part One

I

Adrian

Before the bell sounds and the children surge toward the brightly lit building, he hides among the trees at the edge of the schoolyard. He knows them well, these trees, and can easily tell one trunk from another by touch. He especially likes a trio of tall pine trees that marks the end of the school grounds; if he pushes his way through their low, dense branches that touch at the tips, there is a cozy, silent space in the middle. He waits quietly until the last child has disappeared through the sliding doors, then he slips out from his hiding place and runs quickly across the empty playground. He usually manages to take his seat in the classroom at the exact moment the teacher walks in and presses the door shut behind herself. He sits right at the front, by the window; they decided it was best that way. He likes it there; he can watch the black winter sky weaken into a misty gray, and the barely moving lights of the cars that crawl up toward the motorway.

Sometimes, the flight path is directed over the town, and

he gets to see the planes just after takeoff from Torp, the roar of the engines momentarily drowning out the teacher's monotonous voice. In his mind, he places himself inside the plane as he watches it rise upward, and instead of gazing out the classroom window, he is looking out of the plane's plastic one, down at the school. He knows where each plane that takes off from Torp is going to: he memorized the schedule long ago, so quite often he's already looking out the window by the time the plane appears, anticipating the 0820 KLM City Hopper to Amsterdam, or the 0905 Widerøe Fokker X to Bergen. From his window seat he can see the big, ugly school nestled in between the paint factories by the water, and the patch of trees at the edge of the playground. He can even see the boy among the trees, waiting for playtime to be over, revealed from the aerial vantage point.

The teacher knows that he needs these interludes, these moments of losing himself in thought and gazing out of the window, so she doesn't say anything, just keeps talking and lets him be. The other kids sometimes make a mean comment or emulate the sound of a plane when they see him looking out the window. One boy, Steffen, frequently throws little rolled-up scraps of paper at the back of Adrian's head, but Adrian makes a point out of never responding, never turning around. His mother says that bullies are actually just weak people who try to zap some of the strength out of those they sense are stronger and better than themselves, but Adrian doesn't quite believe her – it sounds like something adults say to make kids feel better.

The teacher talks about different kinds of grain and how they are grown. She draws a rudimentary illustration of various grains on the whiteboard: wheat, barley, rye, corn. Adrian pays careful attention and copies the drawing into his notebook, but he doesn't feel quite right today and his hand trembles as he moves the pencil across the page. It's Wednesday, and he always finds the first day of the week back at school difficult after a peaceful weekend at home with Mama. Yesterday they baked cinnamon buns together, his favorites, and the delicious scent of them lingered in the house this morning when he'd sat at the kitchen table chewing his breakfast, dreading the moment it would be time to go off to school. He watched the crawl of the long hand on the clock on the wall; when it touched the 5 it was time to leave. Mama had already left and he'd have to set off on the twenty-minute walk to school in the dark and bitter cold. These things didn't bother him much; it was more the fact that he'd end up at the school when it was finished.

'Do you know how cross-germination works?' asks Marie, the teacher. Adrian likes her; she's kind to him and makes every effort to make him comfortable. Once, at the beginning of the year, she'd pulled him aside at the end of a particularly bad day, and said softly – *You know, Adrian, it's a good thing to be like you.* He wants to put his hand up and speak, because he does indeed know how cross-germination works, but he knows that it would be impossible. The words wouldn't come. His voice wouldn't be able to carry them. He feels Marie looking at him, and he knows that she knows that he would be able to answer the question, that he is perhaps the only one in the class who could, but he's careful to avoid her gaze. To Adrian it feels difficult and often impossible, to meet the eyes of other people. It's as though the act of sharing a gaze is just too much; it leaves him with the sensation of a burn. Sometimes he can bear to look into Mama's eyes, the eyes that are so like his own that he has the sensation of looking in the mirror, but even then, he has to work up to it, to consciously steel himself for the moment when they fully look at each other.

The bell sounds and he's filled with an instant, visceral dread. It's too soon. He's barely gotten used to being inside the warm, lit-up building after the long walk in the dark and the silent moments between the trees, and now it's time for the first break. The children lurch to their feet and rush from the room. Adrian stands up too, slowly, and shuffles toward the door; as much as he doesn't want to go outside, risking being left alone with the boys in the class, he also can't bear Marie's pity if he stays behind at his desk. If he's lucky, he might be able to slip out from the school's less-used side entrance; it's closer to the far end of the playground and the trees. He turns the corner, avoiding the glances of the other kids, keeping his eyes firmly on the linoleum floor, then on the rectangular window inset into the door at the far end of the corridor. It's just gone nine thirty and there is a beautiful, deep-blue light outside, giving Adrian the sensation of looking into water from the windows of a submerged ship.

'Hey there,' says a voice, close to his ear. He freezes in his tracks, one hand on the door handle.

'He can't hear you,' says another voice, this one ice cold and cruel: Steffen. 'He's deaf, remember?' Adrian moves swiftly forward, using all his force to shove the door open so he can run outside into the freezing blue air, away from them, but he is jerked back hard, by a hand grabbing the hair at the back of his head. It hurts terribly and Adrian crumples to the ground, breathless. He makes himself stay completely still, focusing on stopping the tears that pool in his eyes.

'He's not deaf,' says the first voice, belonging to a boy called Josef, Steffen's henchman, a burly and dumb kid Adrian recognizes by his shoes. 'He's just a mute.' The black, scuffed sneaker in front of Adrian's face suddenly leaps into action and delivers a swift kick into his shoulder. He sits up and tries to get his bearings. If only he could get to the door...

'Fucking weirdo,' says Steffen, laughing. He grabs him by the hood of his parka and drags him back up to his feet. Adrian's knees are trembling and he feels as though he'll fall back down if Steffen releases his vice-like grip. 'Can you imagine being that fucking weird?' The two boys laugh. 'Hit him,' says Steffen, so Josef does, very hard, in the soft pit of his stomach.

'If you tell him to stop, he'll stop,' says Steffen.

'Yeah,' says Josef. 'Just say stop.' Adrian pushes his tongue against his teeth, mouth clamped shut. All he has to do is find the word, that one word, *stop*. But he can't. Josef hits him again, in the face, so hard he topples over and strikes his cheekbone on the window ledge as he falls. They both laugh.

'Why don't you just tell him to stop?' says Steffen, pushing his wide, red face close to Adrian's, his sour breath making Adrian's stomach lurch. 'Look at me. I said, look at me!'

'Hey! Stop! Let him go!' a voice hollers down the corridor. Steffen's grip is instantly released. The two boys shoot out the door, leaving it swinging on its hinges, icy air being sucked into the building. Adrian collapses back on the floor but is picked back up again, very gently this time. 'Oh no. Oh, sweetie,' says Marie, touching a patch of broken skin on his cheek with her fingertip. 'I'm so sorry.'

* * *

They can't get hold of his mother, but after the school nurse has disinfected the cut on his cheek and pressed a plaster across it, he's allowed to sit out the rest of the morning in a corner of the teacher's room, doing exercises in a physics book. Steffen and Josef are sent home, not for the first time. At lunchtime, he tries to eat his lunch, but feels violently nauseous and needs to lie down in the nurse's office. They still can't get hold of his mother.

He must have fallen asleep for a moment because when he opens his eyes again, someone is sitting beside him on the sofa – it's Marie.

'I'm going to drive you home, okay?' she says, softly, taking his hand in her own warm one.

In the car, Adrian looks out of the window. It's just past two o'clock and already the light is reduced to a violet gloom. Marie doesn't speak, but he can feel her occasionally glancing over at him. She knows where to drop him off, that the road doesn't go all the way up to the house; it's not the first time she's driven him. She pulls over in the lay-by tucked in from the road beneath a rocky outcrop on top of which row upon row of new houses are being built. On his way to school, Adrian sometimes takes the longer route up the hill and past the building site, walking beyond the path, close to the drop, looking out at the harbor basin spreading out far below. More than once, he's imagined losing his footing and tumbling down the cliffside, his broken body landing messily in the lay-by where Marie has just stopped the car. He can almost see himself out there, in front of the car on the asphalt, dead.

'Bye, sweetie,' says Marie. 'Please tell your mom to call me, or stop in to see me, okay?' Adrian nods and watches as she pulls away and merges back into the traffic toward the town. He steps onto the steep path that leads from the main road and toward their house nestled high above the western end of the town, on top of the next cliff over from the one where the houses are being built. His mother has told him that the construction company wants to buy their house too, and demolish it to build modern apartments, but that she'll never sell it. The thing she loves about it, which Adrian loves too, is that it sits entirely on its own, shielded from view by a thick line of trees on one side, and by the massive rocky cliff on the other, below which lies a narrow strip of sand, completely unreachable by car. Once it was a summer cabin and the people who owned it used to moor a little boat down on the beach, accessing the house by a narrow, perilous path. Then the new road was built, bringing the house considerably closer to the town, but to access it, you still have to walk the final stretch, up and down, past the beach, through the last steep thicket.

At home, Adrian closes the door behind him, then he begins to cry, unleashing everything he has held inside. His howls tear through the little house, sounding like wind trapped in the chimney. He paces through the house aimlessly, trying to dissolve the feelings he can't put into words, throwing things to the floor as he goes. Clothes from hangers, a framed photograph of himself as a much younger child, newspapers left on the table, books from the bookshelves; all indiscriminately flung to the ground. The glass frame shatters and it's as though its sound brings Adrian back into himself, making him stop in his tracks. He stops crying and stares at the mess he's made. Slowly, he makes his way back through the rooms, picking up everything he has thrown around, placing everything carefully back in its designated place. He sweeps up the glass shards of the picture frame and places the photograph itself between the pages of an encyclopedia in the bookshelf, hoping Mama won't immediately notice its absence.

He feels exhausted, and walks over to the bench beneath the window in the kitchen. He sits there for a long while, looking out over the town, and has the strange sensation that though the world is out there, he's not really a part of it. He can see cars lining up to drive onto the ferry to Sweden, specks of people walking home from work, another plane taking off in the distance, turning east and quickly disappearing into the low gauzy clouds – it's the 1510 Ryanair flight to London Stansted. The people out there all seem to be going places, meeting family and friends, doing things. Adrian never goes anywhere; he's never even been on a plane. He doesn't have family except for Mama. The kids at school are so different to him, even the ones that aren't mean. It's like he's a different species, a strange little bird who should be among other strange little birds in the sky, or sitting in a tree, except he's never met anyone like himself.

The sun has gone down beyond the hills across the inner harbor, leaving the sky a wistful indigo. Adrian waits and waits, feeling empty inside, unable to motivate himself to get up off the bench and do something, anything, like he normally would. Just after four, when it is completely dark and Adrian struggles to tell the lights from the houses scattered on the hills surrounding Sandefjord from the pinprick stars appearing in the sky, Mama's key slots into the lock. He waits for her to drop her bag on the ground in the hallway, kick off her shoes, and to make her way into the open-plan kitchen and living area, letting her discover him. At the sight of his bruised face and sad expression, Mama's expression darkens and she rushes over to him and cups his face in her hands.

'Who did this to you?' she whispers. He won't look at her, but she angles his face so that in the end, he has no choice. 'Tell me, baby. Please.' He shakes his head.

'Let's have a burgers-and-Boeings kind of afternoon,' says Mama, knowing it's the only thing that could make him feel better.

* * *

They walk slowly together down the ice-encrusted path, then along the wooden walkway that leads from the beach, up the rocky hill to the main road. They don't have to wait long for the bus, which pulls into the lay-by where Marie dropped Adrian off hours before, but still they're shivering from the few minutes spent standing still. They sit side by side in silence until they reach the airport.

Outside, it's minus thirteen degrees Celsius and they walk quickly toward the terminal building, holding hands. There's a McDonald's in the arrivals area, with a seating area overlooking the runway. Mama orders the food at the self-serve station, then brings it over to where Adrian is sitting staring out at the flashing red light from the air traffic control tower. He gets to work on his cheeseburger and fries, his eyes not leaving the skies for a moment.

'Look,' he says, the word clear and strong. 'The Amsterdam plane's early.' Mama follows his pointed finger to a pinprick light pulsating above the frosty forested hills to the north. They watch as it moves closer, going from a barely discernible speck of light to a nimble white-and-blue Fokker 70 that perfectly touches down on the runway.

There is a lull in the traffic, but Adrian doesn't tire from staring out the window, waiting. Mama sits quietly, lost in thought. A Boeing 737 from Wizz Air lines up on the runway, its white fuselage twinkling in the glare from the lights at the far end of the runway. Adrian sits rapt, enthralled, entirely still, his fingers hovering above the rest of his fries, careful not to make a sound as the plane revs its engines, sending hot air crumbling from the turbines. It surges toward where they're sitting in the warm terminal building, strangely slowly, as if it is too heavy to take flight, but as soon as the nose lifts, the plane is in its element and it goes from clunky and earth-bound to something other, a thing of the heavens, a beautiful, roaring bird of prey.

Mama stands and motions for Adrian to follow. She strokes his hair, then places his fleece hat back on his head before they step outside. They don't speak all the way back to the house, not even on the walk from the lay-by; they just walk quickly beside each other in the icy darkness of the January evening, gloved hands intertwined. Later, when Adrian is in bed, Mama sits by his side.

'We might go away sometime soon,' she whispers in

their secret language, gently stroking the curve of his brow. Adrian looks at her, and their eyes briefly meet before he feels he has to look away. He realizes she looks different suddenly, but struggles to identify the expression on her face: fear or sadness, or perhaps both?

'Where?' he says, his voice unfamiliar and loud in his little room. Mama smiles and kisses the top of his head, her lips lingering on his skin.

'I don't know,' she says. 'But I know that I love you more than anything and will always keep you safe.'

2

Liv, two days later

Like every day, I arrive before eight, when the sky is still pitch black and studded with pinprick white stars. It's fifteen below zero outside and my breath emerges in visible bursts as I move around my little office getting set up for the day. I turn the heating on and make coffee, staring out the window at the rolling, snow-covered fields shimmering in the waning moonlight as the water in the kettle rises to a boil. I keep my jacket on while I wait for the heating to kick in, sipping my delicious, hot coffee, my laptop still closed in front of me as I look for the first signs of daybreak outside. For a long while, I sit at my desk, just waiting, allowing whichever thoughts drop into my head, until a deep blush appears on the horizon above the furthermost fields, where the farm borders thick forests. Indigo and red streaks of light reach across the sky and the moon recedes, dropping below the line of trees in the distance. A huge, burning sun bearing the otherworldly pink Arctic light appears, casting the snowy fields in shades of rose and gold.

I should get going, I have a lot to do, but I'm mesmerized and moved by the beauty of the sunrise that is unseen by those still sleeping snug in their beds or sitting at desks with less panoramic views than mine. From here in this ancient barn converted into garages and storage units and a single office – mine – all I can see are fields and trees and a small section of a big lake, now frozen solid. The only sign of human activity I ever see from here is an occasional ice-skater venturing out onto the lake, a black speck of a being moving in slow, wide circles, like a fly. I also see airplanes dropping slowly from the sky down toward the runway at Torp Airport, very close by but entirely concealed by the forest. Because I can't see any signs of the airport itself, it looks like a scene from a disaster movie – a passenger plane crashing into remote woodland. When I first came here, I'd almost brace myself for the sound of impact, for flames and thick black smoke rising into the air every time a new plane appeared and then disappeared into the clutch of trees. I was on edge back then, always jumping at any unfamiliar sight or sound, constantly on high alert and running on adrenaline. In many ways I still am, but I've relaxed into this tiny space where I spend most of my days.

I love this view and have been surprised by how healing I find it, to be in such close proximity to nature. I often imagine that I'm somewhere else; this place bears similarity to many other places. I play a little game with myself, in which I'm not Liv Carlsen on a farm on the outskirts of a little Norwegian town, but a woman in Switzerland, perhaps, or Canada, or the southwest of France. This woman is younger than I am, and for her all the doors are still open, every opportunity and imagined future are still available to her. Unlike me, she can get up from her desk and walk outside into the shockingly cold air, carrying the scent of untouched woods and deep, black lakes, and just set about changing the constructs of her life.

When the last trace of the night is gone from the sky, I open my laptop and enter the long series of passwords and disablers on the systems. I wait as my various inboxes scan for new emails and retrieve the two phones from where I've taped them under the first drawer in the desk. I make another coffee and force myself to wait until it is finished before glancing at the screens. Nothing. Usually, nothing is good, but at the moment, I'm waiting for something and for every day that passes without contact, I get increasingly anxious.

I scan the markets from Nikkei to London Stock Exchange to Nasdaq, all looking good. At noon I eat two boiled eggs and two slices of ham I brought with me from home, then I put my jacket on and head for the door. I don't often leave my space in the barn during the day; I make every effort to minimize the chance of bumping into Kai, the farmer I rent the space from. He seems like a nice enough guy, but the less contact we have, the better. I push the wide old wooden door open and it creaks loudly, but when I step out into the farmyard, there is no sign of anybody. The animals are shut inside because of the ongoing extreme cold spell and Kai and his wife are probably running errands; both their cars are gone.

I loop around the back of the barn and walk briskly alongside the field, heading toward the woods. I didn't bring gloves and even though I'm clenching and unclenching my hands in the pockets of my down jacket, they quickly grow numb with cold. I turn around and look back at the red barn with its little grid windows, sills painted white. I imagine myself as I usually am, sitting at my desk, staring out at this woman half walking, half running toward the woods. A loud rumble stirs the air and I follow its direction upward, to a blue-and-yellow jet on final approach, flaps fully extended, wings visibly trembling on the wind, dragging a gray shadow fast across the fields. If Adrian knew that I came here every day, to this place with unrivaled views of his beloved planes, he'd beg me to take him here. I turn back toward the barn and try to picture my son looking back at me from the office window beneath the eaves, but find it difficult to build the image; for his own safety he'll never come here and he'll never know about this place or what I do here.

My face stings with cold and I pick up my pace into a light run; I want a few moments in the woods before I head back to the office. In spite of everything, in these moments, running as fast as I can bear on the hard, ice-crusted snow, taking shallow breaths of pure, icy air, I feel young again. I reach the forest and slip into its hushed, cathedral silence. This place reminds me of home and though I try to banish those thoughts, I can't and I allow the tears that spring to my eyes to run warmly down my face and drop off my chin. As a child I used to spend a lot of my time in the woods, it was my safe space. It still is. I focus on deep breaths and the sense of calm I only ever feel down here, among the tall, snow-laden pines. Adrian is the same; he feels the trees the way I do, and sometimes, in the summers, we pull mattresses out into the clearing by the house and sleep surrounded by trees. I run my fingertips down a gnarled tree trunk, picking at a frozen trail of sap. I pocket a couple of pinecones for the office and, clutching them in my hands, I slip out of the forest and begin the dash back across the fields.

The farmer's car is back in the farmyard, and I slip quickly into the red barn across from the farmhouse. Upstairs, I flick the switch on the kettle and rub my arms hard to regain warmth. I feel much calmer than I did. I'm about to pour myself a cup of peppermint tea when I happen to glance at one of the phones, which, unusually, I left out on the desk. There's a new message from an unstored number, but I recognize it instantly.

Poppy down, it reads.

I sit down heavily in the chair, a surge of adrenaline rushing through me. I immediately stand back up again, scanning the tiny, sparsely furnished office as if for a clue for what to do next. *Poppy down.*

'No,' I whisper out loud. *Please, no. Not now.*

Lilia thrives in warm weather, I write back, then I switch off the phone.

I open the drawer and find a needle kept there for this purpose, and insert it into the side panel of the phone, an older Samsung Galaxy. The panel slips open and I retrieve the SIM card. I cut it into pieces, as tiny as I can manage, before carefully scooping up the debris and depositing it into a clear plastic bag, the kind used for cosmetics at airport security. I open the laptop and reenter the long series of passwords on the various systems. I set up the emergency transfers to the remote servers like I've practiced before, and watch the rainbow wheel spinning as the systems get underway. Everything needs to be off this laptop, now.

I sit down on the floor as the computer works; I need to

focus on not panicking. *It's okay*, I tell myself. This doesn't necessarily mean anything at all. But it does. I know it does. And either way, I can't take any chances. I think of my son, my sweet, vulnerable little Adrian, who in this exact moment will be walking home from school in that slow, thoughtful way of his. It's a long walk home for him, but he never complains, not even now in the depths of winter. He likes to stop and consider his surroundings as he walks and in the evening he'll tell me about what he's discovered: a tree ripped from the ground by the recent storms, a new house taking shape on the housing development he passes, a beached jellyfish on the strip of sand far below our house which sits perched on top of a rocky promontory overlooking the sea.

But not this evening. Because we need to leave.

Twenty slow, deep breaths. My heart rate returns to almost normal. Ten more mindful breaths; I'll never need a clear head more than in these moments. Do I really have to do this, to leave it all behind? Adrian has never known any other life than this one. He's never been on a plane. He's not like other little boys, not at all... I force my mind back to the moments when I last wrote to Poppy. It was over a week ago. A clear, beautiful morning like today. What exactly did I write? I close my eyes, imagine my hands preparing the parcel. The tickets, the money, the note. I wrote it on a blue Post-it and stuck it to the plain white envelope containing the money. I can see it in my mind now, my hand moving the pen quickly across the scrap of paper, and my exact words:

'Tell M Lilia is still safe and at home.'

I go into system preferences on the laptop and select

'Return to factory settings', wiping the hard drive clean. Once it's done, I pour a bottle of mineral water over the keyboard and watch the screen flicker, then blur, then die.

I get up and move quickly around the little space, grabbing the laptop and shoving it into a weekend bag alongside the phones, the portable Wi-Fi router and a few pieces of paper from the desk. I grab some antibacterial wet wipes from my handbag and carefully wipe down every single surface and the metal handles on the door and window. I allow myself a long moment at the window, drinking in this view for the last time. It's not yet three o'clock in the afternoon and already the light is dusky pink and weakening. By daybreak, if all goes well, I'll watch the sun rise again from an entirely different place.

I shut the door behind me silently and pad down the stairs. Stepping back outside into the afternoon, I make myself walk away from the farm toward the bus stop on the main road at a normal pace, not looking back once, fighting a strong urge to break into a run. As I go, I try to call Adrian, but he doesn't pick up. Again and again I try, but there's no answer.

3

Adrian

Adrian sits on the floor with his legs crossed underneath him, the phone propped up against an empty cereal box in front of him. His fingers are nimble and fast-moving, and he wedges his tongue between his teeth in concentration as he slips the last few loose paper ends underneath the plane's undercarriage. He pinches the long nose of the aircraft, nice and elongated and pointing slightly downward, good – optimal aerodynamic velocity. Almost ready to fly. The YouTube tutorial ends in a flurry of drumbeats, and the finished Concorde, identical to the one in his hand, glides beautifully through the air before the screen goes black. Adrian especially likes Madplanez' tutorials because they are set only to music. He doesn't like the ones where he's told what to do: *fold here, tuck this underneath, fold again, blah blah.* Why do they have to say it when they can just show it?

To Adrian, words are like diamonds: hard, difficult to come by, and shouldn't be thrown around. He knows they can be beautiful too, like when Mama sits by his bedside in the dead of night when she thinks he's sleeping and whispers to him in their secret language. My little bird, she calls him, and the words take him from his bed to the skies where he can fly freely, feeling the cool wind tickle his belly, where forests and lakes and cities and people are just a blurry smudge far below, where he can adjust his speed and trajectory with the smallest flick of a wingtip.

Adrian stands up and smiles to himself at the sight of the paper plane in his hand. It's the best one he's ever done. He contemplates waiting until Mama comes home before flying it, so they can watch its elegant, silent journey through the still air of the living room together, but his hand trembles with desire to launch it, and he knows he won't manage to wait. He walks over to the sofa by the window and stands on the armrest, his back to the dark night sky outside. It's only just gone 4 p.m. but now, the second week of January, it's pitch dark. Adrian doesn't like being home alone when it gets dark so early in the afternoons, but it's more manageable since Mama gave him the iPhone and he discovered the paper plane tutorials. The hours he has to wait for her to come home, which used to feel so long and frightening, suddenly seem to melt away as sheet after sheet of paper take on the shapes of F-14s and F-18s and MiG-21s and Typhoons beneath his fingertips.

Adrian stretches as high as he can, pinching the Concorde between his index finger and thumb, aiming for a straight flight path past the dining table, past the bookshelves, into the wide-open space of the kitchen. Then he lets go. The plane glides perfectly through the air, its slender delta wings reaching behind its long, elegant body, and Adrian watches it with his mouth dropped wide open, his mind spinning. He can practically see the tiny pinprick people inside the narrow fuselage, and imagines the sonic booms of the aircraft reverberating through the atmosphere as the Concorde hurtles high above a black, glinting ocean. Mama is going to love this one. Adrian rushes across the open-plan room to retrieve the plane, which has landed perfectly in the middle of the kitchen floor, but is jolted by the unexpected sound of the doorbell.

He stops dead in his tracks, fear washing over him. This has never happened before. Nobody comes here, ever. Nobody rings that doorbell. He turns toward the entrance door; he can see it from where he's standing. A stained-glass window is set into the door, luminated by an outdoor lamp, and Adrian can make out the outline of a large man. The doorbell rings again, shrilly, followed by an urgent knock rattling the flimsy glass pane. Adrian closes his eyes, tries to center his thoughts, to not give into the panic that comes more easily to him than to other little boys.

He glances toward his phone that is still propped up against the Frosties box on the floor. Four eighteen p.m. Mama's usually here at four thirteen or four fourteen so why isn't she back yet? And what is the right thing to do? He could move silently over to the phone and call Mama so she can tell him what to do. Or he could answer the door – it's what people do when the doorbell rings. He knows this because he's seen it on TV, and besides, that's why people have doorbells in the first place. Only, theirs has never rung before.

Adrian fastens the chain on the door, the one they use only at night. His hand trembles visibly, like it did only moments ago, but then it was with excitement over launching the jet. He unlocks the top lock, then the bottom one, and opens the door a crack, making the metal chain snap tight. On the doorstep is a stranger. The man clearly wasn't expecting Adrian because his mouth drops open and his eyes look wild and alarmed, like people in cartoons when they're surprised. Adrian waits for the man to say something, but he doesn't. He must have rung the wrong doorbell.

'Oh, my God,' the man says, finally, in English. Adrian knows a little English because they are taught it in school. 'Is your, uh, mother here?'

Adrian stares at the man and shakes his head slowly. This is true.

'Do you know when she'll be home?' the man asks, but Adrian doesn't quite grasp the words and by now he feels as though he might black out from stress, so he closes the door and flicks the locks, but immediately the man starts knocking, harder now. 'Open the door,' he says. 'You need to listen to me. Please. Please, open the door.'

Adrian takes a few faltering steps backward into the house then he feels filled with a surge of urgency and rushes over to his phone. His mind feels strange and wired, like he is thinking all the thoughts he would normally think in a day all at once. The man, the door rattling, Mama not home, the plane, the pitch-black night sky, fear like a cold bullet in the pit of his gut, Mama, where is she, the perfect, slow glide toward the kitchen floor, the man's voice and wild eyes, the darkness. Adrian opens Facetime and calls his mother.

She answers straight away, her familiar face looking

nervous or maybe sad but it lights up at the sight of her boy, then grows alarmed at the sight of Adrian's terrorized expression. She glances around, and satisfied there's nobody there, lowers her voice to a whisper.

'Where have you been, Adrian? I've tried to call you many times.'

There's a loud noise on the line, and he realizes it's his own strained breathing. He knows what he needs to say but the words won't come. They are like little pebbles in his mouth, clearly discernable, but he can't get them out. His mother looks around again, then whispers for him to use his signs.

'Mmmmmm,' he stutters, and when he manages to wrench his mouth open at the end of the long, humming consonant, only a strange scream emerges.

'Adrian, honey, slow down. What's happening? Baby, stay with me, look at me. Adrian. Breathe. Come on, honey. Breathe.'

Adrian drinks in his mother's face; her big, worried eyes, her painted pink lips held open in a slack O, her dark hair emerging from her wool hat and flying about as she picks up her pace. He can make out the glint of the water behind her, and the masts of boats to her side. She's taking the shortcut across the boatyard; it's not far, she'll be here in a few minutes; she's practically running now, but he needs to get the words out, to warn her.

'Mmmmmm,' he tries again. 'S–s–s–s–s!'

'Adrian, my love, listen to me.' Mama stops, brings the phone very close to her face. 'What you're experiencing is panic. We've talked about this. And how frightening it is. I'm so sorry you're feeling like this. Can you try to take three very deep breaths, and find your words to tell me what is happening?'

Adrian stands entirely still and listens out for the knocking, but it has stopped. He looks into his mother's eyes. They're gray and far apart, like his own, only his are blue. He takes three very deep breaths and feels his heart begin to calm down in his chest.

'A man,' he whispers. 'There's a man at the door.'

'Adrian, listen to me,' Mama says, her voice louder, and she is running again now, the orange streetlights behind her jiggling, 'Do not open the door. Don't open it. Whatever you do, don't open the door. I'll be home in five minutes. Count with me.'

Adrian begins to count in his head to the words Mama says as she rushes home toward him; *one, two, three, four*, but just as she is about to say 'five', a shape, unmistakably a very big man, lurches toward her from the right, where the footpath borders the water, and Mama unleashes a bloodcurdling scream, like a cat that's been stepped on, and the phone screen swoops as Mama drops it, briefly taking in the crescent moon, the side of the storage buildings, the man – whose face is covered, leaving only slits for eyes – and the water shimmering with light from stars and windows and streetlights, before it skids across the boardwalk and the screen goes black.

'Mama!' screams Adrian, again and again, and this word comes easy for him. 'Mama!' But Mama is gone.

4

Anastasia

She sets her alarm for 5.30 a.m. every day. It's a habit instilled in her by her grandmother, who perhaps wished she'd taught her only child the same discipline. Anastasia swiftly flicks the button on the alarm clock to not wake the others; the walls are thin and her tiny windowless bedroom is wedged in between the larger one shared by Xenia and Natalia, and what had once been the dining room, where Micki sleeps. She slips from the bed and goes to the kitchen where she silently prepares a strong, black coffee. She drinks it by the window, watching the cool moonlight sparkle in puddles on the street far below. She runs through the day ahead in her head. Six castings before noon, five after. She takes a step back from the window and takes in her reflection staring back at her. Eyes big, hair wild and piled atop her head, dark hollows beneath her cheeks, her neck like a long, fragile stalk.

When she has finished the coffee, she stays a while at the window, looking out over the sleeping city. After two months here, everything about it still feels strange. The language, the buildings, the people, all like they've been drenched in beauty but don't even notice it. To them, all this beauty is intrinsic, matter of course, how it always was and how it always will be. The language, of course, owns its beauty and shows it off in its impossible lingering successive vowels and irresistible melody, so far removed from Anastasia's tightly structured, sharp mother tongue. The buildings, too, are far removed from the remote countryside environment of Anastasia's childhood, and every day she experiences a deep thrill in her belly as she leaves the top-floor apartment, running her hand along the oak handrail, smoothed by centuries of hands, as she descends five floors, then steps onto via Melzo.

It feels as though there's a somber hush over Milan in the early morning, in spite of the busyness and traffic and rush of people, and Anastasia enjoys the walk from the Porta Venezia district, across the fashion district and the city center to the agency on via Savona. If it rains, she takes the metro, but at this time of year it rarely does, and Anastasia likes to angle her face upward toward the sun as she walks.

Today, she dresses slowly, slipping on a pair of high-waisted jeans that clearly shows off her tiny waist, and a white fitted T-shirt, a variation of what she wears most days.

Let them see you, not your outfit, Graziela says.

She brushes her hair slowly and carefully, teasing out the knots that have formed overnight at the nape of her neck, until her thick golden-blond mane is smooth and shiny, before gathering it up into a high ponytail. It was one of the first things Graziela said to her, at the beginning.

That face is going to change your life, put your hair up so they can see it...

It's not yet seven when she emerges from the turn-of-the-century building with its ornate facade and small balconies laden with flowers, on the top of which lies Anastasia's cramped apartment, once the servants' quarters. She smiles at the man who runs the coffee bar on the corner of via Lambro. Like every morning, he's busy positioning the metal chairs and tables on the pavement, and tips an imaginary hat dramatically at her and says, '*Buongiorno, la russa più bella...*'

She walks quickly, dodging newspaper carts and dogs out for their morning walk, dragging along Milanese ladies hiding bleary eyes behind enormous black sunglasses. She weaves between children being herded to daycare through gridlocked traffic, taking her usual and favored route down Corso Venezia, then across Corso Giacomo Matteotti and up via Monteleone. *The tenderloin of Milan*, says Graziela. For Anastasia, heading across the city to the agency, it's a slight detour, but she takes this route whenever she has time, as a reminder of where she is and where she is going. She passes Bulgari, Louis Vuitton, Dolce & Gabbana, Prada, Salvatore Ferragamo and then comes to a stop in front of Gucci. The window display shows a mannequin posing with a riding crop, its tip teasing the cheek of a male mannequin who has been placed on the ground, face pressed into a dense fake-grass lawn. A sharp stiletto pins the man to the ground, and a bamboo-handle handbag dangles above his head. On the wall behind them hangs a huge poster picturing supermodel Mariana Toledo cradling the same bag in her arms like a newborn. Anastasia stares at the strange scene, then moves her gaze to her own reflection in the glass.

She tries to imagine her own face in the place of Mariana Toledo's, on billboards across Milan, and other cities too, places she dreams of going: Paris, London, New York. Anastasia Nikitina – the newest face of Gucci. An impossible dream only months ago, and yet, yesterday the call came.

'Pietro and Luigi at Gucci can't wait to see you tomorrow,' said Graziela, unable to keep a deep tremor of excitement from her husky voice.

Anastasia takes a deep breath and continues slowly up via Monteleone, but now the upmarket Italian streetscape momentarily blurs in her mind and becomes the sun-speckled forest track she stood on, many months before, when she first met Graziela Marco. The woman had stepped out from a big group of tourists, men and women from all over the world who had stood talking in a cacophony of languages, taking in the golden cupolas of the memorial monastery and the floral tributes deposited for the martyrs. Anastasia had grown suddenly aware of being studied and her actions had gone from automated to self-conscious as she dragged the broom across the steps of one of the smaller buildings. She turned around and came face to face with the woman who'd separated herself from the group. The woman was staring at her, mouth dropped open, as though she'd suddenly caught sight of a mythical creature out there in the vast woods. A slim, olive-skinned hand bearing several gold rings on each finger clutched a camera strung around her neck. A stream of sweat ran from the woman's temple down the side of her face and dropped onto her mustard-yellow blouse.

She said something, but Anastasia couldn't understand what it was. The woman took a couple of steps closer to her and started laughing a little. Anastasia felt self-conscious and disturbed by the woman's strange behavior and looked past her for signs of her grandmother, who, when she last saw her, had been working on the flower beds by the statues, but now there was no sign of her.

Beautiful, said the woman, and this word Anastasia knew. *So beautiful.* She gestured to the camera around her neck and before Anastasia realized what she meant, she'd lifted it to her eye and fired off a series of shots.

Two days later Anastasia and her grandmother took the bus into the city center. Anastasia felt overwhelmed, almost paralyzed, by the big city; though they lived only a few miles outside the urban area, theirs was a life dominated by the dacha and its rambling, demanding gardens, the forests and the rhythm of the seasons, and their work keeping the grounds at the martyrs' monastery. Anastasia couldn't remember the last time she had been to central Yekaterinburg. She retained only a few painful memories of her very beginnings in an especially impoverished part of the city, when she still lived with her mother, before she'd died and her grandmother had come to her rescue, raising her in the wilderness of Krasotski Maga, her cozy, little dacha and its wild gardens.

She and Vera walked from the bus stop on Ulitsa Borisa Yel'tsina toward the hotel, a monstrous mirrored structure looming over the river Iset's left bank. It was June and the river lay languid and silvery across the city like a slinky necklace. The air was hot and humid, even early in the day. Anastasia and Vera stepped into the lobby of the Hyatt

Regency Excelsior and there, waiting for them beneath a strange and modernistic display of oversized light bulbs gathered into the shape of a classic chandelier, stood the woman from Ganina Yama. With her was a skinny young man and another woman. She spoke and the man translated into Russian, introducing himself as Yuri. He explained that the woman, whose name was Silvia Nebbio, was a famous fashion photographer. The other woman was introduced as Graziela Marco, of Gio's Modeling Agency in Milan.

'You are simply exquisite. Special. One in a million,' translated Yuri, as Silvia spoke and Graziela nodded gravely. 'You have to come to Milan.' Anastasia had barely heard of Milan, and would not have been able to locate Italy on a map any more than she would have been able to spot the ninth moon of Saturn in the night sky. She'd left school at fourteen and since then, she'd tended the grounds at Ganina Yama with Vera.

Less than a month later, Anastasia left for Milan. And it wasn't until she was on a plane for the first time ever that Anastasia began to grasp what she was leaving behind. The weeks between that first meeting with Silvia and Graziela and the moment she sat strapped into a narrow seat and watching the Yekaterinburg urban area peter out and get swallowed up by huge swathes of forest, had just flown by. Twice more she'd gone into the city, once to be photographed by another photographer, this one a Russian man who didn't say a single word, merely giving instructions to turn this way or that with a slight wave of his hand; the second to obtain the necessary documentation for her Italian visa, as well as a passport. Anastasia had never left Yekaterinburg Oblast, the city and county of her birth. She'd never had a bank account or a passport or a mobile phone. All of these were now given to her. She'd laid them out on top of the wooden chest in her bedroom and every time she looked at them, she'd be struck by a deep trepidation. She felt as though the predictable future she'd envisioned had simply been erased, replaced by an opaque black hole into which she was expected to leap.

In the evenings, she'd sit outside with Vera on the rickety deck, overlooking the sea of flowers and foliage stretching out in front of them, bathed in the fading golden light of dusk, and bordered by a wall of dark pines beyond. They'd sit eating pistachios and roasted sunflower seeds, swatting at the persistent mosquitoes drifting in clouds into the gardens from the slow-moving twin streams on either side of the property. Anastasia would sit through waves of panic at the thought that soon, all of this would be half a world away and Vera would be here alone, tending the earth as she always had, and she herself would be in a big city where she knew no one, where she would not be able to understand a single word, alone for the first time in her twenty-two years. Vera would sense when she experienced a moment of fear and would lace her fingers through her own soft, warm ones. Anastasia would close her eyes then, and draw in the scent of her childhood drifting into her nostrils from Krasotski Maga's garden: rhubarb, lilies, tomatoes, Siberian orchid, Perovskia sage, Russian Easter lilies, chrysanthemum, bluebells, cardinal tulips...

Lost in thoughts of home, Anastasia drifts through the city, not noticing her surroundings and navigating purely from habit, until she comes to a stop in front of the modern building housing Gio's Modeling Agency, where she presents herself every morning. She allows herself another brief moment holding onto her memories, and summons Vera to mind. If her grandmother could see her now, standing in front of one of the world's leading modeling agencies, about to be seen by the senior casting team at Gucci, her weather-beaten, sweet face would break into a wide smile and she'd reach out and smooth down the stubborn stray hairs that stick up at Anastasia's temples, like she always did.

Krasivaya Anoushka, she'd say. Beautiful Anoushka. For a moment, Anastasia turns her face up to the bright morning sun and closes her eyes. Then she goes inside.

* * *

It's late afternoon. Her limbs and joints ache after a long day of walking between castings, but now the moment has come; the most important one. She walks into the room as another girl walks out; she, too, is unusually tall, angular, striking. They exchange a quick glance, not hostile but not friendly, either.

'Walk, please,' says one of the two men seated on white plastic chairs to the side of the room, a large, empty space at the top floor of a modern building not far from Anastasia's apartment in Porta Venezia. A third man stands behind a camera, ready. Music starts playing. Surprisingly it's Marvin Gaye's 'Let's Get it On', and as she starts to walk in the self-assured, brisk way she has been endlessly practicing with the encouragement of Graziela, Anastasia feels her nerves melt away and her entire focus is on the steady shuffle of her feet, the perfect turn, the moment of eye contact with the men on the sidelines. After her second turn, the older of the two men, a short and balding man with a surprisingly sweet, youthful face, stops her halfway down the imaginary catwalk. He gets up and walks over to where she stands trembling slightly and her nerves return, making her limbs shake and her mouth feel thick and dry.

The man, Luigi, places a slim, brown hand on Anastasia's hip, drawing her close.

'Yes,' he says. 'You.'

5

Adrian

'Mama, Mama, Mama,' Adrian chants. He keeps pressing the call button on his phone but it goes straight to voicemail, of course it does, he saw himself that she dropped it. He has to help her. He hears a strange sound, a pained wailing like a trapped bird but realizes it's coming from himself. He stands on the back of the sofa and from up there he can see the sliver of pebbly beach far below the house, where his mother should have appeared by now. Is what is happening even real? Did he really see what he saw? He knows that a man came knocking and that his mother was ambushed; he caught sight of the man's shape, though his face was covered. The man must have been the same man who knocked and he must have run down the path toward the main road after Adrian shut the door in his face and happened to bump into Mama. He was looking for Mama. He said.

Adrian jumps back down from the sofa and races around the house, grabbing his things. He shoves his feet into his

Wellingtons and pulls his jacket on. He bursts outside into the clearing, not even remembering to shut the door to the house, leaving it swinging open like a lit-up gaping mouth. It's so cold he lets out a loud gasp, then he remembers to be quiet. He's still holding the paper Concorde in his hand, and shoves it in his pocket. He peers around at the familiar trees, at the lights of the town in the distance, and listens for sounds. He hears nothing except the soft lapping of the waves on the beach. He walks over to the cliff edge; he can see much of the path from there by the light of a huge full moon.

The area is deserted as usual and Adrian has to fight the urge to scream 'Mama' over and over. A small sailing boat is the only vessel in the harbor basin, its bow leaving a thin trail of broken surface ice in its wake. Adrian turns around and runs as fast as he can down the path toward the sea, across the stretch of beach, up the hill and down again toward the main road. He's almost there and can see the moving lights of cars in between the bare branches of the birch trees when he hears a loud rustle immediately to his right. He doesn't have time to register what happens before he is thrown to the ground by a large man, and his mouth clamped shut by a strong, cold hand.

6

Selma

In the hour since she pressed 'Send', Selma has been battling an intense nervous energy coursing through her, glancing up every few minutes to try to gauge Olav's reaction through the glass sliding doors of his office. As usual, he's unreadable, though the frown on his face seems to deepen as he scrolls slowly down through her article. Selma feels emotionally and mentally drained after putting the finishing touches on the feature; as always, she's gone all in, combing through every aspect of each case. She was up until the early hours, correcting minor flaws and typos, and every time she scrolled through the five-thousand-word document, she felt the impact of the images of those poor girls. She knew every detail of their faces and their tragic stories by now and felt the weight of responsibility to share them with *Dagsposten*'s readers.

'Selma? Earth to Eriksen...' Olav is standing by her desk, a bemused smile on his face.

'Oh. Hi. Sorry. I was a bit lost in my thoughts there.'

'I'm not surprised. Lots to think about.'

'Yeah.'

'Would you step into my office for a minute?'

She follows behind her boss, glancing briefly out at Øvre Slottsgate through the wall of windows. The usually busy shopping street is practically deserted – it's the third week of January, already dark at 3.30 p.m. and almost fifteen below zero. A light drizzle of icy snow twirls through the air, caught in shafts of light from the streetlights.

'Take a seat,' says Olav. Selma sits down gingerly at the edge of the chair, fighting the urge to start fiddling with the little glass sculptures Olav keeps lined up on his desk. 'Not going to lie, Selma, this was tough reading.'

'Too tough?'

'No. It's fantastic. Just… wow.'

'Really?'

'Really.' Olav presses a key on his Mac and it flickers to life, and Daria Miloszewa's face stares back at them. 'I'm just so shocked.'

'Mmm,' says Selma, and looks away from Daria to the little glass figures. There's a monkey, an elephant and a giraffe glinting in the sharp light from the overhead light.

'I just can't believe what happened to her. And the others.'

'Yeah. It's unbelievable.'

'I'm wondering what we can do with this. We'll certainly run it, but I'm thinking, can we use this to bring change somehow?'

'Well, I've been in touch with Sara Hallin at Interpol with everything I uncovered, though most of it was already known to them. The problem is that the lowly perpetrators get busted and jailed, but the really powerful ones, the ones that actually orchestrate this kind of thing, are so protected, it's almost impossible to uncover who they really are, and who is protecting them. They're untouchable.'

Selma feels a hot stab of anger at the mention of the men who cause the tragic fate of girls like Daria. Billionaires, politicians, counts and Sirs, businessmen.

'Wait. That's it. The title. I think we should call it "Untouchable".'

'Hmm, you're right. Yes.'

They fall silent for a moment. Selma wills Olav to scroll past the feature's main image; of Daria not as an aspiring model but as a young, brilliant schoolgirl, but he doesn't and she avoids looking straight at it, like you'd avoid staring at the sun. In August, eighteen-year-old Daria Miloszewa was found washed up on a beach in Calabria. Days before, she had cruised down the Amalfi coast on a yacht, in the company of much older men and other girls like herself, young and beautiful, mostly from disadvantaged backgrounds in poor countries, who had come to Italy in the hope of a modeling career but ended up being forced into prostitution. Plied with cocaine and amphetamines, Daria had spent the last few months of her life in a cramped apartment on the outskirts of Milan, alternating between attending endless, mostly fruitless castings by day, and entertaining wealthy men at upmarket private clubs or house parties by night. Her parents back home on a farm in southern Poland plastered the walls of their modest home with images of their stunning only child.

'She was a star,' her mother had said to Selma. 'We don't understand how someone could have treated her like trash.'

It took three hours to interview Daria's mother; she was crying so hard she was largely incoherent. Selma tries to rid herself of the image that had alerted her to the story of prostitution and trafficking in the fashion industry in the first place, but she knows it's etched into her mind forever: Daria's skinny, lanky body, naked but for Swarovski-studded bikini bottoms, facedown in the pebbled surf like a small, beached sea mammal, found by local fishermen at the break of dawn. She recalls how her blood ran cold with fury at the headline of one newspaper – 'Another Teenage Prostitute Meets Tragic Death'. *Another teenage prostitute*. Just another teenage prostitute. Selma had pored over the images, both the dead, discarded young woman and the woman she'd been in life: hopeful, gorgeous, easy prey. Selma wanted to bring her justice. Turns out, it wasn't possible – as much as it mattered to tell the story of Daria and the several other girls like her, it was frustrating to repeatedly come up against a wall of protective silence around those really behind the trafficking and exploitation of the girls.

'I can't control how the girls choose to spend their evenings,' said the owner of one modeling agency. 'Money and beauty go hand in hand,' said another. 'You need to stop asking these questions,' said the aide of a high-profile politician who'd recently been photographed amongst several girls younger than his daughters at a villa party at Lake Como.

'Unless you're making covers and major runways, you can't survive without another source of income,' said one of the girls Selma spoke to on her investigative trip to Milan a couple of weeks previously. She was a pale, serious girl from

Russia, who agreed to speak to Selma on the condition of anonymity, introducing herself only as Nastya. Selma had sat across from her at a tiny blue kitchen table in the apartment she shared with four other Eastern European girls in a rough suburb to the north of the city center. 'I have to pack,' she'd said at the end of her conversation with Selma, showing her to the door. Selma had glanced into the bedroom the girl shared with two other models. On the floor was an open Louis Vuitton suitcase. Nastya followed Selma's gaze and said, 'A gift.'

'Where are you going?'

'Maldives. With two men I know. They're okay. Big money. I'll get some amazing pictures for my Instagram. That's how to break out these days, get enough followers on Instagram and the jobs start to follow. I'm walking for Ermanno Scervino at fashion week. They scouted me on Insta.'

What else do you have to do, besides sunbathe and take pictures for social media? Selma had wanted to ask but didn't need to.

She'd followed the girl on Instagram and, as expected, her feed was filled with impressive images of designer bags, private jets, and exclusive holidays. 'Having a blast at Zaiana Resort', she'd captioned one image. And not a single image was posted of either of the men who'd paid for it all. Selma wonders where she is now, that girl, one of the lucky ones who didn't end up dead on a beach or from an overdose.

She'd spoken to other girls too: a soft-spoken Colombian named Tatiana who had been pressurized into escorting but was currently trying to go back to school, having managed to get clean from heroin addiction, and a nervous-looking French girl who kept bursting into tears, saying Selma 'couldn't imagine' what really happens behind the scenes.

'Tell me, please,' said Selma, but the girl just cried more.

'Right,' says Olav, bringing her back to the present moment. 'Anyway. Well done, Selma.'

'I can't quite leave this behind, you know?'

'I can see why. But I think it's important to remember that you've directed a beam of light at something very dark and unsavory that needs to be spoken about. You're making a difference. Daria will be remembered. And Saffiya. And Lianah. Change will happen. It's already happening. Take MeToo. Epstein. Weinstein. The world is ripe for this conversation now.'

'This runs to the very core of society. I'm certain that there are people who know about this, who participate or condone or benefit from the exploitation of these women, who are at the very top of the pyramid. But they have a wall of protection around them, unlike these girls.'

'You're right. And this article more than alludes to that.'

'Alluding doesn't feel like enough, Olav. I want to take them down.'

'But how?'

'I don't know.'

'Sounds dangerous.'

'I'm not afraid of danger.'

'Now, that is a fact.' An easy smile passes between them, and Selma wonders which one of her unorthodox, sometimes dangerous methods Olav might be thinking of in this moment.

'I was thinking I'd keep digging and we could run a follow-up in a few months. I might see if I could get one of my sources to do a profile interview, but none of the girls wanted to go on record. I guess they are afraid of ruining any chance of a fashion career, and afraid of the men too.'

'Okay. But Selma? Try not to get too immersed in this. We have a lot on our plates right now. We need to be versatile.'

'I know.'

'Which brings me to what I wanted to discuss with you. Have you heard about the strange Sandefjord case?'

'The Sandefjord case?'

'Yes.'

'No, I haven't heard. Why, what's happened?'

'I don't have all the details yet, it only happened last night. A mother and her nine-year-old kid have gone missing, apparently without trace. The boy is very vulnerable, said my brief. Probably one of those awful custody situations and the mom's done a runner. The police are giving a press conference at five at the Plaza. Great if you can come with me.'

Selma's mind immediately darts to the disturbing case of seven-year-old Lucia Blix who was abducted from a sleepover in Sandefjord a couple of years ago, and was only recovered eighteen months later at a remote farmstead in the French Pyrenees, through no little effort on Selma's part; she'd directly contributed to solving the case. In the months after, she was mentally and emotionally exhausted, and she knows Olav was worried about her. She hasn't been back to Sandefjord since, and feels uneasy but intrigued to learn that the sleepy little town is at the center of a child abduction case, again.

'Sure.'

'Ready in fifteen?'

'You bet.'

7

Adrian

It was all a dream. The man at the door and the Facetime call with Mama when she was attacked by a masked man and dropped the phone, the run down the hill and across the beach in the dark, the man who threw him to the ground. He's safe. He's at school, by the window, watching the planes. But then the moments at his desk staring at a meek white sky disintegrate, revealing another reality beneath, and Adrian realizes that *that* was the dream. He blinks but can't see anything. It's dark, and he's facedown, his cheek pressing into a scratchy fabric seat. There is a lurching motion, a screech, and then he's jostled around, something firm slicing into the soft skin of his belly – a seatbelt? He tries to sit up, but he's strapped down and his hands are tied tightly behind his back. That sound again, like the wail of a trapped bird. It's coming from him and he stops himself immediately – he instinctively understands that it isn't a good idea to draw attention to himself. It's too late; the car goes from fast to slower and then slower still before coming to a complete stop. Adrian lies completely still, pressing his face further down into the angle between the seat and the seatback.

He counts his breaths, trying to calm the terrified scramble of his heart. It's just like the racing heartbeat of the little bird he saved from a tangled web of plastic ropes washed ashore on the beach last summer. Its heart tapped against his fingertips as he cradled it, so fast he thought it would have to suddenly stop. He tries to imagine that it's Mama driving the car, that they're going somewhere nice. But Mama doesn't drive. And they never go anywhere. Adrian doesn't mind this; he prefers to be at home in the house perched high above the harbor basin, with Mama, just being. All his life, Mama has treated Adrian like that terrified bird he held in his hands after freeing it from the plastic; she cradles him very gently, protects him, whispers to him in her soothing voice in their secret language. He can be himself with her; it's okay to be weird and easily sad and obsessed with memorizing obscure details about aircraft. It's okay not to speak much; she doesn't try to make him talk or get angry when he prefers silence.

'Hey,' says a voice, and Adrian presses his face even further into the little space. It smells of dust and of detergent. The voice says something else but Adrian can't understand what it is; it sounds like another language. He focuses on remaining completely motionless. He can hear a door open and, moments later, the passenger door by his head opens, bringing a surge of freezing air. He feels the man's hands on him, working fast to free his hands from whatever they've been tied with. When they're free, he can't help but flex and unflex his hands, moving all his fingers in turn, and only now he realizes that it really hurt, to be tied up. He feels a rush of tears down his cheeks and angles his face away from the man as he unbuckles the seatbelt and pulls Adrian up into a sitting position. He doesn't want to open his eyes, and doesn't want to see the man, but in the end he does. It's the man who rang the doorbell. Adrian doesn't know his name and can't ask. The man will have to be just The Man.

'Hey,' says The Man again. He places a big, gloved hand on Adrian's shoulder and squeezes it gently. He says something else and Adrian recognizes the language as English. They learn it at school, but Adrian has never in his life been spoken to in English by an actual English person, though he likes languages and knows many words. Sometimes, when he watches American TV, he can understand a lot of what they're saying, but only when he can also read the subtitles in Norwegian. He can feel The Man stare at him, but won't meet his eyes.

He speaks again, and this time Adrian catches the word 'don't' and 'afraid'. How can The Man tell him not to be afraid when he has just thrown him on the ground and tied him up and driven him somewhere in a car? When he has taken his mama somewhere? Maybe she is in this car, in the boot, afraid—

'Mama,' says Adrian, pleased with how forcefully he managed to say the word. The Man nods deeply and says something Adrian doesn't catch. Adrian stares at him but averts his eyes when The Man looks back at him. He has dark hair that falls into his eyes, longer than most men's, and blue eyes with heavy eyelids. He doesn't look like a baddie except for the tattoos on his hands, but Adrian knows from TV that baddies often look quite nice.

'Where Mama?' asks Adrian.

When The Man realizes Adrian didn't understand what he said, he motions to his eyes and raises his eyebrow in a question.

'Did you see what happened to your mama?' he says slowly, several times and Adrian understands. 'See' and 'mama' – he knows those words. He nods. He tries to speak again, to ask The Man if it was him who took Mama and where she is now, but the words won't come; when he tries to say something it's as though they burst in his mouth like soap bubbles.

'I saw it too,' The Man says. He points to his eyes and to himself. 'I,' he says, then points to his eyes, 'Mama. I saw Mama.' As he says 'Mama', The Man's voice breaks and Adrian thinks he might cry. But baddies don't cry. Maybe he's not a baddie. Or he's a baddie and he's pretending to be a goodie, that's the most likely explanation because only baddies take children away in cars. Adrian looks past The Man, who's crouching in the doorway, to the passenger seat, into the night. All he can see is the dark, jagged outline of trees against the night sky. He turns his head and glances at the empty white road ahead, lit up by the car's front lights; the engine has been left running.

'What's your name?' asks The Man and though Adrian knows what this means, his teacher always asks them the same question in English class, he doesn't want to tell The Man his name. He stares down at his hands. There are angry red marks across the tops of his hands where The Man tied him up and Adrian feels a sudden wild flash of anger. Has he tied up Mama too? Is she perhaps in the boot of the car, unconscious, dangerously cold?

'Will you help me find Mama?' Help, find, Mama. Why would The Man ask him to help find Mama if he took her? And how can Adrian know whether to trust him? Mama always tells him not to trust anyone, no one but her. *You can't*, she says. *But you have me.* Adrian nods. He has no choice but to trust The Man and help find Mama, because what if Mama's never found?

He tries to speak again. He already managed to say 'Where Mama?' once; why can't he do it again? Tears sting his eyes. The Man squeezes his shoulder again and stands up. He leans across and buckles Adrian back into his seat, the normal way this time. He gets back into the driver's seat and puts the car back into drive, merging back onto the road without indicating. He speaks a couple of times more, but Adrian can't understand what he is saying over the hum of the engine, and after a while he seems to give up. Adrian can feel his eyes on him occasionally in the rearview mirror and focuses on keeping his face blank and unreadable. He stares out of the window, following the red blinking light of a plane inching across the sky. He doesn't recognize anything outside, or have any idea which direction they might be heading in. He has never left Sandefjord before and has never sat in a car without his mother. He can feel more tears build up but bites down hard on his lip to stop them, and for a while it works.

The Man maneuvers the car from the road onto a smaller graveled track, and the car shudders along, faster than a car would normally drive on this kind of road. If Adrian said something, it would come out staccato and he can't resist the temptation to try. No words come. He tries again and uses his special trick of exhaling slowly, then halfway through, inserting his voice. When it works, all he has to do is form a word with his tongue and lips. He manages to release his voice and it comes out as 'ha-ha-ha-ha' as the car bounces along the narrow track, long, bare branches occasionally scratching its sides. He clamps his mouth shut and avoids The Man's eyes in the mirror. His heart is still thundering uncomfortably in his chest and he feels like the little bird, captured and incapacitated by scraps of plastic waste. He wishes he could fly like the bird did eventually after Adrian released it. It tottered around on the grass for several moments after Adrian gingerly placed it there, twitching and flexing its wings that had sat uncomfortably pinned to its body, before launching into a seemingly effortless, smooth flight. Adrian imagines pressing the button to lower the window and then just slipping through it, ascending quickly through the night air, watching the car on the road far below grow smaller and smaller.

The car stops again. The Man turns around again and says 'come'. Adrian looks outside; nothing but towering black pines reaching toward a narrow slit of sky. He feels a sudden wave of fear – what if The Man is planning on killing him and burying him out here in the woods? The Man must notice his fear because he smiles at Adrian and says something again in a calm voice. He catches 'please', 'don't', 'afraid', 'big', 'boy', and 'Mama'. They leave the car just standing there by the roadside and start to walk. They follow a map on The Man's phone and Adrian watches the pulsating blue dot on the screen that shows their position. He recognizes the two twin peninsulas of Sandefjord reaching out into the sea and the lake near the motorway.

The blue dot is somewhere in the woods above the lake, not so far from the airport.

They walk fast, shoes crunching on hard-packed, gravel-specked snow. It must be early evening by now and the moon appears in the narrow gap between the trees. Adrian steals glances at The Man as they walk along. He has a scar on his check, and another scar traversing it, as though someone has tried to carve an X into his face. His eyebrows are thick and unruly and sit protruding above his eyes like stony ledges above clear blue rock pools. He's unshaven and scruffy but to Adrian he doesn't seem like the kind of man who sleeps rough. He looks more like one of the nice dads from school if they were pretending to be someone who sleeps rough. Adrian doesn't have a dad, and that's okay because he has a mama who will do everything for him forever. She says. Still, he sometimes misses having a dad like almost all the other kids. A dad who'd pick him up from school, smiling widely at the sight of him. A dad who would drive a nice big car that he could toss his bag into before sinking back into a smooth, warm leather seat. A dad who'd kick a ball with him and play rough, pretend-punching him. Adrian sees these kinds of dads on TV, and also at school pick-up, when many of the kids disappear into the waiting cars purring in the parking lot. He quite often thinks about this on his long, lonely walk home.

He used to ask Mama about his dad. When he was little, he didn't know that everyone has two biological parents, and simply accepted that he only has Mama. After becoming aware of how children are created, he asked Mama about his father. She stroked his hair for a long time until he shrunk away from her – he grows uncomfortable if touched for more than a few moments. And he really wanted an answer.

'He's bad,' she said and her face looked so pained and wrought with sadness that Adrian never asked again. He's bad... He thought about what she said many times. It made him afraid, to know that his dad was bad, because he knew how things work; that children receive parts of their parents, a bit from the mother and a bit from the father. Perhaps this explained why Adrian was nothing like Mama, who was so calm and good with words and always knew what people meant by just looking at their faces. Perhaps he, Adrian, was different and wrong and weird like the boys in his class say because his dad was bad.

Adrian realizes he's stopped walking, and The Man has realized too, and turns around to see what's happening. Adrian forces himself to look The Man in the eyes, even though it feels like a kind of burning. He reminds himself of what Mama says, that it isn't true that people can look into him just because Adrian is able to look into them. He maintains eye contact and The Man says something about 'come' and 'Mama' and 'please'. He rubs his hands together, hard, and Adrian can see that little ice crystals have formed amid the stubble on his face and they twinkle in the moonlight. He draws a deep breath. He holds it inside until he can bear it no longer, then releases it slowly and visibly into the freezing air, finally inserting his voice into the flow of air. He can do this. He forms an O with his lips and even doing it hurts in the freezing cold.

'Who,' he says, clearly, followed by 'you'. The Man is still staring at him, his face awash with the cool light of the moon. Adrian is afraid and has the sensation that he might suddenly strike him. He takes a step back and The Man takes two steps forward, almost closing the gap between them. He drops onto his knees on the hard snow and takes Adrian's hand, though he immediately retracts it. 'Who you?' he asks again.

'Look. I... I'm your dad,' says The Man. 'Father. Uh. Dad. Papa.' The moon disappears behind a cloud and The Man's face is steeped in darkness. Adrian feels as though his legs will buckle. He moves his little finger up and down in his pocket. He nods and starts walking again, past The Man. He knows, now, that he's in real danger and that he mustn't trust this man.

He's bad, Mama said.

8

Selma

The press conference was brief, but the details that emerged were disconcerting, and Selma had felt her intrigue deepen as she considered the circumstances.

A woman and her son, identified as Liv and Adrian Carlsen, missing from a sleepy little town. The police had 'indications' of mental health challenges and the search for them is urgent. No witnesses, even though they likely disappeared in the afternoon on a Friday, when the roads would have been full of cars heading to the mountains for the weekend. *Father unknown*, said the police. Passports left behind in the house. Liv Carlsen does not own a car, nor has any evidence of having rented one been uncovered. The mother and her son have not, so far, been observed on any mode of public transport by members of the public, but police are urging people who may have traveled out of Sandefjord on January 14th to reconsider whether they may have seen Carlsen and the little boy.

What would make a mother take her son and disappear without a trace? Selma wonders.

Now it's late, well past midnight, but Selma can't sleep or even relax. She sits in the swivel chair by the floor-to-ceiling windows, looking down into the frozen valley below her apartment building, where a glaze of ice has settled across the Akerselva River. The myriad lights of central Oslo in the distance merge with the vivid stars on the night sky and the temperature on the thermometer on Selma's balcony reads minus nineteen. The apartment is nice and warm, and Selma cradles sleeping Medusa, who purrs dramatically, in her arms. Occasionally her tiny pink tongue snaps out of her mouth and her eyes open then shut again. Selma smiles down at the little cat, gently scratching the spot she likes behind her ear. It occurs to Selma that Medusa is getting old, and that someday she won't be here, sprawled out on the bed when Selma returns from work, exhausted after another grueling day at *Dagsposten*.

She stands up slowly and places the cat down on her bed in the next room. She contemplates slipping into her pajamas and trying to sleep, but decides against it; Selma has always feared long wakeful hours tossing and turning – that's when all the thoughts come, the thoughts she doesn't want to think, so she never goes to bed until she literally can't keep her eyes open. Tonight she feels especially wired. She returns to the main living space and stares out at the city, loneliness settling in her bones like frost. She could eat something; in fact, she probably should. She's had nothing since she devoured a takeaway baguette at her desk for lunch, hours before her meeting with Olav and the subsequent press conference. She's not at all hungry and can't face the prospect of cooking yet another pasta meal for one, the only food left in the house. The new medicines she takes to help her manage her inattention curb her appetite and she's noticed in recent months that she's gone from slim to scrawny. Almost like the girls in Milan, whose bones jut out, whose clothes hang off them. She makes a mental note to order groceries.

She sits down at the kitchen table and opens her laptop. Might as well do some research; the night is still young.

'Liv Carlsen Sandefjord,' she types.

9

Anastasia

The girls squeal and laugh loudly as they are getting ready, crammed into Micki's tiny bedroom space. The sound of tinny Italian pop music playing from Micki's phone reaches Anastasia through the paper-thin wall. Every few minutes, one of the girls raps their knuckles against the wall and screams, 'Anoushka! Hurry! What are you doing in there?'

Anastasia is on her back on her single bed, which takes up almost all the space in the windowless room. She's reading and rereading the letter that arrived today from Vera, the first this month. Her neat handwriting fills two whole pages, and carefully folded in between the two sheets which are thick and of good, expensive quality, is a perfectly preserved, dried Easter lily, Anastasia's favorite. The flower represents resurrection, which is also the meaning of Anastasia's name. When she was a little girl, only four years old, and came to live with Vera at Krasotski Maga after her mother, Nadia, died, Vera planted hundreds of Easter lily bulbs in the garden. *For your mother*, she said, and it's one of Anastasia's earliest clear memories, that following spring, when her mother had been dead in the ground for almost a year and Anastasia had stood on the deck with Vera at sunrise, taking in the lilies which had bloomed overnight in a riot of deep yellows and golds, a symbol of new life.

She holds the flower to her nose, breathing in deeply, but the dried flower smells of nothing at all. She runs her fingertips across Vera's carefully penned words, slowly deciphering them – it still doesn't come easy for her. At school she had to repeat two years before finally leaving at fourteen; too stupid to read, her teacher had told Vera, though Anastasia had an incredible mind for numbers. Vera made it her mission to help Anastasia with her dyslexia, but she was so traumatized by the way she was treated in school that letters and reading bring on a cold sweat to this day.

Grisha and Kolya miss you, Vera wrote, referring to the elderly brothers who worked in maintenance at Ganina Yama alongside Anastasia and her grandmother. *They want you to send pictures of yourself from magazines and I promised you would when you have some.* For a moment, Anastasia tries to imagine the old men, sitting closely together in the living room of the little house they share at Koptyaki, peering at her face cut from a German *Vogue* editorial or the most recent edition of *Sfizi*, in which Anastasia featured in a 'new faces' line-up, but finds she can't imagine it, as though no part of her could still exist in that other world, not even a photograph. It feels as though she has been neatly sliced out of that life, and that nothing of her could possibly remain there, not even her memory.

It disturbs her to think that Vera, the person closest to her, doesn't know who she is now, or the person she can't help becoming. When she was still at home, going through the daily motions of her life – tending the dacha garden, working at the monastery – she was able to stay largely the same, because how much can you grow and change when every day is a repeat of the last? She had a clear sense of herself then. She knew where she'd come from and what to expect from the future.

And then it all changed, herself included. For a start, she can now speak English. Not perfectly, but enough to get by. She has friends. It was a revelation to her to connect with girls of her own age, from different countries and backgrounds, in Milan for the same reason as her – to build a new life and a career from their looks. Xenia, Natalia, Anastasia, and Micki spend countless hours in the apartment together, cooking strange combinations of the foods they know from home, sharing them with each other, speaking a medley of English, peppered with Russian and Micki's Portuguese. Natalia's Ukrainian *holubtsi*, meat and boiled rice wrapped in cabbage leaves, served with Anastasia's favorite *okroshka*, a cold soup Vera used to make every weekend, oddly paired with a side of sardines marinaded in lemon and olive oil, served straight from the can. They drink cheap unlabeled wine, and occasionally champagne gifted from clients.

Every Tuesday and Thursday evening, Anastasia and Xenia have begun to trek across Porto Venezia to Cagnola where they take a free evening class in Italian. Anastasia has been surprised that she has both an interest and a talent for languages; after only six weeks, she was separated from Xenia and placed two levels above.

Xenia is by far the biggest success story of the girls so far, and the one Anastasia feels closest to. Xenia, too, is Russian, but from a sophisticated and cosmopolitan background in St Petersburg. She knew since childhood that she wanted to be a model, and after three years in London and one in Paris, she arrived in Milan last year. She has already walked for Miu Miu and Bottega Veneta and is highly hyped for the upcoming fall shows. Xenia is even taller than Anastasia, and thinner too. She has unruly, light-blond hair that frames her face like a wispy halo, and beautiful, deep-brown eyes. Her lips are thin but clearly defined and a natural, dusky rose color; whenever she smiles, which is often, a row of perfect, unusually sharp teeth are revealed. She is striking and incredibly photogenic, which the new editorial from *ID* magazine shows off to perfection – the girls pored over the pictures spread out on the kitchen counter earlier in the afternoon. Xenia had posed on a beach in Hawaii, wearing nothing but carefully positioned raw gemstones. In one picture, she's reclining in the sand, clutching a ruby the size of a baseball to her groin, as though someone has just pitched it to her. Her small breasts are exposed and Xenia groaned with embarrassment when Micki pointed out that her nipples were sunburnt.

Red boobies, she said, and they all burst out laughing, the sound reverberating around the small kitchen.

'Anoushka,' screams Natalia and they've momentarily paused the music. 'You sleeping?'

She's jolted from her thoughts, and suddenly she feels claustrophobic in the tiny space.

'I'm coming,' she shouts back. She slips out of the jeans and T-shirt that she's been wearing to the castings all day and takes a black Gucci silk dress from the closet, a gift from Pietro after her first fitting. She still hasn't worked for them besides a couple of fittings, but they've booked her for the autumn–winter show. She takes in her appearance in the narrow full-length mirror on the inside of the wardrobe door. The dress is amazing, accentuating all the right places. Anastasia looks into her own eyes, the ones Vera used to mournfully say she got from her mother, and asks herself in a whisper, in English:

'Who are you now?'

* * *

The party is on a roof top on Via Giovanni Berchet, just behind the Duomo. Its lit-up white spires are breathtaking against the indigo evening sky, darkening to matte black to the east. Anastasia almost has to pinch herself, to compute that such a place could exist, and that she could be part of it. The fashion house Strada is throwing the party, and the huge terrace is populated by various fashion types, some of whom Anastasia knows by sight: photographers, journalists, editors, models, designers, and other industry types. Her arm linked through Xenia's, she crosses the wide-open space that will later become the dancefloor and heads for the bar, which is made from purple glass atop which countless bottles of Veuve Clicquot sit in coolers.

Anastasia can feel the eyes of the crowd on her and focuses on walking elegantly in the high heels Xenia lent her for the occasion. She briefly catches the eye of a man sitting at a low table with another man and three girls, models by the looks of them. He's an attractive man, older than her and clad in typical sharp Italian style with beige chinos, a white linen shirt and soft leather loafers. On his wrist sits a huge gold watch glinting with diamonds. His face is rough with stubble and he has unusual, striking light-blue eyes. He looks like a third Casiraghi brother, and Anastasia makes a mental note to point him out to Micki, who has a huge crush on the Monégasque princes and has hung their pictures above her bed in her tiny space. She catches sight of Graziela in the crowd and, clutching the champagne flute someone has handed to her, Xenia in tow, she heads over to where she is sitting with three men.

'Ah, Anastasia, perfect. You came. You must meet Andrea Fiorentini of Strada. And this is Gianni Terenc from *Vogue Italia*. And, this is Tom Kingsley from America. Andrea, Gianni, Tom, meet Anastasia Nikitina, GMA's newest star. Xenia you know, of course.'

'A pleasure,' says the first man, an elegant man in his forties with a thick mane of black hair and warm, almond-shaped brown eyes. 'Graziela has been telling everyone about you.'

'Hi there,' says Tom, a tall man with facial stubble which stands in sharp contrast to the Italian men's flawless smooth shaves. She's barely heard American English before and he reminds Anastasia so much of a grown-up version of one of the guys in the American high school movies she watches with Xenia and Micki that she has to suppress a little giggle, concealing it as a cough.

Gianni from *Vogue* nods and watches Anastasia carefully as she answers Tom and Andrea's several questions. Does she like Milan? Where in Russia is she from? Does she understand any Italian? Is she doing Paris next month? And New York? Anastasia speaks slowly, taking care with the slippery, difficult English l's and r's, and the men nod and smile encouragingly. She feels momentarily powerful and in alignment with being a young and beautiful woman who can retain the attentions of sophisticated and glamorous men like these. She thinks about the girl from Yekaterinburg, the one who lost her mother to a heroin overdose aged four, who grew up at the edge of the forest where the last tsar and his family lay buried for almost a century, who dropped out of school and worked as a cleaner and landscape assistant at the shrine built in their memories at the burial sites. All those long days spent sweeping stairs and walkways, dodging tourists photographing the shrines to the emperor's dead children, all the long evenings spent at home in the tiny dacha cottage with her grandmother, waiting for the cabbage soup to finish boiling, they all melt away into a distant past and Anastasia realizes she's not an impostor, is not *that* girl pretending to be *this* one; not anymore. This is who she is now: a self-assured, eloquent young woman who lives in Milan and is about to walk down the Gucci runway, who drinks Veuve Clicquot from fragile flutes and spends evenings on rooftops overlooking the Duomo.

***

'Got news for you,' says Graziela, as soon as she walks in the door. Anastasia stares at her, at first wondering whether it could be bad news, Graziela's face is somber and her gravelly smoker's voice unreadable.

'What is it?'

'Andrea Fiorentini called. He loved meeting you last night. You were a real hit with Gianni too. They want to shoot you for Strada's resort collection. In the Maldives.

Next week. We're going to have to clear your schedule. This is a big fat fucking deal, my dear.' Graziela stands up and walks around the desk to give her a big hug.

'What does *in the Maldives* mean?' asks Anastasia. Graziela laughs and hugs her again.

'It's basically heaven. Go get some bikinis.'

'Will you come with me?'

'No, sweetie. I'm busy-busy here. You'll be fine.'

* * *

She's pleased to be allocated a window seat and she watches the lights of Milan grow smaller, then get swallowed up by a thick layer of clouds as the plane ascends, shuddering slightly as it climbs. The cabin is softly lit and the engines whirr as the plane settles into cruise and the 'fasten seatbelts' sign is switched off. The TV screen flickers to life and Anastasia selects the map option. In the next few hours, she will travel high above the Adriatic Sea, then Greece and Turkey, Syria and Saudi Arabia, her plane a moving speck in the night sky, before it will land in Doha. Doha – she says it several times in her head; she'd never heard of such a place until the moment she received her flight to Malé and was told she'd have to change planes on the way.

The map rotates on the screen at the touch of her finger, and she turns the globe eastward, so that the vast bulk of Russia comes into sight. A boy at school once told her that you could fly for ten hours and be above Russia that whole time. She hadn't believed him then, but she does now, seeing it dominate the continent from the Norwegian border in the west to the Bering Strait in the east, a final sliver of land reaching into the Pacific as if for its American neighbor. She zooms in on Yekaterinburg. It seems strange to her that it's much closer to Moscow than to the cities of the Far East. She's never been to the capital; it was never even raised as a possibility for her and Vera to go there. And yet here she is, on a plane from Milan to Doha, then heading onward to a place called Malé. And once she gets to Malé, she has to take a sea plane for more than an hour to get to the place she is going.

The most beautiful place on the planet, Andrea Fiorentini said when she met him again at Gio's Modeling Agency's offices the day before to talk through the job. *Suits the most beautiful face on the planet*, he added, and it wasn't until later that it occurred to Anastasia that he'd meant her. For a moment she studies her reflection in the plastic window. She looks tired and slightly gaunt; the last few days have been stressful – as much as Anastasia wanted to feel blasé and excited about the upcoming trip, the truth is that she's been terrified to get on another plane by herself and fly halfway across the world again, to another new place.

She zooms in even further on Yekaterinburg and although the map isn't of a quality that allows much detail, Anastasia craves its familiarity with a sudden, crushing force: to see pictures of its streets and shopping centers and the river Iset and the vast forests surrounding it. She wrote to Vera to say she would be going away to the Maldives to work, but she knows her grandmother won't know what to make of that, perhaps assuming it's another place in Italy she's never heard of, like Milan.

After a long while, Anastasia falls asleep, her head resting against the curved fuselage of the aircraft. When she wakes again, it's dawn and the huge glowing orb of the morning sun is rising from a wide expanse of water stretching as far as she can see, drenching it in pink and purple. She touches the screen and finds the map again. The plane is banking now and she can make out a string of moving lights on a shoreline drawing closer. According to the map they're flying at an altitude of eleven thousand feet, heading across the Persian Gulf toward the airport. She places a hand on the plastic windowpane. It's the first time she's seen the sea.

10

Selma

She's at the gym shortly after it opens at 6 a.m. Recently, she's been unable to shake off the nervous energy she's been feeling since she's been on the new medication, unless she works out first thing in the morning, even though she's the radical opposite of a morning person. On the few occasions she's skipped her session with the punching bag, the long hours at her desk have felt unsurvivable, so she drags herself from bed, day after day, hours before the sun finally appears in the Norwegian January sky. Medusa, who isn't a morning cat either, barely shifts on the pillow next to Selma's head when she gets up.

She pummels the bag after only a cursory warm-up, launching her weight full-force forward, again and again and again. She's alone in the gym; she usually is for the first twenty minutes or so, until a few bleary-eyed people trickle in, glancing in awe at Selma who's already winding her workout down by then. After, under the hot jet of the shower, she feels a new calm settle in her body, and by the time she's out on the street, walking fast toward downtown through a still-deserted, shockingly cold morning, she feels ready for whatever the day may hold.

At *Dagsposten*, it's just after seven when she walks in, and yet Olav is at his desk, turning slowly round and round on his chair, absentmindedly chewing on the cord from his headphones. Olav prides himself on being old-fashioned, from the ancient Nokia he insists on to the shunning of AirPods and social media. He's speaking into the microphone on the cord but gives Selma a little wave as she passes him. She rolls her eyes at him, then smiles; they have an ongoing competition around who gets in to the office first; they're both single and both notorious insomniacs, and it's usually Selma who wins.

She starts the systems and scans through her incoming emails, all the usual alerts flooding in from news agencies across the globe, sharing mostly sad and shocking manifestations of the human condition: a live hostage situation in Bolivia, a planned and imminent terrorist attack in London narrowly averted, floods in northern Norway caused by melting polar ice rendering a whole little village homeless. She scans the highlights specifically selected for her, looking for matches or relevance to any of her ongoing or planned features but nothing leaps out at her. She decides to get started on the morning's steady stream of black coffee and swings her chair around, about to get up, but Olav is standing there and smirks when she jumps at the sight of him.

'Hey there, Eriksen,' he says. 'Looking a little tired this morning.'

'Not as tired as you, Olav,' Selma counters. 'Oh, wait, I take it back. It's just old age.'

'Ha-ha. Look, I need a word.'

'Sure.'

'Coffee?'

Selma nods and follows behind Olav through the empty office, casting a quick glance through the floor-to-ceiling windows at Øvre Slottsgate outside, which is growing busy with the morning rush hour. Soon, the office will be filled with people, the unbroken hum of voices and the constant bleep from their phones the familiar backdrop to Selma's life. Olav fiddles with the coffee machine and they stand awkwardly waiting as it noisily churns the coffee beans.

'So, what's up?' Selma asks as he hands her a steaming black Americano.

'Some bad news and some good this beautiful, chilly morning, Eriksen. Here's the thing. I can't run your piece on human trafficking in the modeling industry.'

'Wait, what?' Selma places the porcelain mug down on the glass countertop much harder than she intended, the sound echoing around the empty, hushed office.

'I'm sorry,' he says.

'Olav, I don't understand. You said yesterday that you thought it was amazing...'

'I do.'

'But...'

'Orders from above, I suppose you could say. Way above.'

'I'm sorry? I really don't understand.'

'You don't have to. I'm telling you that unfortunately I just don't have support to run this.'

'Support from who? You're the editor in chief. The boss. The head honcho.'

'And yet, I don't own this newspaper. It's not like I answer to nobody, okay?'

Selma's mouth is open in sheer shock at Olav's words. *Orders from above.* What the hell does that even mean? 'Shall I tweak it, maybe? I could make it more about the girls' individual stories, and—'

'I think we're going to have to leave it for now.'

'Are you actually giving me a gag order?'

'Selma, look, it's not like that at all. It's perhaps more a case of being sensitive about where to shine a torch at this exact moment.'

'You said yourself, yesterday, that the world is finally ripe for this conversation. You mentioned Epstein, Weinstein, MeToo.'

'I know. Hey, I know this is disappointing. I'm not very happy about it either. Let's have a think about how we could go about it, okay? But for now, I need you to focus your attention elsewhere for a while. Remember, we've talked about versatility, right?'

'So what's the good news?' she asks, draining the last few sips of her coffee.

'I'm going to need you to head down to Sandefjord this morning. Snoop around a bit. Oh, come on, Eriksen. Wipe that look off your face. You know you love a little guerilla reporting.'

'What are we looking for, exactly?'

'Well. My police source is being cagey and strange about this case. I have a funny feeling about it.'

'A funny feeling.'

'Yeah. You know, a funny feeling, like you get sometimes. I know that you know what I mean.'

'A hunch.'

'Mmm.'

'This morning, I heard that the police aren't looking for anyone else but the mother. They keep referring to mental health, insinuating some history there. But then, the closest neighbor to the mother and son gave a brief statement to a reporter from *VG*, saying she'd seen a man lurking around the house at the time of the disappearance.'

'And?'

'Apparently that's very unusual. They lived in their house alone. She's never seen a visitor there before, ever. And she stated quite clearly that the police seemed dismissive about this observation.'

'Right.'

'Speak to her?'

'Okay.'

'Drag some juicy stuff out of her, Eriksen.'

'You know I will.'

* * *

Selma walks briskly from the station through a light drizzle, following the GPS on her phone. Though it's warmer in Sandefjord than in Oslo, the cold air feels raw and insistent and she draws her jacket tighter around her thin frame. She recognizes the large, white shopping center in the middle of the little town, the square in front of it empty of people. It's Tuesday and just after ten o'clock and it feels to Selma as though the day has been long already; it's strange to think that only five hours ago, she got up from her bed at home and went to the gym. On the train on the way down here, she'd read through her article about Daria Miloszewa and the others, tears pressing into her eyes at the thought that she'd failed them. Sadness gave way to fury to think that an editor at a major newspaper in a liberal country like Norway couldn't run an article pointing the finger toward powerful men with possible links to governments and billon-dollar corporations. *What does it say about power and free speech and value and who really controls the world?* she noted on her phone.

For the last half hour before the train arrived in Sandefjord she'd scoured the various Norwegian newspapers for anything new about the mother and child in Sandefjord, but there was barely a mention. She felt annoyed with Olav too, for sending her off to look into it when it wasn't like she didn't have plenty to do back at the office with a backlog of features that needed tweaking and enhancing before final deadline.

She's walking past the shipyard where the leisure boats have been pulled up for winter, concealed beneath weighted-down moss-green tarpaulins rustling in the wind, when she feels her phone vibrating in her hand. It's an incoming message from Olav; a link to an NRK sending, released on the news less than ten minutes ago.

Woah, he's added. She opens the link and Terje Haakonsen, the head of police, is speaking.

'... new information in the case of the missing woman and her son in Sandefjord has resulted in us classifying the disappearance as more urgent than previously thought. We implore members of the public to get in touch if they have any information at all about the woman, now identified as Liv Carlsen, originally from Holmestrand. She is considered likely to have used one or several aliases. Her son, Adrian

Carlsen, is classified as an extremely vulnerable nine-year-old, with very limited communications skills due to his autism. The police have this morning uncovered significant funds at the property in which Carlsen and her son lived, as well as further information linked to their disappearance. If you have seen or believe you have seen Liv Carlsen and her son, please contact your local police without delay. If you observe them, do not make contact under any circumstances, but immediately get in touch with the police.' The screen goes black but Selma keeps staring at it as though it may leap back to life, then it begins to vibrate.

'Hey there,' says Olav.

'Hey.

'Told you this is fishy. Something very odd going on there.'

'Mmm. Sounds like it.'

'You there yet?'

'Walking toward the house. It's bloody freezing. I would have wrapped up better if I'd thought I'd be going on an impromptu field trip.'

'Call me when you've spoken to the neighbor.'

'Okay.'

Selma reaches the beginning of Vesterøya peninsula, and continues along the water, past the international school and up into a residential area. She vaguely knows her way around Sandefjord after spending quite a bit of time here during the time Lucia Blix was missing, interviewing the parents and just driving around, trying to get a sense of what had happened to the little girl. It's strange to think that right now she's somewhere here in this town, sitting at a desk in a classroom, safe and long-since reunited with her family. Selma wonders whether she ever thinks about the eighteen months she was in the custody of another woman posing as her mother, brainwashing her in a remote farmhouse in the Pyrenees. It would be impossible not to be scarred by an experience like that, but Selma also knows how resilient children are. Her thoughts return to the little boy who has been removed from his known environment, seemingly by his own mother. An autistic child with limited language skills. Selma feels a shiver of fear at the realization that a child like him is extra vulnerable to family violence, and especially if his poor mother is all alone and struggling to raise him. Desperate people do desperate things...

The road becomes a path and loops back down toward the water, overlooking the paint factories on the shore. Selma follows the pulsating blue dot on the map and when the road comes to a dead end she has to check and double-check that she's definitely moving in the right direction. She continues on a small path and arrives at a tiny strip of beach, with a soggy boardwalk onto which fat slabs of seaweed have been thrown by the recent winter storms. Scraps of plastic are strewn across the beach and Selma wishes she had time to stop and pick them up. At the end of the beach the path continues up a very steep hill. At the top, she catches sight of a dark-brown timber house with a shiny moss-green tiled roof. As she approaches, she realizes she's not alone.

Three men in plain clothes stand in the little clearing in front of the house, two talking among themselves, one on the phone.

'Selma!' says one of the men, his face breaking into a wide smile. 'No way!'

It takes her a moment to place him, then she remembers him as Gaute Svendsen, the pleasant and very helpful Sandefjord police detective with whom she was in touch several times when Lucia Blix was missing.

'Gaute. What a pleasure!'

'Looking well,' he says as if on autopilot, then he takes her in properly and narrows his eyes in undisguised concern. 'Well, lovely as always. Maybe a little tired? How have things been?'

'Oh, you know. Busy as all hell, to be honest.'

'I bet. I saw you were working on that corruption case. And the PM candidate who tried to kill his wife in that remote cabin in Telemark. Jesus, that was mad.'

'Yeah, that *was* mad,' she says, laughing to humor Gaute but feeling a quiver of lingering stress in the pit of her stomach at the recollection of some of the very demanding cases she's worked on since they last came face to face. 'So, what's going on here?' she nods toward the curious building, more like a cabin than a house, built on one floor with a wraparound porch, close to the edge of an unsecured cliff above the little beach. A strange place to live with a young child, she thinks. The house is so secluded that if you didn't know it was there, it would be impossible to spot it from anywhere. You'd be highly unlikely to stumble upon the path that leads to it from the beach, the only access point. How did the Carlsen woman manage up here without car access and why would she have chosen such a place in the first place?

'It's pretty weird, to be honest,' says Gaute, lowering his voice to a whisper. His colleague fiddles with the police tape securing the scene, which is fastened to a tall pine tree on either side of the house. The other one is still on the phone, speaking in heavily accented English, apparently imploring someone to send him something by email.

'All ears.'

'Well. I can't really—'

'I think you know I can help you out here.'

Gaute glances back at the house, a concentrated expression on his face. He's a good-looking guy, seemingly of South American origin, with smooth, brown skin and expressive eyes with comically long eyelashes. He looks more like a teenage band member than a senior police officer, thinks Selma, not for the first time.

'We, uh, found an iPad. In the house. Some stuff on that.'

'What kind of stuff?'

'She had searched for "how to disappear", for example. She's also conducted a lot of flight searches over the past few months.'

'To where?'

'Lots of places. Miami, especially. But also LA, Honolulu, and Mexico City.'

'Hmmm. I'm assuming you're checking departure logs, that kind of thing.'

'Yep. Her passport is in the house and we've had no matches from any airport in Norway or elsewhere in Scandinavia that she might feasibly have gotten to.'

'Right.'

'There's more, though. We found an online Penzu diary on the iPad. Some suicidal thoughts and stuff on there. It would seem without intent, but still. She had antidepressants and stimulants in the house, but nothing has ever been prescribed to her according to the medical registry.'

'Not hard to get pills online, Gaute.'

'I know. Just, it seems like a lot of covert stuff. She'd booked a one-way ticket for herself and the boy to Miami about four months ago, back in September. Middle of the school year. She changed it three days before departure, to October. Then never showed up for that flight.'

'Odd.'

'Yep. But what's more, get this – she booked first class on British Airways during the UK half-term holidays. The tickets were nine thousand dollars per seat.'

'Woah.'

'She's a single parent and a cleaner.'

'Right.'

'So we keep digging and when we did a sweep of the house, we found that there's a hollow space in the wall behind the fridge. Six hundred thousand dollars in cash. And almost twenty thousand in the bedroom closet too.'

'What the actual hell?'

'Selma, look. I can't tell you anymore at this point unless you promise not to publish anything at all until we have a clearer picture of what's going on. But I know you can help. In fact, I couldn't believe my luck when you came walking up that track.'

'Fine, yes.'

'Nothing. Until I say.'

'Sure. You know I won't if I say I won't. So, what more do we know?'

'She's from Holmestrand. A couple of the guys are there now, with her mother, trying to figure out if she knows anything. I'll keep you posted. The nearest neighbor, who as you can see isn't very near at all, she saw a man on the beach around the time Liv and Adrian went missing. She also thinks she heard a strange scream from the house, but she couldn't be quite sure. She says it sounded like a child screaming "Mama", but she's never heard the boy speak before and according to his teacher at school, he'd be unlikely to be able to scream or say anything, especially if afraid or agitated. Also, there's a football pitch on the other side of that patch of forest, by the new-build estate. They were playing there at the time, so if the wind was carrying from that direction, it's likely the shout the neighbor heard came from there.'

'Right.' Selma takes notes on her phone, quick bullet points like *Scream? Man? Neighbor?* 'What's the neighbor called?'

'May Hansrud. She lives in the yellow bungalow on the opposite end of the beach below us, where the path leads back up to the main road.'

'I'll speak to her.'

Gaute nods. 'Two more things. Carlsen doesn't work where she told Adrian's school she works.'

'I thought we knew she worked as a cleaner?'

'No, it's what she'd put on the registration papers for the school. It's also what she told Barnevernet when they were involved with the family, first in 2019 and then again last year.' Selma sighs. It's never a good sign when someone lies to Barnevernet, the child protection services, about what they do for a living. 'We checked, naturally, with her purported employer, the deaf school up by Kodal. They'd never heard of Liv Carlsen.'

'What's the last thing? You said two more things.'

'We had a guy call in this morning, saying he'd rented

an office in one of his farm buildings to a woman fitting the description of the missing woman and that she left in a hurry on Friday just after three p.m. He said she practically ran toward the bus stop and that when he went to check, the office had been completely emptied.'

'Hmmm. When did the neighbor say she saw the man?'

'Around ten to four on Friday. She said it was definitely totally dark and that she'd seen him by the light of the moon, which was very bright that afternoon, being full.'

'Okay. I'll do some research. Ask around. Let me know if you come across anything else I could look into.' Gaute gives Selma the name of the farmer and turns around, allowing her to take a few quick pictures of the house on her phone.

'Who owns the house?' she asks.

'We're looking into it. Strangely, it's classified as a business address rather than a private residence. Unusual.'

Selma writes 'house owner!' in her notes.

'Last thing, Liv Carlsen is deaf.'

'Deaf? Are you sure?'

'Yes, Adrian's teacher and the farmer both say that.'

'Right, have you checked whether she's a member of the National Society for Hearing Disabilities?'

'Not yet. But I will, this afternoon.'

'Let me know. She'd have a lot of rights as a single parent with a hearing disability. She'd likely be receiving benefits. And they might be able to shed some more light on her work situation.'

'Got it.'

Selma shakes Gaute's gloved hand, a warm smile passing between them. She can't quite believe her luck, either, that what might turn out to be Norway's next big story is unfolding in Sandefjord and that it's her old acquaintance working on it. She nods at the two other men, who watch her carefully as she heads back down the narrow, icy path toward the beach. The rain has let up but it's bitterly cold, a strong wind jostling the trees and whipping the murky surface of the inner fjord into pointy white crests. She finds her way to the opposite end of the bay and walks through steep terraced gardens up to the yellow house, that of Liv and Adrian Carlsen's closest neighbor.

'Hi,' she says, smiling disarmingly when a stooping, sour-faced lady opens the door. 'I'm Selma. You must be May. I know you've already spoken to the police, but I was just wondering if you'd give me a couple of minutes of your time.' May sighs and looks past Selma, down toward the water. Satisfied there's no one out there about to point a camera in her face, she lets her into a sparsely furnished, pine-clad hallway.

'They're not taking me very seriously, you know. The police. I told them exactly how unusual it was to observe a stranger loitering here. He was down there on the beach, pacing back and forth, muttering to himself. A very strange man.'

'Did you see him actually head up toward Liv Carlsen's house?'

'Yes. And then I heard a strange scream a few minutes later.'

'Had you seen Liv that afternoon?'

'No, but I saw the boy. He came walking home around two o'clock. Not that I look out for them or generally tend to notice their comings and goings.'

Yeah, right, thinks Selma. 'Anything unusual about that?'

'No. He walked slowly, stopping to pick up bits and pieces from the sand as he usually does. He's a strange kid. I feel sorry for him, living on top of a cliff with that deaf mother. She usually comes home after him, rushing along the shore, carrying bags of food. Why doesn't she just go and live in a terraced house in town with driveway parking like a normal single mother would?'

'Have you ever seen other visitors to the house walking past?'

'Never. They keep to themselves, those two. They don't often go anywhere, either. They're up at the house, or down on the beach, collecting things into plastic bags and pointing out birds in the sky.'

'Do they always use sign language among themselves when you've observed them?'

'Yes.'

'So you've never heard Liv Carlsen speak?'

'Never. Though she waves at me sometimes. Seems nice enough, just odd. She left me a note once, when I'd broken my hip, saying she'd be happy to help with anything if I needed it.'

'Did you observe the man leaving again on Friday?'

'No, that's the strange thing. I thought I heard someone run past, down on the beach, just moments after the scream, but by the time I'd opened the front door to get a better look, it was all quiet.'

'I see,' says Selma opening the taxi app on her phone. She won't get anything more out of May. It's obvious that she would be only too happy to talk if she actually knew something. It is a long walk from the station and if she's going to have time to speak to the farmer before she heads back to Oslo, she's going to need to get a move on. She thanks May and steps back outside, hopping quickly down the stone steps toward the path running alongside the beach. It's a beautiful and secluded place, and Selma totally understands why Liv would have chosen to live here, rather than in a boxy modern terraced house in town.

The taxi waits in a lay-by on the main road and Selma sinks gratefully into the back seat. After her conversation with Gaute and May, her interest in Liv Carlsen's disappearance has increased tenfold and her mind is spinning with all the new information. It's a long car ride, all the way across central Sandefjord and up to the E-18 motorway, across the other side of it and toward Torp Airport. The farm sits entirely on its own at the edge of Fevang, encroached on by forests. It's not as remote as it might look; when Selma steps out of the taxi she can hear the hum of cars on the motorway beyond the trees and as she walks toward a cluster of modest farm buildings with its characteristic red barn, like those peppered across the Norwegian rural landscape, the roar of a jet taking off from Torp rips through the air. She discreetly shoots a couple of pictures of the farm buildings but as she's about to ring the doorbell of what seems to be the main house, she realizes she's being watched by a very large man in muddy blue overalls, peering at her from a side door of the barn. She smiles her most disarming smile and gives the man a light wave. He steps out from the barn into the snow-covered courtyard and slams the door very hard behind him with a loud metallic bang.

'What do you want?' he barks.

'Oh, hi there, you must be Kai Oserød?'

'Who's asking?'

'I'm Selma Eriksen. I work for *Dagsposten*.'

'You need to leave. I've already told the police everything. And they promised they'd keep reporters away from here. This is a working farm. Now get out of here.'

'Sir, if you'd just give me—'

'I'll call the police.'

'Kai. Wait. Listen. I promise I won't publish anything at all. I just have a couple of very minor questions. Look, a mother and her very vulnerable child are missing here. I like to think I might help find her. It was me who helped find Lucia Blix. Please?' Kai flinches at the mention of Lucia Blix, but doesn't answer. He glances back at the barn briefly, and Selma looks in the same direction, but there's nobody there.

'You've got two minutes.'

'Thank you. I wondered whether the woman who rented the office space from you came here every day.'

Kai nods. 'Yes she did. Approximately nine to three.'

'Did you often speak to her?'

'Almost never. She's deaf.'

'Right. Did she wear a hearing aid or any other visible aid?'

'Not that I ever noticed.'

'How did you communicate with her if you almost never spoke to her? You must have had some dealings, in terms of rent, bills, that kind of thing.'

'By email. She always pays on time, cash. Which is very annoying. Thankfully Norway will soon be the world's first cash-free society. What kind of person would rather use cash? Anyway. She's polite. Nods at me and my wife whenever she comes and goes.'

'Did you have any indication of what she does here? Or why she wanted to rent an office in such a remote location?'

'She said she was an online therapist for the deaf in her first email to me two years or so ago. You know, she's quite odd. Didn't even want the code for the Wi-Fi which was included in the rent, saying she had her own.'

'Ah. And did you ever see her drive a car? Or in the company of anyone else?'

'No.'

'What did she look like?'

'Dark hair, dark eyes. She looked kind of, uh, foreign. You know. Portuguese maybe.'

'Portuguese?'

'Yeah. Dark hair. Thick lips. Very tall. Didn't look like a mom from Sandefjord.'

'Kai, I've noticed that you have a CCTV camera over there, above your front door. Do you think there's any chance the camera could have caught imagery of Liv Carlsen at any point?'

'No, I had it put up last year, after a burglary. Smashed my fucking window in, they did. Gypsy thugs.'

'Right.'

'Your time's up now.'

'I won't bother you any more, Mr Oserød. Thank you so much for your time. One more thing. If you think of anything at all that might be of some importance, can you please get in touch with me? Here's my card.' The hand that grabs the card is meaty and red from the biting cold. Kai shoves it into the chest pocket of his overalls, then turns around and heads back toward the barn without a word of goodbye.

***

Selma jumps on a bus that thankfully happens to come along as she reaches the main road; she realizes it must be the same bus Liv Carlsen would take back into Sandefjord after doing whatever it is she did here at Kai Oserød's farm. She pulls her phone from her jacket pocket and messages Olav, her fingers stiff from the freezing cold.

Hey. I'm going to stay for a day or two. You were right about fishy. Call me tonight.

Back in town, she checks into Hotel Kong Carl and is given a lovely plush room on the top floor overlooking the ground-floor terrace and a large primary school at the end of the road. She stands at the window as the final bell rings and the children file from the building in a blur of padded jackets and wooly hats. She thinks of the little boy who is somewhere a little further along the same spectrum as herself, on the run with his mother, who is perhaps depressed and suicidal or caught up in something unsavory and criminal, from what she can surmise so far. Selma knows the feeling of being trapped in her own body, unable to speak of what's happening inside of her; it wasn't until she discovered writing in her teens that she was ever able to truly connect with other people and put meaning into words.

ADHD with mild Aspergers was the diagnosis she'd eventually received in her late teens, and she'd felt a mixture of relief and confusion; she'd known that she was different from the other kids but she'd also instinctively felt that this difference was an advantage. It was disturbing to be told that it was, in fact, a spectrum diagnosis. These days, Selma manages it well with a combination of a healthy lifestyle and medication at times of stress. She still believes that her neurodiversity directly benefits her career. She may not be able to sustain focus on tasks that don't interest her, but she has a vivid inner life and the ability to build richly detailed scenes in her mind that often cast new light on the cases she's working on.

Selma concentrates on evoking an image of where the boy might be in this exact moment, and a vision comes to her like she hoped it would, so that when she looks down, it's onto small milky white hands clasped tightly together. She has the sensation of fast movement as a snow-laden landscape blurs past outside. Jagged breath, a dull ache from an empty stomach, the familiar feeling of not being able to eat even the tiniest morsel anyway, a huge painful lump wedged in the throat. So vivid is the construction of the scene in Selma's mind that when she touches a hand to her hair, she can feel the short, silky hair of the boy in her imagination, even the tiny flick of a severed curl behind her ears. She keeps focusing, trying to gain a sense of who he might be with, but there is nothing, nothing but a dense and silent white space between the boy and the world.

'I'm going to help you,' she whispers into the deepening blue afternoon, her breath forming a patch of steam on the windowpane, in which she scratches a perfect 'S', like a snake, with her index finger. Then she retreats to the king-size bed, grabs her laptop from her bag and gets to work.

II

Liv

It's nice, to be rocked like this. So gentle. It's warm and dark and there is a strange sound, *click, click, click*. I think of a fetus in the womb, snug, sheltered, rocked.

I try to open my eyes, but I'm so tired. No. Not tired. I can't open my eyes because they're stuck together.

A voice, muffled, far away. A man, laughing.

I try to sit up and only then do I realize that I'm not tucked in or snug, but bound by chains. It seems like I'm inside a sleeping bag and that metal chains have been wound around me on the outside. I try to move my hands and the movement prompts intense pain – I'm handcuffed. I instinctively open my mouth to scream, but stop myself before a sound emerges; I don't want to draw attention to the fact that I'm conscious.

My left eye opens a crack, but it hurts as if someone has pummeled me in the face and left me covered in bruises, which I realize is most likely the case. I can't see anything at all; it's dark like inside a coffin.

Adrian. His name appears in my aching mind like a flash of lightning, and it is this that makes me unleash a cry, I can't help it. My boy. I need to get to my boy. I remember something now. His face, terrified, on my phone screen as I was rushing home. *A man had come to the house*, he said. And then a man lurched at me from out of nowhere.

Could it be…? I begin to pray in my head, desperately and obsessively: *please, please, please*, I say, over and over, *please, no…*

I hear the strange sound again. *Click, click, click.* I can barely move an inch. The boot of a car? No, a different kind of movement and no engine sounds. Somewhere nearby, above me, the man laughs again.

Click, click. Waves. The clicking is the sound of waves licking the bough of a boat and I'm inside the boat, sailing away from Sandefjord, my baby, my whole life.

Please, no, I whisper, feeling the sting of tears in my eyes. *Not like this.* The boat rolls on, and I feel my life with Adrian, this quiet, careful life with my boy in a Norwegian seaside town, slip away from me, the past having finally come for me.

Part Two

Part Two

12

Adrian

They emerge from the gravel track in the forest onto a pedestrian footpath running parallel to a floodlit main road. Cars zoom past in a streaky blur of white and red light, as they continue for a while toward a cluster of buildings in the distance. They look vaguely familiar to Adrian and he wonders if this could be somewhere the bus passes when he and Mama go to the airport. The Man walks fast but makes sure Adrian is keeping up.

'Come on, kiddo,' he says. Adrian won't look at him, not after what he said. His thoughts feel jumbled and strange, as though they've been souped together inside his head and he can't think a single one of them to a conclusion. Either The Man lied or he did not. If he lied he is probably very dangerous, and if he did not, then he is definitely very dangerous. Adrian feels as though an ice-cold claw is clutching his heart. Could he alert someone in a passing car? They're driving much too fast. And besides, even if he managed it, how would he ever explain what has happened?

Adrian clenches and unclenches his hands, but they are so cold he barely manages to move his fingers. He digs his fingernails into his palms, he feels another wave of wild anger, a fury he's never felt before, at what's happened. For a moment, he considers dropping a few more steps behind The Man, then running full speed into him and pushing him in front of an oncoming car at exactly the right moment, but even as he visualizes the moment The Man is catapulted into the air and the sickening sound as metal meets flesh, Adrian knows he wouldn't be able to gather enough force. If he tries something like that and fails, The Man will surely kill him right there and then by the roadside. And Mama, too, when he finds her.

'Stop,' says The Man. They are standing at a bus stop lay-by in front of the huddle of buildings. Now they're close, Adrian realizes that they are derelict factory buildings. He scans the empty parking lot and the upper floors of what looks like an office building, but there is nobody in sight. The Man motions to the road, where a pair of headlights are drawing closer. As the bus approaches, Adrian reads the lit-up sign: Oslo S, it says. The Man sticks out his hand and the bus indicates toward the lay-by. Adrian glances up at The Man, shocked. Oslo. He's never been to the capital, though it's only an hour and a half away. Marie has talked about it sometimes in school, showing images on the projector of the king's yellow palace atop a hill, the famous marble opera house half-submerged in water, and the red-brick twin towers of the somber-looking town hall.

The bus is half empty and The Man walks behind Adrian past the few other passengers; some of them are slumped over and sleeping, some gazing out the window at the frozen blackness, a couple briefly glancing up at them as they pass. They sit down almost all the way at the back, The Man urging Adrian into a window seat. He feels trapped there, pushed up against the cool window, The Man's big, bulky body blocking any chance of escape. He could scream, right now. Adrian considers this. He tries to imagine the sound of his voice piercing the air, how the man across the aisle would jerk awake, and the young girl two rows ahead of them would remove her AirPods and turn around to peer into the dark back of the bus, how everyone on the bus would stare at him. *It's okay*, he tells himself. *You have to do this.*

For Mama. He draws a deep breath and as he begins to release it from his lungs, does his trick of adding his voice gradually to the air until it becomes audible. The Man turns sharply toward him as he realizes Adrian is making a noise and grabs his right leg very hard in his hand, his fist closing around Adrian's bony knee.

'Shut up,' he hisses into Adrian's ear. Adrian won't be deterred; he needs to draw attention to them so the bus will pull over and the police can come and take The Man away. Then they can go find Mama.

'Heh–heh–' stutters Adrian, half of 'help', almost there. 'Heh–' The Man tightens his grip around Adrian's knee, so hard he can feel a ligament slip. It hurts so badly he can barely breathe, let alone scream.

'Shut the fuck up,' whispers The Man. Adrian understands this; it's the kind of thing he hears kids like Steffen and Josef say in the schoolyard. 'Listen. Mama. You want Mama. I want to find your mama. Help me. Please help me.' Adrian's eyes fill with tears, both from pain where The Man is still gripping his knee, and at the mention of Mama. He has no choice but to trust The Man. He nods. The Man releases his grip. Adrian looks out the window but feels afraid of the look in his own eyes reflected back at him. He closes his eyes and leans his head back against the headrest.

He must have fallen asleep because when he wakes the bus is no longer moving. He sits up and realizes it's parked in a bay alongside several other Norway Express buses, beneath a motorway flyover. The last couple of passengers are leaving the bus and The Man stands up.

'Come,' he says, giving Adrian his hand to help him out from the seat. Adrian doesn't take it, but when he stands up, his knee hurts terribly and he remembers how it felt as though it would be crushed in The Man's hand. His face must show how much it still hurts, because The Man says, 'I'm so sorry.'

They leave the bus and walk into a brightly lit metal-and-glass building. There's a 7-Eleven kiosk inside and Adrian's stomach growls loudly at the sight and scent of row upon row of thick, glistening hot dogs wrapped in scorched bacon, turning slowly on the grill. The Man follows his gaze and orders two. He also buys two Cokes, paying cash. Adrian is surprised that the young girl behind the counter doesn't seem to find it at all strange that The Man spoke in English. She answers in English and smiles at Adrian and The Man. They sit down on a metal bench and eat in silence. The hot dog tastes even better than Adrian could have imagined and he slips from the present moment into one of his visions, where he sees himself from the outside. To passersby, he's just some kid enjoying a hot dog on a bench in transit with his dad, probably going somewhere he's looking forward to going. Visiting grandparents in Lillehammer, maybe. He sees himself clearly, as if he is one of the people rushing past who happen to glance at him; dark jeans, a thin black down jacket, ears still red from the cold, short blond hair prone to a curl at the tips, a pale wan face and big red-rimmed eyes, jaw churning, a thin line of mustard running down his wrist and disappearing into his sleeve. He knows he looks younger than nine, and is often mistaken for a seven-year-old. *A tired and hungry little boy*, people would think. Not *An abducted and terrified child who has watched his mother disappear and now finds himself in the company of a dangerous stranger.*

As soon as they've finished, The Man stands up.

'Come,' he says, and Adrian dutifully follows him through the terminal building to where a huge screen projects all the upcoming departures. The Man peers briefly up at it, then they head to the far end of the terminal, where a bus driver is just unlocking the front door of another Norway Express bus. Its sign is blank but as the driver turns the key in the ignition, several other passengers emerge from inside the heated building and gather in line. Adrian wants to know where he is being taken now and anxiously keeps his gaze on the sign, but then the bus driver motions for them to start boarding and as he and The Man are first in line, Adrian has no choice but to start climbing the steps.

They sit near the back again, and Adrian has a strange sensation of reliving his trip on the first bus. The Man hands him a chocolate bar and fumbles through his jacket pocket to produce a small blue pill. He snaps it in half between his teeth and hands Adrian one half. Adrian shakes his head; he's never taken a pill before in his life and this one has touched The Man's lips, which makes him feel queasy. The Man insists, pressing it into his hand. 'To sleep,' he says.

Adrian would quite like to sleep, and maybe when he wakes up, Mama will be there. He swallows the pill dry. 'Good boy,' says The Man. Then he says, 'God, you are so much like your mother.'

The bus starts moving and Adrian leans his head against the window, the murmur from the engine reverberating slightly through the glass. He feels pierced by what The Man said, about being so much like his mother; it's as though he inserted a knife between two ribs and twisted it around. He begins to feel very tired and his thoughts slip and drift. He unwraps the chocolate bar and the last thing he clearly remembers doing is bringing it up to his face to take a bite, then everything fades away: the bus, the rumble of the road, the sensation of The Man's bulk next to him, the cold uncaring stars piercing the sky, the road ahead.

13

Anastasia

When she finally arrives, it's over twenty-four hours since the first plane took off from Milan. The noisy, tiny seaplane that made Anastasia's stomach lurch at the sight of it but was actually an exhilarating experience to fly in, slows to an almost silent glide and makes a final turn toward a thin, narrow island fringed by coral reef. The only other passengers are a Malaysian couple who bear a remarkable resemblance to each other, with huge black sunglasses and matching haircuts and white linen clothes. Anastasia presses her face to the window, her mouth dropping open in disbelief at the color of the ocean: a medley of turquoises and the brightest aqua blues, in contrast to the bone-white strip of pristine sand. Houses fan out into the Indian Ocean from a wooden walkway linking to the island, and each house has a pool on the terrace above the gently lapping waves. The plane lands directly in front of the houses and a small speedboat arrives to take its passengers and luggage. Anastasia squints at the sun, blinking hard, it feels like being in a dream and knowing it.

That night, Anastasia walks slowly from her villa toward the restaurant on the beach, drawing the fragrant, humid air deep into her lungs, willing it to become a part of her; she can't bear the thought of ever forgetting such a place. She can't quite believe it could even exist, that heaven has an actual name – it's called Drift Velaga. She whispers the strange name out loud into the night and laughs a little to herself. She feels refreshed after a long nap and a shower, and gets ready slowly, drinking a glass of white wine from the mini bar and blow-drying her hair into voluminous curls. She's meeting the team for dinner at eight, and wants to impress; she'd hate for the brand to have flown her all the way here and take one look at her and wonder why they bothered.

There's a live band playing in the restaurant and the ambience is buzzy but relaxed. Everyone looks sun-kissed and happy, their laughter reverberating around the domed, canvas-roofed space. The tables stand in silky sand and the moon-streaked ocean is just inches from the tables at the furthest edge of the restaurant.

'Anastasia,' someone calls. It's Andrea Fiorentini, sitting at a round table laden with an extravagant orchid centerpiece. He stands to greet her and kisses her firmly on the cheek, looping his arm around her waist to draw her close. He smells good, and looks good too, wearing a white linen shirt and loose navy chinos. He's in his early forties, she'd guess, but retains a slightly rueful, boyish look about him. She's glad to see him; it's nice to see a familiar face. 'You made it.' She nods and laughs. Andrea enquires about her travel, what she makes of Drift Velaga, whether she's ready for tomorrow's shoot. She answers thoughtfully, conscious of her English pronunciation.

'Oh, here they are,' says Andrea, as two other people approach the table. 'Anastasia, meet Catalina, our photographer, and Sam, our make-up magician.' The new arrivals kiss Anastasia's cheeks in turn, then Andrea's, then they sit down as the waiter brings a round of impressive cocktails presented in hollowed-out coconut shells. Anastasia takes a sip; it's delicious: watermelon, lime, sours, some kind of strong spirit that stings the back of her throat.

The conversation flows and Anastasia is able to follow most of it, and she feels confident and happy in the company of Andrea, Sam, and Catalina. Andrea regales them with tales of his childhood on the island of Ischia, where his parents ran a tourist sightseeing boat. Catalina says it's her first time to the Maldives, that she lives in Paris and has done for years. Anastasia says it must be so beautiful, that she hopes to visit someday.

'Wait,' shouts Sam above the music, that is growing faster and louder as people start to dance barefoot in the sand after finishing dinner. 'You've never been to Paris?'

'No,' smiles Anastasia. 'I've never been anywhere.' And the three almost-strangers listen in awe as she speaks of the dacha at the edge of the woods, the woods that hid the tsar and his family for the best part of a century; they've all heard of the place, it's been in the news fairly recently. She tells them about how Vera, who is an incredible gardener and horticulturalist, was hired by the state office for historical preservation to oversee the maintenance of the grounds of the monastery that was constructed at the burial site to commemorate the imperial family martyrs. Anastasia stumbles and struggles for words a few times, the English words making her tongue curl, but the three of them listen enraptured, and Andrea gently coaxes her when needed.

'Wow,' says Sam when she's finished speaking and the waiters clear away their dessert plates. 'Isn't it insane, that we're sitting here together, the three of us, in the middle of the Indian Ocean? I think about that often, on these kinds of occasions, you know, when you're just thrown together with random, interesting people from all over the place.' Anastasia nods and smiles, thinking about how it is indeed insane that this is her life now. She listens as Sam goes on to tell them about his early life in Alaska, how he loathed every moment of it until one day he got on a Greyhound bus and somehow managed to get to LA. He still lives there now with his boyfriend, who he repeatedly refers to as 'sexy Swedish Viking, Gulliver'.

More drinks arrive, then Andrea gets up and pulls Anastasia to her feet, breaking into a smooth waltz and shuffling her over to the open space where many other couples are dancing. He's a good dancer, and so is she; ballroom dancing was the one activity she practiced throughout her childhood and teens. Every Tuesday, Wednesday and Thursday after school, Anastasia and Vera would take the bus to Naberezhnaya Street, where Anastasia would spend the afternoon at Sveta's Dance Studio while Vera waited on a plastic chair outside, knitting or reading. She feels a lump thicken in her throat at the memory and swallows it back, forcing herself back to the current moment. Andrea is holding her very close and she can tell he's impressed by her dance skills. At one point he pulls back and dramatically raises an eyebrow and laughs, his perfect teeth glinting in the moonlight.

'Where did you learn to dance like that, Miss Nikitina?'

'At Sveta's Dance Studio in Yekaterinburg,' she says and he laughs again, spinning her around before lowering her into a dip, clutching her hand tight, the metal of his wedding ring cool against her skin. Some of the other couples have stopped dancing now and stand watching Andrea and Anastasia, clapping and cheering. The music dies down momentarily before the band launches into another tune, and Andrea leads Anastasia back inside the main restaurant space.

'Let's call it a night, shall we? You'll need your beauty sleep for tomorrow. We can party more tomorrow evening.'

Andrea, Anastasia, Sam, and Catalina walk back through the resort and down the wooden jetty to the villas together in comfortable silence, taking in the black ocean and the wash of stars, which appear to be entirely different out here, no longer having to compete with the glare from cities or the haze of pollution.

Back in the villa, Anastasia lies awake for a long time, listening to the whoosh of the fan spinning on the mahogany ceiling and the lap of waves beneath the house, smiling to herself in the dark, the memory of the music and the quick, assured dance steps still pulsating through her.

※ ※ ※

They shoot for several hours in the morning before the sun is blisteringly hot, on a remote stretch of the beach at the western end of A'Hava Fushi island. Anastasia is placed in the surf, in the sand, across a large, flat stone jutting out into the water, which is so clear they can see stingray babies chasing each other like submerged birds, their wing-like fins flapping. She's been photographed enough in the last few months to know her angles by now, and understands that a fraction of an inch this way or that sometimes makes all the difference. When she first came to Milan, she spent several days in Silvia Nebbio's studio on via Artigianale, building an initial portfolio. Graziela came along and watched as Silvia fired away the shots, and afterward, the two of them stood closely together and watched the results on Silvia's Mac, both of them nodding sagely.

Catalina is standing in the sea, and Anastasia lies on her front in the surf, face turned toward the camera. Sam has carefully pressed a line of ruby crystals along her hairline and accentuated her large, slightly slanting eyes with winged eyeliner. Catalina holds the camera lens close to Anastasia's face and Anastasia focuses on maintaining the look Graziela says is so unique to her; innocent and fierce at once, she calls it. Like an untamed horse. Behind Catalina stands Andrea, watching. He's wearing a pair of light-blue Vilebrequin swimming shorts with a lobster pattern. Anastasia is wearing a gauzy pink cover-up from the Strada Resort collection, encrusted with row upon row of twinkling faux gemstones. It strikes her as absurd that in this moment they are all at work: she half-submerged in the warm Indian Ocean, covered in crystals; Andrea in his swimming shorts, watching her; Catalina taking pictures of Anastasia in the strangest contortions, wearing expensive clothes that will be ruined by the saltwater; and Sam, scrolling on his phone beneath the shade of a palm-frond parasol and waiting to be called upon again.

When they wrap up, Andrea satisfied they have what they need, the skin on Anastasia's fingertips has shriveled from the several hours spent mostly in water. She feels exhilarated by the morning; this is her first campaign and it has been both fun and challenging. She spends a couple of hours by the pool on her private terrace, skimming through one of the complimentary magazines, not even attempting to read an article. If she's dyslexic in Russian, she is most certainly dyslexic in English. She never enjoyed reading anyway, to Vera's chagrin; she preferred the predictable order of numbers. *What kind of life awaits a girl who hasn't read the great Russian classics,* Vera would muse. *Well, look at me now,* thinks Anastasia, gazing out over the Indian Ocean. She smiles to herself and tries not to think about Vera. Sometimes the longing for her is so strong it momentarily takes her breath away. Soon, she thinks. Soon, Verushka can come to Milan. She only has to earn a little more money to make it happen, and then they can walk up via Monteleone until they get to the Strada flagship store, and there they'll pause and stare at Anastasia staring back from the building's huge billboards. They'll go to the Duomo and to the Vittorio Emmanuele galleries, and perhaps they can take the train to Como; everyone keeps saying to Anastasia how beautiful it is and that she must go.

There is a knock and Anastasia gets up from the sun lounger and slips on a Strada Resort cover-up, this one in white linen with jade stones sewn into the neckline.

'Madam,' says the porter outside, holding out a black clothing bag to her. 'For you.'

Back inside she unzips the bag to reveal an exquisite light-pink evening dress and a note.

For the most beautiful woman, from Andrea x, it reads. It strikes her as a little strange that it's signed from Andrea and not from the Strada team, but she's flattered and lays the dress on the bed to take it in properly. It is as detailed and structured as many wedding dresses, with a firm satin bodice and a full chiffon skirt studded with discreet Swarovski stones at the hem. She reads the note again and has to fight the urge to giggle at being called a woman, though she knows that is of course what she is. To herself, Anastasia is still a girl, a girl who, it must be painfully obvious, has very little life experience. She wasn't so aware of it when she was still at home in Russia, because back then everything was just what it was, and what she'd always known. In the months since she came to Milan, she's been exposed to more diversity and experiences than in all of her life up until the moment Silvia Nebbio discovered her at Ganina Yama.

Anastasia had never been to a restaurant until Graziela brought her to a trattoria wedged down a narrow lane off via Melzo on her first night in Italy, when she was fresh off the plane, walking around in a half-daze and shaking with nerves. Anastasia had barely been to a shop besides the roadside stalls that pop up by the roadside in the summertime at Koptyaki and sell everything from counterfeit perfumes to cheap clothes to Russian cigarettes to fat cabbages pulled from the ground the day before. Anastasia had never been to a party or drunk alcohol before arriving in Italy, when she discovered that both were perfectly normal things to do, and rather fun.

She slips back out of the cover-up and spends another hour out on the deck, watching the sun descend toward the horizon, setting it ablaze. She drinks a glass of white wine and plays Manu Chao on her phone, swaying to the music. She's looking forward to another dinner with the team; last night was so much fun. She steps into the dress and manages to do the buttons up herself with some effort. She studies herself in the mirror, feeling almost embarrassed to be so done up, like some kind of princess when, really, that couldn't be further from the truth. She tries to imagine what Anastasia aged, say, eight, would have made of Anastasia aged twenty-two, in this moment, and finds she can't. She didn't dream much as a child, or aspire to anything in particular, she was always well aware that she already had more than what was a given after Vera saved her from a life in an orphanage when her mother died.

She's aware of a hush when she enters the restaurant, of people looking at her and then doing a double take. The band is playing again, and she has a sense of déjà vu as she walks over to the table where Sam and Andrea are waiting, careful not to trip on the layers of chiffon swishing around her feet. Sam raises an eyebrow and forms an O in the air with his thumb and index finger as she approaches, and Andrea looks mesmerized, his eyes glazed, like a hungry man staring at a bloody steak. Anastasia feels a current of power rush through her and smiles widely at the men as they rise to kiss her.

'Where is Catalina?' she asks.

'She had to return to Paris earlier than expected. Another job, I think. She's really hitting the big time. She used to be Gianni Terenc's assistant, so she's learned from the absolute best. Cool lady,' says Andrea and Anastasia nods. A round of cocktails arrives, the same as yesterday, and Anastasia takes several long sips, and feels herself mellow and relax.

'The pictures are incredible,' continues Andrea, beaming at her across the table and raising his coconut in a toast. 'Here's to the new face of Strada Resort.' Another round of cocktails, some food – sashimi and oysters, followed by carpaccio and seared tuna. Two bottles of champagne. Like yesterday, the beach turns into a dance floor and Anastasia can feel her feet begin to almost itch to get out there, swaying to the beats through the warm and humid night air.

'I'm going to hit the sack,' says Sam and though both Anastasia and Andrea protest, he gets up and leaves after kisses and hugs and promises of staying in touch. Anastasia wonders if it's always like this, that you have a few days of intense bonding with a group of people, so much that you feel like old friends and then they just leave and you might never see them again. Catalina didn't even say goodbye, and it had stung Anastasia a little; she felt like they'd gotten on really well. Like she knew he would, Andrea leads Anastasia to the dance floor and pulls her close, very close. She lets him, she feels safe in his arms, that this is a man she can dance with like this without inviting unwanted advances. He's an attractive man and she enjoys his company, but he's much too old and she's well aware that he's happily married; earlier in the day he told her about his wife, Giulia, and two little boys, with whom he lives in a suburb of Milan.

After several energetic dances, Andrea whispers something in her ear but she can't make out what he's saying and says 'what' several times, until he leads her by the hand away from the restaurant tent and the loud music.

'I said let's take a little break,' he says, still holding her by the hand and she nods, realizing she's a little woozy from all the wine and dancing. Andrea leads her away from the domed canvas tent into the night, to a deserted section of the beach bar, and they sit closely together on a low, white sofa. A waiter appears, swiftly stepping out from the darkness and Andrea orders more champagne.

'And water, please,' adds Anastasia. She realizes she needs the bathroom and untangles her hand from Andrea's and walks back to the restaurant. When she's finished and on her way back, she watches Andrea's silhouette in the moonlight for a long moment before he sees her. A strong nose, thick, unruly hair, a serene and relaxed expression on his face, his arm casually slung across the back of the sofa as though someone is sitting there. In this moment, Anastasia feels as though she is living a life other than her own, that something strange is happening and she can't quite make out what it is. She feels suddenly nervous, then realizes that's ridiculous, she's merely having one more drink with a man that has been nothing but kind to her and has taken her career to the next level in a big lurch.

Andrea hands her a new glass of champagne and clinks his own softly to hers.

'You really are something else, Anastasia-from-Yekaterinburg,' he says. She laughs. She feels nervous again and wishes she was back at the villa, tucked into bed. She takes a few big glugs from the glass, willing the alcohol to soothe her. But everything goes black.

* * *

She's in bed. It hurts to open her eyes, like someone has glued them together. The room is bright, sunlight streaming into the vaulted space from the open terrace doors. She can make out a flash of bright blue and beyond it, a deeper blue. Something is strange. This is not her villa. She tries to sit up but her head pounds with the effort and she feels strangely tender, as though she's been pummeled. There is a sound, a kind of whooshing, and she realizes it's rushing water. She tries again to sit up and this time she manages it. She realizes she is completely naked and can make out the silhouette of the pink Strada dress on the floor. She draws the bedsheet up to cover her breasts and just then the bathroom door opens and Andrea stands there, a white towel tied around his waist, droplets of water scattering from his hair onto his shoulders and the floor. At the sight of her he breaks into a wide smile. She wants to scream. She looks away from him, can't bear the satisfied look in his eyes. They can't have... She tries to recall what happened after she sat back down at the beach bar, but her memory is simply empty. The last thing she can remember is the soft clink of Andrea's glass touching hers. But what happened between then and now?

'*Buongiorno*, sleeping beauty,' says Andrea, walking over to her side of the bed and bending to kiss her. She turns away from him; his breath smells of stale alcohol and she feels a mounting sense of panic.

'Andrea, what happened?'

'What do you mean, what happened?'

'Did we...' She can't even say it. Anastasia has only slept with one person, her first boyfriend, Konstantin. He moved away to Khabarovsk to study the summer they were nineteen and she missed him terribly at first. Though he wrote frequently to begin with, eventually his postcards dried up and she found herself thinking about him less and less.

'I must say you like it hard, Miss Nikitina,' says Andrea, winking at her. As he speaks, she becomes aware of a dull ache between her legs.

'I... I didn't agree to... this,' she whispers. 'I didn't want sex.'

He laughs a little, incredulously. Cruelly. 'Yes, you did. You begged, in fact.'

She closes her eyes, feels a rush of tears. 'No.'

'Anastasia, look. You made a lot of noise. Seemed to me like you enjoyed it, that's for sure.' He laughs again. The tears keep coming, even faster now. A vague image takes form in her mind, growing out of the opaque emptiness. Andrea on top of her, grunting, moving fast, a searing pain between her legs, Anastasia saying, *No, no, no, please*, Andrea clamping her mouth shut with a big, sweaty hand, moving harder.

'No,' she says. 'No. It's not true.'

'What the hell are you talking about?' Andrea throws his hands up in exasperation, as though he is dealing with an unreasonable child and she is so repulsed by him that she can feel bile rising from her stomach and she covers her mouth with her hand before quickly removing it again: it reminds her of when he forced her mouth shut, and she knows beyond any doubt then that it is a real memory and it really happened like that.

'I didn't want sex,' she says, her voice trembling with emotion.

Andrea turns away from her with a big sigh and in the bright light streaming in from the terrace doors, she can make out a long, raw scratch down the side of his neck. She must have clawed him, trying to get him off. 'You did. So I fucked you. And you loved it.'

She shakes her head, and tears drop from her chin onto the crisp duvet cover. 'No. You're lying.' She gets up off the bed, taking the duvet with her to cover herself and as she steps away from the bed they both see a couple of splotches of blood on the sheet.

'As I said, you liked it rough,' says Andrea, smirking. He closes the gap between them in a couple of steps and tears the duvet from her, leaving her naked. She tries to writhe away from him, but he grabs her hard by the jaw and makes her look him in the eyes. It occurs to her that during those two evenings of carefree, suggestive dancing, they would have emulated this pose almost exactly; pressing into each other, staring into each other's eyes, bodies aligned. 'Now you're going to listen to me. We had some fun. You enjoyed it. In fact, I can prove it. Got some video. I asked first, of course. I'm a gentleman, which you should know by now. Let's leave it at that, shall we?'

'No,' she hisses through clenched teeth.

'No? Yes, Anastasia. Let me be really fucking clear with you. This ends here. Or you'll never work again. You'll be dropped by Gio's. No one will touch you, not ever. Do you understand? Who do you think people will believe? Me, a respectable, married man with an extremely successful career, or a whore like you? Here's what happened. You got booked for a great job. You did good. Very good, in fact. You'll get booked again if you learn how to play the game. You got drunk. Wasted. You passed out. You got cleaned up and went home. You got booked again, and again. Your star rises. Do you understand?' Andrea tightens his grip on Anastasia's jaw, his thumb digging into her trachea. She can see red swirling shapes dancing on her retina when she closes her eyes. She nods.

14

Selma

She's on the laptop late into the evening, stopping only to dash down the road to McDonald's, which she'd noticed earlier was close to the hotel. She eats a Big Mac sitting on the bed, only then realizing how ravenous she was, failing to pick up the signals of hunger during all the hours she rushed around Sandefjord, first to Liv Carlsen's house, then to the farm near the airport. Selma pores over every bit of information appearing in the press about the disappearance. According to *VG*, Liv Carlsen's son was 'almost taken into care by Barnevernet in 2019 because she refused to pursue a diagnosis for the boy even though he was very obviously on the spectrum.' Sensationalist *Osloposten* writes, 'Another Barnevernet fail? Suicidal mother disappears without trace with child in tow.' And *Aftenposten*: 'What is it going to take for a real conversation about failing single parent support structures to begin?'

Selma comes across a heartbreaking public Facebook

post by a woman named Marie Hem, who she gathers is
Adrian's school teacher.

Dear Adrian, (and Liv),

Someday I believe you'll read my words, sitting back
at your desk over by the window. Today was a hard day
without you, yesterday too. None of the kids were able
to focus. Many cried. I cried too. It breaks my heart that
you don't think you belong here, and that you don't
know just how big of a part of our community you are.
When you first joined my class four years ago, I was
thrown by how you express yourself, until I learned that
you do so in the most exquisite way – your own. I didn't
immediately understand how you could focus intently,
storing every word I speak inside of you, while keeping
your eyes glued to the planes coming in to land. People
used to say that all kids should be the same, that the ones
who didn't quite fit the narrow mold should be forced
into it, slicing off bits of their precious selves, just to fit.
It didn't sit right with me and when I met you, Adrian, I
realized why – it's the differences that make us beautiful.

Your mother knows this. I've never met a mother
who sees and knows and loves her child more than
yours does. You're safe with your mama, this I know. I
hope that you both have a place to be safe in the world,
somewhere that holds you and nourishes you and gives
you the time to just be. And remember, you have a home
here, a community that wants to help you hold whatever
might feel too heavy to carry. It's never, ever too late to
come home.

Every day you remind me of why I became a teacher. When I've had a bad day, or a bad week, or a bad year, you have helped me to find purpose and joy every time you give me that wry smile of yours, and every time you hand me your sweet notes with a drawing of a plane, and the words 'thank you'. You never needed to thank me, Adrian, because it is such a pleasure to be your teacher. It's me who should thank you – so thank you for everything you are. I'm sending all the best thoughts in the universe out there for you and your mama tonight.

Marie

Selma cries too. How lucky the little boy is to have a teacher like Marie. She clicks on her profile and studies the few pictures she's made public. Marie Hem is young, probably in her early thirties, with a plain, pleasant face framed by light-brown bouncy bangs. In one of the pictures she holds a Norwegian forest cat which looks remarkably like Medusa, and that makes Selma instantly like her. She presses the message icon.

Hi Marie,

I'm working for *Dagsposten* and also in close contact with Sandefjord police with regard to the disappearance of Adrian Carlsen and his mother. I was wondering whether you could spare a few minutes of your time for a chat? I sense that you could really add something to the picture. This would, of course, be entirely off record.

Best, Selma Eriksen

Selma finds it interesting and noteworthy that Marie, a teacher who has clearly known Adrian and Liv for four years speaks out in such a supporting way. If Liv were an unhinged or unfit mother, which certain corners of the media are insinuating merely based on the fact that she has previously come into contact with the child protection services, surely Marie would have an inkling of that. Selma's phone beeps, just minutes after she sent the message.

Hi Selma,
I know who you are. I followed the Lucia Blix case intently, like all of Sandefjord. It was incredible, what you did. Happy to speak. Free tomorrow between nine and ten if you wanted to stop by school?
Marie

Selma confirms and messages Olav to share the good news that she's uncovering quite a few pieces of the mystery.

Have you seen this? he replies, with a link. She clicks on it, and it's another headline from *Osloposten*.

'Sandefjord Mother Has Gone Missing Before!' screams the headline, followed by a picture of a young woman. She's a striking woman with straight, jet-black hair and hazel eyes, accentuated by dramatic eye make-up. Selma zooms in and out of the main picture, feeling as though there is something vaguely familiar about the woman staring back at her. She's already extensively googled 'Liv Carlsen' but it is a fairly common name and no interesting recent hits have come up, and none matching these images.

Police don't suspect foul play and are focusing the investigation on a theory of a mental health breakdown, as missing mother's family confirm a complicated and tragic past history, including drug abuse and suicidal ideation. It is considered likely that Carlsen and her son have left Norway. The above images of Liv Carlsen, dating from 2010, when she was last in contact with her family in Holmestrand, were released by police this evening, and police are hopeful more leads will follow these. Several interesting lines of inquiry, both domestic and international, are currently being explored as Norway holds its breath, praying for the little boy to be recovered safely. 'All efforts are being employed to locate the mother and her son who most likely went missing from Sandefjord on the afternoon of Friday, January 14th, and members of the public are urged to remain on the lookout for anyone who could feasibly be Liv Carlsen and Adrian. Their appearances may have been altered, so please remain alert,' says Gaute Svendsen, senior investigator at Sandefjord Politi.

Selma scrolls down to 'G' in her contact list and calls Gaute, even though it's past eleven.

'Ummmm, hello?' he says when he finally answers after a long while.

'Gaute, it's Selma.'

'Do you know what time it is?' He doesn't sound annoyed, more bemused.

'I do. And I apologize. I assume you weren't sleeping?'

'I wasn't, no. My phone is going mental after we released the images of Carlsen.'

'I thought you were going to give me a heads-up?'

'I would have, but this came from above. Kripos went to speak with her mother and sisters in Holmestrand this afternoon. Concerns for the boy are growing by the day, and apparently they're well founded. Her own mother didn't have much good to say about her. And they've never even met the kid.'

'Sounds messy.'

'Definitely. They haven't seen their daughter since 2008. They remained sporadically in contact up until 2010 when she went missing in Italy.'

'In Italy?'

'Yes. Then it would seem she turned up again later that year, having returned to Norway. Her son was born here, at Tønsberg Hospital in February 2011. She's been in touch with her family on and off since then, but she's apparently very difficult and wants little to do with her family.'

'Maybe it's the family that's difficult.'

'Hah. Maybe. I wasn't there so couldn't tell you, but the report I've had definitely suggests some deep-rooted tension.'

'What was she doing in Italy?'

'She was a model, apparently. In Milan.' Gaute might as well have punched Selma in the gut full force, such is the effect of his words. She is literally speechless. She balances the phone against her chin and brings the images of Liv Carlsen back up on her computer, and now she's surprised she didn't guess when she first saw her. Liv has that look quite typical of runway models: angular and striking, more than classically beautiful. 'Selma? Hello? Are you there?'

'Uh. Mmm.'

'Terrible industry for young, impressionable girls, I imagine. Her parents said she always was a handful, but going there just broke her. Got hooked on drugs. Bad men. That kind of thing.'

'Who's Adrian's father? Do the parents know?' Selma's voice emerges as barely a whisper.

'They have no idea. Like I said, they've never even met him. We still haven't been able to find a picture of Adrian. Strangely there were none at the house. And he has been away sick every time the school photographer has come. Weird in itself, don't you think?'

'Mmm.' Selma utters a few polite phrases, then hangs up. The shock of Gaute telling her that Liv Carlsen was a fashion model in Milan just won't release its grip and it feels as though she's looking through a long tunnel at a tiny image at its end, unable to get any sense of a bigger picture. It might be a random coincidence that Selma has spent the last few months working on the feature on the fashion industry, but Selma doesn't entirely believe in random coincidences and feels profoundly shaken to suddenly discover such a concurrence. She types 'Liv Carlsen Milan 2008' into Google and finally she gets the hits that eluded her before. There she is, a young catwalk model stalking down the runways of several prestigious fashion houses, from Loewe to Versace and Miu Miu. She doesn't uncover any magazine covers, except for one for *Elle Serbia*, in which Liv sits facing another girl, each biting suggestively into an apple positioned between them. Their hair has been styled identically, slicked back from their foreheads, and the overall impression is that they could be two sides of the same girl, mirrored.

Selma is frustrated at coming across a revelation this big close to midnight; she feels the irresistible urge to get out and move her body in order to clear her head. She wants to go straight to Liv's parents' house and to Marie's, right now, bombarding them with questions; she can barely stand the wait for tomorrow. She closes the laptop and considers the inviting bed, but knows she's just too riled up for any chance of sleep. Luckily she wore her running shoes to work today, and her workout kit from the early morning's boxing session is at the bottom of her work bag. She puts it back on, quietly goes downstairs and slips into the night. The only sound in the deserted town is the soft, rhythmic thud of Selma's shoes slapping the sidewalks as she breaks into a run.

15

Liv

I wake up. No. I come to; I wasn't asleep but unconscious. It takes a long while to recover fragments of memory; my mind feels entirely blank like the mirrored, silver surface of a lake. I can't move, or see. I'm in pain, though I can't locate its source; it seems to be coming from all over. There's a searing ache running down the side of my head, culminating in an especially tender spot on my jaw, and I vaguely recall the moment before the side of my face slammed into the boardwalk down by the water. I run my tongue around the inside of my mouth and taste the faint metallic aftertaste of blood. My left arm feels dead and when I try to wriggle my fingers, I can only manage the slightest response. My stomach hurts too, and an image seeps into my mind, of being punched hard several times, then losing consciousness.

I manage to shift my weight forward a little but as I move a sickening stench rises into my nostrils and I begin to retch, acidic bile shooting into my mouth. The air smells like oil and rotting fish and urine. I'm on my stomach, my face pressed into a cold, smooth surface, my hands tied tight behind my back. It feels as though I'm enveloped inside a carpet or a sleeping bag, with something heavy placed on top, pinning me down. I recall the gentle rocking I felt earlier and realize it's stopped almost completely, though there is still slight movement and an occasional soft thud from the hull, as though it is nudging against a mooring.

Before, there were voices too, the muffled voices of men speaking urgently, but now it's eerily silent. I manage to turn my head an inch and angle it upward and this enables me to see a small sliver of my surroundings. I am indeed wrapped inside something; a thick black material extends past my head like a funnel, but beyond it I can see the curved white shape of a hull meeting in a pointed bow. The space is softly lit by a yellow electric light but I can't make out its source. It feels as though it is the middle of the night and I am definitely on a boat, a small sailing boat, judging by what I can make out of the size of the space. I imagine it's the kind of boat that you see docked by the hundred in Sandefjord, big enough for four people to enjoy a day out on the fjord or an overnight trip down to Sweden, with a narrow deck and a galley and a couple of bunks down below.

Adrian. The thought of my son sends a bolt of terror down my spine, more painful and insistent than the aches from my injuries. I *have* to find a way out of here and home to my son. Could he still be inside the house, pacing around and muttering to himself in the middle of the night, or have they come for him too? I see him so clearly in my mind, his pale little face, his straw-colored hair that sticks straight up from his head where it's short at the back, his beautiful blue eyes, set apart widely like mine, framed by long, dark lashes. The thought of him in the hands of someone intent on harming us makes me feel faint and numb with terror. *Someone knocked on the door*, he said. He said he shut the door in the man's face. But what if, moments after I was knocked to the ground, the man came back and forced his way into the house, taking Adrian? It isn't possible, nobody knows about Adrian. But what if the man who came to the door looking for me took one look at Adrian and put two and two together? I know that I've placed myself in danger, that I've made choices that have made me a target but knowing that those choices could kill not only me, but my child, too, is unbearable.

I begin to cry; I can't help it. Sobs tear out of me, and I bite down on my lip to stop any further sound escaping but it's too late. I hear the sound of footsteps approaching, rocking the boat. There is a loud creak as a door opens and then I sense someone standing here in the tiny space with me. I hear a soft whistling sound, then a low chuckle. I make myself lie entirely still, though my instinct is to scream and fight, clawing at the eyes of whoever is standing there. I've never felt more powerless in all my life. A sharp kick lands in a soft hollow on my back, just below my ribs. The pain is astonishing and I can't help but whimper. Another kick, straight in the ribs this time. I feel more movement and there is a muffled shuffle and more laughter.

'She's playing dead,' says a man, in Italian. *Sta facendo la morta.*

'Fucking bitch,' says another. *Porca troia.* I feel something come undone inside of me at the sound of the soft, melodious language; for many it's a language of beauty and of love, but for me, it's no doubt a death sentence. I'm overcome by a primal panic and begin to writhe and shake inside my constraints, and whatever is tying my hands together chafes into my skin, drawing blood. I can feel it slither hotly down my wrists and this makes me even more hysterical, my cries growing into hoarse hiccupy bellows. And underneath all the noise I'm making I can hear the men who are standing there watching me, laughing. Another blow lands, this one in the soft cave of my stomach. Then another. Everything goes black and all the sounds melt away and I'm floating gently on the warm surface of the sea, Adrian's plump baby hand snug in my own.

***

I come to again and now everything is different. There is a cacophony of sound coming from several different places at once, and a lurching motion that makes me instinctively reach out for something to hold on to and now I can feel about a little bit. I'm still restrained with my hands bound behind my back, and I've been blindfolded, but I'm no longer wrapped inside whatever I was inside before. Instead, it feels as though I'm strapped into a seat by a three-point belt meeting painfully in the middle of my stomach. I wish I could press my fingers into my ears to partially block out the metallic rapid-fire sound that is rising in intensity, but I feel too disoriented by the blindfold to immediately identify its source. There is another lurching motion and the sensation of being turned around, and then the sound gets even louder and the whole space I'm in shudders and lifts off and it is only then I realize I'm in a helicopter.

I remember the first time I ever sat in a helicopter and I could howl to think of that girl pressing her young face to the window, her mouth dropping open in awe at the sight of white-capped mountains biting into the sky in the distance. Back then, the unfamiliar motions of flying in a helicopter had felt wonderful and terrifying in equal measure. But I'm not that girl anymore. I'm a grown woman, and what's more, I'm a mother, Adrian's mama, the only person he has in the whole world. I can't die and leave him behind, though I know that is exactly what will happen if I don't find a way out of this. If it weren't for my son, I would pray for this helicopter to drop from the sky, to smash into fragments on a remote hillside, bursting into flames on impact; I'd rather meet death like that than the death I'm heading toward.

We touch down softly and my mouth is swiftly taped shut and then I'm dragged like an animal from the helicopter. As soon as I catch a breath of fresh air carrying the scent of the mountains and the deep, clean lake water, it's instantly familiar and though I haven't breathed this scent into my lungs for almost a decade, in this moment it's as though I never left. A door is opened, I'm dragged again, another door, a flight of stairs. I try to cry out; I'm certain I have fractured ribs from where I was kicked earlier. A sudden, visceral image insists itself into my mind: the feel of loving hands on broken skin, when I'd get hurt as a child. A homemade poultice of yarrow leaves, carefully pressed to the wound. Made-up rhymes whispered straight into my ear until my sobs subsided. I haven't known much kindness, but I've retained all of it inside of me and it's what has kept me from giving up for all of these years, and it's what will get me through this, because I am going to, I have to; I am going to hold my boy again. I imagine those hands carefully tracing the swells and bumps on my back now, massaging calendula oil gently into the skin in circles. I can hear that sweet voice whispering, medicine in a memory.

At the bottom of the stairs I'm picked up and carried over someone's shoulder. Whoever is carrying me must be a big guy; I'm five foot ten, but he walks briskly and apparently effortlessly, his footsteps echoing around me. The air is stale and cold. The sound of metal clanging, then another door is opened, creaking on its hinges. The man carrying me seems to stoop down as we enter into a new space. There's a murmur of voices coming from somewhere over to the left. The man has stopped, leaving me dangling over his shoulder. I want to wrench myself free and make a run for it but of course I know I never could. From this place, there's nowhere to run. The only way out is death.

Someone says something I don't catch and the man carrying me takes a couple of steps forward, then throws me to the ground with such force I can feel my left elbow fracture on impact with the stone floor. My face, too, hits the floor. I bite my tongue and my mouth floods with blood. I spit and splutter and whimper, trying to press myself up against the wall, winning as many centimeters as possible between myself and my attackers. For several long moments, nothing happens and the space we're in is entirely silent. With the blindfold on, I can't be sure whether I am here with two people – the man who carried me and the other with whom he just spoke – or if there are many of them.

I use the last of my strength to just breathe steadily through my nostrils, clearing my head, bringing my terrified heart rate down. Nothing can happen to me here that hasn't already happened to me, I tell myself. I survived all of that.

I will survive again, for my son. All my focus needs to be on him; I know what I'm living and fighting for.

I hear footsteps advancing before coming to a stop somewhere close to me and my instinct is to wince; it feels as though a loaded gun is being pointed at me, and perhaps it is, but rationally I know that if the goal was to simply kill me, they would have killed me within minutes of locating me in Sandefjord and not gone through the trouble of transporting me here in secret.

A pair of hands brush against the side of my face. I instinctively draw back, but the hands follow, firmer now, holding my head still. They fumble with the ties of the blindfold, then it drops away. My eyes are clamped shut; I want to protect myself and draw out a few last moments of not fully irreversibly knowing, but the instinct to identify and assess danger is stronger and I open my eyes. I'm in one of the basement storage rooms. I recognize it immediately: a huge space with a low ceiling and a dirt floor. There's a man over by the door, a burly, red-faced man with spiky blond hair, wearing a suit stretching comically across his expansive chest, clearly the guy that carried me here. He has cold, gray eyes staring at a spot somewhere just above my head, and a handgun sits visibly in a holster at his waist.

'Welcome back,' says a voice from somewhere over in the far corner of the room, steeped in shadows. The blond man over by the door immediately snaps to life at the sound of the voice, like a dog. He takes a couple of steps forward until he's standing directly in front of me. He then unzips his flies and unleashes a long, warm stream of urine onto me. It stings the cuts on my neck and face and I begin to retch uncontrollably. When he's finished, both men leave the room without another glance at me, laughing and joking as though they've just popped down to the wine cellar for a nice bottle of Meursault. The initial warmth of the urine dissipates and a raw cold settles into my bones. The smell of fresh and concentrated urine is unbearable and my stomach spasms repeatedly, bringing fresh bursts of bitter bile to my mouth.

16

Adrian

'Hey,' says The Man, nudging Adrian's shoulder. 'Wake up, kiddo.'

Adrian opens his eyes and looks straight into The Man's clear blue ones. He immediately looks away, but it's too late; he can feel a deep, uncomfortable burning sensation in the pit of his stomach. Whenever someone looks directly into Adrian's eyes, it feels like they're climbing inside his head as if his eyes are little doors. Nobody else is inside the bus and it's parked in a vast lit-up space, like an underground parking garage. There's a rumbling sound followed by several metal clangs and then the whole world rocks strangely.

'Boat,' says The Man. A boat? It can't be.

'No,' whispers Adrian, surprising both himself and The Man with the ease of the word. 'No,' he says again and stands up, pushing past The Man. The bus driver is standing by the open door at the front of the bus and motions for Adrian and The Man to get off the bus.

'*Kom igjen*,' he shouts in Norwegian, his fleshy face

anxious and ruddy. *Come on.* As Adrian passes him leaving the bus, the driver does a double take and looks at him more carefully, as though noticing him for the first time. Adrian turns around and makes himself meet the man's eyes even though it's difficult and it burns, but the driver quickly looks away and doesn't seem to notice that the boy in front of him isn't quite like other little boys.

On the ship, they climb a series of steep narrow steps until they emerge into a quiet cafeteria. A couple of people are slumped over and asleep as the ferry purrs across the strait to Germany. The Man points this out to Adrian, saying, 'See those lights? That's Germany.' Adrian knows a lot about Germany; that it used to be at war with Norway, about its Luftwaffe, which he did a school project on, and, of course, various airport codes. He soothes himself now, in this strange moment, by going through them in his mind. FRA for Frankfurt, STR for Stuttgart, the strange SXF for Berlin-Schönefeld... The Man breaks his train of thought by speaking in a low voice, glancing about as though someone may be hovering and listening.

'Look, all we need to do is avoid suspicion. I think I know where your mama is.'

17

Anastasia

She steps back off the runway into the backstage area and is enveloped by numerous hugs, people placing kisses on her head, her forehead, her cheeks. She blinks but can't see anything; the cameras are still flashing on her retinas, adrenaline rushing through her veins. People are chattering and laughing; she can discern the voices of Luigi, Pietro, Graziela, Xenia, and Natalia from the cacophony.

'That was fucking crazy,' shouts someone. Micki? And inside her head, another voice, her own – *Anastasia, you just closed the Gucci show in Milan.*

At the afterparty people mill around her. She drinks champagne, but not much; she's been careful with drinking for weeks now, ever since she got back from the Maldives. As she stepped out onto the runway earlier, her focus razor sharp on delivering the perfect walk, she fixed her gaze on one of the huge wrought-iron lanterns strung from the ceiling in Museo del Novecento's hall of windows where the catwalk had been constructed overlooking the piazza del

Duomo through enormous wall-to-wall vaulted windows. She avoided even a single glance at the crowds seated in rows on all sides. She knew the entire elite of the fashion world would be sitting there, scrutinizing her, drinking in the two-piece baby-blue suit she was wearing, cut to perfection and tailored exactly to Anastasia's frame.

Editors from *Vogue*, *Harper's Bazaar*, *Elle*; celebrities, fashionistas, and all kinds of other industry types, including Andrea Fiorentini. She knew this, because earlier in the day, after the final run-through, she'd stepped out from the backstage area and walked quickly between the rows and rows of carefully positioned chairs, now complete with name tags stuck to their backs and goody bags placed on the seats. She'd been casually handed one, too, by one of the backstage PAs, and had been shocked to find a new iPhone, tickets to a special showing of *Madame Butterfly* at La Scala, a Gucci bracelet, and his and hers Gucci perfumes, among other things. And there – on one of the chairs at the far end of the front row was his name: Andrea Fiorentini.

Her heart had begun to race in her chest but she'd made herself breathe slowly and calmly until it settled down again. In spite of what happened in the Maldives, Anastasia knew she had no choice but to learn to play the game Andrea had referred to, but it hadn't been easy. Often she'd wake in the night, her face wet with tears and her pulse sky high. Or she'd experience a sudden panic walking back home to via Melzo in the evening, as though someone might lurch from the darkness and hurt her. She'd gone to parties with the girls, of course, but she'd been constantly looking over her shoulder, keeping an eye out for *him*. Xenia, in particular, had noticed that something had changed and kept asking Anastasia if something was wrong until one night when only the two of them were at the apartment, watching a reality show on television, Anastasia had burst into tears and told Xenia what had happened between her and Andrea Fiorentini. Xenia had looked at her for a long while after she'd stopped speaking, catching a few tears that careened down Anastasia's face with her fingertips, clasping her trembling hand in her own.

Shhhhh, she'd whispered. *I know how you feel. But now, you must forget.*

But Anastasia couldn't forget. A couple of weeks after the Maldives, after several nights in a row with hardly any sleep at all, Anastasia turned up at the office on what should have been her first day off in over a month. She waited for a while in the reception area for Graziela; she was on a phone call, according to the receptionist. Also waiting was a man who seemed vaguely familiar, dressed smartly in polished brown shoes and a blue suit. At first she couldn't think where she'd seen him, but just as Graziela came to fetch her, she realized it was the American, the one who'd been with Andrea Fiorentini and Gianni Terenc when she'd been introduced to them by Graziela. When he caught her eye, the American smiled at her in an open, friendly manner but she gave him a cool glance – she wasn't going to be especially nice to one of Fiorentini's buddies.

'Hi Tom,' said Graziela to the man. 'Giorgio's been caught up in traffic but will be here in a few.' The man nodded and smiled at Anastasia again as she followed Graziela down the corridor. In her office, Graziela looked suddenly small and nervous about Anastasia's unannounced appearance.

Good, thought Anastasia. For several long moments she observed the older woman, the person who'd turned her life around in so many ways. *Did you know what would happen and just sent me there anyway?* she wanted to ask. Instead, she did what she'd decided she would on her long walk over here – get straight to the point.

'Graziela, Andrea Fiorentini raped me in the Maldives.'

Graziela took an exaggerated inhalation, then sat down in her chair, nodding sadly and motioning for Anastasia to take a seat. She remained standing. 'Look. Anastasia. I'm really glad you've come to see me. We need to talk about this, absolutely. Though what you have just said is a very serious allegation.'

'It's the truth.'

'I'll be honest with you. I've been waiting for you to talk to me about this. Andrea Fiorentini already has, pretty much right after you returned, and it's imperative both for Strada and for the agency that we're able to iron out this misunderstanding.'

'Misunderstanding?'

'Well, yes.'

'I just told you I've been raped. I haven't slept through a whole night since. I can't stop crying. I can feel his disgusting clammy hands on my body, and—'

'Anastasia. Like I said, Andrea told me what happened. Sadly it's not the first time I've heard that story or one like it. Being far away, drinking too much and then regretting what happened in the heat of the moment. You know, it's actually happened to me too, in the past.'

Anastasia stared at Graziela in sheer shock. 'I'm telling you that he raped me.'

'And I'm telling you that you need to stop calling it that.'

'Graziela, he drugged me and had sex with me against my wishes.'

'Anastasia. Enough. You like it here, no? You're doing well at work. Everybody seems to think you really are that one in a million. So don't ruin it. Let it go.'

Anastasia stalked out of the office, through the reception area, and took the stairs two at a time until she got outside, where a light, warm rain was mercifully falling. She angled her face up to the sky, letting the droplets wash her tears away. Only then did she realize someone was standing beside her, having followed her out onto the street from GMA's office building.

'Anastasia, hi, I'm sorry to bother you. I saw you, uh, up there and you looked really upset and I guess I just wanted to make sure you were all right.' The American.

Anastasia drew a deep breath, ready to shout at the guy and tell him to go to hell, today really wasn't the day for some opportunistic come-on, but then she noticed the unmistakable kindness in his eyes, and she exhaled deeply, and with the effort came a low sob and more tears, but Tom didn't look fazed at all, merely concerned.

'Come,' he said, and steered her gently across the road to the park, the same park she often gazes at through the wide windows in Graziela's office during the morning meetings. A huge oak tree stands on its own at the park's far end and a round bench has been constructed around the tree, entirely sheltered beneath its dense, low crown.

'If you feel that you can tell me what's going on, I swear I won't tell anyone unless you want me to.'

'Just a bad day.'

'I think I've seen enough of the industry you're in to know that some pretty challenging stuff can happen.'

'What do you know about modeling?'

'Not that much, you're right. I'm in business. But I've been around Milan for a while now and it seems to me that people, girls, aren't always treated that well.'

'Someone... Someone attacked me. Sexually. When I was away on a job abroad.'

'Oh, my God, I'm so sorry. Were you...'

'Raped. Yes. And my own manager doesn't even care. She just told me to let it go if I want to keep working in Milan.'

'What the hell?'

'Yeah.'

A thick vein begins to pulsate at Tom's temple and Anastasia can tell he's truly furious at what she's just told him. She feels grateful, suddenly, that he followed her and offered to listen.

'Look. Thank you for listening. I appreciate it. Maybe what I needed was to tell someone and feel understood.'

'You should tell the police.'

'No, I—'

'He'll do it again. To someone else.'

Fresh tears meandered down Anastasia's face and she let them drop onto her jeans. 'I know,' she whispers.

'You know the guy's name, right?'

'Well, yes. We were working together.'

'Will you tell me?'

'No.'

'Why not?'

'Because you'll tell someone.'

'I told you I wouldn't.'

'Swear.'

'I swear. But why are you protecting him and not yourself?'

'It was Andrea Fiorentini.'

Tom looked truly shocked at Anastasia's words and immediately stood up as though he were going to barge through Milan and hunt Fiorentini down. 'Fucking scumbag,' he said at last.

Anastasia nodded and they sat a while in silence, though Anastasia was aware of Tom's phone vibrating non-stop in his suit trousers. He ignored it.

'So what were you doing at GMA?' asked Anastasia.

'I have a meeting with the owner. Giorgio. That's probably who keeps calling me.'

'You have to go.'

Tom nodded ruefully, but withdrew a business card from his jacket pocket.

'I, uh, live here alone. I have a lot of time on my hands. I can be a good listener. Give me a call sometime.'

Anastasia nodded but she knew even as she placed Tom Kingsley's business card into her handbag that she never would.

* * *

Seeing Andrea's name there on the chairback, Anastasia realized she hadn't forgotten, no matter how hard she'd tried. Not at all. But he wasn't going to ruin this for her. And he hasn't. It felt like a triumph when she finished walking, knowing she'd done so perfectly, that she'd been able to do that even though he'd have been sitting there, watching, wanting, smirking.

Graziela hovers near Anastasia all evening at the afterparty, filtering out the various people trying to speak with her. Anastasia feels as though she's been more protective of her since the conversation they had that day when Tom Kingsley followed her out onto the street, but Graziela has never referred to the conversation again, or apologized to her for telling her to get over it. At one point, Anastasia briefly catches the eye of Andrea, who is seated at a table with a beautiful, petite brunette – his wife, presumably, but she lets her gaze travel quickly onward and ignores the dull ache in her stomach at the sight of him.

'God, they're like vultures,' says Graziela, grabbing Anastasia by the shoulders and pulling her into a little sideways hug. 'You were fantastic.'

'What is vultures?' asks Anastasia. She's never heard the word before.

'Big ugly birds that want to eat you alive,' says Graziela, deadpan, lighting a cigarette and inhaling deeply. 'That's what happens when you hit the big time, babe. Everyone wants a piece of you.'

***

Weeks pass, more shows, another campaign, a trip to London. Anastasia walks, awestruck, through sodden, foggy streets, taking pictures of the Queen's palace, the brown river, the red buses, the throngs of people, and the famous bridges on her day off. Then she walks some more, up and down the various runways of London Fashion Week. Burberry, Alexander McQueen, Matthew Williamson. A shoot for British *Vogue*. On her final day, before catching an evening flight back to Milan, she takes a train out to Richmond and follows the signs across the beautiful meadows by the river to Petersham Nurseries.

She buys three packets of *Nelumbo nucifera* seeds, which she has to ask for specifically and which have to be brought out from a storage vault, costing a fortune, and slips them into the lining of her new Gucci hold-all bag, another gift from Pietro. When she returns to Milan, she posts them to Vera in Yekaterinburg along with a letter saying she will try to clear some space in her diary in the next couple of months and come home for a visit; she could more than afford it by now.

She wakes at five thirty, moments before the alarm goes off, her body having long ago integrated the early start to the day. She has a day off and no plans for once. She decides to start the day by going for a run, something she always plans on doing, yet rarely does. She dresses quickly and quietly, conscious not to wake the other girls. They were out late last night at a party in Navigli district. Anastasia didn't go; she still feels tired and run-down after show season; out of the four of them, she's easily the one who has worked the most.

'Next season, you'll be doing Paris and New York on top of it,' said Graziela, beaming, when they last sat down together in her office a few days ago, numerous pictures of Anastasia on the various runways fanning out on the desk between them. 'Gucci adores you. Bulgari and Bottega Veneta have been in touch. You're hot shit in Milan, my dear.'

Xenia also did a few of the big Milan shows and Micki landed a cosmetics campaign for a big American company, sending her to New York for a couple of weeks. She came back glowing, proclaiming she wanted to move there. Natalia, who is only just eighteen and from Ukraine, is still going from casting to casting, hoping to get booked for something other than an occasional editorial for some obscure online journal. She's a willowy, striking girl with dark eyes and thick auburn hair. Her face, which is angular and dominated by a strong Roman nose and thick eyebrows, isn't traditionally beautiful but is the kind you don't easily forget. Natalia photographs well and Anastasia doesn't for a moment doubt that someday she'll be gazing back at her from major billboards with that sulky, defiant look.

'Sometimes I just want to go home,' she said to Anastasia the other day, when the other girls had gone out and it was just the two of them in the apartment. Anastasia had made dinner for them, a simple but tasty salad with walnuts, beetroot, and figs, something Vera had often made with fresh produce from the garden. Anastasia nodded at her words, and sat down across from her, placing the food down on the table. She knew that feeling, of wanting to go home. Though she loved the excitement of Milan and meeting so many fascinating people, she missed the simple comforts of just being in her most familiar space; falling asleep to the sound of the wind tearing at the tall trees across the clearing, waking up to the sun pouring through the gridded window and turning the timber walls of her room a shimmery golden blond.

'But I can't ever go home,' continued Natalia. 'Not until I'm rich.' As they ate the salad, she told Anastasia more details about her early life back in Mykolaiv, a shipbuilding town on the banks of the Pivdennyi Buh River, not far from the Black Sea. The only child of a single mother, she'd lived in a run-down communal apartment block, her mother working long shifts as a cleaner at a nearby factory to put food on the table. Natalia had never met her father and they had no family other than each other. At fifteen, Natalia got pregnant, giving birth to a little daughter, Sofia. Anastasia stared at Natalia across the kitchen table in disbelief, she hadn't known she had a child, she'd never mentioned her before. She was the most guarded and private of the girls, and the one Anastasia knew the least, but she'd seemed carefree and confident. Natalia had come to Milan after becoming runner up on Ukraine's Next Supermodel and was signed to Gio's around the same time as Anastasia. Sofia stayed in Mykolaiv with her grandmother, a repeat of Natalia's own early life, but Natalia was determined to turn her life around and bring little Sofia to Italy.

'I just need to get work,' she added softly. Anastasia had reached for her hand across the table and squeezed it. 'Rich girls like Xenia don't understand. This is my only chance.' Anastasia saw something steely in her face, a vein of determination. Since that night, she's barely seen Natalia; she's been out in the evenings a lot, but she's thought about their conversation several times, wondering whether there is anything she can do to help her.

Anastasia shoves her feet into her running shoes and slips out of her bedroom space soundlessly. She approaches the front door when she realizes that someone is trying to open it from the outside, fiddling with the key in the lock, which can be tricky. Anastasia unlocks the door and opens it. Natalia stands outside, a strange smile on her face, key held suspended in the air.

'Oh, hi, Natalia,' says Anastasia. 'Are you only just coming home?' She laughs, it's almost 6 a.m. and her own day has already started. Natalia stares at her, then nods absentmindedly. She smells of alcohol, but taking in the glazed look in her eyes, Anastasia realizes she's high.

'What... What have you taken?' she asks, softly, helping Natalia into the tiny entrance space. Natalia turns around to face her, that strange smile still playing on her lips and then she sits down straight onto the floor.

'Don't worry your pretty head, Anoushka,' she says, laughing loudly, a hollow tinny laugh that is likely to wake both Micki and Xenia.

'Shhhhhh,' says Anastasia, gesturing down the hallway at the hushed, silent apartment. Natalia laughs again and fumbles with the zipper on her over-the-knee boots. Anastasia bends to help her, and when she's done, she realizes that Natalia's laughter has turned into crying and huge, silent sobs rack her bony frame. Anastasia pulls her into a hug and Natalia allows herself to be held.

'My baby,' Natalia says, over and over. 'I just want my baby.' Anastasia manages to get Natalia to her feet and leads her down the hallway to her own tiny space. She figures it might be best to let Natalia have some space to herself and not wake Xenia, who'll be working all day. As soon as her head hits the pillow, Natalia's eyes roll back and then shut, a deep sleep dragging her away. Anastasia stands a while in the doorway, watching her. She's about to leave for her run when the sun's first rays appear above the roof of the building opposite, shining a sharp beam straight onto the figure on the bed and she can clearly make out dark, splotchy bruises running up the length of Natalia's left arm.

* * *

Anastasia shoots a major campaign for Bottega Veneta, photographed against the snowcapped mountains behind the Bard fortress in Valle d'Aosta. She transfers the entirety of her fee to Vera's bank account; it's enough to buy another plot of land, or even an apartment. She also sends her a beautiful cashmere sweater and a Bottega Veneta leather handbag by registered delivery, though she knows Vera will ponder these items with a look of amusement on her face before placing them in her old Siberian wooden chest, once carved by Vera's beloved father. Anastasia includes a series of images, cut from magazines, of her most recent work. Anastasia imagines Vera poring over them before meticulously gluing them into the album she purchased from one of the street stalls at Koptyaki the week before she left.

'So I can look at you every day,' she said, blinking away tears.

The apartment is quiet this evening, Anastasia is home alone. The other girls are all out somewhere, probably wrapping up castings, though they've arranged to meet at the cocktail party thrown by the agency at Palazzo Parigi in less than an hour. Every couple of months, Gio's throws a party to keep the girls in contact with clients and prospective clients, as well as other industry people, from photographers to casting agents. Anastasia only returned from Valle d'Aosta last night and has spent the day sorting through her belongings, washing her clothes at the laundromat down the road and napping.

She's putting her make-up on, accentuating her gray

eyes with a discreet line of kohl, when her phone begins to ring. She can't immediately locate it; it's buried somewhere underneath the pile of laundry on her bed, and by the time she's rifled through it and managed to grab the little mobile, it has stopped ringing. It's unusual that it rang in the first place; the only person to ever call her is Graziela on the rare occasion that a change has been made to her schedule. She presses the 'Home' button and feels a sudden terror spread out in her stomach when she sees the +7 (343) area code, for Yekaterinburg. What if something has happened to Vera? It can't have been her calling; the dacha doesn't even have a phone line installed and it's not like her grandmother has a mobile phone. She's about to return the call when her phone starts ringing again, the little screen flashing green, the tinny sound of Vivaldi filling the room.

'Hello?'

'Ah. Anya. Anoushka.' It is Vera. Anastasia can't believe it.

'How—'

'I got a phone installed, sweet girl. With the money you sent. I wanted to hear your voice. Oh, Verushka, I miss you so much. I wanted to say be careful. We can't speak long because I have bought a special calling card to call another country and it was quite difficult but I just felt like I had to call you and tell you to be careful. It was just a feeling I had.'

'I am careful, Verushka.'

'Good. And thank you for the *Nelumbo nucifera* seeds. What a special thing to receive. I pray they shall grow.'

Anastasia feels momentarily struck dumb, intensely

moved to think of Vera kneeling in the dirt, digging a row into the black earth with her trowel, her dear, rough hands expertly pouring the seeds from Petersham Nurseries into the moist, fertile soil of the Urals.

'Yes,' she whispers.

'I—' begins Vera but there's a series of loud beeps and the line goes dead.

***

She drinks glass after glass of champagne. She feels fragile tonight, unsettled by the shock of suddenly hearing Vera's voice. She makes a mental note to look into getting Vera a different kind of phone contract, one that doesn't cut them off after two minutes, then they can speak every day. The thought of it fills Anastasia with a gentle warmth and she makes an effort to return to the conversation. She is standing with Xenia and Natalia and a couple of casting agents they all know. One of the agents, an American woman called Irene, pronouncing it as though she is Italian (ee-*ray*-neh), tells a funny story about a German girl they booked for a big show a couple of seasons ago who dropped out at the last minute because she decided she didn't agree with the label's fur policy.

'Can you imagine?' she shrieks, then drains her champagne glass and looks around for a top-up. 'What a fucking snowflake. I swear, the poor girls are always the easiest to deal with. Don't turn their noses up at work.' She winks at Natalia, Xenia and Anastasia before turning on her heel to chase a waiter circling the room pushing a magnum bottle of Krug on a drinks trolley. A momentary silence ensues after the other casting agent also drifts away in pursuit of the first.

'Wow. Toxic,' says Xenia.

'Toxic as fuck,' says Anastasia and the three of them laugh. Her friends always find it funny on the rare occasions she swears. Just then, she catches the eye of Tom, who is talking with another man she's never seen before. The other man is laughing at something Tom is saying and Anastasia finds herself wanting to stand there too, laughing. She makes a mental note to go over and say hi when there is a lull in the conversation.

'So. I got a job,' says Natalia, switching to Russian now that the three of them are alone, pulling Anastasia back in.

'Wow! That's great,' says Xenia.

'Yeah. See that guy over there? By the door. Yes, him. That's Roman Ulyanovich. Oligarch.'

'Mmm, I know who he is,' says Xenia.

'He's paying me ten thousand euros to go to the Monaco Grand Prix with him.'

'Wait, what?' says Anastasia. 'On a shoot?'

'No, no. As his date.' Xenia and Anastasia both stare at Natalia for a long while. She's looking particularly striking tonight in a high-necked black velvet-and-lace dress and she throws her head back and laughs as though this whole exchange with her friends is very, very funny. The man, Ulyanovich, turns toward them, and when his eyes meet Natalia's he breaks into a smile, revealing a jumble of uneven brown teeth beneath a bushy gray-specked mustache.

'Natalia. That man is easily sixty years old,' says Xenia.

'So? It's not like I have to do anything with him. It's

literally a question of standing on a balcony and watching some cars, he says.'

'You don't think you have to do anything with him for ten thousand euros?' Anastasia says, still staring at the balding man who seems to think it's okay to offer a desperate teenager ten thousand euros to accompany him to Monaco.

'I don't care, even,' says Natalia, a defiant look on her face. 'Besides, it's hardly the first money date I've been on. Not everyone can be on the cover of *Elle*, Anoushka.' She spits out Anastasia's pet name and Anastasia is taken aback by this sudden venom. She had no idea Natalia even knew about the *Elle* cover job; she only learned yesterday that she landed it.

'Look, I'm sorry,' says Natalia, reaching down to give Anastasia's hand a quick squeeze. Anastasia nods, still looking across the throng of people at Ulyanovich and his companion, who's partially obscured by other people.

Ulyanovich stares back, unashamed, and the man he is with steps forward and turns around, following Ulyanovich's gaze to the three girls across the room. Anastasia realizes with a start that it's the same man whose eye she briefly caught at the Strada party weeks before, the one who reminded her of a Casiraghi brother. Thinking back to that night, it feels like half a lifetime ago. It was also the first time she met Andrea Fiorentini, before she went to the Maldives and the awful thing happened. She feels like a different person from the girl she was before, though she can't quite put a finger on how this difference manifests itself. She makes a daily effort to never think about what happened or about Fiorentini himself, though occasionally their paths cross and Anastasia feels a visceral nausea for hours afterward, as though he left something inside her that poisons her from within.

'Who's that guy? With Ulyanovich?' she asks, keeping her voice neutral. Now both Natalia and Xenia break into giggles. 'What is it? Who is he?' Anastasia doesn't yet know that this is one of the defining moments of her life, that everything that does and does not happen to her from this point onward will be because of this man. The man's eyes are locked on hers, ice blue and mesmerizing, and he raises an eyebrow slowly, as though he's questioning her very existence. Ulyanovich appears to say something to him, but the man doesn't react or respond; he's entirely focused on the woman across the room – Anastasia.

'Anastasia, that's Giorgio di Vincenzo. You must know who he is? GMA's founder!' says Xenia.

'You're basically Giorgio's bitch,' Natalia says, giggling. 'We all are.'

'Except now you're Ulyanovich's bitch too,' says Xenia.

'Well, yes.'

'Wait,' says Anastasia, feeling strangely liquid, still locked into Giorgio's gaze. '*That's* Giorgio di Vincenzo?' She's heard of him, of course, the elusive billionaire philanthropist and founder of Gio's, but has never been introduced to him or even come across him except for that time on the Strada roof terrace when their eyes had briefly met, when she didn't know who he was. She remembers that night clearly, how the spires of the Duomo glinted in the evening sun like shards of bone emerging from the earth, how she was brand new to all of this, then. She remembers, too, the feeling of a moment passing between her and the stranger as she walked past, but it was nothing like this; this current of electricity rushing through her, as though he has passed it from him into her just by looking at her.

'Uh huh,' says Xenia, now aware of the strange look on Anastasia's face. 'He's a hottie, isn't he? Elusive, though. Doesn't often come to these things, and from what I've heard, he can be… difficult. Can't believe you haven't met him before.' Anastasia forces herself to look away from Giorgio and focus on her friends' faces but her heart is hollering in her chest and her hand holding the champagne flute has grown cold and sweaty, so she places the glass down on a windowsill and is about to excuse herself to go to the bathroom when Graziela appears.

'Ah, my favorite Russian dolls,' she says.

'I'm Ukrainian,' says Natalia, smiling sweetly and somewhat falsely, but Graziela pretends not to hear her. Anastasia realizes she's not going to pay the most attention to the girl bringing in the least money. She swallows and smiles at Graziela, trying to get rid of an image of Natalia pinned beneath Ulyanovich's hairy, flabby body in bed, her flame-colored hair fanning out on starched white sheets beneath her.

'What are you tittering about then? I've been watching you girls watching the boys.' She gestures to Ulyanovich and di Vincenzo across the room, who are talking intently.

'We're talking about men,' says Xenia, revealing those little sharp teeth in a smile.

'Ah. Anyone you like?'

'Nah,' says Xenia. 'I have a boyfriend, Marco. He's Italian. A real stud.' They all laugh.

'What about you, Natalia?' asks Graziela.

'Oh, I'm young, wild and single. But I only like them super rich,' says Natalia. Anastasia feels uncomfortable and wants a moment to herself in the bathroom, to hold her hands under the cold tap to center herself. She glances at Graziela, who has clearly just said something about her; she caught her name. She feels uncomfortable around Graziela still, like she can't trust her. When she first came here she had no choice but to trust Graziela with everything – she had nobody else – but after the Maldives, the trust is gone.

'What?' says Anastasia.

'Oh, Xenia just said I should ask you what kind of men you like, since you're so secretive and I told her that's not necessary.' Anastasia has the sensation that she doesn't quite understand what Graziela is saying, that her grasp of English, which by now is pretty solid, has momentarily lapsed.

'Why?'

'Why what?'

'Why is that not necessary?'

Graziela pauses for a long moment, watching Anastasia, a slight smile on her lips and a look Anastasia can't quite decipher in her eyes; pity, empathy, or perhaps triumph?

'Because you're Giorgio's.' She plants a wet kiss on Anastasia's cheek before swiftly merging back into the crowd, leaving Anastasia with the intense sensation of wanting to rub her face hard where Graziela's mouth touched her skin. Xenia whistles softly between her teeth and Natalia stands entirely still and silent besides her, like a statue. Anastasia knows what will happen next, as though she has no control over it. She'll turn her head a fraction, she'll move her gaze from Xenia toward the door, and her eyes will meet Giorgio's again and she won't be able to look away again, no matter how much she might want to.

Because you're Giorgio's.

She can hear Graziela's husky voice echoing in her head. And then, Vera's too, crystal clear – *be careful, Anoushka.*

18

Selma

Adrian's school, Sandøya Primary School, lies in a quiet residential neighborhood on the edge of a patch of pines and birch trees meandering down a hillside, bordering the playground. When Selma arrives, the playground is deserted, a few footballs lie scattered about and someone has piled several plastic inflatable sleds atop each other at the bottom of a small snow-covered hill. She wonders if Adrian is the kind of kid who likes to play with a ball, but concludes maybe not; being on the spectrum he's likely to prefer his own company over engaging in team sports.

'Come through,' says Marie, meeting Selma in the vestibule, where hot air whooshes toward her when she steps inside. She's short; Selma imagines she can't be much taller than the fourth graders she teaches, and her eyes look red and sore. She shows Selma into an empty classroom decorated with children's drawings and a huge colored-in map of the world.

'Thank you for meeting with me, Marie,' says Selma.

ALEX DAHL

'I… I just want to help in any way I can. Like I said in my message, I followed the Lucia Blix case, like everyone else. It was incredible what you did in that case; more than the police, I'd say.'

'I'm not sure about that, but—'

'I'm happy to be of any help I can.'

'I read your post to Adrian on Facebook. I was really moved by it.'

'Oh. Yes. I've had a lot of messages about that. It was impulsive of me to post it, perhaps, but I've felt so affected by what's happened, we all have. It seems surreal that something like this could happen in Sandefjord, again. And at all. I grew up here and it always just felt like the absolute safest place on earth.'

'Yes. I can see that.'

'And Adrian really is a very special little boy. You've probably gathered he's not quite like everyone else. Though in my work as a teacher, I've come to understand that there most definitely is no "everyone else". We're all beautifully different.'

'Yes. It's lovely to speak to an educator who really understands that. It wasn't my own experience in school, unfortunately.'

'Nor mine.'

'Would you mind telling me a little bit about Adrian and his mother, as you've observed them over the years?'

'Sure. So, Adrian started first grade here, as the only child in his year who hadn't attended any of the local nurseries. Maybe his mother sensed early on that Adrian was different to the other kids and wanted to shield him from them for as long as possible. I remember she once told me that she'd made the decision to stay at home with him up until school age, and was able to do that because she'd inherited some money.'

'Did she say from whom?'

'No.'

'How did she tell you this? In person?'

'Yes.'

'Can you confirm whether or not you believe Liv Carlsen to be deaf?'

'Oh yes, Liv was deaf, from birth.'

'So, how—'

'When I was at university, I did two semesters of audio-visual communication as part of my teaching degree. I also hold a master's in special needs. This was the main reason Adrian was placed in my form as opposed to one of the other two.'

'I see.'

'So, as Adrian and Liv communicate mainly by sign language, it made sense for him to be placed with me. It soon emerged that there were other issues with Adrian, and it was pretty obvious that he was neurodivergent.'

'How was it obvious?'

'He has little to no interest in interacting with other children. His interests are very narrow and he is best reached through creating analogies to those.'

'What is he interested in?'

'Airplanes. So, for example, when I give Norwegian homework to write a story, I'll ask Adrian to specifically write a story based at an airport, involving a variety of different types of aircraft. Then it's no problem and he'll produce a lovely, richly detailed story. If I'd told him to just write any old story, or about something outside of his field of interest, he'd struggle.'

'I see.'

'It's the same across most subjects. I tailor as much as I can to his interests and make sure wider learning can be accessed from within that, if that makes sense. Recently, the kids did a history project about World War II. Adrian, of course, chose to do his on the Luftwaffe, and it was just wonderful. He's a very intelligent boy. And very sensitive.'

'How much would you say you've had to do with Liv over the years?'

'Not that much, to be honest. You know what Norwegian schools are like, pretty hands-off. I don't get the impression most of the parents know each other or socialize outside of school. And Adrian is unfortunately on the periphery of the social dynamics of the class anyway.'

'Right.'

'He gets picked on, a lot. I keep an eye out for him, try to make sure certain kids don't get near him at break times, that kind of thing. But he has a very tough time socially.'

'Poor kid.'

'Yeah.' Marie stares off into space, her eyes flooding with fresh tears. 'You know, I keep seeing him in my mind, the way he was that last week. On Wednesday, two of the other boys in the class attacked him on the way outside for breaktime. He had a nasty cut on his cheekbone. He looked so tiny and broken in the nurse's office, I offered to drive him home. I've done it on a few other occasions too. Liv doesn't drive.'

'Have you ever been to their house?'

'No. You can't drive all the way there. I dropped him

in the lay-by over by Vesterøysvingen. It's just a couple of minutes' walk from there, I think. I asked him to tell Liv to get in touch with me so we could talk about what had happened and he said he would. I also messaged her directly, asking her to get in touch, but she never called, which was unusual. She always follows up when it comes to his school stuff. On the Thursday he was home from school, unsurprisingly. On the Friday, he was back but I was so busy preparing for a seminar that I barely had a chance to speak to him all day, and a substitute teacher handled the class for the final two hours. I just wish I'd had a chance to pull him aside and ask if everything was okay at home, whether something had happened…'

'Marie, you mustn't blame yourself. It sounds as though Adrian knows you care about him very much. Did you ever speak to Liv about work?'

'I believed she was a cleaner at the Sigma school. She filled that out on a form so I had no reason not to believe her. That being said… it did, perhaps, strike me as a little bit odd that she worked as a cleaner for a living. Mainly because she clearly only worked during school hours; she was with Adrian the rest of the time, and wouldn't the cleaners at the deaf school work in the late afternoons after everyone has gone home? Also, Liv is quite a glamorous type, though she plays it down. Beautifully kept nails, groomed eyebrows, that kind of thing.'

'Did you know she used to be a model?'

'No. No, I didn't know that. Oh wow. Yeah, now you've mentioned it, I can't say I'm surprised.'

'I found it really moving, the way you spoke of her as

a mother in your post. It sounded like you were confident that Adrian was safe at home with his mother.'

'Yes. Absolutely. I have never doubted that.'

'Are you aware that Liv was reported to Barnevernet twice?'

Marie looks uncomfortable, then a flash of anger travels across her gentle face. 'Yes. It was the headteacher at the time who reported her. There was a big hullaballoo about it, actually. I gave a statement to Barnevernet in support of Liv, and actually worried I might get fired for it. It felt like a witch hunt.'

'Why was she reported?'

'It was to do with the school wanting Adrian to have a formal diagnosis so we'd be awarded more funds to provide tailored provision for him.'

'Sounds reasonable.'

'Yes. I was in favor of that too. Sometimes it really helps to have a label that goes some way to explaining why we are how we are, but Liv felt very strongly that while Adrian is different, there isn't anything wrong with his way of being. And I agree with that too. Getting a spectrum diagnosis at that age is a very lengthy, invasive process and I think Liv might have felt like there was no need for that, so early on, especially as Adrian had no academic struggles or problems keeping up with the curriculum.'

'Right.'

'So the headteacher at the time reported her to Barnevernet saying Liv didn't have her son's best interests at heart.'

'Sounds difficult to be caught in the middle of all that.'

'Yes, but I knew I had to defend her. Just like I knew I had to speak to you. It isn't true what some of the papers are saying, that she is crazy or whatever. I have never known Liv to be anything other than a loving, competent mother. I think something bad must have happened to them. That someone has taken them.'

'Can you think of any reason why anyone would want to do that?'

'No,' she says softly, looking stricken. Just then, a shrill bell rings and Marie jumps to her feet. 'I'm sorry, I have to go. I have lessons in just a minute.'

'Thank you for this, Marie. Do you mind giving me a call if anything else comes to mind?'

She nods and reaches across to squeeze Selma's arm, then she disappears down the hallway, the rubber soles of her shoes squeaking as she goes.

***

As the train pulls away from Sandefjord station, Selma looks out at the empty streets through lashings of rain. She's glad she went, and it feels exhilarating to be so filled up with a story that there's almost no space in her mind for anything else. She likes it that way, and always tells her father that she keeps her personal life simple so her work life can be wild. The rain thankfully lets up by the time she arrives in Holmestrand.

Liv's mother lives in a modern apartment just a couple of minutes' walk from the railway station. It seems unbelievable to her that it could be possible to choose to live less than an hour away in Sandefjord with your son and never want to see your own family. What would Selma give to see her own mother one last time? Everything, she thinks, lifting her finger to the doorbell that reads 'Carlsen'.

She's buzzed in without being asked who it is and she takes the stairs instead of the elevator, a modern glass box fixed to the outside of the building that gives Selma vertigo just looking at it. On the third floor, a door is ajar, and the smell of cooked meat seeps out into the hallway, making Selma's stomach growl; she hasn't had anything to eat since the McDonald's burger almost twenty-four hours ago.

'Hurry inside, Lena,' a woman's voice shouts from inside, 'it's getting cold in here!'

'Umm,' says Selma, pushing the door open. 'Hello?'

'I said close the door! It's been left open since the last girl left! Close it, now! It's so damned cold!'

Selma steps into the hallway and shuts the door, trying to think what to say next.

'Uh, Mrs Carlsen? My name is Selma. May I please come in?' A thick silence ensues, only broken by an occasional low wheezing sound, like an old dog trying to hobble up a flight of stairs.

'Lena?' asks the voice again, thinly. 'Is that you?'

Selma slips her running shoes off next to the other shoes meticulously lined up in the hallway and proceeds toward what she assumes is the lounge. A woman is half reclined in a black leather sofa, clutching an electric blanket to her chin with one hand and the remote control with the other. At the sight of Selma a look of annoyance crosses her face.

'Who the hell are you?'

'I'm sorry, my name is Selma—'

'Why hasn't Lena come? Is she working overtime again?'

'Ummm.'

'You're not from the council medical team, are you?'

'No. I work for *Dagsposten*.'

'Oh for fuck's sake. A reporter. Can you please leave?'

'I was hoping I could speak to you for a moment—'

'And I was hoping someone had come to help change my catheter bag. It's full.' The woman, who appears to be in her sixties but looks much older thanks to the thin, greasy gray hair plastered to her pink skull and the huge puffy bags beneath her eyes commonly seen in people with alcohol addiction, stares at Selma with thinly concealed hostility. Then she glares at a metal stand on the floor next to her, from which a large bag of dark-yellow urine hangs suspended. 'You're trespassing. I'm going to have to call the police.'

'I'm sorry. I've come about Liv. Please let me stay, only for a few moments.'

'Liv, Liv, Liv, it's all I've heard for days. Unsurprising perhaps. She always was attention-seeking.'

'You must be very upset about Liv going missing. And little Adrian.'

'No.'

'No?'

'Excuse me, whatever your name is, but my daughter disappeared from my life a very long time ago. By choice.'

'That must have been really painful.'

'Are you a therapist as well as a reporter?' she laughs, a cruel little bark.

'Do you mind sharing with me what happened the last time Liv went missing?'

'It wasn't once. It was repeatedly. She's a loose cannon.'

'Look, Mrs Carlsen, I just met with someone in Sandefjord who knew your daughter and little Adrian quite well, and she seemed to be of a very different opinion about Liv. I can appreciate, though, that there is a long and painful family history here. I just wanted to mention it, in case it gave you some comfort that Liv seems to have got her life in order and cared very well for Adrian.'

'I'd be surprised. Couldn't even care for herself.'

'She's the youngest of four girls, am I right?'

The woman nods. 'My husband, bless his heart, always said we should have stopped at three. It was too much to ask to produce four healthy girls and for all of them to turn out to be lovely people. Liv was always difficult. Challenging, obstinate, argumentative, cut from a different cloth than the rest of us. They're good girls, my daughters. Kaja's a veterinary assistant, Tone is a conductor on the train, Silja's got a very good job in marketing in Drammen, big office with coffee machines and things like that. They're all married mothers, modest and hard workers. And what's wrong with that?'

'Nothing, of course, I just wonder—'

'Nothing was ever good enough for Liv,' continues the mother, interrupting Selma. 'Not this family, not this town, not even this country, no normal job or normal man. It all had to be so bloody special. *She* always had to be special.' Selma wonders if Liv was ever made to feel special at home, as the youngest of four, born to a mother like this one, and concludes probably not. 'When she was spotted on the train by a model scout, we thought she was making it up at first. But then off she went to Oslo and started working straight away. We couldn't believe that she'd be paid as much as her father to parade around in ridiculous, overpriced clothes. She went to Paris for a season, but hated it. Can you imagine? Even Paris wasn't good enough for that girl.'

A sudden image comes to Selma's mind, as forceful as a punch. Liv stepping out onto a runway, blinded by lights, her heart beating so fast it feels like the desperate scramble of a caged bird for freedom, her face sculptured by dramatic make-up, very loud hip-hop music coursing through her as she begins to walk. And after, alone in a prep room backstage, smoking thin cigarettes and removing all the make-up from her young, flawless face, the feeling of being liquidized inside, a vast disparity between appearance and feeling. And later still, walking home to her tiny bedsit through quiet, rain-lashed streets, crossing a vast, beautiful square, feeling untethered from everything she'd known in her life.

'Do you know why she hated it?'

'Hard work didn't come easy for her. Liv was very lazy.'

'I'm a little surprised you refer to her in the past tense.'

'I think of her as in the past. Dead, even.'

'What about the boy? Aren't you curious about your grandson?'

'I have seven other grandchildren. Their mothers bring them here to see me several times a week, so I've more than got my hands full, really.' She indicates to a long stretch of orange yarn spooling out from a pair of knitting needles on the table in front of the sofa.

'Right.'

'Anything else?'

'Was it hard for Liv as a child, being deaf?'

'Whatever do you mean?'

'I just wonder whether it was challenging at times. You know, raising a child with a disability?'

'I have no idea what you are talking about. You really are a very odd girl. Now, would you please leave.'

Selma stares at the woman, and at the revolting heavy bag of urine dangling from the stand above her, feeling a visceral pity for Liv, who came into the world with this person as her mother. Selma knows that it is infinitely better to have had a mother like her own for seven short years, than to have a mother like this for a lifetime. She understands now exactly how it's possible to live less than an hour away and yet choose never to see your own mother. She nods and turns around, hurrying back out from the apartment with the stale smell of cooked meat and urine lingering in the air.

***

Back home, she picks up Medusa gently in one hand and carries the Mac through to the living room in the other. She's messaged Olav twice, asking him to call ASAP, and has also left two messages for Gaute Svendsen. Her head pounded with swirling, discombobulated thoughts all the way back from Holmestrand, she felt completely shaken after the meeting with Liv Carlsen's vile and vicious mother. The enormity of what she told her echoed around Selma's mind, growing and growing. *Whatever are you talking about?* she said, her face etched with genuine surprise when asked about her daughter's deafness. It could mean several things, of course. Liv could have been lying about being deaf, but why? Or she could have become deaf in the years since she last saw her mother, but why would she invent a lie about that, telling Marie she'd been deaf since birth?

An email comes through on her phone and Selma glances at it briefly before doing a double take. It's from Kai Oserød.

Hello,

It occurred to me that the camera might have caught something. Liv came knocking about a month ago. She'd slipped on the stairs leading up to the office in the morning when it was still dark and was bleeding a lot from a cut above her eye. She needed a bandage, which I gave to her. When she stepped onto the porch, the camera was activated and started recording. I remembered it was just before Christmas, so I went back and had a look, and managed to recover the recording, attached to this email. Not sure it's at all relevant, do you think I should also send it to the police?

Kai O.

Selma is about to click on the attachment when the doorbell rings, making Medusa snap to attention, her yellow eyes blazing.

'What the...' she mutters to herself, glancing at the time on the clock above the cooker. It's eight o' clock sharp. Then she remembers. Olav.

Come to mine after work. Bring takeout, she'd written. Her stomach groans at the thought of a Thai green chicken curry, laced with chilies and served with steaming white jasmine rice. She opens the door, and there's Olav, holding a large paper bag from which a delicious smell emanates.

'Special order from Yaya's,' he says, smiling widely, tiny snow crystals settled among the strands of his dark curly hair, and Selma is surprised at how glad she is to see him.

'You're not going to believe the crazy stuff going down in Sandefjord this time,' she says, shutting the door behind him.

19

Adrian

They sit on red plastic chairs in the cafeteria. The Man glances around a lot, as though making sure no one he knows is there. The sun rises slowly from the black surface of the sea, rinsing the horizon blood red. Adrian stares out of the windows which wrap around the entirety of the lounge at the front of the ship. After a while, The Man gets up and buys a newspaper, a steaming black coffee for himself, and a hot chocolate for Adrian. The Man doesn't appear to understand the newspaper; he quickly flicks through the pages which rustle loudly, pausing briefly to glance at a photograph here and there, until he gets to a page with crosswords and sudoku. He pulls a pen from his jacket pocket and starts the sudoku, his brows knitting together in concentration. Adrian likes sudoku, and can solve this one after a brief glance from across the table. The Man pauses for a long while over one of the empty boxes. Adrian holds up four fingers on his right hand. The Man looks up at him and at the sight of Adrian, his face breaks into a smile.

'Ah, yes,' he says. 'Of course. Thanks, kiddo.' Adrian instinctively smiles back, then realizes what he's done and forces his face back to blank and unreadable.

'Hey,' says The Man. 'What's your name? Please. I'd like to know.'

Adrian puts his hand in his pocket and touches upon the crumpled paper Concorde. He feels jolted to think about what has happened in the short space of time since he was on his knees in the living room at home, watching Madplanez' tutorial, carefully folding the sheet into flaps and ailerons, waiting for Mama. He swallows hard, trying to dislodge the painful lump in his throat. He pulls the Concorde out of his pocket, smooths down the paper until it is almost right again. He takes the pen from The Man's hand and writes his name on the plane's fuselage.

'Adrian,' says The Man. Ay-dree-un, he says. 'Beautiful name.' Adrian looks at him, it seems a strange thing for him to say, that his name is beautiful. He shakes his head; The Man said it wrong. The Man understands what he means and repeats his name, getting it right this time – Ah-dree-ahn.

'Adrian,' he says again, 'of course.' His eyes look sad. Adrian wants to talk to him now, to ask more questions. He unfolds the plane and smooths the sheet down repeatedly with his hand. He picks the pen up again and writes *Where Mama*.

'I will do everything to find her,' says The Man, very slowly and Adrian understands 'I' and 'find' and 'her'.

Who take Mama, writes Adrian.

'Bad people,' says The Man. Adrian stares at him, and even when The Man stares back, Adrian manages to maintain eye contact. He has to find out if this man is a bad man too. *Why you help me*, he writes.

'Because I love your mama,' says The Man and looking at him, at the way his eyes are awash with tears, at how his mouth twitches strangely downward as he speaks, at the way his words emerge barely in a whisper, Adrian knows this is true. Then, The Man lowers his voice, and in Adrian and Mama's secret language, which no one else knows in the whole world besides them, he says: 'And because I love *you*, more than all the stars in the sky.'

Adrian stands up, almost knocking over his hot chocolate. He walks away from the table and stands by the floor-to-ceiling window, pressing his nose against the cool glass. He can see a line of lights in the distance, curiously stretching out across the water, then he realizes it's a bridge. He looks up at the sky, now a deep violet as the day takes over from the night, hoping to see a bird, because they calm him down. It's to do with their freedom – Adrian craves freedom. He feels trapped in his own mind; he's not like anyone else and he wishes he could fly away. He scans the sky, but there are no signs of any birds, not even a seagull. Adrian especially likes seagulls even if everyone else finds them annoying. How great would it be to be that comfortable making lots of noise? He likes their eager faces and hungry, open beaks too.

His heart is beating so fast in his chest he worries he could faint. How is it possible that The Man knows the secret language? He has a strange way of pronouncing the words, as though he's speaking them underwater, but there is no doubt he knows it. It must be true that he knows Mama, and it must be true that he's his dad, but his dad is

bad, so how can he trust that he wants to help find Mama?
I love you, he said. No one but Mama has ever said that
to Adrian before, because no one but Mama loves him. He
feels a heavy hand land on his shoulder and give it a gentle
squeeze. He turns around and The Man draws him close
into a hug and only then does Adrian realize he's crying,
big trails of tears meandering down his face. They stay like
that for a long while, Adrian letting The Man hug him. He
doesn't usually like being touched or hugged; sometimes it
can feel like something is left on his skin from whomever
touched him and he doesn't like it. Once Marie hugged
him after Steffen was mean to him and her hug made it
worse so Mama had to call the school to say, *Please don't
hug Adrian.*

'Come,' says The Man. They sit back down at the table.
From his jacket pocket The Man pulls a couple of folded-
over sheets of paper. 'You like planes?' Adrian nods. 'Me
too,' says The Man and he smiles, showing a row of straight,
long teeth. Adrian takes a piece of paper and starts to fold,
watched by The Man. It takes a long while to complete
the plane from memory, but when he finishes, tweaking
the wingtips and vertical ailerons into distinct sharp flicks,
and holds it up for The Man to see, it's certainly a very
impressive aircraft.

'Woah. An F-14 Tomcat. Impressive.'

Adrian raises an eyebrow. He didn't anticipate that The
Man would know the name of the plane. The Man takes
a sheet of paper and Adrian watches as his hands expertly
fold and tuck the ends into an ever more complicated
construction, his eyes widening as he realizes he's making
an SU-30. He hands the finished aircraft to Adrian, who

holds it gingerly, unable to keep a look of sheer awe off his face.

The Man stands up and motions for Adrian to follow. They leave the cafeteria and walk toward the back of the ferry. They pass a few other passengers, a couple of men playing cards at the table of a closed restaurant, several sleeping, heads resting upon bags, and a man staring out of a window in the corridor, at a long strip of land barely discernible from the still, dark sea. They take a flight of stairs down to a lower deck and turn a corner to a long, empty corridor lined with lit-up cabinets showing items for sale from the duty-free shop.

'Perfect,' says The Man and lifts his hand holding the SU-30. 'A fantastic plane,' he continues, in a tinny pretend voice, like a plane commentator speaking on the radio, and Adrian is amazed to realize he understands what he says in English more easily now he's getting used to listening carefully to it. 'Fast as all hell.' He releases the plane and it takes flight swiftly, slicing soundlessly through the air before descending in a slack line and veering off to the left. 'Boom.' They laugh. Adrian raises his hand and gives the Tomcat a good push. It careens uncontrollably and crashes with a thud into a cabinet containing stacks of Marlboro Reds. He feels his face flush with embarrassment but when The Man laughs, he can't help but join in. They pick the planes back up and fly them again and again, not interrupted by anyone, until they feel the ferry slow down, the engine backing noisily against the current, making the floor vibrate and the glass fronts of the cabinets tremble.

A loud voice crackles through the loudspeaker system, saying something in several different languages, none of which Adrian can understand. The Man draws his eyebrows together in concentration, then nods his head, and points downward to the belly of the ship, where the bus waits on the car deck. When they have settled back into their seats, Adrian motions for The Man to hand him the pen by making a writing motion with his right hand. He takes the Concorde back out from his pocket, finds a white patch without any writing on it and writes *Will bad men kill Mama?*

The Man clenches his jaw and shakes his head curtly.

No! he writes. *We are going to stop them.*

OK, writes Adrian, forming the word with his lips too, first the puckered O, then the smiled K. He hands the pen back to The Man as the engine rumbles to life and the bow door splits open, revealing a bright-blue sky outside. The Man takes the pen, and his hand, and Adrian lets him hold it.

20

Anastasia

I t's Friday morning, less than a week after the cocktail party at Palazzo Parigi. Anastasia wakes with a start at twenty past five and, for once, decides to try to sleep longer – she doesn't have to get up early today. A current of nervous energy rushes through her at the prospect of what awaits her: at eleven she will be picked up from the apartment and brought to Giorgio di Vincenzo's home in Como, for lunch. Two days ago, as she got up at the end of their morning chat, Graziela handed her a small envelope the blue color of duck eggs.

'For you,' she said, winking. Anastasia stuck the envelope into her handbag and didn't open it until she turned a corner, walking briskly away from the agency on via Savona toward a fitting at Bulgari headquarters on via Montenapoleone.

Dear Anastasia,
    I would like to invite you to lunch at my home in Como on Friday. Please say yes.   Gio x

She stood a while on the street corner, just thinking, trying to discern how she actually felt about the invitation. She knew she'd like to look into those eyes again, but Giorgio di Vincenzo frightened her – never had she spent time in the company of someone with such vastly different life experience to her own. The day after the cocktail party, she and Xenia had sat close together on Xenia's bed, drinking fresh mint tea and googling everything they could find about Giorgio on Xenia's laptop. He may not be one of the Monégasque princes he resembles, but he's an aristocrat nonetheless; born Count Giorgio Giuseppe Raffaele von Michaelisburg di Vincenzo, the oldest son of an Austrian princess and socialite, Serafina von Michaelisburg, and her Italian husband, Count Gianfranco di Vincenzo.

According to a rare interview he'd given *Paris Match* a couple of years ago, and translated into Russian by Google Translate, he split his time between homes in Como, Palermo, Anacapri, and Umbria. He was 'too busy' to get married and 'utterly devoted' to his work, and in spite of being linked to numerous models and members of European high society, he remains single. Apart from running Gio's Modeling Agency, an agency committed to taking care of its girls, he was the founder and chairman of Audire, a charity supporting deaf children across Italy and providing them with life-changing surgery, or if that is not possible, access to hearing aids and education about managing deafness.

The article featured a series of images of Giorgio posing among a throng of smiling children giving thumbs-ups to the camera. Anastasia had felt a sliver of trepidation just looking at his picture. Another article, this one from *Hello!* magazine, showed Giorgio at an aristocratic wedding in

Germany, where he'd been best man. In one of the images, in which he stood under an archway of white roses, waiting next to the groom for his bride to arrive, he appeared to have been unaware of the cameras and had a wistful look on his face that made him look young and somewhat forlorn.

One of Europe's most eligible bachelors, Prince Constantine of Bayreuth and Anstruther-Schaall, is now firmly off the market after marrying Ana Victoria Vazquez at the Marienkirche in Munich today, read the article. *Another high-profile bachelor, Count Giorgio di Vincenzo, of Palermo, served as his best man.*

'How do they even remember their own names?' Xenia had asked and they'd laughed and laughed, repeating the strange names as if introducing themselves. 'Oh, hi there, I'm Prince Constantine of Bayreuth and Anstruther-Schaall. Nice to meet you, Count Giorgio Giuseppe Raffaele von Michaelisburg di Vincenzo...'

Anastasia and Xenia had never heard of any of these people but had spent a few amusing hours peering into their world through the magic portal of the internet. They'd uncovered one further article about Giorgio that featured some pictures, in which he was doing some conservational work concerning marine life off the coast of Sicily. In one image he stood on the deck of a trawler holding a dead bird who had yards of blue plastic rope wound around its neck. His face was serious and haunted, his dark-blond hair wet with seawater and whipped by the wind. It was this image of Giorgio that came to Anastasia's mind when she received the invitation to lunch with him in Como; not the smooth, smartly dressed businessman whose eyes had locked on hers across the room at Palazzo Parigi, or the suit-clad prince of the wedding article, but this guy – the philanthropist holding the poor bird, a look of sadness etched across his face.

***

She's picked up in a black Range Rover by a courteous driver who nods at her and holds the door open, revealing a pristine white leather interior. She gets into the back seat and immediately, a screen on the back of the seat in front leaps to life with the message, *Buongiorno, Anastasia. Looking forward to seeing you soon, G X.*

She leans back against the seat, watching the busy streets of Porto Venezia slide by outside. It's a beautiful day, not too hot, but sunny and mild and lots of people are out and about. Normally, she'd be one of them, walking from one client to another. They stop at a red light, and she watches a lanky girl with a serious expression, who looks like she's only in her mid-teens, cross the street clutching the telltale black portfolio book to her chest. Anastasia smiles to herself, thinking of how much like that girl she was when she first arrived in Milan. Daunted to navigate the chaotic Italian traffic, trying to figure out how to get from here to there, rushing to get to the next appointment in the hope of getting seen by the right people at the right time. Now, she's someone who knows Milan like the back of her hand, who has friends from Brazil and Ukraine and France and even America, who works for Gucci and Bulgari, on her way to lunch with an actual count.

After less than ten minutes, the car pulls off the main thoroughfare of corso Venezia and into what looks like a suburban industrial area. Anastasia was expecting to spend over an hour in the car and looks at the driver in the mirror. He nods to a hangar, outside which stands another man, this one big and blond, smartly clad in a sharp suit. The driver walks around the car and opens the door for Anastasia.

'Your next ride, madame,' he says. The blond man steps forward and hands Anastasia noise-canceling headphones with a microphone. She frowns, not understanding, but he leads her gently by the arm away from the car and around the side of the building, where the hangar's enormous doors are folded back and in front of the building stands a small white helicopter with a blue-and-gold crest on the tail cone. Anastasia feels a sudden terror and the man must sense this, because he smiles kindly at her and tells her not to worry in perfect American English.

'I'm Ron,' he says, 'Giorgio's aide. I'll be looking after you up to Como, okay? Let's go.'

Anastasia gets into the helicopter next to Ron, careful to smooth down her skirt so it doesn't crease against the leather seats.

'You're gonna love this, kiddo,' says Ron, but whatever he says next is drowned out by the rotor blades leaping to life. The pilot, a young man wearing sunglasses, turns around and gives Ron and Anastasia a thumbs-up, then the little helicopter begins to turn and taxi out into the open space between buildings. Anastasia puts her headphones on to cancel out the deafening roar of the helicopter, and is surprised to find Ron's smooth voice speaking into her ear, clearly audible.

'Short flight this morning,' he says, as the helicopter rises steadily, slowly upward. Anastasia sits with her face pressed against the window, watching the huge Range Rover become smaller and smaller until it looks like a toy car. She laughs a little. 'I need to run you through a few things, okay? Rules, if you will.'

'Rules?' asks Anastasia, turning to look at Ron, who suddenly appears somewhat frightening, with his huge bulky frame and stern expression. What is she doing here, trapped in a tiny, trembling helicopter, flying to an unknown destination with this man she's never met before?

'Yes, rules. Look, Giorgio is a cool guy. He leads a big life, very busy. A kind of life that is perhaps difficult to understand if you're not from that world, do you understand?'

Anastasia nods, then shakes her head. 'No, I'm not sure I do.'

'Don't worry. You'll have fun. Giorgio's been excited you're coming. He doesn't do this often, you know. Never, actually.' Anastasia laughs a little, incredulously, but Ron nods as if to further reassure her. 'It's true. He likes a party as much as the next guy but he doesn't often bring guests to the house.'

'Okay,' says Anastasia softly, knowing even less what to expect than before. In the distance, the green hills grow into brown-and-green mountains, then behind them, bigger mountains, some snowclad even now, at the end of May. She waits for Ron to continue and to explain what these rules are, but for a while he doesn't.

'The Alps,' says Ron, following her line of sight. The helicopter zooms above a small lake, then another one, with shimmering, azure water.

'Is it Lake Como?' asks Anastasia.

'Not yet.' They both look out of the windows as the helicopter flies above a verdant green mountain, its peak not far below. 'Here's what you need to know. The most important thing is, never speak to him without direct eye contact. Do you understand?'

She considers this for a moment. 'Can I ask why?'

'It's common courtesy to look someone in the eye when you address them.'

'Yes, but—'

'This one is important, Anastasia.'

'Okay. But what if we're walking side by side, or he's turned away from me when I speak, or—'

'Then wait until you have eye contact before speaking again. It's to do with respect. Look, I know it sounds a little odd. But in Giorgio's circles, it's completely normal.' Anastasia is well aware that she knows very little of the kind of world Giorgio inhabits, but she's a fast learner; she's proven that in the past year, going from junior horticultural assistant at Ganina Yama to a model in Milan, navigating a new life bearing almost no similarity to her old one. Even her own face in the mirror has been subtly altered, and the girl looking back at her reflected in the helicopter's window isn't the same girl she grew up seeing in the mirror above the wash bowl at home, the only mirror in the dacha. This girl looks sharper, cleaner, her eyes a little harder, as though every part of her has been brought into focus.

Anastasia realizes she hasn't responded, so she nods again, more firmly this time, and smiles at Ron as the helicopter lowers itself down toward the surface of another lake, this one even bigger than the last one, with crystal-clear aquamarine water along its shores, deepening to shades of cobalt and indigo further out. Anastasia can't make out where they're going to touch down; all she can see beneath them is water. When they are so close to the water that she can make out individual creases on the lake's surface, the helicopter turns in a tight circle suddenly revealing a huge house directly in front of them, its gardens rolling all the way down to the water. The house is a dusky pink with light-green shutters. It has numerous terraces and a sprawling, meticulously kept vibrant green lawn onto which the helicopter softly lands. Anastasia stares out of the window as the rotor blades wind down, at the house, at the man emerging from a lower floor onto the terrace and waving at her, at the several speedboats moored off a jetty jutting into the lake.

'Welcome to Villa Serafina,' says Ron, clearly enjoying the stunned look on Anastasia's face.

***

She didn't expect Giorgio to cook for her, though she isn't sure she knew what to expect at all, but he does, slicing fat red onions and chopping garlic, throwing them into a sizzling pan. The kitchen is large but cozy and clearly lived in, and two black Labradors lie in the corner, thumping their tails every time she so much as looks at them, occasionally getting up and ambling over for a few strokes.

'They like you,' Giorgio says.

'Labradors like everyone,' she counters, disentangling herself from the dogs' energetic cuddles, making sure she has full eye contact with Giorgio every time she speaks. It was strange that Ron had been so adamant about how to speak to Giorgio, who seems so relaxed and normal. She feels comfortable and at ease in his company, the conversation has flowed easily from the start, even though they realized that they had actually never spoken before Anastasia emerged from the helicopter and they impulsively kissed.

She smiles to herself, cheeks aching, to think that they kissed before they ever spoke.

They eat slowly, a simple pasta dish with olives and thyme from the garden, talking so intently they barely remember to eat. At one point Giorgio looks almost sad while she's telling him something, and she pauses and asks whether something is wrong.

'No,' he says. 'Just. You're beautiful. Too beautiful.'

He picks her hand off the table and holds it in his own, turning it over and tracing the lines on her palm. He smiles, but his eyes are serious and pensive. He looks young, much younger than thirty-seven, and when she says that, he laughs and asks how she knows his age.

'Don't worry, I googled you too,' he adds, squeezing her hand again when he senses her embarrassment, and they both laugh. 'It would seem you're Yekaterinburg's most successful export to Milan...'

He asks her to tell him about Yekaterinburg, about growing up out there in the forests, about her grandmother and the dacha. So she does. He asks her to tell him something she's never told anyone before and she tells him about the time when she was ten or eleven years old and she decided on a whim not to go straight back to Vera's after school, but to the apartment building she lived in with her mother before she died. It was a run-down building on Ulitsa Khabarovskaya, and she knew how to get there because it was on the way to Sveta's Dance Studio and Vera had pointed it out to her from the bus window more than once.

'I can't believe she's really gone,' Vera said once, softly, staring at the building through crumbling columns of exhaust as the bus stood in gridlocked traffic for a long while.

'On that particular day,' Anastasia continues, looking into Giorgio's eyes as she speaks, 'I got off the bus at the vaguely familiar stop close to Ulitsa Khabarovskaya. I ran straight across the street through a lull in traffic, prompting honks, my feet shuffling on a thin layer of ice on the road. As I walked toward the building it felt as though I was walking straight into a memory, the only clear one I had of Nadia. My mother. We were walking together through fresh snow and she was tugging on my hand, making me go faster and faster, my feet barely touching the ground. When I couldn't go any faster, my mother paused, annoyed, and picked me up. Then, it was as though her tone changed and she smiled at me, taking time to kiss my cold cheeks. *Vorobushek,* she said, whispering the word straight into my ear.'

'What does that mean?' asks Giorgio.

Anastasia pauses, looking for the right word, then it comes to her. 'Little sparrow.'

'So, what happened next? On that day when you went there after school?'

'Nothing, really. Just that memory of her came to me. Before that, I had nothing. It was as though she was returned to me, and I never lost her again; she was seared into my mind, every last detail of her face, the way she moved, the sound of her voice.'

'Do you look like her?'

'No. I don't think so. Vera says I look like the men in the family. My own father, and Vera's.'

'You look nothing like a man,' says Giorgio. They laugh.

'What about you?' asks Anastasia. 'Who do you resemble?'

'My father, I think. I wish I could say my mother; she was very beautiful. Like you.'

'What… What happened to your mother?'

'I lost her in childhood. Another thing we have in common, Anastasia.'

'I'm so sorry,' she whispers. He nods and looks stricken. He opens his mouth as if to continue but doesn't, and Anastasia doesn't prompt him further.

He reaches across the table and pours another smooth column of rosé wine into her glass. He stands up and picks up both of their wine glasses.

'Come,' he says. 'I'd like to show you the gardens.'

They walk around for a long time, pausing occasionally to sit admiring their surroundings at one bench or another, most with views of the lake. They kiss again, this time slowly and consciously, only breaking apart after a long while to laugh a little, at the turn the day has taken, the ease of each other's company.

'Let's go out on the water,' he says, and from the jetty they glide out onto the lake in a gleaming Riva. Far out, when Villa Serafina is a mere pink speck on the distant shore, Giorgio throws an anchor and they lie down close together on the sun deck at the front, Giorgio pointing out the sights to Anastasia, leading her hand with his own to point them out.

'That's Villa Mascia over there with the bronze statues, that's Monte Crocione, that's Bellagio, that's George Clooney having his afternoon espresso on the terrace of Grand Hotel Villa Serbelloni, just kidding…'

* * *

It's days before she leaves. Her stomach hurts from all the laughing. Other places too, reminders of all the sex, pleasure bordering on pain. Giorgio drives her himself in a little sports car with a roaring engine, and they sit in comfortable silence, his right hand resting on her thigh, suggestively high up. Every time they glance at each other, one of them bursts into laughter again, struck by the craziness of the weekend, that such a time could be conjured up by a couple of strangers and some serious chemistry. It might have made her uncomfortable, the way he sometimes stares at her, so intensely that it feels as though he is trying to inch his way inside her soul, but there is a steadiness there that she likes. It's not only a sexual current that runs between them, but something more than that, a tenderness. He kissed her within moments of her stepping out from the helicopter, Ron trailing somewhere behind them on the lawn. He'd clearly intended to kiss her cheek but she intentionally moved her face, offering up her lips, surprised at her own brazenness, but pleased he read her signs correctly. She opened her mouth and the tip of his tongue flickered against hers.

Anastasia has never done anything like this before, has barely kissed a man other than Konstantin, whose memory is so blurred by now that she might struggle to pick him out of a crowd. But then, she never wanted to. She'd felt content being alone, keeping her life small and neat and predictable, until she came to Milan and started wanting more, the more she got. So she let herself go with it, this unfamiliar but exhilarating current of wanting.

It's Tuesday morning and raining lightly when they pull up outside her building on via Melzo. The man who runs the café on the corner is positioning his metal tables and chairs on the sidewalk underneath a stripy awning and he raises an eyebrow and smirks as he catches sight of Anastasia in the sports car. Giorgio maneuvers the car into a tight space and turns to her. She opens her mouth to say something – *Thank you,* perhaps, or, *Don't go.* He closes her lips with his own, his quick, warm tongue nudging hers. She pulls him even closer and feels her body immediately respond to his touch. His hand moves up the inside of her leg, higher, until it reaches her underwear, then it moves it aside and pushes two fingers slow and hard inside her.

'Now, go to work,' he says, kissing her passionately several more times.

She walks upstairs in a daze, hugs Micki and Xenia, who burst from the bedrooms demanding the full lowdown, extricates herself and stands a long while under the lukewarm trickle of the shower, running her hands up and down her body, imagining them to be Giorgio's. When she emerges from the building after drying and styling her hair, she feels light and happy and beautiful. All day, she can't stop smiling, even when the photographer on the shoot she's working asks her to look 'angry and kind of aggressive, like you want to punch me'. Anastasia nods and regains her focus, and they manage to get the shots in the end, but as soon as they have, she's smiling again.

Now, in the silent darkness of her bedroom, Anastasia lies wide awake, still smiling, replaying the last three days. It's as though her consciousness has been heightened; she retains far more details from each day than she normally would, as though everything was recorded and she can watch each moment again. From the way the rays of sunlight spiraled into the depths of the lake as the helicopter came in to land, to the ornate frescos on Villa Serafina's facade, to the puckered scars on Giorgio's torso, from a car accident when he was a boy, Anastasia's mind vividly reproduces every single detail.

She wakes from the alarm at five thirty. She stares at the darkness, blinking, trying to determine whether the weekend was just a dream. Her lips still feel raw from all the kissing. Yesterday, she woke in Giorgio's arms and at the memory of it she feels a surge of longing for him. What if he's one of those guys who makes a girl feel like the most special woman in the universe, and then, as soon as he's had his way with her, he never calls again? She's seen it herself, with some of the other models. Pursued by wealthy men, showered with gifts, flown here and there, then dropped like a piece of trash when they tire of her. She can't imagine what it might feel like, never to see Giorgio again, and she doesn't have to. By the time she's out of the shower and dressed, her phone is vibrating. It's a text message from Giorgio.

When can I see you?

* * *

For weeks, Anastasia's tiny room at the apartment stands mostly empty. Once or twice, she stops by to get more clothes between jobs and for a catch-up with the girls. One day, over a cup of fresh mint tea, Xenia asks Anastasia if it's okay if Micki moves into her space so they each have their separate area.

'I mean, it's not like you actually live here anymore,' she adds, winking affectionately.

Every morning she is chauffeured or flown in the helicopter into Milan for work. Sometimes, at lunchtime, Giorgio takes her to one of the casual, fun, family-run restaurants on via Nino Bixio or for something more special, to Joia or Latteria Maffucci. When neither Giorgio or Anastasia are working, they go back to Villa Serafina, cooking simple dishes together in the kitchen and walking the dogs around the garden.

Anastasia goes to Paris for the Dior show and Giorgio comes with her, staying at Le Crillon. On their last morning in the city, Giorgio hails a taxi and takes her to rue Mouffetard where they meander from shop to shop, eating croissants and cheese and firm baby tomatoes straight from paper bags. They sit under a stripy black-and-white awning at a café on place de la Contrescarpe as warm summer rain crashes to the ground, kissing and laughing, then they walk back to place Vendôme, soaked to the bone, still laughing.

Back in Como, Giorgio throws his annual summer party. On the morning of the party Mariangela and Sofian from Gucci come to dress Anastasia. She wears a light-blue silk taffeta evening gown with a hand-sewn crystal-encrusted train commissioned specifically by Giorgio. When she takes in her reflection in the mirror the effect is practically bridal, she realizes. She wishes Vera could see her like this and makes a note to call her that afternoon. They speak frequently now, but Anastasia is often left feeling wistful and low after their conversations; it feels as though Vera's life remains the same and Anastasia's has moved on from that shared life at lightning speed, creating a vast and uncrossable gulf of references no longer shared between them.

'We'll bring her here to Como,' Giorgio has said several times but Anastasia explains that Vera won't ever come; she can't leave the plants.

'We'll get her a gardener to look after them for her while she's here,' he'll say. And Anastasia will nod and change the subject, because she knows it won't happen. It's not just the plants that need Vera; Vera needs them just as much, if not more. Her grandmother is wed to the earth at Koptyaki and leaving it even only for a while would be as unimaginable as leaving her own body.

'Anoushka,' says Giorgio, now, his voice thick with emotion. He's entered the dressing room without her noticing and is watching her watching herself in the mirror. Mariangela and Sofian step back and marvel at the vision in the dress, then they discretely leave the room. When Giorgio drops down on one knee, Anastasia realizes it was all planned, that they knew what was about to happen. He takes a small box from his jacket pocket, his hand trembling violently. Inside is a huge pink diamond surrounded by a circle of white diamonds.

'I've never loved anyone like I love you. Will you marry me?'

She nods. 'Yes. Si. Oui. Da.'

They laugh and cling to one another, tears traveling from his face to hers and back. He frees her from the dress and carries her naked back into the vast bedroom suite overlooking the lake. He's inside her urgently, and Anastasia feels like she is being carried away from everything she once was on a strong current of love, beauty, sex, and money. She closes her eyes and lets him take her away.

At the party, Giorgio sticks close to Anastasia, steering her around the various groups gathered on the lawns, drinking Bellinis and eating canapés, watching the last blood-red streaks on the sky. He introduces her to politicians and actors and other important people, their smiling faces blurring together in her mind. Tom Kingsley is there too, and Gio tells her he's a very brilliant entrepreneur who's launched a start-up that Giorgio is considering making a major investment in. They chat for a few moments, Giorgio steering the conversation, then he leads her away to be introduced to someone else.

She's able to spend a little time with Micki, Natalia, and Xenia, who fawn over her ring. She feels a sense of standing beside herself, watching the scene unfolding. She's happy, happier than she's been in all her life, and yet she feels untethered, drifting uncontrollably away from that other life. She's hyperconscious of the ring on her finger; the sheer weight of it seems to drag her hand down. Giorgio keeps grabbing it and holding it up to show the ring off to some person or another and she laughs along, posing for endless photographs. A potbellied man with swollen, watery eyes takes her hand in his own and strokes the ring. Anastasia wants to pull her hand away from him, but is aware of Gio's calm presence next to her.

'It's incredible,' says the man in heavily accented English. 'To see Giorgio di Vincenzo like this, a man in love.' Hours later, Anastasia walks toward the house to use the bathroom and passes the same man sitting wedged in between two very young girls on a sofa beneath lashings of bougainvillea on one of the terraces. She watches him snort a line of cocaine off the bared breast of one of the girls and glances around to see whether anyone else has seen. There is no one else around, and the man catches Anastasia's eye and winks conspiratorially at her.

Later, in bed, she and Giorgio lie in comfortable silence in the dark, Anastasia going back over the incredible events of the day in her mind.

'Who was that man we spoke to for a bit down by the jetty? Do you remember?' she asks Giorgio, but he doesn't answer. 'Gio?' she whispers again, prodding him. He switches on the bedside lamp and they both blink at the suddenly sharp light.

'Did you say something?'

'Yes, I asked about that man we spoke to down by the jetty. Who is he?'

'Ah, that was Michele Uragni. Head of Sicilian police. He loved you, I could tell. And it's true what he said, that it's incredible to see me like this, in love.' Giorgio reaches for her and nuzzles her neck.

'I saw him, much later, with two really young girls. Teens, almost. They were doing coke.'

'Ah. Yes. Not surprised. Uragni is a naughty boy, has a bit of a reputation. He's a very important man to keep sweet, though. You'll learn all of this. So we make sure to book him a couple of girls, Macedonians, you know what they're like—'

'Wait, what? What do you mean *booked* them?'

'They're escorts, Anoushka. They're signed to GMA but really, they're working girls.'

She's so shocked she's unable to speak, and she has to

make a conscious effort to keep a neutral facial expression. He speaks for another couple of minutes about the party, what a success it was, how much everyone adored her, and she responds with an occasional 'mmmm' and Giorgio doesn't seem to notice she's grown quiet. Then his voice trails off and is interspersed with a few drawn-out yawns before he falls silent, his breath a steady, gentle purr. She switches the light off, mind spinning.

'Gio,' she says, in the darkness. Then, louder, 'Giorgio.' But he doesn't respond. Anastasia fingers her ring for a long while, her mind too wired to settle into sleep.

* * *

They spend summer in Anacapri. Anastasia believed that she had seen most of the beauty the world could offer by now, spending her time at Villa Serafina and having traveled to Paris, Milan, the Alps, the Dolomites, and the Maldives, but Capri is otherworldly and profoundly affecting. Anastasia feels a connection to it she's never felt to any place before, and imagines this is how Vera feels about the land she was born on and tends so carefully. At the end of their first week at Giorgio's villa – a huge, whitewashed compound overlooking the western cliffs, the Pino Fort, and the lighthouse – Giorgio unveils the new signs he's had commissioned for the property, in hand-painted local ceramic, reading 'Villa Anastasia' in blue letters, changed from Villa Girasole.

'When we're married, you'll spend your time between here, Villa Serafina, and Palermo,' he says, passing her a glass of rosé with chunks of ice floating in it, as they watch the sun slip into the ocean in fiery bursts.

'And Milan and Paris and London for work.'

'Babe, you don't have to work another day in your life.'

'But I want to. And I want an education, later.'

Giorgio smiles and raises his glass in a toast. 'I'm sure you'll be very busy with children and travel. By the way, I've instructed Graziela not to book you for any of the spring–summer shows at fashion week.'

'But… why?'

'I'll be spending all of September at the house in Palermo. Business. Going to need you there with me.'

'I think I'm likely to be booked by Gucci again, though, and Valentino too. Graziela said—' Giorgio silences her with a swift wave of his hand. He holds her gaze and touches his crystal whiskey tumbler to her wine glass in a loud clink.

'Anoushka. Baby. Graziela answers to me.' She takes this in, staring at the darkening ocean, and like a strong current deep beneath the surface, something starts to churn inside her, a very first tremor of disquiet.

21

Selma

The green chicken curry is left in its bag, cooling as Olav and Selma sit down close together on the sofa, clicking on the attachment from Kai Oserød. The image flickers to life and it takes Selma a moment to realize what she's looking at. The camera is positioned directly above the porch and is soundlessly filming the top of a woman's head. Her hands are gesticulating, presumably attempting to explain something to someone out of shot. A hand appears, passing something to the woman.

'The bandage,' says Selma. 'It sounds so odd, what he wrote about her falling on the stairs.'

'Mmm,' says Olav.

The woman in the CCTV footage turns around and just before she steps off the porch, she looks up and straight into the camera for a long moment. Selma leaps forward and stabs the pause button with her index finger, perfectly freezing the image.

'Woah,' says Olav.

'Bingo.'

'Indeed.'

The woman looking back at them is young, younger than Selma would have expected her to look; Liv is about to turn forty in a couple of weeks. She's unusual-looking, with wide-set eyes and dark hair scraped up in a bun. Like Oserød said, there's a vivid gash on her forehead from which blood runs in several tributaries down her face, and in the still she is raising her hand toward it, clutching a tissue. There is something wild about her, in her expression, as though she might be about to bolt from the porch into the fields behind the farm, like a rare, fabled animal suddenly caught on camera. It could be that she's agitated due to the injury, but the guarded, nervous look seems more ingrained in her than just the result of the present moment. Selma presses Play again and the last couple of seconds of the footage unfold; Liv steps off the porch and takes a couple of steps into the farmyard. Before she disappears from view, she quickly turns back, pausing for a moment, the side of her face caught by the camera again as she looks straight up, cocking her head as if listening to something distant. Then, she begins walking again, and the camera cuts off.

Selma rewinds to the first still of her face and pauses again, catching a slightly different expression this time, and stares at Liv so intently that the strange thing that sometimes happens to her from time to time and which she used to find so disturbing, happens now. It's as though Selma can step into the image, into another dimension, where she is able to move around within the image as though she is really there herself. She looks down and sees a leather-gloved hand clutching a large, brown sticking plaster, wrapped in plastic. She feels the pressure of her other hand holding moist tissue paper to her brow, and even the sensation of cold kitchen roll touching her skin feels crystal clear. She hears the rush-hour whirr from the motorway, and the crunch of her boots as she crosses the farmyard back toward her office in the barn.

Olav says something, but he's far away. He's at her apartment in Nydalsveien, absentmindedly stroking Medusa and looking at the two-dimensional image of Liv Carlsen and Selma's here, in the frozen farmyard, as Liv Carlsen herself. The way she suddenly stopped and cocked her head, she heard a sound and stopped to listen, Selma is sure of it. What did she hear? Selma closes her eyes, brings forth the sounds she herself heard in the farmyard: the distant clang of machinery, the buzz from the road, the jet taking off from Torp. That's it. It was loud, the roar of the jet engine – the farm is very close to the airport. This woman heard a plane and looked up, following its trajectory across the still-black morning sky.

'She's not deaf,' she says. 'I'm not even sure this is the same person.'

'It looks like her. The pictures her parents had are over a decade old.'

'There's a resemblance, yes. But is it the same person? I'm not sure.'

Selma screenshots the still of Liv's face from CCTV and emails it to herself.

'I'm going back to Sandefjord.'

'What, now?'

'In the morning. You can crash here if you want. We've

got lots to do. I want to compare this image to the others more carefully, and—' Selma feels a stab of embarrassment for offering Olav to sleep over – while they've been friends for years, he's her boss. She just thought it might be easier; he lives miles away at the top of Holmenkollen. He's raising an eyebrow, his face etched with amusement, and he's placed a big, warm hand on top of Selma's bony one, still hovering above the trackpad on the Mac.

'Selma. Selma, shhh. Do you ever stop? Even for a minute? Come on. The food is getting cold. Let's eat.'

'But—'

'That's an order.'

Selma has to consciously stop herself from gulping down the food. It's delicious and she forgot to eat for so long – she realizes she still hasn't eaten since that Big Mac. She makes herself chew slowly and feels herself relax, listening to Olav telling her a funny story about his son. Conversation flows easily between them. It always has, and Selma knows that in a different universe, Olav might be exactly the type of man she would like. Not in this one, though; Selma doesn't have time for dating, and has always been content with her quiet, predictable life in her tidy apartment with Medusa. Since she turned thirty in November, she has noticed a slight shift in herself, though; a flicker of yearning for something more. Now, she watches Olav's face lit up and animated when he speaks of his son, who's ten and whom he shares amicably with his ex-wife, and wonders what it might be like to one day have a child of her own. She has also felt very affected by the plight of little Adrian, especially since she learned that he's on the spectrum. She imagines he's the kind of child she might one day have, and felt moved by Marie's descriptions of Liv's attitude to her son.

Olav has said something and is clearly awaiting her response.

'Earth to Selma...' It's an ongoing joke between them, that Selma has a tendency to disappear into the far corners of her mind, completely unreachable.

'I'm sorry. What did you say?'

'I said, have you had a chance to think about those holiday dates you're going to need to take within the next month?'

'Nope.'

'You're going to lose them if you don't.'

'I don't want time off, Olav. I'm best when I'm going full speed. You know this.'

'Maybe it's time to take a little more care of yourself, Selma. Or—' He looks down, suddenly looking like a much younger man.

'Or what?' asks Selma, aware of a shift in the atmosphere. She knows he is going to say something that opens up another dimension between them, and suddenly realizes that she wants him to say it. He hesitates, his face flushing red, and then he seems to gather courage, looking her straight in the eyes, his green ones playful and warm, and she feels it then, that surge of feeling that people talk about, as though something is being dragged out from inside of her.

'Or... You could let me take care of you.'

She swallows hard, her eyes still locked on his. 'I'd like that,' she says, then closes his mouth gently with her own. His hands travel into her hair, rubbing at the knots at the nape of her neck, pulling her even closer, his tongue playfully touching hers. She places her hand on his heart in the sliver of space between them, feeling its steady, reassuring thud. For a moment, she pulls back and looks into his eyes, then she kisses him again, harder.

22

Adrian

The bus drives out of the ferry terminal area and onto a straight, wide road slicing through flat fields as far as Adrian can see. The Man seems restless, checking his phone apps and then the map and then the apps again repeatedly. Adrian's stomach groans with hunger, so loudly the Man can hear and he smiles at him absentmindedly before handing him a Bounty bar produced from his pocket.

The sun is huge and cold in the winter sky, its rays bouncing off the roofs of oncoming cars, stabbing Adrian in the eyes. He makes himself sit completely still, looking out over this strange new land, so unlike Sandefjord. It's entirely flat, with soggy brown fields, earth upturned in long, gaping rows stretching toward the sea in the distance.

The ferry has already set off again, and Adrian watches it slide into the shallow brown waters of the bay. A few houses dot the roadside, strange houses unlike any he's ever seen before. These look like gingerbread red-brick cottages from a fairytale, some adorned with ivy, others with curious round window features, as if half house, half ship.

There are signs by the side of the road, advertising things to buy, something Adrian has never seen in Norway. One poster features an enormous picture of two children around his age, biting into big, juicy burgers, both kids holding their thumbs up. He tries to read the words under the image but the bus is driving too fast.

The bus slows down, then comes to a stop. The Man shifts in his seat next to Adrian, craning his head to get a view of the road ahead through the bus's front window. A revolving blue light streaks through the dimly lit bus. The Man places his hand on Adrian's knee. Adrian shrinks back in anticipation of another violent squeeze but it never comes; a warning suffices now.

The bus driver opens the door and it swings outward, bringing a mishmash of noise into the hushed cabin. The driver speaks to someone in a foreign language that sounds clipped and harsh in Adrian's ear, their voices seeping all the way back to where Adrian and The Man sit at the back.

The whirr of cars zipping past on the road merges with the sound of the men's voices and the distant echo of seagulls screaming in the port. He saw them as the bus drove off the ramp from the ferry, swarms of them circling the pier and its few low buildings, hoping for the ship's bins to be emptied.

'Polizei,' says a voice. It's an angry voice, and the word is repeated several times, at first from the front of the bus, then moving closer as two men advance down the aisle. One is shining a torch, letting it sweep across the faces of the passengers.

'Sleep,' whispers The Man into Adrian's ear, barely audible. He clutches Adrian's head to his chest and Adrian closes his eyes and lets his mouth drop slightly open. Mama always thinks he's asleep when she checks on him and he makes this exact face. Then he'll get back out of bed and sit on the floor of his room, folding planes, watching Madplanez' tutorials with the sound muted as the house falls silent and the moon climbs high in the sky.

'Sir,' says a voice, very close. 'Sir.'

The Man pretends to jerk awake and talks to the other man for several moments. He speaks so fast that Adrian can't tell if he's speaking English or something else entirely.

'Now,' says the new man. 'Now.' Adrian glances up. There are two men standing there, both wearing black suits and earpieces. One is holding out a name badge to The Man, who looks very angry.

One of the suited men reaches out and grabs the top of The Man's arm.

'Let go,' he shouts. Adrian can feel the eyes of every person on the bus, searing his skin.

'Now,' says the man in the suit. The Man takes Adrian's hand in his own and it's clammy and cold. Adrian hides his face with his jacket sleeve as he's pulled down the length of the aisle, then dragged outside into the bitterly cold air.

A small white car stands at the edge of the lay-by, a rotating blue light on its roof. One of the suited men opens the back door of the car and says something, motioning for Adrian and The Man to get in. The Man doesn't move. The two suited men exchange a quick glance. One of them waves the bus away in irritation and as it begins to move, Adrian can still feel the eyes of the passengers staring from the windows. The suited man repeats his command, louder this time, his voice hollering above the roar of traffic.

The man who brought him here, the man who says he's his father, pulls hard on Adrian's hand, pulling him from the lay-by into the field alongside the road, dark and still as a lake.

'Run,' he says, dragging Adrian along. The two men shout out in surprise and Adrian can't quite tell what happens next, but then a series of loud raps tear the air and he knows beyond doubt they're gunshots, he recognizes the tinny rap-rap sound from his cartoons, and feels a splash of something hot and wet pouring down the side of his face, then The Man's hand goes limp in his own and now it's no longer The Man dragging Adrian forward, but Adrian trying to drag The Man. A wild screeching sound fills the air; it's Adrian's own voice breaking free from his chest as he tugs with his entire force at The Man's heavy hand. Within seconds, the suited men are upon him, slamming him to the ground, one quickly taping Adrian's mouth shut with duct tape, pressing the cool mouth of a gun forcefully to his temple. A stinking, wet rag is shoved into his face so he has no choice but to breathe into it. Then everything goes dark.

23

Anastasia

In Palermo, the days are long. After all the months in Milan going from casting to casting and job to job, Anastasia's schedule is suddenly clear. She's expected to dine with Giorgio every evening, but otherwise he pays her little attention as he rushes between business meetings. They go to restaurants most nights, but sometimes they eat a simple plate of fresh pasta on the roof terrace, balancing the plates on their knees and drinking Messina beer straight from the bottle. She feels content, then, listening to his voice in the warm evening, looking out over the myriad patterned lights of the city.

On more than one occasion, Giorgio is gone for several days. Claudio, Giorgio's butler from Villa Serafina, has come to help manage the house during their stay, as has Ron, Gio's aide, but Anastasia feels deeply lonely and cut off from everything she knows, whiling away day after day inside the somber fourteenth-century Palazzo di Arcimboldo in the town center. The property has been in the di Vincenzo family since the seventeenth century and she enjoys hearing about its history from Claudio, who sometimes shares a few anecdotes with her between tasks, as she perches on a stool in the kitchen and sips from a steaming-hot macchiato.

In the afternoons Anastasia likes to sit outside, under the orange trees in the internal courtyard, teaching herself a variety of subjects, but even at the end of summer the heat is so intense she doesn't even last an hour. She doesn't tell Giorgio about her learning pursuits; she wants to someday surprise him by having fully acquired his language, and more knowledge about the world, like he has.

Toward the end of the month, they're invited to a party at the home of Michele Uragni on the outskirts of Catania and travel there by helicopter. Anastasia looks out of the wide windows at the changing landscapes of rural Sicily far below. Built-up Palermo gives way to a patchwork of sunstruck ochre fields, then, as they head southwest, the land rises into lush hills, then barren mountains peppered by scraggly trees. Giorgio points out a monastery far below, a huddled jumble of buildings high up in the mountains.

'Parco delle Madonie,' he says, his voice tinny in her ear through the headphones.

At the party, Anastasia stays close to Giorgio, doing the rounds of strangers, smiling and being introduced, making small talk with dukes and designers and magnates. By the pool house, a group of girls stands together, holding champagne flutes and laughing self-consciously in the way people do when they know they're being watched, and Anastasia remembers the parties in Milan, at the beginning, when she'd been one of them. One of the girls turns around, her thick, auburn hair flowing around her shoulders, and Anastasia realizes with a start that it's Natalia. She excuses herself and pushes her way through the crowd toward her. Natalia is speaking animatedly with another girl, a sullen-faced and very thin girl with huge gold hoop earrings and a slicked-back updo. The lights from the dance floor occasionally roam over the crowd by the pool house, casting deep shadows across the girl's gaunt face. Natalia looks more striking than ever, wearing a black velvet gown and matching gloves that reach beyond her elbows, the corners of her eyes elongated dramatically with thick black eyeliner.

Anastasia is excited to see her; she hasn't seen her or the other girls in ages, not since the party at the beginning of summer in Como, the day she and Gio got engaged. As she gets closer, she waves at Natalia when she catches her eye. Natalia doesn't wave back, but says something to the other girl and they both laugh. Anastasia slips through a pocket in the crowd and then she's standing in front of Natalia.

'Hi,' she says, in Russian. 'Long time.'

Natalia, who would normally answer her in Ukrainian, looks her slowly up and down as though they've never met before.

'Oh, look,' she says to the other girl in English, 'it's the princess.' They laugh.

'Natalia, hey, what's up?'

'Oh, wait, now you want to be my friend?'

'What are you talking about?'

'You haven't exactly shown much interest in the last few months. Did you even know I got kicked out of via Melzo—'

'No, I—'

'Mmmm. You were busy.'

'Natalia, look—'

'Don't you have somewhere to be? Some duke to chat to? Wouldn't want to spend your evening talking to a couple of escorts, would you?'

'Hey, Natalia, that's quite unfair.'

'Life is unfair, Anoushka, that's pretty damned obvious.' Natalia gives Anastasia a cruel, lingering look of disdain before linking arms with the other girl and dragging her away.

'Hi there,' says a voice behind her. She turns around and it's Tom Kingsley standing there, smiling.

'Oh, hello,' she says, smiling back. She's glad to see him; she has often thought of his kindness toward her all those months ago after her meeting with Graziela.

'Great party, huh?' says Tom, glancing around at the glamorous crowd gathered around an enormous pool flanked by Roman columns and ivy-clad archways. She nods, but feels disturbed by the encounter with Natalia. 'So, Anastasia. You never called me. How have you been? I worried about you.'

'Thank you. I... Well, I met Giorgio and, you know, life has just been pretty crazy ever since.'

'I see. Well, I do hope you are happy and that he takes great care of you.' Giorgio has suddenly appeared behind Tom and, smiling brilliantly, grabs his shoulder and pulls him into a half-hug.

'Kingsley, my man,' he says, and they both laugh. 'Found my beautiful woman in the crowd, I see.'

'I did. You're a lucky man.'

'Indeed.' They make small talk for a few moments before

Giorgio makes an excuse about having to catch up with someone, steering Anastasia away.

'Nice guy, Tom,' he says. 'Not your typical tech founder, is he? I'm sure he told you I'm going in big in his company. Ten million.'

'Mmm,' says Anastasia. She's about to ask some more questions about Tom and Gio's investment in CoreTech, when a series of loud bangs rips through the warm air and she spins around to see fireworks light up the sky. Giorgio has walked ahead of her into the main house, not even pausing for the magnificent display shredding the sky into rainbow colors, so she stands alone for a long while on the vast, beautiful terrace, face angled up to the sky, watching.

* * *

When they return to Como, there is a delicious chill to the air that reminds Anastasia of home. Every day, she takes her morning coffee down by the jetty, her feet dangling above the clear, green water, wrapping herself in a cashmere shawl, watching wisps of fog tumble down the mountainsides on the opposite shore. Sometimes Giorgio joins her, but he seems increasingly busy and is traveling on an almost weekly basis between Palermo, Milan, Como, and the house in Umbria, which Anastasia has not yet even visited, but which has been selected as the wedding venue. 'I want it to be a surprise,' says Giorgio. 'It's one of the most spectacular properties in Italy, if not in the world, and soon it will be yours…' Giorgio enlists a wedding planner, a stern German woman named Henny, who comes almost daily and demands hours and hours with Anastasia in the library, poring over mood boards and minute details of the ceremony and reception.

One evening toward the end of October, when Anastasia and Giorgio have enjoyed a casual, simple dinner alone in the kitchen, she decides to broach the subject of work with him. For months now, since the engagement, he's instantly dismissed any mention of Anastasia working, even instructing Graziela to turn down Gucci's new perfume campaign, one of the biggest Italian jobs of the year. Anastasia has wanted to discuss this with one of her friends, but Micki has returned to Brazil for family reasons and Xenia is constantly traveling, booking bigger and bigger jobs across the globe, opening the Chanel show in Paris, fronting Louis Vuitton's winter campaign and gracing the cover of American *Vogue*. Every time she sees her friend smiling back at her from a billboard or an advertising campaign, Anastasia feels a stab of envy as well as a surge of pride.

Anastasia is still earning an income from reprints of her campaigns, and makes sure to send almost all of it to Vera. She tries not to think about how much more she would likely be bringing in if only she were still modeling full-time, though it's not really about the money, it's about a feeling of purpose.

'I'd like to go back to work,' she says, giving Giorgio a soft smile, reaching for his hand across the gold-veined marble kitchen island, but he retracts it and runs it absentmindedly through his sandy-blond hair.

'Why don't you wait until at least after the wedding, Anoushka?'

'Because... I'm bored.'

Giorgio laughs incredulously. 'You're bored? What the hell? I give you everything.'

'Yes, but—'

'Yes, but what? What more could you possibly want? You live in a palace. You want for nothing. You can go into any store on via Montenapoleone or Vittorio Emanuele and buy whatever the hell you want.'

'Gio. Honey. I know. And I'm so very grateful. For that, but most of all for you. But I miss having a sense of purpose. I need to feel like me again.'

He stares at her for a long while, eyebrows drawn close together in concentration, as though he is really making an effort to comprehend what she's saying. 'Look, I wasn't going to tell you yet. I wanted to surprise you. But we're going on a trip.'

'Another one.' Anastasia smiles and tries to look excited but her heart sinks at the mention of another trip.

'You're going to love this. You'll need to pack for the cold, darling. You see, this is the kind of thing we wouldn't be able to do if you were wasting your time walking the runways.'

'Where are we going?'

'Home.'

24

Adrian

When Adrian wakes, he's slumped against a plastic window, a terrible ache insisting itself into his skull when he opens his eyes, and he has to blink several times to make sense of the world outside. At first, he assumes he is still on the bus; there is the gentle sound of an engine murmuring, but that notion doesn't line up with what he is seeing with his own eyes. The terrible memory of the gunshots tearing through the night air returns to him and he shudders in his seat, closing his eyes. Still, the image of The Man who took him from Sandefjord stays in his mind, how he crumpled to the ground, dead, his blood spraying Adrian's face, neck, and clothes. Adrian opens his eyes again and still, the strange vision he thought he must have imagined remains the same outside. And it is so very beautiful, more beautiful than he has ever known it before in all his life.

Adrian is on a plane, flying smoothly high above a smattering of pink clouds. Beneath the clouds, Adrian can make out a landscape of rolling, sparsely populated gray-and-emerald hills that grow more dramatic until they become small brown mountains, then big white ones. He quickly scans the cabin and realizes that one of the two suit-clad men, the one who grabbed The Man by the arm on the bus, is sitting directly opposite him in a wide, white leather seat. His seat is reclined, and he's placed his feet on the armrest of Adrian's chair. He is staring hard at Adrian and in his hand sits a menacing silver gun, held casually. Adrian draws a sharp breath and feels his heart leap, then rush uncontrollably. Before the day before yesterday, when his life was still predictable and calm, Adrian had never known any real stress that hadn't originated in the frightening corners of his own mind. He's always been a child prone to anxiety and frustration; he was born with a mind that produces vivid and wild imaginings, sometimes in such quick succession he isn't able to discern between them, or indeed reality. And he was born with the inability to put what he sees in his mind into words. Now he finds himself in a situation where his circumstances far outweigh any nightmarish situations his mind could possibly create.

Adrian stares out the window, still in disbelief that he really is up here, on a plane. He feels a vicious pang of longing for his mother: the feel of her touch upon his brow, the sound of her voice humming the strange songs she loves as she moves about the house, always drifting from room to room, busying herself. His mother rarely sits down and just relaxes; she likes to be active. Sometimes, when she doesn't realize he's watching, she pauses a while in front of the mirror in the hallway as she passes, lingering and locking eyes with herself, studying her own face as though it is that of a stranger. It was Mama who was going to take Adrian on a plane for the first time, soon; she promised, but now he's here with dangerous strangers and not Mama.

He leans forward and, looking out the window toward the back of the aircraft, can just make out a jet engine held snug against the fuselage, set back from the wings. Adrian scans the cabin quickly, avoiding the man sitting opposite; there is no sign of anyone else, but he can make out a figure moving back and forth up in the galley behind a partially drawn thick white curtain with intertwined gold letters on it. The plane has been configured to seat eight passengers in white leather seats identical to the one Adrian is sitting in, as well as a few more seats on a long white sofa running toward the rear. The cabin is so well insulated he can only just make out the faint whoosh of the engine; he imagined riding on a plane would be much louder. Adrian, who has spent several hours a day since he can remember watching airplane videos, guesses the aircraft is a Gulfstream g550, a long-range aircraft that can fly over 12 hours or 12,000 kilometers non-stop. This plane could take him halfway across the planet, away from Mama. He clutches the upholstered and warmed armrest and returns to the view, hoping to see something, anything that might give him a clue as to where they might be going. Mountains, reflecting the pink and gold rays of the sun on their steep, snow-drenched sides. Adrian summons the map of the world to mind. He likes to study world maps; it's easier to understand borders and lakes and continents than many less tangible things a kid has to learn, like how to read people or why people have decided to govern themselves in certain ways. A lake is a lake, a mountain is a mountain.

Could this be the north of Norway? He's seen pictures from there, of row upon row of pointy mountains. Adrian decides it isn't likely; it is clearly morning but the sun is too high in the sky to be close to the Arctic circle. They've learned in school that places like Tromsø hardly get any daylight at all in the winter. Could this be the Pyrenees or the Alps? Or, if he's been knocked out for longer than he thinks, somewhere in North America? A deep, narrow valley comes into view, its bottom gloomy and obscured, the surrounding mountainsides drenched in morning sun. Adrian presses his face against the window and can make out tiny buildings flanking the hillsides, and a couple toward the top of the mountains, reached by cable cars; he can make out the tiny compartments suspended between the valley and the ski resorts higher up. Adrian imagines being a bird of prey, flying low over the peaks, a brisk wind tearing at his feathered face. He'd alter his course with the smallest flick of a wingtip, spinning on the air, catching sight of a Gulfstream streaking across the sky high above. He'd land on a mountain ledge overlooking the ski runs and clutch the cold rock with his clawed feet, watching children weave slowly down the forest-fringed beginner runs.

'Hey,' says a voice and Adrian is shaken from his reverie. A lady is standing in the aisle, next to his seat. For the briefest of moments, Adrian manages to convince himself that it's Mama standing there, that this is all a terrible mistake, and refuses to look up to dispel the fantasy. The lady places something on the gleaming, polished table that separates Adrian from the bad man with the gun. He catches a whiff of something delicious and glances at the tray, which is laden with pancakes, bacon, and a bowl of plump, crimson raspberries. He feels his mouth begin to water. 'You should eat something,' says the lady, in strange Norwegian. Adrian looks at her. She's very young and wearing a tight bright-blue uniform. She's beautiful, like a lady in a magazine, but she looks nervous, and a splotchy rash creeps from her starched collar up toward her jawline. As she places a tall glass of orange juice on the table in front of Adrian, her hand visibly trembles. Adrian looks at the man sitting opposite. He is leaning back in his seat, watching the lady, who really is more of a girl, his face contorted into a strange grin Adrian can't decipher. The look on his face reminds him of the lions in nature movies when they come upon unaware water buffalos drinking from a river, the moment they realize nothing will stop them from tearing them to pieces.

'Don't be afraid,' the lady says to Adrian, placing a napkin in his lap. He realizes it isn't Norwegian she's speaking, but Swedish. She has a name tag pinned to her uniform that reads 'Ylva'. The man says something to her in another language in a brisk voice and she nods, disappearing quickly up the aisle toward the galley. Adrian anxiously shifts in his seat and wishes she'd come back. He gingerly reaches out and takes a raspberry, feeling the man's eyes on him. There are bloodstains on Adrian's wrist and he feels violently nauseous at the sight of the other man's blood on his skin. He puts the raspberry back down on the plate in front of him and beneath the table, rubs hard at the patch of skin where the blood was with a moist serviette that came in a sealed little parcel on the tray. Then he eats the raspberry.

The plane banks heavily toward the left, its wingtip reaching down toward the mountaintops. Adrian feels a tremor in his stomach as he feels the plane drop a little; they're descending. He eats more raspberries and two rashers of bacon to appease his stomach's incessant rumble. The man has placed the gun on the table between them, its gaping mouth facing Adrian. He is scrolling on his phone and drinks a steaming-hot drink from a tall white mug. Adrian pictures himself reaching across the table, as fast as a lion pouncing on a water buffalo, grabbing the revolver and firing it straight at the man. This man killed The Man, who Adrian had begun to like even though he must have been bad for taking a boy from his home and for crushing his knee. The Man, who said he was his daddy. Adrian thinks about this, that he finally met his father, but only for a night and a day. No matter who he was and how bad he was, Adrian knows right down to his bones that the man sitting opposite him now is much worse. The plane banks again, heading toward a charcoal layer of clouds ahead. Adrian gazes back at the mountains; he knows he will never forget the sight of them from up here.

For a long while the plane shudders through the layers of gray clouds with the occasional sharp jolt, making the slim white wings reverberate, and when it reemerges, Adrian realizes they've descended thousands of feet and are only a few minutes away from landing. From the window he can see green, rain-lashed fields, houses on hilltops, wide motorways webbing the floor of a vast, flat valley, more mountains in the distance, their peaks disappearing into the low clouds. The man takes the gun from the table and holds it demonstratively in his hand for a while, turning it around, running his fingertip down the length of the barrel, holding it so it points straight at Adrian. He feels the pressure of a trapped scream in his chest, a terrible pain as it grows in his lungs with nowhere to go. He opens his mouth as though he has no choice but to release it, but no sound will come, not even the faintest squawk.

He stares at his hands as the landing gear rumbles from the hull. He's missed a spot; there's a fleck of dried blood in the crook of his thumb. He pictures the paper Tomcat sitting there in that exact same spot, poised for flight, fuselage pinched between his thumb and index finger. He can't believe it was only hours ago that he and The Man flew the paper planes up and down the corridor of the ferry and now he's dead, his blood on Adrian's skin, and Adrian is here, on a plane with The Man's murderer pointing a gun at him, about to land in an unknown place. He makes himself believe that Mama will be there when he arrives, wherever it is he's going.

* * *

The plane touches down so smoothly Adrian can't be sure it has actually landed until he feels the reverse thrust of the engines and the aircraft slows to an amble. They taxi for a long while, Adrian knitting his hands tight together as if he is praying, his heart sloshing blood from its chambers around his veins so fast he can hear it in his head. Other planes take off but for once Adrian doesn't sit transfixed, watching them. He feels as though the very essence of who he is has left his body and the boy in the seat is only a shell, an inanimate puppet. He's up there in the sky, flicking his broad wings, swooping low over valleys and black, deep lakes, little bird feet held tight to his feathered belly. As the plane slows to a crawl and slowly turns on its axis, Adrian is filled with the most vicious dread and uncontrollable tears begin to pour from his eyes. He hears a sound, and realizes it's the man across from him, laughing.

When the plane has made a full turn, Adrian can see a vast terminal building with rows of mirrored windows on the other side of a runway. Closer to the plane are several windowless hangar buildings, one of them with a series of large blue letters across its top.

'Orio al Serio,' it reads, and instantly Adrian knows where he is. Bergamo, Italy, airport code BGY, also known as Il Caravaggio International Airport. Adrian tries to summon the map of Europe to mind, mentally locating Italy toward the south. Bergamo is in northern Italy, in the southern foothills of the Alps. He draws a sharp breath, focusing on the scene unfolding outside, trying to decipher clues as to what might happen next. He knows nothing about Italy, nothing except its airports, just like he knows all the other airports and their codes.

The engines switch off but nothing happens immediately. The man scrolls some more on his phone, the lady is still out of sight in the galley, the only sound is the tinny hum of the electronic system. Then a sound begins to insist itself into Adrian's consciousness, a faint chopping sound drawing steadily closer. Adrian watches as a tiny round helicopter with a long, thin horizontal stabilizer tail fin bearing an intricate gold crest comes into view. Adrian is lifted from his seat, not by the man sitting across from him, but another man, the second suited man who took him and his first companion from the bus. He must have been here all along. The man is huge and carries Adrian on his front like a baby monkey, Adrian's heart scrambling like a wild animal caught in the sliver of space between their bodies. The man with the gun follows behind them and Adrian drops his gaze to the floor to avoid looking at him. He's carried quickly down the aircraft steps into cold air and a blustery wind that seems to come from all directions. He's outside for no more than a few seconds before he is deposited into one of three seats at the back of the helicopter, the suited men settling on either side of him. Within moments, the little helicopter takes noisily to the air, lurching strangely before propelling forward, heading northwest.

25

Selma

When she wakes, Olav is gone from the bed and Selma feels a visceral disappointment, a feeling of loss so overwhelming that tears press into her eyes. Did it all mean nothing to him, did he wait until she fell asleep before gathering his clothes together and slipping out into the night? She sits up; it's light outside and, looking at her phone, she realizes that it's eight thirty. Half the day is gone already. She swears and gets out of bed, placing her feet on the heated parquet floor; how could she have forgotten to set her alarm? Again, she remembers last night, how Olav made love to her so gently, making sure she was okay, that she really was present with him in the moment and fully enjoying it. The door swings open, and Olav is standing there with two takeaway coffees from Kaffebrenneriet, and a brown paper food bag in his other hand, a wide smile on his face, red from the cold.

'Hey you,' he says.

'Olav, it's eight thirty! I thought you'd gone. We're both late, we should have been in the office ages ago—'

'Oh, shush. First coffee. Then croissants. Then back to bed. Then, and only then, you can go to Sandefjord and I'll grace the office with my presence.' He kisses her firmly, shutting out both her laughter and any protest.

* * *

On the train, she finds she's focused and relaxed, unlike the way she's been feeling since she started taking the new meds, in spite of the fact that she hasn't been to the gym this morning. She makes a mental note to speak to her doctor before logging into Facebook. She sends the CCTV still to Marie on Messenger, asking her to confirm that the woman in the picture is the same as the woman she knows as Liv Carlsen. She doesn't immediately respond; she's probably teaching her class, and Selma feels a pang of sadness at the thought of Adrian's empty desk. She compulsively checks for messages every few minutes, then thinks about what a calming effect the time she spent with Olav had on her, and forces herself to recenter, slowing her breathing right down and listening to the rhythmic sound of the train hurtling down the track, heading south.

She scans the news sites for any developments in the Liv Carlsen disappearance, but finds little news, except for a short mention in *Aftenposten* saying, 'The police remain confident this is a tragic case of a mother removing herself and her son from the country to escape the scrutiny of Barnevernet,' and that they urge Miss Carlsen to come forward.

Selma calls Gaute.

'Why do I get the feeling that you're giving up on Liv Carlsen and Adrian?' she says as soon as he says hello.

He sighs. 'Selma. What a pleasure.'

'I'm on my way back to Sandefjord. Can we meet? I have quite a few new insights into Liv Carlsen; some of them are really quite disturbing.'

'The thing is, the Carlsen case is being handed over from us to Interpol. There have been a couple of very reliable sightings of Liv and Adrian in Vienna. She had friends there, according to her family.'

'So what happens next?'

'They'll go on a generalized missing persons list. Once we consider it overwhelmingly likely they've left the country of their own volition, there's not that much we can do, really.'

'Gaute, I'm totally sure something very strange is going on here. She was a model; she had ties to an industry that has well-established links to organized crime.'

'Well, according to her mother, she didn't make it as a model. Apparently she had a drug addiction and may have turned to escorting and prostitution.'

'I've just written a big feature on the industry, and specifically in Milan. Liv worked there. Believe me, I know quite a bit about the kinds of dangers she may well have encountered. Many of the girls that don't make it are funneled into a really nasty world of escorting and drug trafficking. There are mafia and 'Ndrangheta networks who have major stakes in it all, procuring girls for powerful men, getting them hooked on heroin and then they drift back and forth between the smuggling trade and prostitution.' Selma lowers her voice, aware that she's practically shouting and a couple of older ladies across the aisle are staring at her, mouths open. 'And on the surface it all looks kosher, because they're signed to a reputable agency that really does manage top models, the very lucky few who actually make it onto magazine covers and the catwalk.'

'Selma—'

'Gaute, I can feel that there is a link here. Do you know what? I'm not even sure Liv Carlsen is who she pretended to be. According to her son's school, Kai Oserød, and the neighbor, she was deaf. Her own mother had never heard of such a thing. What the hell? Something strange is going on. Then, I got CCTV footage from Oserød—'

'Selma, wait, what?'

'I'm sending it to you now, as we speak. Look closely at her. At her face.' Selma forwards the video to Gaute on WhatsApp and waits as Gaute sighs heavily, his patience with her clearly wearing thin. 'Now compare those images to the others. Is it her? I'm not so sure.'

'It's her. It's very obviously her. But Selma, I'm not very happy about you procuring CCTV footage directly from a police source in an ongoing investigation, and then not even immediately sharing it with me.'

'Sorry. I just received it. I got sidetracked, that's all. Gaute, please. Don't give up on this one. Besides, what about the man the neighbor observed loitering near the house that afternoon?'

'My personal theory is that he might have been a boyfriend or something, and that he drove Adrian and Liv across to Sweden before they were even reported missing. Almost impossible to trace by then, and they would have arrived wherever they were going long before we were even on the alert.'

'Okay, but what if he wasn't a boyfriend? What if he was someone from that other world that she clearly once lived in? You said it yourself, that her own mother said she might have been escorting. Do you have any idea what kind of men rule that world? No? Well, I do. And I can promise you they are extremely dangerous with close ties all the way into the upper echelons of society. Politicians. Billionaires. Royalty. You piss these people off and believe me, you're in trouble.'

'Look, I don't doubt that. But that fight isn't one that you and I can take on by ourselves, is it? All the evidence points to Liv Carlsen voluntarily leaving Norway with her son to escape from Barnevernet.'

'Yeah? What about all that money in the house? That is an absolutely insane amount of money to have stashed behind the refrigerator, wouldn't you say? And to then choose not to take it with you?'

'Yes,' he says. 'Selma, I agree with you that it's very strange. I'm afraid that whatever she was involved in is something that will get looked into by Interpol, not us, moving forward.'

'You and I both know something is going on here. Please will you do one thing for me? Just one? Can you obtain the CCTV footage from the ferries leaving Sandefjord and Larvik for Sweden and Denmark on the Friday evening and the rest of that weekend?'

'That's hours and hours of recordings.'

'I'll look through it if you won't.'

'Selma.'

'Please.'

'I'll see what I can do. But then you have to promise to drop it. It's someone else's problem now.'

'It's not a problem we're talking about here. It's a mother and her little boy. And if you can produce CCTV evidence that they went happily and voluntarily off with some boyfriend, I'll drop it. I promise.'

'They could have left by lots of different routes—'

'Gaute, if they were leaving Sandefjord that day or the day after without getting on a plane, it's overwhelmingly likely that they'd drive onto one of the two car ferries in the area, saving hundreds of miles.'

They ring off and Selma slumps back in her seat, head spinning, staring out at the stark wintry landscape rushing past in a white-and-gray blur.

A thought occurs to her and she types 'Liv Carlsen Milan agency' into Google. There are several hundred hits but none that seems to be what she's looking for. She pauses momentarily at a picture she hasn't seen before, showing Liv standing to the far left in a group of girls, tall and beautiful, if a little same-y, likely all models. Liv's posing with her head cocked, pinching a champagne glass between her index finger and thumb. The four other girls except one are blond, in contrast to Liv's raven, tightly pulled-back hair. The angle the camera has caught her face is slightly similar to the angle of the CCTV still Selma screenshotted, and she pulls this image back up on her phone, glancing between them in comparison. Because the image is slightly grainy and because the image of the group of girls is twelve years old, it's hard to ascertain whether they really are of the same person. *It's very obviously her*, Gaute said, but Selma knows people see what they want to see. Beneath the picture, Selma notices a caption that makes her heart beat faster in her chest.

'Liv Carlsen, Marsha King, Dawn Obermeier, Clio Amaury, and Ria Mazar of GMA Models, at the opening of Storm nightclub in Acquabella, Milan.'

She googles 'GMA Models Milan' and clicks on the website. Headshots of young men and women shuffle across the screen, all shot in black and white and bearing similar serious, almost defiant expressions. She clicks on the English flag in the corner, then 'About us'.

GMA Models, short for Gio's Model Agency, is one of Milan's top model agencies. We represent some of the world's most in-demand models, from iconic Xenia Aliyeva, to Marsha King and Elula Hudson. Our models are regularly booked by clients such as Chanel, Gucci, Dolce & Gabbana, Valentino, Strada, Vogue Italia, LVMH, and Bottega Veneta, among many others. The agency was founded in 1999 by Giorgio di Vincenzo. For bookings and general enquires contact general manager Graziela Marco on **Graziela@gmamodels.it**

Selma returns to Google and types in 'Giorgio di Vincenzo', producing several thousand hits. She clicks through several gossip press articles, lauding di Vincenzo as an aristocratic billionaire philanthropist, involved in everything from marine conservation on Sicily, to various charity foundations. She scrutinizes his pictures, mostly dated several years ago, finding only a couple more recent ones, in which di Vincenzo made appearances at charity functions and most recently, last year's Monaco Grand Prix. Selma clicks on that picture, and according to *Monaco-Matin* newspaper and Google Translate:

Once a party boy, di Vincenzo has been largely reclusive in recent years, directing his focus toward the preservation of marine life in and around Sicily. He's thought to split his time between homes in Como and Palermo and has long been considered one of Europe's most eligible bachelors.

She scrolls and scrolls, clicking her way through numerous articles, trying to build an image of this man who seems to have successfully lived a high-profile life while remaining an enigma. She makes a mental note to go back over her sources for her Daria Miloszewa feature and find out whether any of the girls were signed to GMA Models. She goes to Instagram and searches for Giorgio di Vincenzo. He comes up instantly, his profile verified with a blue tick, and followed by almost six hundred thousand people. Mostly women, Selma surmises, taking in his light-blue eyes, sun-kissed, smooth skin and wide, perfect smile. In most of the pictures, Giorgio himself features, posing with pale, serious children, while handing over some monetary gift or another, or holding an endangered bird on a beach, beaming as he frees it from a web of plastic. The images are captured with glowing accolades of Giorgio's philanthropic commitments in four languages; Italian, German, English, and French, clearly written by a skilled PR. She scrolls further and finds him posing with several internationally known politicians.

Selma composes an email to Graziela Marco.

Hi,

I am a reporter at *Dagsposten* in Oslo, Norway. I am currently working on the disturbing disappearance of one of your former models, Liv Carlsen, a Norwegian citizen. I'd be very grateful if you could get in touch with me with regards to Liv's time in Milan.

Selma Eriksen

Within just a few minutes, Selma's phone rings and her heart lurches when she realizes that the incoming call is from Milan, +3902.

'Hello, Selma speaking.'

'Hi there. This is Graziela Marco calling from GMA Models in Milan. I wanted to get in touch right away when I received your email. I was very concerned to read your words.' Graziela Marco's voice is the husky, graveled voice of a heavy smoker, and heavily accented.

'Right. Uh, do you know Liv?'

'I do, yes.'

'When did you last speak to her?'

'Oh, several years ago. She's, uh, Liv has had some problems.'

'Problems?'

'Drug problems.'

'I see.'

'Are you sure she is missing?'

'Yes, absolutely. She's been all over the media here in Norway. Both she and her son have disappeared without a trace.'

There is a silence on the other end of the line. Then, 'Look. Selma. I need you to drop this.'

'Drop this?' she spits the words out, incredulous. 'Drop this? No way am I going to drop this. A woman and a young child have disappeared—'

'I'm only going to say this one time. Please. Focus your efforts elsewhere.'

'Are you serious? No way in hell am I going to drop this. I am, in fact, going to dig and dig until I uncover exactly what is going on here and with GMA, and believe me, I will.'

The line goes dead and Selma is so shocked the phone drops from her hand into her lap, from where it slips to the floor with a loud bang. She's aware that the train has been standing still, people shuffling down the aisle, dragging bags and chattering while she was on the phone to Graziela, and it's now pulling away from a station. It's Sandefjord, too late to get off. She stands up but sits back down immediately, her legs are trembling violently.

After a while, she tries again, and this time she makes it down to the exit doors, where she stands watching a foggy early afternoon slip past as the train continues south toward Larvik.

26

Liv

I lie awake most of the night, shaking with cold and retching. My hands are still tied and every half hour or so I make myself get up and pace the room for warmth and to keep my blood flowing. I move my hands around as much as I can, but any movement brings an onslaught of pain. At one point I must fall asleep because I jerk awake propped up against the wall, shaking with cold. I strongly feel someone's physical presence, and I scan the room, feeling disoriented. I locate him over in the far corner of the room, gazing out of a narrow window overlooking a section of the rain-drenched gardens and the lake beyond, glowing in the light of the moon. He's alone this time and this makes me even more afraid.

For so many years I have refused to allow even the most fleeting thoughts of him into my mind and life, training myself to let go, to focus on my boy and what I set out to do. There is, after all, no greater revenge than rendering someone completely meaningless; a nothing.

He realizes I'm awake and turns toward me with a brilliant, fake smile on his lips. His eyes are cold, like they always were.

'Ah, the princess is awake,' he says, crossing the room until he stands in front of me. His smile fades and a look of disgust settles on his face. I don't want to give him the satisfaction of showing him I'm afraid of him, that I always was, so I make myself meet his eyes. I'm not embarrassed by how I appear, humiliated like an animal, beaten and bloody, drenched in urine; I want him to see that underneath all of that, I'm still me and he can't break me, not ever. 'I'm sure you'd like to know why I've brought you here.' I don't respond. 'Fine. Don't speak. Let me tell you. You can imagine it was a shock to discover what you've done. I won't lie, I was surprised, I wouldn't have given some stupid uneducated bitch like you enough credit to think you could fool me. But you fooled me, you really did. So, congratulations. I hope it felt good, while it lasted. Did it feel good?' I make myself hold his gaze, though it sends ice-cold shivers down my entire spine. I nod and give him a little smile; I can imagine how angry it will make him to see me unrepentant and defiant.

'Now, I'm sure you want to know why I've brought you here and what I want.' I shrug, and watch as a vein distends at his temple and pulsates as his fury mounts. Apart from the fine lines at the corner of his eyes and the thick sandy beard he's grown since we last met, Giorgio di Vincenzo has barely changed at all in the decade that has passed since we last met. He still has that arrogant, entitled air about him, and I can see how much he is enjoying these moments, standing in front of a broken, bloody woman he is keeping as his prisoner.

'You've stolen from me,' he says, pointing a finger in my face so close its tip brushes against my nose. 'You stole from me, you fucking bitch. And now it's time to undo what you've done. God damn you!' He screams the last few words and I realize how completely out of control he is. He grabs my upper arm and squeezes hard, then lets go and steps back. He paces around several times before coming abruptly to a stop in front of me again.

'How did you do it?' he hisses. I laugh softly to taunt him, and wince, awaiting another blow. It doesn't come. Giorgio, too, laughs softly, and in another life we might be mistaken for old friends, standing across from each other, fondly recalling a shared memory. 'Okay, fine. I get it. You don't want to tell me. But here's the thing, you're going to. Either you speak and tell me exactly how you did it and every single fucking name I ask you for, or you can spend the rest of your life in a bare basement, do you understand? I said, *Do you understand?*, you fucking bitch?' Giorgio bellows the last few words, his breath sour and familiar in my face. I shake my head slowly. He must be insane if he thinks I'll give him even a single name.

'Let's begin with Tatiana Osorio, shall we?' The mention of her name jolts me, and I'm brought back to that moment days ago when I read '*Poppy down*' and I realized it could only mean one thing and that my whole life would come crashing down around me. 'If it wasn't for Osorio, I might never have found you, so thank God for that stupid girl and the fact that she is still a druggie, huh?'

'What...'

'Indeed. Didn't anybody tell you not to trust the Colombians? They'll do anything for money. Most dumb, poor girls will, as you well know yourself, but the Colombians? Easier to corrupt than most.' Giorgio laughs dramatically, circling me as he speaks, like a lion around its prey, and that is of course exactly the case. 'Osorio worked for me. She was a crack whore. Wait, you didn't know that? Oh no. Let me guess. You thought you'd saved her, that you'd gotten her clean, that she'd go on to live a cute little life somewhere. Awww. That is what you thought. Well, I'm sorry to burst your bubble.' I try to take in his words, to compute what he's saying. I think of Tatiana; we knew each other for many years after meeting during my first season in Paris. She was a quiet girl from Cartagena with big, green eyes and a shy, genuine smile. When she first came to Europe, she graced the covers of several major fashion magazines, and walked the runways of Paris and Milan before she suddenly disappeared. We'd met a few times, those first few seasons, and I remember wondering what had happened to her. She turned up again, several years later, having become addicted to heroin and crystal meth after being groomed into prostitution, a shell of her former self. I decided to help her.

She was a crack whore. Well, she was a hell of a lot more than that, she got clean and helped so many other girls like herself and I don't believe for a second that she worked for Giorgio.

'How did you do it?' His voice is calm again, almost pleasant. I stare at him hard, my face giving away nothing. He reaches out and brushes a strand of hair from my face and I recoil from his touch. This makes him angry, so he touches me again, grabbing me violently between the legs. 'I can't believe I'm looking at you,' he says, his eyes drinking me in for a long while. Then he spits straight into my face, and turns around and leaves the room.

***

The moon has disappeared, and dawn brings a thick, milky fog rolling in from the lake onto the sweeping lawns. I stand a while by the small window separating me from the world outside, from freedom. My legs hurt, my mind hurts, my heart hurts. I lie down on the stone floor and have only been there for a few moments when Giorgio returns, bringing two other men with him. The blond man who urinated on me is here and the sight of him makes my stomach turn violently; I have to swallow back bile at the back of my throat. The second man looks south Italian, with shiny black curls, wild bushy eyebrows, and a thick scarred neck, and glances at me with a menacing scowl. Probably a criminal Giorgio enlisted in Palermo; it wouldn't be the first time.

'Make her talk,' says Giorgio, to the darker of the men. *Farla parlare.* The man smiles, revealing surprisingly straight, white teeth with the exception of his two front teeth, which are a glinting metal, dark like onyx. The man rubs his hands together and I notice that his wrists are strangely thin and white, like a girl's. He must notice me staring at them because he aggressively steps toward me then glances back at Giorgio, awaiting orders.

'Now, you're going to take a little trip down memory lane. I want the name of every single girl, do you understand? Names, dates, transactions, every last detail. Do you understand? Give me that and I will let you go.' I laugh incredulously. Even if I were to give Giorgio what he's asking for, I know he'll never let me go. Why would he? He has nothing to lose by killing me and I know that's exactly what he'll do. I need to buy time and figure out a way of getting him to release me without compromising the others. There must be a way, and I have to find it, for Adrian.

'Names. Now.'

'No,' I say, my voice low but clear.

'No?'

'No.'

Giorgio raises his eyebrows in exaggerated surprise and the three men laugh. 'She tells me no, Mario,' he says.

Mario, the curly-haired southerner, laughs, and I can tell that in another life, he might have been quite nice. Perhaps he'd have spent his days pulling fat tuna from the azure Ionian Sea in Marzamemi, going home at dusk to a gentle wife with thick auburn braids and a couple of children kicking a football in a dirt yard.

'Nobody tells you no,' says Mario.

'No.'

'Names. Now. Give me a name and I'll give you a meal and a shower.'

I shake my head again.

'Okay,' says Giorgio. 'Fine. Mario, fuck her.'

'No!' I shout, but already strong hands are on me, pushing me hard back down onto the cold stone slabs, clawing at my clothes, then pinning me down, and I can feel Mario's panting breath as he struggles with his flies. For a brief moment I catch Giorgio's gaze and he watches coolly, and my eyes flood with desperate tears. I'm twenty-two again, trying to fight someone much bigger than me off, but

I couldn't then and I can't now and I can't stop screaming as Mario manages to wrestle me out of my trousers so I'm naked from the waist down and flings them into a corner of the room. He flips me over onto my stomach and pushes my face hard into the floor. I'm still screaming but now a word separates itself out from the unintelligible cries, as though I have no say in it, and it becomes clearer and clearer until it is a name without a doubt.

'Clio,' I splutter.

'Stop,' says Giorgio and Mario lets go of his grip on my face.

'Clio Amaury,' I whisper, my voice reduced to a feeble croak, and I see her in my mind's eye: the striking, skinny girl from Corsica whose parents were sheep farmers in the mountains and who couldn't believe their luck when she was discovered as a model and moved to Milan.

Most of the girls who manage to get out tend to disappear, needing to sever any link to that other life. But Clio never stopped thanking me for what I did for her, and still finds ways to get in touch with a token of her appreciation.

'Clio Amaury,' repeats Giorgio, then nods. The three men leave the room. I pull my soiled, wet trousers back on and huddle in the corner, my teeth chattering, my stomach aching and groaning. After a while, the door opens again and this time I recognize the man entering. It's Claudio. He's carrying a plate of hot food and makes his way carefully across the gloomy room. He avoids glancing in my direction and places the food down on the floor over by the window. On his way back toward the door he looks at me, then does a double take, and covers his mouth with his hand in shock at the sight.

'Oh,' he whispers. '*Dio mio.*'

'Hi, old friend,' I say, attempting a smile, but the moment is too sad, and tears flood my eyes. *Ciao, amico vecchio.* The Italian still flows freely, though I haven't spoken it a single time in a decade. Claudio nods softly, his eyes, too, filled with tears. Then he leaves me alone in the afternoon's deepening darkness.

27

Adrian

On the helicopter, Adrian is unable to get his bearings as the men on either side partially block his view and he doesn't want to lean across them to better see outside. He's frightened; he doesn't love helicopters the way he loves planes, though he knows quite a bit about them too. Adrian imagines the helicopter dropping like a stone from the sky, shattering against the gray mountainside, himself squashed inside, his blood seeping from him and pooling together with the blood of the men flanking him, the cracked upturned fuselage circled by birds of prey. The men occasionally speak among themselves, not directly to one another, but into microphones attached to their headsets. Their language is unlike anything Adrian has heard before, and he assumes it must be Italian. Unlike the flat monotonous Norwegian he's used to hearing, or the fast, fun secret language he speaks with his Mama, the way the men speak is like a mix of singing and talking. It's as though most of the consonants have been removed from this language, leaving long series of melodious and consecutive vowels. At one point the man with the gun says something that's apparently so funny that the other man takes several moments to recover from his fits of laughter. He snorts like a pig, his eyes stream, and he clutches his considerable gut, his whole body shaking. Adrian inches away from him, desperate to create some space between himself and the grotesque man.

He leans forward, elbows on his knees, and stares at the back of the pilot's head. He hasn't turned around a single time; all Adrian knows of him is that he is wearing a red baseball cap with a headset placed across it, and that he has short-cropped ashy-blond hair. If Adrian screamed, might this man help him? Adrian wonders who he thinks he's flying, and why. After a while, the helicopter begins to descend, not quietly and smoothly like the Gulfstream, but noisily and uncomfortably fast, and as it turns, Adrian catches sight of water far below, its metallic surface shimmering in the sun, green hillsides rising from its shores. The man with the gun taps Adrian on the shoulder. He turns slowly toward the left and, as he faces him, the man presses the stinking rag to Adrian's face again, making him gag, then slump back in his seat, a line of drool running from the corner of his mouth toward his chin.

* * *

Blue walls, high ceilings, frost creeping across tall windows, the distant sound of barking. A strange smell lingering in the air – he can't tell if it smells good or bad. The light coming in from the windows is waning, a deep gloomy blue-gray. Adrian sits up in bed. He's on a narrow single bed propped against the wall. There is only a narrow strip of wooden floor between this bed and another identical, empty one. He remembers the ferry, the plane, the blood on his hand, the lady with the flushed red neck, the helicopter. He looks at the palms of his hands; they hurt, commanding his attention, and he realizes it's because he's dug his fingernails into them so hard he's left deep, violet little half-moon shapes. His eyelids feel puffy and heavy; every time he blinks he has to make a concerted effort to wrench his eyes open again.

He stands up and immediately sits back down on the bed again, his legs feeling weak and like they might just buckle beneath him. He'd crumple to the ground, like the American, his dad, when he was shot. He tries again and this time he makes it over to the door. It's a huge double door, a strange size for such a small room, in textured blond wood. Adrian runs his hand across the wood, getting the strange sensation that it's still part of a living, breathing tree. He pushes the curved iron handle down but the door doesn't budge; it's locked from the outside. He kneels down and peers through the keyhole, his view blocked by the key still sitting in the lock.

He gets up again and walks over to the window. There is a desk in front of the window, but no chair. Adrian climbs onto the desk and presses his face against the frosty glass pane. He's up high, probably the third floor. The window faces out onto the top of a majestic tree, its longest branches almost touching the wall beneath the window. It is the strangest tree Adrian has ever seen; it has been cut to a precise rounded shape so that it looks almost exactly like a giant broccoli. From his vantage point it is like looking out over dense verdant green florets. Adrian almost laughs. He peers up the length of the window; there are clasps to open it, old-fashioned ones that need keys, but they're locked and the keys have been removed.

Beyond the tree there is a stretch of lawn hemmed in by tall hedges. From the hedges, two very tall and thin trees rise some distance apart like watchtowers from a fortress wall, these, too, carefully trimmed to appear entirely smooth and tamed. Beyond the hedges rises a very steep hillside covered in trees and bushes. Adrian cranes his neck to catch sight of a slit of gray sky above its rounded summit. He presses his face hard against the glass trying to get a view beyond where the hedges turn at an angle, but he's clearly at the back of the house and the outlook from the room is limited.

In the corner of the room is an ornate plaster arch leading to a tiny separate space in which stands a toilet and sink.

Adrian gets back into bed and tries to think. He brings the crumpled-up Concord out of his pocket and smooths it out on the bedsheet.

Will bad men kill Mama, he'd written. It felt like years ago that he'd sat there in the ferry's cafeteria with the first man.

No! wrote the American, The Man. His father. Adrian feels sure, suddenly, that The Man was his father. He feels sure, too, that he wasn't a baddie even though Mama said his father was one. Maybe she didn't know him that well. *We're going to stop them.*

But now he's dead, and Adrian is here, locked in a room. How will he stop them on his own?

He hears murmuring voices from somewhere nearby and realizes someone is standing right outside his door. He fights the urge to flee, to launch himself from the window into the welcoming branches of the broccoli tree. He'd have to smash the glass but it would make so much noise and surely whoever is outside would reach him before he could escape. Besides, if he didn't make it into the tree and fell to the ground, he might get killed; he's up pretty high. At the very least he'd break his legs and that would make everything even worse.

He straightens up on the bed, tries to calm his heart, steadily increasing its beat. He crumples the Concorde in his hand and shoves it back in his pocket just as the door swings open. A man stands in the doorway. Adrian can't help but look at who's there and when their eyes meet it's as though a powerful bolt of energy courses between them. The man seems to notice it too, averting his eyes quickly to the floor. He mumbles something then nods, as though he weren't standing there alone. The man is wearing a smart white shirt tucked into pressed beige trousers with a black belt. The black belt has a large golden G on it. On his feet are white woolly slippers that look as though he's stuck his feet into a pair of clouds, and Adrian thinks the man's bare ankles look unnaturally thin and pale.

'Hello,' says the man, in English. He is fixing Adrian with his eyes now as though he is trying to read his thoughts. Adrian focuses on his carefully honed blank expression. It's the look he gives his bullies whenever they speak to him. *Nothing makes them more annoyed than being ignored*, says Mama. *Pretend like they're air.* From outside, the barking starts up again, much closer now, and it is more than one dog unleashing hoarse, guttural barks. Big guard dogs, thinks Adrian. The man doesn't react or look past Adrian toward the window. He walks across the room and sits down opposite Adrian on the other narrow bed.

The barking is reaching hysterical proportions and is interspersed with long, wailing howls. The man doesn't even glance away, so neither does Adrian.

'What's your name?' asks the man. Adrian doesn't answer, just focuses on a spot on the blue wall directly behind the man.

'I'm Gio,' says the man. Gee-oh. *Stupid name*, thinks Adrian. *Sounds like a dog's name*. At the thought of this, he allows himself a tiny, delicious smile and he can tell it makes the man angry, a vein bulging at his temple. The man pulls a phone from his back pocket and takes a picture of Adrian, the flash making his eyes smart. 'Fine,' he says and stands up, turning toward the door. From outside comes the rhythmic chop of the helicopter's rotors; it's clearly about to take off again, and underneath, the hysterical cacophony of the dogs. Adrian has a strange and niggling sensation as the man walks toward the door, it's like knowing something but not being able to grasp it, the feeling of trying to remember a secret from a dream. He draws a deep breath, releases it slowly, uses all his power to insert his voice. It works, and it emerges raspy but loud, almost a bark.

'Where Mama!' he shouts, in English. The man doesn't react. 'Where Mama?' Adrian shouts again, louder this time, his heart pummeling in exhilaration at the easy release of the words. The man pushes the door open, bringing a slice of yellow light into the room, then he turns around slowly, an unperturbed and still expression on his face and Adrian realizes with complete clarity that the man is deaf. He gives him a wave, and then signs 'wait', holding up both his hands, palms open and facing him, wriggling his fingers. The man's expression changes from relaxed to one of surprise, his mouth dropping open to reveal the soft pink lining of his mouth, then horror, his face flushing deep red, then a recovered composure. He quickly closes the door again. Adrian has his full attention now. He spreads his hands out and moves them back and forth, then taps his index and middle finger into the palm of his left hand twice.

'Where's Mama?' he mouths. The man's eyes widen, fresh shock on his face. He laughs, a nasty, incredulous laugh, high-pitched, like the girls' in Adrian's class, and he can tell that this man is probably crazy. He spins dramatically on his feet, then pushes the door open and leaves the room.

***

The afternoon light fades from the sky and the only light in Adrian's room is the meager glow coming from a lamp attached to the wall of the house far below his window. It's a cloudy night, no moon, and Adrian sits atop the desk, staring out at the darkness. There is a ceiling light but Adrian couldn't find the switch; it was nowhere to be found on the wall. His stomach aches and growls; he's been given nothing to eat all day. Could it be that the crazy man plans to starve him to death here? His thoughts keep returning to the pancakes and the crisp rashers of bacon presented to him on the Gulfstream, as though he were a valued guest and not an abducted child. The house is quiet now, except for the occasional sound of barking in the distance. The air holds a distinctive smell, strangely familiar, but Adrian can't put his finger on what it is, and whether it's coming from inside the house or the world outside. There's a knock at the door. Adrian leaps off the desk and sits on the bed as the door swings open. He can't make out who's there. Whoever it is, is outlined against the bright light of the hallway. The light in his room comes on; clearly the switch is on the outside.

A short, older woman stands in the doorway, her gray hair swept back into a stern bun from which not even a single hair strays. She's holding a tray, which she places down on the desk. She lifts a metal lid off a plate and a delicious aroma fills the air. The woman speaks gently, but Adrian can't understand a single word. She stops talking and looks closely at him, as though she's only now noticing him. She shakes her head and wrings her hands, reaching out to touch the side of his face where he scraped it when he and the American dashed into the field. She touches her heart, says something and shakes her head again. Adrian feels sorry for her even though he realizes that it's she who pities him.

When the woman has left the room, Adrian eats quickly, gulping down the potatoes and delicious tender meat, similar to a dish Mama makes and serves with stewed cabbage. There's a big wedge of blue-veined cheese on a side plate and Adrian wonders if whoever prepared this food didn't know it was for a kid. He picks it up and takes a careful bite, scrunching his nose at the sharp smell, but he's still hungry after all the hours without food, and finds that it actually tastes good. In a bowl covered by cling film is a dense, dark chocolate cake. He eats it slowly, savoring the rich flavors, and the sensation of a full stomach. He lies back on the bed and drifts off into a deep sleep. When he wakes again, the man from before is sitting on his bed, watching him.

He sits up fast, eyes scanning the room. It looks different

in the bright daylight. A widescreen TV, much bigger than
the one he and Mama have at home, has been brought in
and stands on a table over by the door. Also on the table
is a stack of paper and a brand-new box of coloring pens
and pencils. Another tray has been placed on the desk, with
two croissants, a couple of small pots of jam and a glass
of orange juice. There is also a plain white envelope on the
tray. The man motions for Adrian to open it. Inside is a
photograph of a woman. She's facedown on a dirt floor,
pale and ghost-like in the bright light of the camera flash.
Her eyes are firmly shut and her face is bruised along the
jawline. Her dark hair lies plastered to her skull and her
lips are cracked and bloody. Her hands are tied behind her
back, her elbows protruding upward at an unnatural angle.
It's Mama.

Adrian's mouth drops open, but no sound escapes.

'Is this your mama?' asks the man, speaking clearly and
deliberately. Adrian nods. 'She's fine,' says the man. Adrian
understands what he's saying, in school they always have to
say, *Hello, how are you? Thank you, I'm fine.* Mama doesn't
look fine. She looks half dead. 'But I need your help. Do you
think you can help me?' Adrian nods. He'll do anything
to help Mama. 'Do you have everything you need?' The
man asks, but has to repeat it several times, Adrian only
understands a couple of the words. Adrian asks him to
repeat using sign language, but the man won't sign, though
he clearly understands. 'I need you to tell me about Mama,
okay?' Adrian pauses, then nods again. Mama always says
that if someone comes and asks questions about her and
about their lives in the little house on the cliff, he mustn't
tell them anything, not ever. But he always wondered what

he'd tell them. He knows their lives are unusual because there is no daddy and because his mama is deaf, except she isn't really, but he's the only person who knows that in the whole world.

When they're out together in the town or at the airport or at the shops, they always sign. He's glad, because it means he doesn't have to struggle so much to speak when other people are watching. At home, when it's only him and Mama and they can speak their secret language, which Mama invented herself, the words flow easily, but it's entirely different out there in the world. Adrian makes himself look at the man. He's thin, more like a boy than a man, and has thick, curly, dark-blond hair. His face is smoothly shaven and his eyes are a striking light blue. He wears a chunky gold watch and gold rings on two of his fingers.

'Will you help me?' asks the man again. 'Will you tell me about Mama?'

Adrian signs, 'Why?', bringing his hand down from the side of his head, folding in his three middle fingers.

'Because if you don't, she dies,' says the man, dragging two of his fingers across his neck slowly.

28

Anastasia

It's a late afternoon in October when they descend through layers of darkening autumn sky, shuddering through a few thick clouds, then touch down at Koltsovo. As the plane taxis toward the commercial airfield and onward toward the terminal buildings, the old one and the new modern one standing side by side, Anastasia's heart begins to race again, as it has done intermittently ever since Giorgio told her they were coming here. In the year since she's been in Italy, Anastasia's life has changed so radically it feels impossible that a semblance of the old life could still exist simultaneously, like a crooked tooth underneath a gleaming white veneer. That it is simply a matter of boarding a plane and then she can be here again, breathing the same air that carries the Siberian cold in on a brisk wind. Anastasia can't compute that her legs will carry her down the airplane steps into the waiting car, and when she leaves it, she'll see the dacha, and inside it, Vera will be waiting.

Giorgio clutches her hand in the car as it inches

northwest on the ring road through rush-hour traffic, watching her carefully as they get closer. They're staying at the Hyatt Regency, the same hotel Anastasia and Vera went to just over a year ago to meet Graziela Marco and Silvia Nebbio after they spotted her at the monastery, but Anastasia insisted on going straight from the airport to the dacha to see Vera. As they leave the main road and continue onto Old Koptyaki Road, tall, silvery birch trees line the road, which is covered in a light dusting of fresh snow. It's still only October, but the difference in temperature from Milan is significant. Giorgio stares out of the window.

'This must be the same road the truck carrying the bodies drove down that night,' he says, pointing to a road sign signaling the turn off for Ganina Yama, the burial site of the last Russian imperial family.

'What?' says Anastasia, transfixed by the familiar sight of the dense forest outside.

'The Romanovs,' says Giorgio. 'I'm actually distantly related to them. Through the house of Hessen-Darmstadt on my mother's side.'

'Mmm,' she says, 'I know,' her voice distant and strange as though she is speaking under water. The car turns off the tarmac road and onto the dirt track that leads to the garden village, going slowly to avoid the cracks in the road surface and the many potholes. A tiny figure is caught in the beam from the Range Rover's headlights, standing by the roadside next to a red metal fence, the fence swallowed up and embedded into a wild, waxy hedge. The little old woman is wearing what she always wears, a green cotton wrap dress and a starched white apron, a handmade embroidered kokoshnik on her head. A thin, white braid emerges from behind each ear and a wide smile divides her face.

Anastasia watches her hand on the door handle as the car slows to a halt. It's as though it doesn't belong to her, as though she's no longer herself, but a stranger to the woman standing outside, waiting. The moment evaporates quickly and Anastasia wrenches the car door open and rushes into Vera's tight embrace.

* * *

Later, the tears just won't stop. He holds her, kisses her shoulders, her forehead, her wrists, and still they flow, soaking them both. She drifts in and out of a fitful sleep and at dawn she gets up from the bed and stands at the window looking out at Gorodsky lake and Dinamo Park, where she used to come on Sundays with Vera as a child. White smoke streaks from the factories in the distance, bleeding into a meek, milky sky. Their suite is on the twenty-first floor and she's looking straight across at the golden cupolas of the Church on the Blood, *Khram-na-krovi*, constructed on the site where the Ipatiev House once stood, where the last tsar and his family were murdered in 1918. She moves her gaze along, taking in the iconic green Sevastyanov House, known as Yekaterinburg's most beautiful building. Between each golden cupola glinting in the morning light from the city's churches, and each, rare ornate mansion in the old pre-revolutionary style, new modern office buildings stand close together, many with mirrored facades reflecting the silvery river, as well as a jumble of communist-era crumbling apartment buildings and brand-new high-rises.

'Hey,' says Giorgio, embracing her from behind. He

catches a tear cascading down her face with his fingertip, then another. 'It's okay to belong to more than one place.'

* * *

They go back to the dacha every day of their stay. Vera pours black tea from her prized silver teapot, inherited from her father's mother, into frail cobalt porcelain cups with hand-painted gold rims. To Anastasia, Giorgio is like an animal taken from its habitat and placed in a new and impossible one. Though he's not a big man, he feels too big for the tiny house, as though the walls have shrunk and are pressing down on him. She wishes she could be here alone with Vera, that she could sleep in her own bed next to the curved, familiar blond-timber walls, instead of the modern white box at the Hyatt Regency, that they could just sit out in the crisp autumnal morning air on the deck, watching steam rise from the river's twin tributaries, coiling itself around the stems of the birch trees at the forest edge.

Anastasia is seeing the dacha and her old life with Vera through Gio's eyes and it's both uncomfortable and wistful because she knows he'll never understand how she could have been happy here. But she was. Happier than now, even, and this realization is like a swallowed lump of ice in her stomach.

'Tell her we're taking her to Troyekurov tonight,' says Giorgio. Anastasia hesitates, then translates. Vera shakes her head.

'I think she would prefer to stay here.'

'But it's Yekaterinburg's best restaurant. Tell her.' Giorgio smiles and Anastasia thinks that it's less a smile and more the facial expression of someone who wants their way.

Anastasia translates again. Another shake of the head, a few softly-spoken words.

'She says she's pulled beets from the earth and wants to make soup for us.'

Giorgio shakes his head abruptly. 'Troyekurov is booked, Anoushka. We're going.'

* * *

Anastasia watches her hand bearing the huge diamond ring pick up the silver fork from the damask tablecloth. This hand belongs to someone else. Giorgio talks fast, defiantly carrying the whole conversation, pretending he hasn't noticed that Anastasia isn't saying much. She pointedly glances at the empty third chair and zones out, making sure she occasionally nods. The buzz of voices chattering around them is loud and merry as the restaurant fills up and Anastasia feels herself relax at the sound of her native language, rather than the medley of Italian, English, and occasional French or German she's grown used to in Milan.

'Marvelous,' says Giorgio as the first dish, *pelmeni* – Russian dumplings – with Kamchatka crab, is placed on the table. 'Aren't you glad we came here?'

Later, back at the hotel, Giorgio wants sex. His breath carries the bitter aftermath of vodka and red wine and Anastasia feels tender and tired, yearning for a dreamless sleep. She removes his hand from her breast, but he puts it back and she removes it again, and he puts it back again, twisting her nipple between her fingers. She's liked it when he's done it before, but not now and she inches away from him in the bed. He follows, hands increasingly eager, his breath short and hot in her ear. She lets him, in the end, but has to turn back around so he's on top of her; she needs to see that it's him and remember he's the man she loves, not Andrea Fiorentini.

***

In the morning Giorgio goes on a guided Romanov-themed walking tour.

'I'm related to them, you know,' he says, 'distantly. But still.'

'Mmm. You've said,' she murmers. As soon as he's left the room, having given up trying to persuade her to come, Anastasia dresses quickly and calls a car. Traffic moves slowly eastward from the city center and Anastasia shifts anxiously in her seat, aware that her time alone with Vera will be short.

At the dacha, Vera is in the garden when she arrives, on her knees in the dirt, placing bulbs in a neat line in the moist black soil.

'Ah,' she says, when she sees Anastasia, 'there you are.' Vera doesn't seem surprised she's come, though they said their goodbyes yesterday, before she and Gio headed back into town to dine at Troyekurov. 'Do you want to help me?' Anastasia nods and sits next to Vera like they used to, placing the bulbs with the pointed ends up into the ground, patting the earth gently shut around them.

'*Voskresheniye*,' says Vera. *Resurrection*. Anastasia nods again, she knows what her grandmother means. Resurrection is the meaning of her name and also the meaning of the Russian Easter lilies they're planting. 'It's why Nadia named you Anastasia. You were her second chance. Her resurrection.' Anastasia thinks of her mother,

Vera's only child who grew up here like she herself did. 'You were mine too, you know.'

***

She's grateful for the darkness when the plane surges from the runway into low clouds, so she doesn't have the option of pressing her face to the window and attempting to identify Koptyaki and the swathes of forests that run for hundreds of miles west of the city, as the lights of Yekaterinburg web out far below. It feels physical to leave, as if the air is being sucked from her lungs. When she bid her second farewell to Vera, she felt as though there was a finality to it that they could both sense, standing there on the wooden steps of the dacha, hugging closely as exhaust curled into the air from the waiting car.

'It's never too late to come home,' Vera said. 'You're not his, remember that. You're only ever your own.'

Anastasia glances over at Giorgio, reclining comfortably back in the wide, white leather seat opposite, reading the *Financial Times*, a frail pair of glasses perched on the thin, straight bridge of his nose.

He'll be the death of you. It's as though Vera's voice is speaking to her, and though she didn't say that, Anastasia had felt her concern and disapproval over flamboyant, entitled Giorgio. Anastasia wishes they could have had a shared language, that there was a way for her grandmother to see what she herself sees: relaxed, knowledgeable Gio who devotes much of his time to rescuing animals threatened by climate change and secretly donates millions of euros every year to deaf children.

'Will you come to my wedding?' she asked Vera and her

grandmother had nodded. She tries to imagine Vera on a plane, Vera in Italy, Vera walking on smooth cobblestones beneath a stone archway covered in white roses at a hilltop castle in Umbria, but finds she can only envision Vera in Koptyaki, the creases on her soft, smooth hands black with dirt. She looks at Giorgio again, and this time he feels her gaze and looks up from the paper and smiles at her.

You're not his, remember that. You're only ever your own.

29

Selma

It's late when she knocks on his door. She had to wait almost a whole hour in Larvik before the train back toward Oslo arrived. There would be no time to stop in Sandefjord now; Marie and Gaute would have to wait. Selma knows that when her gut instinct is as strong as it is now, she'd be crazy not to follow it. On the train back to Oslo, she kept browsing through images of Giorgio di Vincenzo and the girls working for him. She learns he's an actual prince, that he leads a jet-set life between several homes, that he keeps his romantic life cloaked in secrecy. She memorized every detail of his face and when she closed her eyes and leaned her head back against the headrest, he was still there, smiling at her with those icy-blue eyes.

At home, she quickly grabbed the essentials: a couple of changes of clothes, Medusa, and her passport, then she rushed back outside, and it was already three o'clock and getting dark.

'Selma, hi,' says Olav, peering out from the door. 'How did you—'

'I looked on 1881.no. Your address is listed.'

'Ah. Okay. Why didn't you just call?'

'Can I come in?' Olav hesitates for a moment and glances back inside the brightly lit hallway. Then a voice speaks from inside the house.

'Daddy!'

'Coming!'

'Sorry to disturb, I really am, but I need to speak to you and I couldn't tell you what I have to say on the phone.'

'Come inside, Selma. You'll meet him sooner or later anyway. Why not now?' He leans in and quickly kisses her on her cheek, smiling warmly at her, and she feels the painful lump she's had in her stomach since the disturbing conversation with Graziela begin to thaw. Olav doesn't notice the little cage in Selma's hand until she's inside the hallway, shrugging her jacket off.

'You brought Medusa? What, are you moving in?' They laugh.

'Not today.'

Olav leads her through into a cozy, brightly lit living room with spectacular views over Oslo. In an armchair facing the TV sits a young boy bearing a strong resemblance to his father, with big green eyes, a slightly upturned nose, and a friendly, open expression.

'You must be Mikkel,' says Selma. 'I've heard a lot about you.'

'I've heard about you too,' says Mikkel, smiling wryly. When he notices Medusa peering out from the metal bars of her travel case, he lights up and leaps from the chair. 'Oh! Can I hold your cat, please?'

'Sure.' Selma gently releases Medusa from the cage, gives her back a few long strokes, then places her into Mikkel's lap, where she instantly settles. 'She likes you.'

Olav leads her through to the kitchen, and proceeds to make her a pitch-perfect black Americano with his fancy Italian coffee machine.

'Selma. Seriously, what's going on? Are you okay?'

'You know how you said I should take some time off?'

'Yes?'

'Well, I decided to listen. I'm going on a little trip. Right away.'

'A little trip where?'

'To Milan.'

'Selma, seriously, I need you to tell me what's happening. Please. I meant what I said last night; let me be there for you.'

'I'm onto something, Olav. Something big. Please can you look after Medusa for me?' They can hear Mikkel chattering away to Medusa next door, and Olav leans in and kisses her firmly on the lips, then nods.

'Promise me you're not getting yourself involved in something dangerous.'

'I'm not going to make promises I can't keep,' she counters, winking at him and giving his hand a quick squeeze. 'But I'll do my best.'

* * *

She catches the 0620 Lufthansa flight to Frankfurt, then onward to Milan Malpensa, landing just before midnight.

Selma feels as though she's having an out-of-body experience, her senses entirely overwhelmed by the events of the last few days. She gets in a taxi and leans her head against its window as it weaves through traffic that is still heavy due to numerous roadworks on the outskirts of the city. It drops her off at an anonymous-looking budget hotel near the city center that she found on Hotels.com as she was waiting in line for the security scan at Oslo Airport. She checks in and purchases a bag of peanuts, a single-serving bottle of red wine and two bags of potato crisps from the woman in the reception, a perfect snack to keep her going another couple of hours.

In her room, she connects to the Wi-Fi, then gets to work. She googles the names of each of the girls she spoke to or came across during her extensive research for her feature article on the model industry, in combination with 'Gio's Models' and 'GMA Models', procuring a match for both Tatiana Osorio and Leana Fletcher. She recalls Osorio well; she met with her twice on her previous research trip to Milan last autumn. She was soft-spoken and pale, with translucent, bony hands that fidgeted with the pack of cigarettes on the café table between them. Both times, they met on the street terrace of a little café in the hip Porta Venezia district. Her eyes were red-rimmed and sad, and Selma remembers how she wanted to give her a hug, especially when she began to speak of the horrific abuse she'd endured. Her story was similar to so many of the others – she'd arrived in Milan from Colombia aged sixteen, having been scouted after winning a regional modeling competition, full of hope and hell-bent on making it all the way to the top of the game.

Tatiana wouldn't name any names or point her finger

in any one direction, but said that when she failed to earn enough as a model, it had become too tempting not to take the generous payments the girls would be offered to attend parties on yachts and in private villas.

Leana, Tatiana, Liv, Selma writes on her notepad. What do they have in common, besides being aspiring models signed to GMA? Escorting and drugs, but what else?

She pulls her phone out and recovers Tatiana's phone number.

Hi Tatiana,

Selma Eriksen here. I'm back in Milan. It would be great to meet with you again if you are able to spare the time.

Selma x

She continues searching using a combination of search words such as 'escorts', 'di Vincenzo', 'modeling', 'Milan'. She clicks on an article which is over ten years old, written by a Will Marlow, which ran in the *New York Times*.

'Why Won't the Mafia Rumors Around Italy's Billionaire Playboys Go Away?' reads the headline. She scans the text until she sees Giorgio di Vincenzo's name.

Di Vincenzo prides himself on his philanthropy, which unfortunately often comes off as a narcissistic ego trip devised to make people look the other way from his more unsavory pursuits. While he certainly puts his money where his mouth is when it comes to protecting marine life off Sicily's northern coast, less is written about his purported ties to the local mafia. He is known to nurture a close friendship with Michele Uragni, the head of the Sicilian police force, a good friend to have in times of need should you be engaging in activities that may otherwise be of interest to the police. In 2005 and again in 2007, di Vincenzo's properties in Anacapri and Como were searched by Interpol, though no formal charge resulted.

In 2009, di Vincenzo made several trips to Colombia on his private jet, trips that were covered up in the flight logs and only revealed as a result of a whistleblower among his staff members. The staff member said di Vincenzo cultivates fear among his staff, exercised violence toward a woman in the staff member's presence, controls a network in Albania responsible for procuring girls into prostitution, and is directly linked to the drug route running from Northern Africa through Sicily and Calabria toward the rest of the European continent. In spite of these very serious allegations by a highly credible former member of staff, no investigation was launched into the myriad dealings of the Sicilian businessman.

Sounds like a piece of work, thinks Selma, and it aligns with the initial vibe she'd had from this guy anyway. There's something serpentine and slippery about him, a steeliness beneath the affable, slick, princely appearance; a complete absence of warmth from his eyes.

She must have drifted off into a thick sleep, because when she wakes, it's five thirty already, and she gets out of bed, momentarily disoriented before standing a long while at the window, looking out at the unfamiliar view: a narrow street with graffitied houses, the golden cupola of a church glimpsed over the rooftops, a stooping figure noisily dragging a newspaper cart along the cobblestones, occasionally pausing to press a paper through a letterbox. She changes into her running clothes and slips from the room. Outside, it's much warmer than in Oslo – Selma guesses around ten degrees – and she breaks into a fast, easy run, heading toward the Duomo. From her two previous trips to the city, she more or less has her bearings. It takes her less than ten minutes to get there and she allows herself a few moments to catch her breath and take in the incredible building. Then she begins running again, feeling her mind sharpen with every step she takes.

Back at the hotel, she stands under the hot shower for a long time, feeling more relaxed than before the run. She dries her hair and gets dressed, putting on a pair of tight, black trousers, high heels and a white fitted blouse; she knows that in Milan, your clothes speak as loudly as your words. She's about to leave the room when she checks her phone, finding two missed calls from Olav and a text message saying *Call me*.

'Hey,' she says when he picks up, grabbing her bag and heading for the door.

'Hey you,' he says and she can hear him smile at the sound of her voice. 'So. I think I've found something.'

'Really?'

'Several days ago, I saw a mention on a German news reel that a man had been shot somewhere in northern Germany. I didn't think much of it until this morning when the police launched an appeal for witnesses to the crime as the man hasn't been identified.'

'Right.' Selma walks down the hotel's narrow road and

onto a bigger road that's getting lively with the beginning morning rush, and looks around for a taxi.

'And here's the thing. They're saying initial reports state the man was in the company of a young boy. Who's vanished.'

'Oh, my God.'

'Indeed. I think you might have been right about the police looking in the wrong direction. I'm trying to find out more as we speak.'

'Call me as soon as you do.'

'Yep.'

Selma settles into a taxi and begins to Google 'man shot in Germany', and after some effort, manages to find a brief mention on thelocal.de website: 'An unidentified man was found in a field near Puttgarden with several gunshot wounds. Police appeal for any witnesses to urgently come forward.'

'We're here, signorina,' says the driver, pulling up on the sidewalk outside a modern building on via Savona. Selma pays him, then stands outside for a moment, staring at the building. It's strange to think that Liv Carlsen would have stood in this exact spot many times, perhaps steeling herself for a tough day of endless castings, crisscrossing the city on foot. It occurs to Selma that Tatiana hasn't responded to her message and makes a mental note to follow up when she's done at GMA's offices. She presses the buzzer for the agency and instantly, she's let inside. She rides a glass elevator to the sixth floor, the top of the building, ignoring a tremor of anxiety in her stomach as it labors through the pit of the building. A CCTV camera in the top-left corner points straight at her and she has a terrible, uncomfortable premonition that someday soon, a junior at a local police station will come across her image, sitting up straighter in his chair, rubbing exhaustion from his eyes and calling his boss – *Hey, come, quick, I've found her!*

The elevator grinds to a halt and Selma banishes her ridiculous thoughts. She's done a lot of work on herself in recent years and rationally she knows that there is no connection between her thoughts and reality – just because she thinks of something, it doesn't mean it will actually happen like that.

Behind the desk in a smart, sparse reception area sits a young lady wearing a headset, speaking fast in Italian, the words tumbling from her mouth like water, each drop impossible to separate from the next. She acknowledges Selma with a nod and keeps talking for a long while, veering between sounding furious and laughing merrily. Selma walks around the large space, looking up at the huge photographs featuring GMA's models that cover every inch of the wall. She recognizes a couple of faces from the covers of magazines and adverts.

'Hi,' says the receptionist in English.

'Oh hi. My name is Selma Eriksen, from Oslo, Norway.'

'Right. Who's your appointment with?'

'Uh. I don't have one. I spoke to Graziela Marco yesterday. Is she here?'

'No.'

'Oh. Do you know when she'll be back?'

'Let me check.' The girl picks up the phone and speaks rapidly into it in Italian, nodding, the smile fading from her lips, her expression growing stern. She's a beautiful girl, Selma notices, with thick auburn hair and perfect white teeth; she looks like she could be a model herself. A little sign pinned to her black polo-neck reads 'Natasha'.

'So,' she says when she's terminated her call. 'Graziela Marco no longer works here.'

'What?'

'Sorry I can't be of any help.'

'But I spoke to her yesterday.'

'She doesn't work here as of today.'

'Umm. I'm sorry, but that sounds really strange.'

The girl smiles a tight little smile, and looks pointedly past Selma toward the door.

'I have another question. Does the name Liv Carlsen mean anything to you?'

'No,' says the receptionist, not even pretending to consider the question properly.

'What about Tatiana Osorio?'

A flicker of recognition, a moment's hesitation. 'I'm afraid not. Now, unless you have an appointment, I'm going to need to ask you to leave.'

'I'd like Graziela's contact details, please. I'm going to assume she no longer has access to her GMA email address.'

'I'm afraid I don't have them.'

Selma is about to turn around and call the elevator, return to the hotel to recenter herself and consider what she's just been told about Graziela. It makes no sense. From her endless searches, Selma has gleaned that Graziela has been Giorgio di Vincenzo's right-hand woman for years and years; the two were repeatedly pictured together at various agency functions as far back as 2005. Behind where Natasha sits is a long wall made from frosted glass and Selma catches sight of a shadow moving at its far end and, without thinking, she quickly sidesteps the reception desk and rushes in the direction of where she saw movement.

'Hey!' shouts the receptionist, leaping to her feet and running after Selma.

'Hey,' shouts Selma, so loudly her voice reverberates down the corridor which is lined with individual little offices with glass doors. The receptionist grabs Selma's arm very hard and forcibly yanks her back toward reception but, just then, a man rounds the corner, walking casually with his hands stuck in the pockets of his beige chinos, as though he hasn't heard any commotion at all.

'*Buongiorno*,' he says, smiling. 'What's going on here, ladies?' Selma stares open-mouthed at the man as she recognizes him as Giorgio di Vincenzo himself. He's not particularly tall or menacing-looking in real life, and his piercing blue eyes look playful and mischievous rather than cruel as she sensed from the pictures. The receptionist speaks fast to di Vincenzo in Italian, almost shouting with indignation. He nods, his face unreadable.

'What is your name?'

'Selma. Selma Eriksen.'

'From Norway, huh? Beautiful country. Look, Selma, I understand you have some questions. I have time for a coffee this morning, so follow me to my office.' His English is flawless; she imagines he grew up in some damp, ancient boarding school in the English countryside and a vivid vision appears in her mind of Giorgio as a young boy, wearing his school uniform and gazing out from a window onto sodden fields separated by hedgerows. She shakes the image from her mind and focuses on the moment unfolding; she can't believe that she has managed to barge her way straight into an audience with di Vincenzo himself and doesn't quite know whether to be excited or afraid. Giorgio stalks down the hallway ahead of her and when he's not looking, Selma starts the voice recorder on her phone. He shows her into a huge office opening out onto an expansive roof terrace with a row of palm trees shielding it from view from the building across the road.

'What can I do for you, Miss Eriksen?'

'I was hoping to find some information about Liv Carlsen,' she says. Di Vincenzo's face is blank, giving nothing away at the sound of her name. 'She was signed to GMA, I believe.'

'Hm. Yes, you're right. I vaguely remember her. Dark hair, Norwegian too, am I right?'

'Yes, that's her.'

'It's a long time since she worked here.'

'Yes. The thing is, she's gone missing.'

'Well, it wouldn't be for the first time,' says di Vincenzo.

'What do you mean by that exactly?'

'She disappeared without trace back in 2009 or 2010. She'd gotten herself into a big mess. Many of the girls do.'

'Let me guess. Drugs?'

'Yes.'

'Where do the girls get all these drugs from? Who gives them to them? And more importantly, why?'

'Modeling is tough. I expect the temptation to take the edge off can be quite persistent.'

'Mmm. What about Graziela? I came here hoping to speak to her.'

'I'm happy to pass on your best regards.'

'Where is she?'

'What do you mean by that?'

'Where is Graziela, right now?'

Di Vincenzo laughs and looks out of the wide windows, and Selma can tell he's trying to buy time. He seemed genuine when speaking of Liv and that she's disappeared without trace before seems to be a fact supported by several people. But when she mentioned Graziela, Selma sensed him sharpen and grow careful.

'I said I'm happy to pass on your regards. I'm sure I will see Graziela very soon.'

'I wondered about another girl too. Someone who also used to be signed to the agency. Tatiana Osorio.' Di Vincenzo looks straight-up uncomfortable now, but quickly gathers himself together and contorts his face into a strange little smile.

'Yep. I knew her. It was terrible what happened to her. I expect that's why you're asking about her.'

'What do you mean, "what happened to her"?'

'She's dead.'

Selma feels a terrible chill right down to her bones and has to fight the urge to get up, run out onto the roof terrace and scream at the top of her lungs.

'No...'

'She was found dead from a heart attack in her apartment. She was another girl who had some troubles, unfortunately. Her heart just gave out in the end. Poor girl. She was lovely.'

'I don't believe you.'

'Oh, she really has passed away, sadly.'

'I don't believe that she had a heart attack. Look, I don't know what you and your chums get up to but I know that something is very wrong here. And I'm going to find out exactly what.'

'Well, let me know if I can be of any further help. I'd be happy to answer any questions. I'm actually heading back to my house in Como shortly, but why don't you come out for lunch tomorrow? As I'm sure you can imagine, I'm a very busy man but I can always move some things around to make room for lunch with a beautiful woman.' He winks at her and now she can see she was right about the cool calculation in his eyes. Di Vincenzo makes her feel sick to her stomach, she feels so attuned to the negative energy she picks up from him.

'Thanks, but no thanks.' She gets up and moves toward the door.

'I must admit, Selma, that girls who play hard to get are a special weakness of mine. I guess I don't get that treatment so often.'

* * *

She walks back to the hotel. It wasn't far in the taxi, only a few minutes, but on her high heels, it takes her over a half hour. She's grateful for the fresh air and the light rain that has started to fall, loosening the curls she worked into her hair with the round brush this morning. Tatiana Osorio is dead. She can't believe it; it's less than two months since she sat with her at the café, listening to her lovely, soft Spanish accent as she spoke.

She fishes her phone from her bag, presses End on the recording and forwards the file to Olav. She follows it up with a message reading *Call me.*

She calls Tatiana Osorio's number several times, but it

goes straight to voicemail. She calls the number Graziela used yesterday but hangs up when Natasha picks up the phone saying, 'Gio's Model Agency, *buongiorno*'.

It's not yet midday when she lets herself back into the hotel room. She collapses onto the bed and allows the tears she's been holding back to come, in giant hiccupy sobs. She feels a deep yearning to go home, to take the metro all the way back up to the quiet neighborhood where Olav lives on the edge of the woods overlooking the city, and just fold herself into his arms and stay there. They'd lie on the sofa, watching movies and holding each other close and she might be able to forget all of this. She yearns for Medusa too, for her little skull in the palm of her hand, the sound of her purring softly in the night. Maybe she was crazy to come here, thinking she could take on someone like Giorgio di Vincenzo and the men like him, who are disproportionately powerful and who don't believe any laws apply to them. But Selma knows this: nobody is above the law, and the truth always wins.

She leaves the laptop where it is for a bit and stands at the window, consciously ordering her thoughts and trying to make sense of them. Liv Carlsen is still missing. A man was shot in Germany and was reported to have been in the company of a little boy, who is now unaccounted for – Selma is convinced the boy is Adrian; the coincidence is simply too big. Graziela, who has worked at GMA for over fifteen years and was working there yesterday, no longer works there and apparently can't be contacted. Tatiana Osorio is dead, having supposedly had a heart attack around the exact same time Liv Carlsen went missing from Sandefjord. She needs to find out if they knew each other.

Selma returns to the bed and opens the laptop. An idea occurs to her. She rereads the article from the *New York Times* and though it's almost a decade old, Will Marlow clearly spent a lot of time digging into the dealings of di Vincenzo and his associates. After a little search, she manages to uncover Will Marlow's email address.

Hi,

I work for *Dagsposten* in Oslo, Norway, and recently came across your article, link below, on Giorgio di Vincenzo and his associates. I am currently investigating the disappearance of a woman who used to be signed to GMA, and have just learned of the death of another. Would it be at all possible to be put in touch with whoever wrote this article in the hope of potentially uncovering a link between these crimes?

Best, Selma Eriksen

She's hopeful that with the time difference to New York, Marlow might get in touch in a couple of hours when the east coast has woken up and started picking up emails. She sits for a long while, staring at a generic black-and-white photograph of a man and a woman walking hand in hand along a beach at sunset, and when she imagines that it's herself and Olav, suddenly the picture, which would have previously made her gag with its innate cheesiness, seems sweet.

She falls asleep on the bed. The last week has brought little sleep and long hours, but she wakes after less than an hour with a start, realizing what she needs to do next. She picks up her phone and enters Giorgio di Vincenzo's phone number, which is printed in ridiculous gold letters on the crisp card he handed her as she marched out of his office.

'I've changed my mind about lunch,' she writes. 'I'd love to join you tomorrow. Selma.'

She leans her head back against the pillows and closes her eyes. She can't tell if this is a very good idea or a very bad one. But she knows that the key here is di Vincenzo himself. So why not use it?

Part Three

30

Liv

I've been here three days and two nights. It's been mostly quiet, though I've heard the helicopter come and go, and once I heard a woman laughing, her voice hollering merrily down the vaulted hallways on the ground floor. I wondered who she was; probably a young Russian girl, Giorgio's usual preference. He used to say the accent turned him on, and that Russian girls have a certain toughness about them he finds irresistible. Whoever she is, I feel intense pity for her.

It's late afternoon, judging by the waning light. Every day, Claudio brings me one meal. He hasn't looked at me or spoken to me again since that first afternoon after I gave Clio Amaury's name to save myself from Mario. He puts the plate down on the floor, then quickly and soundlessly retreats. This morning I shuffled over to the door as he placed the plate down over by the window in a square of brilliant sunshine, the first nice day since I've been here.

'Please,' I pleaded with him as he made to leave. 'Claudio,

you know me. Please help me. Don't let me die here.' He removed my hand very gently from where I'd placed it on his arm and refused to meet my eyes. When he opened the door I caught sight of the burly blond man and Mario waiting outside.

'Step back!' barked Mario when he saw me standing there.

About an hour ago the helicopter touched down on the lawn. I caught a brief glimpse of it as it came in to land, golden sunlight bouncing off its tail cone. It took off again shortly after, the rotor blades shredding the air, sending birds scrambling from the trees and hedges.

I resumed my pacing around the room, and I'm still doing it now, hours later, moving compulsively in an attempt to retain warmth and control my thoughts. What will Giorgio do with the information about Clio Amaury, and how can I prevent myself from giving any more names? I had no choice. Mario would, without doubt, have brutally raped me, had I not given them a name. I went into full-on panic mode and chose to save myself, and for that I'm ashamed.

I stop for a while and watch the last of the sunlight fade from the surface of the lake. I do something I haven't done since I was a child: I bow my head and close my eyes in prayer. I pray for Adrian. Since I've been here, I've been staving off wave after wave of black panic at the thought of where and with whom my son is. I have to believe that he was able to alert the police or someone, anyone. Perhaps he thought to call his teacher, Marie; she's been fantastic with him and he might be there now, at her home, being taken gentle care of. A thought occurred to me last night as I paced around: what if Giorgio's men saw him on the screen in the moments before they ambushed me? I was speaking to him on Facetime when the man flew out of the darkness and knocked me to the ground. He could have reported back saying I'd been speaking to a boy and Giorgio would no doubt have sent someone after him. And yet, Adrian said someone had come knocking, but that was before I was attacked. I can't figure it out, and my mind isn't working as it usually is; my thoughts feel disjointed and slippery.

There's the sound of the door latch sliding aside, a metal key turning in its lock, then another. Giorgio enters the room, smiling. His beard has been trimmed and he's wearing a light-blue cashmere polo-neck sweater and dark jeans. If it weren't for the cool, mean look in his eyes, he would bear an uncanny resemblance to one of the princes from the society pages of *Monaco-Matin*.

'You know, you still take my breath away,' he says. 'Even when you're in your dirty thirties and lying on the ground, soaked in piss. Come with me. I thought you might like some time out of this little cell.' I want to tell him to fuck off, but at the same time I know that my chances of escaping are much, much higher if I can get out of this room. Perhaps there are other people in the house, people who have no idea how Giorgio di Vincenzo really operates, someone I could alert, who in turn might help me. This house was always full of people; girls, mostly. Girls like me, like Tatiana Osorio, like Clio Amaury and the others. Playthings for a charmed billionaire aristocrat and his friends.

'Where are you taking me?' I ask as he steers me down the long hallway.

'Time for a shower,' he says. 'Then it's showtime.'

'What do you mean, showtime?'

'You'll find out.'

At the end of the hallway is a door that opens up into a courtyard I vaguely recall – it's where staff would hose down Giorgio's dogs when they came back muddy from walks in the woods or from hunting across the border. The courtyard is entirely enclosed, its sheltered core paved with rough cobblestones, and overlooked by the windows on the villa's north side. I look up at the sky where the first stars have appeared. It's bitterly cold, colder than I remember this part of the world ever getting, more like the bone-chilling cold of my childhood.

'Strip,' says Giorgio.

I turn to face him, shocked. 'What?'

'You heard me. You stink. It's time to clean up.' Mario appears in the doorway, holding some folded garments, which he places on a stone windowsill. He comes over to me and cuts the plastic strips tying my hands together with a pair of shears. The relief of being untied is unbelievable, but a vivid, raw pain shoots up and down my wrists and lower arms from the restraints, which have left deep, bloody groves in my skin. 'Do you want to undress yourself or do you need Mario to help you?' I turn away from the men and slowly peel off my clothing, trembling violently in the cold, my hands still slow and uncooperative. When I have finished, I make myself play the game Adrian plays, the one where he leaves his body and looks down upon himself from a different vantage point, or merely flies away.

'Turn around,' says Giorgio. I know there is no point in disobedience, so I do and make myself meet his gaze square on. Giorgio hands the hose to Mario, who winces visibly as his eyes roam my bruised naked body. Ice-cold water spurts from the hose and Mario directs it straight at me, and I can't help but gasp as it hits my frozen, broken skin. I force myself to focus on a spot high up on the wall where there's a little ledge from which a drain pipe emerges. I'm a little bird, perched upon the ledge. My stomach is full and my feathers keep me warm and the scene unfolding far below in the courtyard is nothing sinister, and nothing at all to do with me. I chirp and ruffle my feathers, dunking my beak in the water flowing from the pipe. Then I fly away.

Giorgio shuts off the water. I'm shaking uncontrollably and trying to return to the fantasy of being a little bird, free to fly away, but now it doesn't work. Mario meticulously and slowly dries me off with a scratchy, dirty gray towel that has clearly been used on the dogs – there are visible mud streaks and coarse hairs on it – paying special attention to my breasts and between my legs. I bite my teeth hard together and stare Giorgio straight in the eyes. He's smirking, enjoying it. When he's finished, Mario hands me a red silk cocktail dress. Giorgio nods and motions for me to put it on.

'I can't bear for you to look like a dirty, broken wreck.' I have no choice but to put the dress on. 'Come,' says Giorgio, stepping back into the house, followed by Mario and me. 'Almost time.' I feel a mounting sense of dread at what he's planning; I know that this man is capable of absolutely anything. He leads me toward the small elevator at the far end of the hallway, the one staff use, between the wine cellar and the kitchens. Mario is left behind, and Giorgio and I stand crammed together in the tiny, wood-paneled space as it glides slowly between floors.

'You look beautiful,' he says. 'For a whore.' I swallow

hard and ignore him. I am still so cold, frozen to the very core, that I wouldn't be able to speak even if I tried. The doors slide open and both Mario and the blond man are standing outside. I glance past them and recognize the corridor on the top floor of Villa Serafina, the old servants' quarters, now mostly used for storage. Claudio used to live in a separate loft apartment in the house's west wing, inaccessible from where we're standing, separated from the east wing by the large sweeping marble staircase, and I imagine he still does, having devoted his life to Villa Serafina and Giorgio di Vincenzo, whom he's looked after since childhood.

'Through here,' says Giorgio, opening one of several identical doors. The room is small and plain, with a blue sofa and a low table in front of it, the window shutters firmly closed. On the wall hangs a large white screen covering most of it, and above the door a projector hangs, pointing at the screen. Giorgio gestures toward the blond man and Mario.

'The boys come up here and watch movies,' he says. They both nod solemnly. 'Hollywood,' adds Giorgio. 'So I thought we could come up here for a little date night. It's cozy, no?'

There's a bleep from Mario's phone and he glances at it, then holds his index finger and middle finger up, palm facing outward as though he were making a peace sign. '*Due minuti,*' he says.

Giorgio sits down on the sofa and pulls me down next to him, uncomfortably close, but when I try to edge away, he pulls me back so hard I don't attempt to fight. I need big-picture thinking here, not to win every little battle. Maybe if I let him believe that he could have me, that he could truly possess me, he'd be appeased and when his guard is down I could—

We're interrupted by Mario's phone ringing shrilly.

'And we're live,' says Giorgio. Mario taps into his phone and moments after, the screen flickers to life, showing his phone's Facetime app in widescreen. I try to make sense of what I'm looking at but it's difficult at first, the image is moving and it's dark, then I realize it's a residential street and whoever is filming is walking briskly, moving in and out from the overhead glare of streetlamps. Bright, dark, bright again. 'Bodycam,' says Giorgio. 'Do you know where this is?' I stare at the unfolding scene and make out a couple of low, white bungalows set back behind fences. The road is fringed by tall palm trees planted in terracotta pots and between the trees old, small cars stand parked close together. The road begins to rise and as the man wearing the bodycam turns around to look back in the direction he's come from, the camera catches a long black sweep of sea in the distance, the curve of a wide bay marked by blinking lights in the night. He walks a little further, past a row of identical ochre-colored townhouses and a closed gas station. I shake my head and glance at Giorgio. He's glancing from the screen to me and back, enraptured.

'It's a suburb of Ajaccio,' he says casually. 'Corsica. Beautiful place, as you know.' A violent shiver runs down my spine. Giorgio rests a hand on my upper thigh, wedging two fingers under the hem of the short red dress. 'You have a friend in Corsica, I recall?'

'No,' I whisper. 'Please. No.'

The man has come to a stop in front of a pleasant double-fronted cottage with potted roses on the porch, all of its windows lit.

'Confirming position Alpha One,' says a voice in English. 'Awaiting order.' Giorgio turns toward me and presses his index finger to his lips, before dragging it slowly and menacingly across his throat.

'Proceed,' says Mario. The man takes a few more steps toward the cottage, then his knuckles rap on the wooden door. The quality of the streaming is so good that I can make out the individual ancient lines in the surface of the wood, and we can clearly hear voices chattering inside. A man laughs, a woman says something, a child shouts. The door opens and a woman appears, carrying a little girl on her hip.

'*Bonsoir*,' says the man wearing the bodycam. I understand enough French to understand that he says he's from the *gendarmes* and wants to ask her a couple of questions with regards to a recent burglary in the neighborhood. She acquiesces and agrees to bring the little girl into the house. She returns and confirms that she is Clio Amaury, of Porticcio. I watch in horror as her dark-blue eyes change from unsuspecting and friendly to terrified as she takes in the gun the man suddenly points to her face. She has no time to run, or even to react before three gunshots ring out in rapid concession. The screen begins to shake and blur as the man breaks into a run, then it goes dark and the sounds of the chaotic scenes in Ajaccio are replaced by Giorgio's laughter.

* * *

I'm half pulled, half dragged from the room with the screen back to the elevator, then shoved into it. This time it's Mario who rides back down into the basement with me and he visibly enjoys making me uncomfortable by pushing his lower body into mine and picking a strand of my still-wet hair up from my bared shoulder and rubbing it between his fingertips. Tears are streaming from my eyes, and to escape the sensation of Mario's fingers on my collarbone, I focus on how they fall to the elevator floor.

I just can't believe what I've just witnessed. How will I ever unsee poor Clio's last moments, that look in her eyes as realization dawned? What was the last thought that went through her mind? Her child, I'd imagine, that poor beautiful little girl who would have jumped at the sound of gunshots. It's my fault – I might as well have pulled the trigger myself. I think about the others, all the girls like Clio, so many of them now finally living meaningful, peaceful lives after escaping terror at the hands of Giorgio and his buddies, helped by me, and now in the gravest danger. No matter what, I can't give Giorgio another name. But... Mario. I'll have to let Mario do to me what he'll do; I'll learn to become that little bird again, like Adrian, my precious boy who knows how to leave himself and fly away when it's too difficult or dangerous to remain in his own incarnation.

Back in the dirt cellar, two chairs have been brought in and placed across from each other. Giorgio sits on one, sipping from a large glass of whiskey on the rocks, a look of elated triumph still on his face.

'Now, onwards,' he says as I slump into the seat, teeth chattering with both cold and terror as Mario recedes into the dark shadows behind me. 'Next name, please.'

'I'm never going to give you another name, Giorgio.'

'Never?'

'Never.'

He laughs softly and whistles between his teeth, his face ghoulishly lit up by the screen of his phone, which is balancing on his thigh. He takes another sip of his drink, swilling the liquid around his mouth in a way that's instantly and repugnantly familiar. How many little details of someone's behavior are lost when they disappear from our lives, then revoked with a vengeance when we see them again? I suddenly recall how Clio used to carry a funny little pink handbag, which she told me was a gift from her boyfriend back home, even after her career started taking off and she was gifted beautiful handcrafted leather bags from major fashion houses. I wonder whether she married that same boyfriend, whether it was with him she'd made her life in that sweet cottage on the outskirts of Ajaccio, whether he'd fathered her child, and whether she still had that pink pleather handbag.

'I should have guessed she was one of your girls,' says Giorgio. 'I remember her a few years back; I couldn't even pimp her out to Albanians. Haggard as fuck, hooked on H, didn't exactly cut it as a top model. Then you stepped in like some fairy fucking godmother.' He looks momentarily so angry I'm afraid he could smash the crystal tumbler in my face. 'I hope it felt good while it lasted, saving old hookers with my money. You're going to tell me exactly how you did it. But first, you're going to give me another name.' I open my mouth to say, *No, hell no, I'll never give you another name*, but I stop myself and shut it again, running my tongue around the back of my teeth, buying time.

'Giorgio, look. I'm sorry. I know you don't believe me, but I really am. For everything.'

'You can shut the fuck up unless you're going to give me another name.'

'The girls – Giorgio, it's not their fault. It's mine. Please don't punish them.'

'I said, shut the fuck up unless you're going to give me another name. Here's the thing, the thing you clearly never understood: we can play this game forever and you know it. You won't win with me. You never did. Now, you're going to give me the names. Every single fucking name. And you're going to tell me where the money is. Every fucking cent of it.' Gio wouldn't be able to understand that the girl I was then could grow into the woman I am now. He wouldn't be able to grasp that I can take one euro and turn it into twenty. And he wouldn't believe that I can and will stand up to him – I'm not giving him another name.

'No.' Giorgio stares at me for a long while, then drains the last inch of his whiskey in one big gulp. He stands up and hurls the tumbler to the wall where it shatters, its shards glinting in the cold light of the moon streaming in from the tiny window. 'Fine, have it your way. Mario, get rid of the boy.' Mario nods and turns toward the door, where the blond man is standing guard.

'Wait,' I shout. 'What… what boy?'

'What boy?' repeats Giorgio, mocking my accent and laughing. 'What boy? *Your* little boy, of course. He's upstairs in the blue room, two doors from where you and I just had our little movie night.'

'No,' I whisper. 'No. Gio, please. Please, I beg you—'

'Shut up,' he screams, taking a lurching step toward

me and it seems like he is about to punch me but decides against it at the very last moment. The man at the door, Adrian's face visible on the screen as the man ambushed me, the sound of the helicopter coming and going repeatedly, the kind of power Giorgio possesses; I should have known that there was no way I could keep my baby safe from him.

'Is he okay? Is he—'

'Jesus Christ, shut up. He's upstairs. He's fine. You know, the fact that he even exists explains quite a few things doesn't it? A love child. Cute.'

'Giorgio—'

'I couldn't believe it when I heard, as you can imagine. But I was able to put two and two together, as one learns to do when one is accustomed to dealing with a bunch of conniving, lying whores on a daily basis.'

'It's not—'

'It's not what I think? It's exactly what I think. I was very pleased when I discovered this kid, believe it or not. A rather fine way of leveraging my will with her, I thought. Am I right?' I don't answer him, my brain is working desperately to figure out how to move forward. My son is in this house. He's fine, says Giorgio. If nothing else, I might be able to save him. And I will do anything, absolutely anything in this world to save my child.

'Prove it,' I say. 'Prove that you have him. I don't believe you.'

'Very well.' Giorgio taps on his phone and quickly locates what he's looking for. He turns the screen toward me, and there's my boy, a look of terror and bewilderment on his sweet, pale face. He's sitting on a narrow single bed pushed against a royal-blue wall. He has a bruise on his cheekbone and the corners of his mouth drag downward as though he's about to weep. I reach for the phone; I want to run my fingertips across his image, I want to kiss his face, more than I have ever wanted or needed anything in all my life, but Giorgio swiftly moves it out of reach. 'Now, you're going to listen to me very carefully. It's been a long day. You're going to give me another name, right now, or I send Mario up there to the blue room and he will fuck that kid up, do you understand?'

I nod, tears streaming from my eyes at his words.

'Leana Fletcher,' I whisper, my voice shaking through sobs. Giorgio smiles, brings his palms together and bends forward in a little bow.

'*Grazie*,' he says, and makes for the door. 'Now, that wasn't so difficult, was it?' He motions to Mario to unlock the door, then he turns back around. 'Oh, by the way, I almost forgot. I took care of your baby daddy. Fucking waste of skin.' He strides back over to me and shoves the screen in my face and this time, I'm looking at a picture of the man I love on his front in blood-sprayed snow.

31

Adrian

Adrian watches TV all day, Italian cartoons and cooking shows and a documentary from an airshow. He doesn't especially care that he can't understand a single word they're saying; he's used to not relying much on words. His gaze flits from the screen to the big wooden door; he's expecting the man to return any moment. This morning after he showed Adrian the picture of poor Mama and asked for his help so she wouldn't die, he told him to eat his breakfast and that he'd come back later. But he hasn't yet come back. At lunchtime the old lady returned with another tray, delicious food this time: chicken in mushroom sauce and a little apple tart for dessert. After he finished eating, he went from feeling okay and calm to suddenly overwhelmed and terrified. He hated the blue of the walls, and the confinement of the little room. He tried all the latches on the windows again, but they were all firmly locked. Finally he slumped back on the bed, where he remains, apathetically staring at the cartoons.

The metal clang of a key inserted in the lock. He jerks

violently, drawing the blanket up against his neck as the man from before enters the room.

'Hi,' he says. 'Are you okay?' his voice is kind now, showing no signs of the menace from this morning when he drew a finger across his throat and said his mama will die.

Adrian shakes his head. He's not okay. Nothing is okay, what kind of question is that?

'I'm sorry,' says the man, and he looks so normal and innocent, nothing like the other thugs he's had to deal with since he was taken from Sandefjord, that for a moment, Adrian almost believes him. 'Can I show you something?' He walks over to the door, opens it and motions for Adrian to follow. Adrian pauses at the threshold and looks at the man, as if to ascertain that he really may leave the room. The man nods and smiles, showing Adrian down a long corridor. At the end it opens up into a massive gallery with a chandelier the size of an SUV suspended from the ceiling, which goes up the height of several stories. Adrian is in a palace, for the first time. A turquoise carpet runs down the middle of the stairs, held in place by brass stair rods and at the bottom of the stairs, in the vaulted hallway, stands a grand piano. Adrian leans over the banister, peering down at it, and the top of the head of the man that's playing it, sending a gentle trickle of piano music through the interconnecting rooms and up to where Adrian and Gio stand watching.

The man places two fingers in his mouth and produces an impressive whistle. Adrian wonders why until he hears the thunderous sound of large paws hurtling down the corridor toward them.

'Brutus!' shouts the man. 'Get down!' and, 'Godiva, say

hello. That's it, nicely.' Adrian likes dogs but doesn't often get to spend time with them. He crouches and lets the large animals lick his face. 'Will you help me walk them in the garden and we can talk?' Adrian nods. The man casually hands Adrian the lead for the smaller of the dogs, Godiva, a Hungarian Vizsla with slanted, aquamarine eyes and a vigorous, friendly tail wag. The other looks like an old, black Labrador. Godiva stares at him for a moment before appearing to accept his command, then walks obediently by his side down the three flights of stairs, past the piano man and outside through huge, heavy double doors into which a much smaller door is inserted.

It's chilly outside, though not cold like it was in Sande-fjord. Adrian and the man are standing in a vast court-yard with several cars parked in the driveway. They walk down a path around the side of the house, passing the huge, gnarled trunk of a very big tree and, looking upward into the coiffed crown, Adrian realizes it's the broccoli tree. They continue alongside the hedges and turn the corner to the front of the house, and Adrian can't help but gasp at the sight. Huge gardens, meticulously tended, run all the way down to the water, whose surface is indigo and silver in the late afternoon light. The sun has recently dropped between two huge green mountains on the opposite shore. A long jetty reaches into the water from the property's shoreline, several boats moored from it. Adrian turns back toward the house, and he was right about it being a palace. It's like no house he has ever seen before; the only comparison he can come up with is the king's yellow palace in Oslo, which he's seen so many times printed on postcards and projected onto the classroom screen. This house, while certainly nowhere near as large as the royal palace, is easily as ornate, with stuccoed pink facades, a large wraparound terrace with pillars supporting balconies on the second floor, and two square turrets flanking the main part of the house.

The park is filled with strange trees Adrian has never seen before; there's another broccoli tree, as well as several palm trees down by the water, their fronds swaying on the chilly breeze, and cypresses as tall as buildings. There are vast lawns and one of them to the side of the house has a circle with an H painted white in its middle. This must be where the helicopter touched down, though Adrian can't recall arriving here, nor being brought into the house. Godiva eagerly pulls on the lead, dragging Adrian down to a sheltered, pebbled beach. The black mirror of the lake stretches out in front of him and he picks up a pebble and flings it into the water, cracking its shimmery surface, then another and another. Gio joins him, flinging rocks far out on the water, the dogs watching and halfheartedly pursuing each rock until they realize they couldn't possibly fetch them.

'Who is your father?' asks Gio suddenly, making Adrian drop the stone he was about to fling. He'd began to relax slightly in Gio's company; it was a bit like when he and the American launched paper planes in the ferry corridor. Adrian feels a surge of anger at the thought of the first man, The Man, his father, and how he was shot by this man's helpers. He makes himself turn to face Gio, and signs, 'American. You killed him.'

'Mmm,' says Gio. Adrian wonders if he was born deaf or became deaf. He says something else, but Adrian can't decipher the meaning. How strange language is, he thinks, how absurd that people managed to develop speech and communicate with one another. Well, everyone except for him. He tries to focus even harder to make sense of what the man is saying; he has to, to help Mama. Gio rephrases and now Adrian understands.

'Does Mama have a man?' 'Mama' and 'man', a question. Adrian shakes his head firmly.

'Are you sure?'

Adrian nods.

Gio runs his hand through his hair and stares out at the lake, surface still rippling gently from the rock-throwing. Adrian can't read the look on his face; for a moment it looks angry, then sad, then something else entirely. The man starts throwing rocks again. Adrian crouches down on his knees in between Brutus and Godiva, watching. He feels an eager tremor beneath the dogs' skin every time Gio flings a rock out across the water, like they are actively fighting the urge to charge into the cold, deep water.

'Do you know Mama's family?' Gio asks after a while.

Adrian shakes his head. Mama doesn't have any family. She was born somewhere in the north and both her parents died when she was a little girl and Mama had to go and live in an orphanage. Adrian asked her about it a few times but it was one of the things that made Mama sad; he could tell by the look in her eyes. *We need to focus on the good things, Adrian*, she'd say. *And the best thing in my life is you. Think about how, out of all the billions of people in the world, you and me found each other. How lucky is that?* He'd nod and snuggle into the crook of her arm, drawing in the scent of her, Adrian's favorite in the world. Sometimes, when the bullies at school were especially bad, he'd bring that smell to mind, and it had the power to transport him away from the moment to that place of complete safety.

The man says something else, and he catches the words 'brother' and 'sister'.

He shakes his head again.

'Are you sure?' asks Gio and Adrian raises his eyebrow. Of course he's sure; he would have noticed by now if he'd had a brother or sister. He has wondered about it sometimes, whether Mama would have liked to have more children, but she'd need a man for that and she didn't have one. He had asked her once and Mama had laughed and said, *My little birdy, how could I ever ask for more than you?*

'Does Mama work?'

Adrian nods.

'Where?'

Adrian explains, using signs, that Mama is a cleaner and that she works at a school for the deaf. He's still explaining when the man interrupts him.

'For fuck's sake,' he says. Adrian knows the f-word. 'A cleaner,' he shouts, his voice hollering across the water. 'Damn right!' Then he laughs. Adrian wonders if perhaps he used the wrong sign, maybe the man doesn't know sign language very well since he pretends he isn't deaf. Adrian doesn't understand why he can't just admit it; there's nothing wrong with being different, Mama tells him that every day. But Adrian also knows that it feels hard and maybe the man feels that it's too hard so it's easier to pretend. He watches him as he throws his head back and laughs theatrically again. The dogs watch too, alert, awaiting their master's next command. Gio stops laughing, his face suddenly pinched and angry. He turns on his heel and snaps his fingers at Godiva and Brutus who leap into step next to Gio as he walks briskly up the path toward the house, leaving Adrian on the beach. He looks around in bewilderment and, just then, a man steps out from the shadows of one of the large trees by the tall hedges.

It's the man from the plane, the one with the gun, the man who shot his father. He must have been there all along, watching. Adrian scans his surroundings, calculating the chance of escape, but realizes it's less than zero. The house is built on an enormous plot jutting into the water, a private peninsula with water on three sides and impenetrable hedges on the fourth. The man takes a few steps toward him, beckoning for Adrian to follow him back toward the house. In spite of the cold, the man is wearing only a white shirt tucked into black suit trousers, the gun visible and attached to his belt in a holster. Adrian feels tears spring to his eyes just looking at the man and remembers how cruelly he laughed at him when he cried after they'd landed at Orio al Serio.

He gathers all his strength and bites down hard on his bottom lip to stop the tears, then he charges past the man, up the path in the direction Gio went, making him have to half-run after him to catch up.

'Hey,' shouts the man, his feet crunching on the gravel. Adrian rounds the corner and slips back into the house through the small inset door which has been left open. The piano player remains at his stool and doesn't even look up when Adrian appears. A series of rooms open up from the hallway, one after the other, and he takes in opulent cornicing, shining parquet de chêne, chandeliers with live flickering candles. The man catches up and grabs Adrian's arm violently, dragging him toward the stairs. Adrian hears voices coming from one of the rooms he glimpsed and decides that now is his chance. If there are more people in this house, chances are they don't all know he's here and someone could rescue him, and Mama too... He unleashes a wild, bloodcurdling scream, so loud the piano player instantly stops playing, his hands hovering and trembling in the air.

'Mama!' screams Adrian, 'Mama, Mama, Mama!' and then, 'Help!'

Adrian is picked off the floor by the man from the plane and briskly carried up the first flight of stairs. He keeps shouting but the pianist starts playing again, an energetic piece that drowns out his hoarse voice, which is quickly running dry from lack of use. Adrian kicks and pummels the man with his fists as they keep climbing the stairs, but he doesn't appear to even notice it. The man shoves the door to the blue room open with his shoulder and drops Adrian onto the floor like a sack of potatoes, then slams the door shut. It hurts to land on the wooden floor and his screams become sobs, then hiccupy, raspy gasps of breath. When he wakes, hours later, the moon is framed at the top of the tall windows, white and still almost full, and Adrian is still on the floor. He sits up and in the shaft of light spilling into the room, begins to draw.

When he was little, long before he discovered airshow documentaries and paper plane tutorials, Adrian used to draw to calm himself down and sometimes it's still the only thing that works. It's as if the process of bringing the images in his head onto paper helps make sense of them. Mama gave up trying to get him to talk about what he was thinking a long time ago; now she knows that the way to get him to express himself is through the drawings. He draws for a long while, bringing the images of everything that's happened to him in the past few days onto sheet after sheet of paper. As soon as he's finished one, he starts the next. There's the drawing of Adrian on the floor at home, folding the Concorde, the man outside the front door, hand raised in a fist, poised and about to knock. There's the one showing Mama walking alongside the inner harbor, holding her phone, mouth open in speech, the moment before she was ambushed from the left. Adrian spent a long while on getting the details exactly right, down to the clasp on Mama's handbag and the fuzzy faux fur on Mama's hood.

There's a drawing of Adrian and the American man walking through the woods, away from a little white car, and another of them on the bus, the man's hand encircling Adrian's knee in his huge fist, Adrian's expression sad and frightened. There's one of Adrian and the man flying paper planes on the ferry, faces smiling, and one of them running away from men in suits pointing guns at them. His drawing is fast and self-assured, not even stopping when his right hand begins to ache. After several hours, he's drawn almost everything that's happened to him, including a detailed drawing of the helicopter that brought him here that he's especially pleased with. He only stops when the moon has moved too far along its trajectory to send any light into the blue room and when his hand aches so badly he has to flex and unflex it every few seconds. He crawls into the bed and lies awake for a long while, feeling more relaxed after transferring all the images from his head onto the paper. He has a sudden feeling that Mama is somewhere close, very close, held prisoner somewhere within this house, like himself. He whispers into the dark in their secret language, as though he is speaking directly to Mama, and the words come easily then.

I'm going to save you, Mama, he says. And, *I'll never ask for anything more than you.*

* * *

The light comes on. Gio enters the room. He picks up the drawings, one after the other, scrutinizing them as if he is trying to decide which ones to have framed and hung from the wall. There is no sign of his bizarre behavior from yesterday afternoon when Adrian told him that Mama cleans at the school for the deaf and the man erupted into exaggerated fits of laughter. Perhaps it isn't true that this is the man's house and that he's a prince; perhaps he is a patient, and this is a hospital for very crazy people – Adrian has heard of places like that. Steffen even once said to him that that's where Adrian himself would be sent, to the loony bin. But it can't be that Gio's a patient in a loony bin because all of the other people in this house, the old lady, the men in suits with guns, the pianist, seem to follow his command.

'Wow,' says Gio, holding one of the drawings up to the light, his expression looking genuinely impressed. 'How did you—?' It's the drawing of the helicopter; Adrian has placed it on the lawn in front of the house though he's never seen it there in real life. Its round body gleams in the sunshine and the pink bulk of the house is visible in the background. The helicopter is eerily lifelike and richly detailed, sketched in charcoal. The tail cone even bears the correct registration number, OY-GDV, glimpsed by Adrian for a split second and retained in his mind. He shrugs, doesn't want to attempt any more conversation with Gio. He wants to know why he's here, where Mama is and when he can see her.

'Where Mama,' he says.

'It speaks!' says Gio.

'Where Mama?'

'Look. I said I need your help. Will you help me?'

Adrian nods.

'I need the truth. The proper truth. How about you tell me everything about your life with your mother in Sandefjord and I'll take you for a ride in the helicopter?' It takes them a long while to establish this exchange, Gio making sure Adrian has fully understood what he's asking. Adrian draws a breath, focuses on slow, steady exhalation and inserts his voice.

'I want Mama. I want see Mama.'

'Fine,' says the man. 'Now, talk.' So Adrian talks, at first falteringly in a jumble of English words, Norwegian words, and occasional sign language. The man watches him intently, reading his lips, only occasionally asking him to repeat something. Adrian tells him everything, all the things Mama said he must never tell anyone, but what else is he supposed to do? All he wants is to see Mama, to snuggle in the crook of her arm and have her whisper *My little birdling* into his hair in their secret language. Adrian tells Gio that Mama pretends to be deaf but isn't actually, that she keeps money in the house, a lot of it, and that he sometimes used to play with the bills when Mama was out. He explains that they never go anywhere, except to the airport to look at the planes. He says that no one has ever come to the house and that if Mama has any friends, then he hasn't met them. He quickly adds that it's okay, they don't need other people, they're happiest the way they are, just the two of them. And Mama is the best Mama in the whole world.

32

Anastasia

The winter months pass slowly, spent mainly at Villa Serafina. Anastasia pretends that she could just pop into Milan to work or see friends whenever she wants to but it's increasingly obvious that she's expected to stay put unless she's accompanying Giorgio to something. He doesn't say it; he doesn't have to anymore. He's just automatically dismissive of any plans she might have and, in the end, it's easier to just stay where she is. After all, it's not like she wants for anything. She lives in the most beautiful surroundings imaginable; she knows she simply wouldn't have been able to conceive of such a place as Villa Serafina in her old life at the dacha – her brain couldn't have built such images of opulence and wealth. Weekly, cars arrive with various gifts. Claudio's wife, Patrizia, spends hours gently releasing exquisite items from their dust bags and hanging them in Anastasia's closet room, which is larger than the apartment on via Melzo. She places handbags from Chanel and Gucci and Valentino in rows on built-in shelves, expensively lit from within like in a shop.

Anastasia drinks her coffee on the jetty, almost no matter the weather; in fact she especially likes it when the wind hurls itself across the water, turning her cheeks red. She reads in the library, and meets with Henny, whose stress levels around the impending wedding are reaching feverish proportions, causing a rash to redden her pale neck in patches. She walks the dogs on the beach and sometimes down to the pretty village with its pastel-colored houses jutting into the water on the cape. She waits for Giorgio, who comes and goes and sometimes disappears for days. When they're together, it's mostly good; they come back together like two pieces of a puzzle that could never be slotted in with any other piece, making love long into the night, taking the boats out on the lake, cooking together, and occasionally attending the glitzy parties of Gio's friends and associates.

He likes to bring her out, then, showing her off to the world like a rare bird whose vibrant feathers might fade under the scrutiny of too many eyes. She puts on whichever dress he asks her to, and laughs when someone says something intended to be amusing, and dances slowly and closely with Giorgio, drawing in his full attention after all the time they spend apart. Sometimes, she bumps into Graziela or Xenia at a party and she catches a glimpse of that other life, another one she isn't living, but every day she's reminded of her tremendous fortune, to be living in Villa Serafina, enveloped in Giorgio's love.

* * *

He wakes her at five thirty, and getting up when the sky is still dark feels strange after months of having adapted to Gio's habit of sleeping until past eight. She sits up in bed, alarmed.

'Is something wrong?' She imagines Vera keeled over in a patch of Russian sage, tiny baby-blue flowers kissing her dry cheeks.

'Surprise,' says Giorgio, laughing and kissing her forehead. 'You're going to have your picture taken.'

Maya Kennedy, one of the best make-up artists in Milan, is waiting for her downstairs in the garden room and spends the next hour perfecting Anastasia's skin with dewy, shimmery foundation. She enhances her naturally wide-set eyes with taupe eyeshadow and expert flicks of eyeliner. When she's finished, Patrizia brings an enormous brown clothing bag into the room, so heavy Claudio helps her carry it. Watched by Anastasia and Giorgio, a dress emerges, made from layer upon layer of cream duchess satin and exquisite panels of lace.

'My mother's wedding dress,' says Giorgio, his voice thick with emotion. Anastasia recalls the painting hanging above the fireplace of the dining room at Palazzo di Arcimboldo in Palermo, of a woman in a white dress standing beneath the vaulted archways of Villa Serafina's terraces and gazing toward the violet surface of the lake as the sun emerges above the mountains. *His mother*, Claudio had said once when she'd stopped a while in front of it, making her jump. *Serafina*.

Giorgio rarely speaks of his family, other than to say that they have all died, with the exception of his brother Francesco, who lives on a ranch in Uruguay and who

Anastasia hasn't yet met. He lost his mother in the car accident that scarred him as a young boy, and his father died of Alzheimer's a couple of years ago after spending two decades lost in the cruel haze of his own mind.

Anastasia is uncomfortable stepping into the dress and seeing the look on Giorgio's face as Patrizia does up the last few of a long line of lace-covered buttons running from her lower back up to the nape of her neck. There is something feral about the way he looks at her, his teeth bared in a painful smile, his ice-blue eyes swimming with tears. She walks over to him, the cool silk swishing at her feet as she moves, and places a hand on his wrist. He stares at her, mouth open, as if this vision of Anastasia standing in front of him in his mother's dress can't be real.

'Come,' says Alberto, a photographer she's worked with several times before, including on the Bottega Veneta campaign, motioning toward the glass doors leading to the terrace. 'The light is just about right.' She passes the series of mirrors paneling the wall inside ornate gilded frames and is taken aback at the intense similarity to the woman in the painting. Her hair has been coiled around itself and placed on top of her head in the same loose bun from which wavy strands emerge, framing her face. Her make-up has carefully accentuated her gray eyes, emulating Serafina's almond-shaped ones with the eyeliner. Her eyebrows have been nudged into perfect thick arches, her cheeks made to glow with rosehip oil.

Giorgio watches as Anastasia is placed into position with the help of Alberto and Claudio. Claudio, too, is staring at her strangely and it occurs to her that he's been working for the di Vincenzo family for so long he would have known Serafina herself, back when Giorgio was a child.

'Unbelievable,' whispers Giorgio, inclining Anastasia's face slightly toward the light, the first rays of the emerging sun burning the sky red above Monte Crocione, and casting Anastasia's face in a golden rose glow. Alberto starts taking pictures, but Giorgio interrupts twice, slightly adjusting Anastasia's pose. She feels a sharp twinge in her gut, followed by a dreadful nausea at the strangeness of the scene. The dress is heavy and tight, the bone shards of its corset digging into her flesh. Claudio watches through the vast windows of the garden room, a look of discomfort on his face.

'Stop,' she hears herself say, at first quietly then again, more forcefully. 'Stop.' She steps back from where she's been made to lean against the balustrade and rubs her lower arm where the uneven stone of the balustrade has pressed into her skin. She turns around and walks quickly into the house, past Giorgio and Alberto and Claudio. She runs down the hallway and up the first flight of stairs, fighting wave after wave of nausea until it erupts in a streak of vomit across the white carpet of the bedroom she shares with Giorgio. He's followed closely behind her and grabs her arm and jerks her back up into a standing position, though she is doubled over and still throwing up.

'What the hell was that?' he hisses in her face. 'They're all down there, waiting for you. Do you have any idea what this cost, to bring Alberto Vangese and Maya Kennedy here, at the crack of dawn? Fuck, Anoushka, get yourself cleaned up and come back downstairs. I want a lot more pictures than that.'

'No.'

'No?' Giorgio laughs incredulously, then sneers at her.

'It's weird. I don't know what you're trying to do. But it felt weird.'

'You're just unbelievable. I try to do something nice for you and this is how you thank me?'

'Something nice for *me*? This seems to be very much for you, Gio.'

'You little bitch. Nothing is ever good enough for you. Nothing ever impresses you. You're always just aloof and spacey, as though you were born into all of this and barely notice it. But that's hardly the case, is it, Anastasia?'

'Please leave me alone for a bit. I need to lie down. I don't feel well.' It's true, she still feels nauseated, and underneath that, a visceral dread is rushing through her caused by his cruel words, making her ears ring and her head feel strangely light. He seems to snap back into himself and nods, turning toward the door. Then he spins back around and punches Anastasia full force in the stomach, smashing his knuckles into the protective wall of the corset. He screams, a wild guttural scream that echoes down the hallway through the open door. She's sure the people downstairs in the garden room will have heard it and will come rushing upstairs to help. Realizing he has hurt himself more than her thanks to the corset, he grabs her by the neck and squeezes so hard Anastasia begins to see swirling red clouds in her field of vision. He pushes her backward and slams her into the closed bathroom door, her skull striking the solid wood with a loud bang. He squeezes even harder and doesn't let go until she almost loses consciousness, crumpling to the floor.

Claudio stands in the doorway and Giorgio pushes past him.

'Can you help Miss Nikitina to bed, please?' he asks, stepping over her motionless body, then rushing toward the stairs. 'She's not feeling very well.'

Anastasia comes to, Claudio gently patting her cheeks and whispering to her in his incomprehensible Sicilian dialect. She vaguely notices the sound of the helicopter taking off from the lawn but drifts away on an irresistible thick wave of sleep. She stirs again and the sun is going down, and she hears the whirr of the incoming helicopter again. Patrizia comes and helps her to the bathroom and back to bed, but her legs shake so badly she can barely walk. Patrizia goes away for a while, then returns with a light linen cloth soaked in hot lavender water, which she gently presses to Anastasia's neck. Anastasia opens her eyes a crack but doesn't have the energy to take in what's happening and is so disoriented she thinks she's back home in the dacha and it's Vera holding the cloth to her neck. She tries to speak, to say thank you, or help me, or what do I do now, please help me, but no words come, only a thin croak.

'*La paura*,' says Patrizia, stroking her forehead.

It's two days before she is well enough to get out of bed unaided. She walks across the room and opens the door to the balcony directly above the terrace where the strange episode unfolded. Now its memory is hazy and impotent, like a nightmare recalled in the reassuring light of day, but Anastasia knows she'll never forget the sensation of Giorgio's strong hands closing around her neck, squeezing her trachea shut.

When she goes back into the room, rubbing her arms from the sting of the morning air, Giorgio has returned and is sitting on the baroque black velvet sofa at the foot of their bed, his head cradled in his hands, hair wild and unkempt. When he hears her approach, he looks up at her, his eyes full of remorse.

'I could die from shame,' he says.

'I wish you would.'

'Anastasia. I'm so sorry. I have no excuses. Maybe an explanation. But what I did was unforgivable, I know that. But Anoushka, please, please, will you let me tell you something I haven't ever told anyone? Please. I beg you.' He pauses for a moment; she stares out at the violet, hazy lake. He clearly takes her silence as a sign to continue.

'I want to tell you about my seventh birthday,' he says. 'We were living in Palermo back then, as you know. It was the second day of the summer holidays and we were busy preparing the house to close for August, getting ready to go to Anacapri. We'd celebrated my birthday in the morning with cake and presents in bed. I remember my father taking lots of pictures and the strange thing is, I've never found out what happened to those pictures; they were lost forever. I got a red plastic remote control car I'd wanted for a long while and Francesco and I rushed after it from room to room, laughing and shouting. We ate lunch at home – *fritto misto*, my favorite meal as a child.

'We slept for a while after lunch, tucked up beneath cool sheets with the shutters closed against the sun. Then, my mother and brother and I decided to spend the afternoon on the beach in Mondello. It was a sweltering hot day and the heat in the city was unbearable, bringing with it an unescapable rancid stench of sewage and garbage. My father was off somewhere in meetings, as he usually was. We called for the car and I remember the drive so well, every moment of it, as the dusty, dirty streets slipped past grand graffitied townhouses already shuttered and closed for the summer, their owners long gone to Puglia or Sorrento or Levanto.

'We were heading from the Centro Storico toward the port; my mother preferred the coastal road to Mondello and didn't mind the detour. We'd just passed the cathedral when the car carrying the bombs pulled up next to ours. I remember the seconds before it detonated; it was as though I *knew* on some level, but of course that's a trick of the mind with hindsight. But there was a stillness to the air, a slowing down. I smiled at my little brother, and I've thought about that so many times, that I'm glad I did. My mother was leaning her head against the window, beads of sweat gathering at her temples, her blue-gray eyes the exact color of the sea and her hair the deep honeyed hues of the sunstruck stone houses of the old town. It's how I remember her most clearly, like the most beautiful parts of Palermo on a hot day incarnated.

'The bomb was meant for my father, who had made members of the mafia extremely angry, and ironically, he was the only member of our family who escaped entirely unscathed. Nobody could understand how I lived. There was almost nothing left of them.'

'Them?' Anastasia whispers, her voice still won't carry sound. Giorgio nods, tears streaming down his face.

'The driver. My mother. Francesco.'

'But—'

'I know.'

'You said Francesco lives in Uruguay. I don't understand...'

'I can't bear the truth, Anastasia.'

'I—'

'Don't say anything. It's okay. It is what it is. I'm so sorry for what has happened between us. I am not trying to excuse it, I only wanted to make you understand. I don't know what happened. I – it seemed like a normal, nice thing to do at first. To recreate the picture of her. You remind me of her, very much; you always have, there is a strong physical resemblance between you. I didn't want to say that to you in case you thought that I didn't love you for you. I do, more than anything else. It was more that it was an added bonus that you reminded me of her, a bittersweet and lovely fact known only to me, and, I suppose, to Claudio and Patrizia. They were very fond of my mother.

'When you put the dress on and posed for the pictures it was as though something inside of me came crashing down, no, detonated, pulverizing my insides and I just completely lost control of myself. Then it made me so angry that you denied me the continuation of the incredible pleasure of seeing her again, watching her standing there in front of me, resurrected, alive and so very beautiful, as though she'd stepped from the painting. When you ran for the stairs, I would have done anything to stop you. I went completely crazy.'

'I'm not her, Gio,' she says, more softly now, but the raspiness in her voice is a stark reminder of the violence that caused it.

'I know that. You're you. Thank God for that. And you're mine. Anastasia. Please say you'll still be mine, I love you more than anything.' He gently takes her hand in his own, fingering the bare patch of skin where the engagement ring usually sits. 'Please.'

'Is it what made you deaf?'

Giorgio's facial expression drastically changes, from sad and hopeful to shocked, angry, then back to shocked.

'How did you know? Nobody knows. Only Claudio.'

'I guessed. A long time ago.' At the beginning, Anastasia hadn't been able to put her finger on what it was with Giorgio, but she had known long before he told her what had happened to him. She imagines everyone around him knows deep down.

'But how?'

'The thoughtful way you watch people when they speak; I realized you were lip-reading. The devotion to Audire and to making life easier for deaf children across Italy. The instruction to speak to you only when I have your full attention. The way you often watch the helicopter land on the lawn without an ear guard. I whisper something to you in the dark sometimes, and you don't answer even though I'm sure you haven't fallen asleep yet. The way you quite often claim to have not been told something, when I have definitely told you. One day I googled the school you went to, in England, you'd mentioned its name. I saw that as well as its mainstream program it had an award-winning program for deaf children. Something just clicked. What I don't understand is why you pretend not to be deaf.'

'Because talking about it or acknowledging it is a

constant reminder of what I've lost. So I pretend. I pretend that Francesco is in Uruguay, playing polo at Punta del Este, not dead at four. That my mother is upstairs in her room, reading in bed, and that I can hear like everyone else.' He begins to cry again, fat teardrops landing on the back of his hand, which is clutching hers. 'My father sent me to England to learn to live as a deaf man, but I made it my mission to get out of there having learned to live like a man who nobody knew was deaf. I just can't bear it. Please don't leave me, Anastasia.'

'Then you have to let me in. All the way in.'

She signs it as she says it and Giorgio stares at her in disbelief and awe at her demonstration of love, his eyes overflowing with tears. He signs, 'I promise.' And, 'When did you learn to sign?'

She signs back, 'That first summer in Palermo. I taught myself, for weeks.'

She'd thought about confronting him gently about it many times, but she felt the kinder thing to do would be to wait for him to tell her himself. Over the time they've been together, Anastasia has adopted many strategies to protect Giorgio and make his pretense easier, like sometimes repeating something when someone else has spoken without him catching it, or pointing to something when its sound didn't alert him. She'd told herself that she was doing all of this out of kindness and consideration, but she wonders now if, on some level, she also knew to be afraid to ask Giorgio about her suspicion.

Giorgio pulls her close and she lets herself be held and, though it feels good, as if they've reconstructed what was shattered between them, Anastasia knows that even though its shape may have been resurrected in their close embrace, deep cracks run beneath the surface.

You're mine.

Don't forget you're only ever your own.

33

Selma

Selma is picked up from the hotel and driven to Como in a gleaming black Range Rover by a friendly driver called Mario. He tells her about his village in Sicily, apparently the prettiest village in the whole country, and how, next year, he is marrying his childhood sweetheart and moving back home. When the car stops at a tollgate and Mario reaches his arm out of the window to scan his credit card on the card reader, his white shirt creeps up to reveal a huge tattoo on his lower arm and wrist and Selma has the strange sensation that he's entirely covered in ink beneath the smart tailored suit. He goes on and on about his girlfriend in almost incomprehensible English and in the end Selma nods and smiles politely, zoning out of the one-sided conversation while firing off emails and messages, catching up on her considerable daily correspondence. There's a message from Olav which makes her smile.

Checking in with my favorite Bond girl. You okay?

Yep. Only on my way to Como to lunch with di Vincenzo himself. Will keep you posted.

Jeeez, Eriksen. Be careful.

On arrival in Como, Giorgio is waiting for Selma in a huge, glass fronted room opening out onto the terraces, the doors closed, presumably for winter. He has a bemused smile on his face, his arms crossed in front of his chest. He is wearing a sharp white shirt, well-cut black woolen suit trousers, and loafers with a gold GdV monogram. Selma feels acutely underdressed in dark jeans and a moss-green polo-neck.

'Not that hard-to-get after all, it would seem,' he says, leaning in for a kiss on Selma's cheek, but she sidesteps him and extends her hand for him to shake instead.

'This is a business meeting, Mr di Vincenzo.'

'Of course. But please, call me Gio.' Giorgio leads Selma through to a formal dining room with a feature wall made from what looks like real zebra skin and a very large chandelier hanging low above an enormous, polished mahogany table that could easily seat twenty but is set for two.

'Nice crib,' she says.

'Excuse me?'

'Your house. Cute.'

'Ah. Yes. Cute, huh. That's a first. Thank you, Selma, I do like it here.'

'Do you live here alone, if you don't mind me asking?'

'I have live-in staff, people like Claudio, whom you met. His wife, Patrizia. Others.'

'Girlfriend? Wife?'

'Very direct aren't you? Typical Scandinavian.'

'Sorry. Just curious for a living, that's all.' Giorgio laughs and Selma takes a seat, feeling almost relaxed in his company. What a strange situation to be in, she thinks, letting her eyes roam around the room, doing a double take at the sight of what is without doubt a Picasso above the fireplace. She's never been anywhere like this before, and this is most likely the only glimpse she will ever have into this kind of world. She imagines what it might be like to live here with Giorgio, spending your whole life in such gilded, ostentatious opulence, and wonders whether, after a while, you'd just get used to it and not really notice much. Her thoughts continue to Olav's cozy cottage on the hillside high above Oslo; it isn't big but the views are to die for and there is something intensely comforting about it. She feels a sharp twinge of longing for him and for an imagined future which is starting to grow like a fantasy in her mind.

She wonders what it must have been like to grow up here, surrounded by staff, taking boats out on the lake and traveling between several homes by private plane or on a helicopter. What kind of grasp of normal life is it possible to have when that is the only world you've ever known? She studies di Vincenzo with some pity.

'Since you ask, you shall receive an answer.' Giorgio winks at Selma and takes a seat opposite. A woman appears from a side door and pours San Pellegrino into very thin square glass tumblers, then rosé wine onto ice in big wine bowls. When she slips soundlessly back out from the room, Giorgio continues. 'I'm having some woman troubles at the moment, if I'm honest. Unfortunately for me, I have a weakness for sulky Eastern Europeans. It's like I become a little boy again around these girls; I'm just desperate to win them over and make them smile. It's surprisingly difficult to please these women. I don't know if you've ever had a Russian girlfriend yourself, Selma; I'm going to assume not.' She shakes her head and laughs a little, in spite of herself. 'They're like magpies. Anything bling-bling and they're on it. They love this room, for example.' He laughs and touches his wine glass to hers in a melodious clink. 'Magpies, with cold hearts.'

Sounds like you, thinks Selma. 'So, you're single.'

'I'm not sure I'd call it that exactly. I have friends, if you will. A few very close friends.'

'Mmm. What about Liv Carlsen?'

'What about her?'

'Was she one of your very close friends?'

'No. Not my type.'

'No? From what I've seen, she was stunning.'

'They all are.'

'So what's your type?'

'I like mellow girls. Relaxed.'

'Girls who don't ask lots of annoying questions?'

'Check.'

'Girls who are easily appeased by a five-thousand-euro handbag?'

'Check,' he says again, raising his wine glass to her. They're clearly both enjoying the banter, and Selma is conscious of keeping the tone light. Giorgio takes a long sip of his wine and the woman reappears, placing a beautifully presented plate of confit duck on the table in front of each of them.

'What about Graziela?'

'What about her? Definitely not my type.' He laughs,

draining the rest of his wine glass and immediately the woman reappears to refill it, cradling the bottle in a thick white serviette before placing it back in the silver cooler and disappearing.

'I meant, have you spoken to her?'

'Why do you want to know about her?'

'Because I'd really like to get in touch with her.'

'Yes, me too. In fact, I'd kill to get hold of her, but alas, I've been unable to.'

'So you haven't spoken to her.'

'Selma, let me ask you something. Why are you really here? As much as I'd like to fool myself into thinking this could be the beginning of something wonderful, I have the feeling you're after something else entirely.'

'Mr di Vincenzo—'

'Gio.'

'Okay. Fine. Gio. Cut the crap. Please. A woman is missing. And her young son. I'm here to try to find out what might have happened to them. I'm aware of the dark destinies of several of the girls who have been signed to your agency and feel confident there is a link between Liv's past history in Milan and her disappearance.'

'Dark destinies? That's a little dramatic, don't you think?'

'It seems to me like a disproportionate number of young women working for you end up addicted to heroin, or as prostitutes, or dead.'

'Has it occurred to you that the majority of the girls who work for me are teenagers with limited life experience from disadvantaged backgrounds who suddenly find themselves in this kind of world?' He gesticulates around the room, at the gilded mirrors, the soaring, intricately painted ceilings, the twinkling crystal chandelier. 'And that they naturally often succumb to temptation and make bad choices?'

'Mmm, or are they lured in with false promises, then groomed and taken advantage of? Plied with drugs and forced into sexual service to pay off their debts?'

'You know, Selma, you're a really pretty girl. A little plain, perhaps, but definitely an attractive enough girl. But when you talk like that, you sound like one of those washed-up old lesbian feminists who hates men and can't accept that women are the masters of their own fates, just like everyone else.'

'Wow.' He's getting angry, she can tell by the way he's gone from relaxed to noticeably controlled, a tight smile on his lips, his eyes frighteningly cold. She needs to change the subject and decides on a risky question from left field, with no idea how di Vincenzo might react; in her experience those are often the ones that yield the best results. 'Anyway, interesting debate. Gosh, this food is just absolutely delicious.' Deliberately taking her time, she dabs the last morsel, a mouthful of perfectly seared shiitake mushroom, into a rich jus of brandy and thyme, then pops it in her mouth. When she's finished, she leans back and watches Giorgio across the table. He's still agitated, probably trying to figure out how to get rid of her. 'One more thing I wondered about. Can you tell me about Will Marlow?'

What happens next happens so fast Selma has no time to react before it's over. Giorgio leaps from his seat, knocking his chair back, grabs his wine glass from the table and flings it very hard in her direction, shattering it on the wall behind her.

'That's enough! For fuck's sake! Get out! How dare

you come into my home and ask me about that fucking scumbag?'

'Mr di Vincenzo, Gio—'

'Get the fuck out!' Giorgio turns on his heel and storms from the room, and instantly, two men appear from the side door, flanking Selma, who remains seated at the table. She recognizes one of them as Mario and the other is a tall Germanic-looking guy with a buzz cut and an earpiece into which a voice is shouting so loudly she can hear its crackling, muffled echo.

'No problemo,' says the man into a microphone, then he turns toward Selma, yanking her hard up from the chair by her upper arm. 'Time to leave.'

Mario drives her back to Milan, but this time he doesn't say a single word. Occasionally he stares at her in the rearview mirror with a hostile look and she makes herself meet his gaze square on. She's itching to call Olav to tell him everything, but settles for a quick WhatsApp message: *Omg. The guy's insane. Fact. Went COMPLETELY nuts when I asked about Will Marlow. Can you dig? Call you in an hr.*

She's almost surprised to be dropped safely back at the hotel and not taken to a dark alleyway somewhere and beaten up, or worse. The car drives off in a dramatic hurry, tires screeching, and Selma runs upstairs to the hotel room. She'll grab her things and leave; enough is enough.

When she's locked the door behind her and fastened the chain, she pulls her phone back out from her handbag and sees six missed calls from Olav. Her heart begins to race as she returns his call.

'Hey,' she says. 'What's going on? You okay?'

'Are you okay, Selma?'

'I'm fine. Tell me what you've got.'

'This is seriously next-level stuff. I know why you haven't been able to get hold of Will Marlow.'

'Why? Olav, tell me!'

'Because he's in prison for murder.'

34

Liv

I'm left alone for several days and nights. Carefully watched by Mario or the blond, Claudio brings food once a day at dusk, disgusting scraps of meat swimming in fatty broth, and he doesn't meet my gaze even once. Giorgio is smart enough to not leave me alone with him, a man I once considered something of a friend. I hope he looks after Adrian up there. There is no sign of Giorgio, but I hear the helicopter coming and going, sometimes several times a day. One morning I hear laughter from outside, close by, and catch sight of a woman's ankles as she runs past. She is pursued by another woman, then a man; they're all laughing and shouting. The man is Giorgio, I can tell from the exquisite cognac-colored hand-stitched leather shoes. It's easy to picture the scene unfolding up there. The elusive billionaire prince, once one of the most eligible bachelors in Europe, entertaining a couple of stunningly beautiful girls barely out of their teens, whose lives have been absolutely nothing like Giorgio's own.

I know these girls because I was one of them, once. They arrive in Milan from Barranquilla, Coimbra, Thessaloniki, Malmö, Yekaterinburg, with a one-way ticket and nothing to go back to anyway. At least, that's what they're told. *What you had, back there in the cramped apartment with your people, it was nothing. What you can have here is worth so much more.* The parties, the jewels, the champagne, the cars, the travel, the clothes; all freely exchanged for that one irresistible thing money can't buy: beauty. The inexhaustible beauty of the girls stalking the catwalks, arriving in their thousands, expendable and exploitable. They navigate this new gilded world awestruck and grateful, and this new world has its way with them, taking most of them not to the promised cover of magazines and top catwalks, but to endless fruitless castings, followed by paid nightclub appearances and yacht parties, where they are considered by the middle-aged politicians, oligarchs, and businessmen watching them like goods lined up on the softly lit shelves of via Montenapoleone's finest boutiques. They learn to dance suggestively, to put a couple of lines of coke up their noses to find the energy to stay out night after night in the company of these men who fund them until they make it big. They unlearn consent and what it means to value themselves. They smile, but their eyes grow cold.

Upstairs, Giorgio will be showing those girls what life could be like. He'll be indirectly telling them that what they had didn't matter, that they have to give themselves over entirely to men like him and his associates, only to be discarded; that this life of excess and beauty is all they should aim for.

They'll laugh and drink his champagne and marvel at the

priceless art at Villa Serafina, staring out at the glimmering cerulean lake, and celebrate the loss of who they once were. They'll get into his bed, sometimes one by one, sometimes together, and they'll pretend to love the way he moves inside them, the way the coarse, now graying hair on his chest rubs their breasts raw. They'll get chauffeured home to cramped apartments in run-down buildings in Bovisa or Quarto Oggiaro, and never be called back to the pristine Belle Époque palazzo on the banks of Lake Como where they once took part in a cocaine binge culminating in a threesome. They were promised fun, shared apartments with roof terraces in Porta Venezia or Navigli, just like they were promised Dolce & Gabbana and Gucci, and now they're learning that it might just be that they're not the one in a million. They'll pore over editorials featuring the biggest stars from Gio's Model Agency, girls like Xenia Aliyeva, Marsha King, Adrienne Suva, and Anastasia Nikitina. They'll keep going to the castings and the parties, and before long they'll need more and more drugs to keep up, helpfully provided by the men who then start to ask for some kind of compensation.

They'll get sent on the travels they dreamed of, only not exactly as models, but still, they'll get to go to private islands and some of the world's largest yachts and they'll lounge around shimmering pools drinking cocktails and at times like that, it will feel worth it, that the price they're paying for the tiniest slice of another world than the one they came from is worth it.

Every day, whiling away endless hours locked in this dirt cellar, I cry. I stand at the window, watching the world go on without me. I am in no doubt that Giorgio and his henchmen will have gotten rid of Leana Fletcher too. Her blood is on my hands, like Clio Amaury's. And Will Marlow's. Will didn't understand what he was up against; I endlessly tried to deter him from involving himself in a world that could only ever kill him. And it did.

I cry for him, and for me, and for Adrian and everything that won't ever be. The other day, I picked up a shard from Giorgio's smashed tumbler from over by the window and sliced a long, shallow line into my skin; it was all I could manage. I thought about my son, how horrified he would be to learn that I'd bled to death at my own hands. It helped release some of the overwhelming feelings and terror I hold inside, though, and I decided that it would be okay to do it again, only not with intent of taking me away from here forever.

I find myself pacing from corner to corner, my mind spinning wildly for hours on end. Where is Giorgio, why hasn't he returned, why hasn't he forced more names from me, what has he done to Adrian, why am I just kept here like a death row prisoner?

One night, a perfect silver moon creeps from the folds of a bulbous cloud and hovers for a long while in the narrow window. I raise my hand to the glass and feel myself gain strength and grow centered in myself.

'The kingdom is within you,' I whisper to myself, feeling self-conscious at first, then emboldened. My face is reflected back to me in the window, and I think that I look more beautiful and real and valuable in this moment as a prisoner at breaking point, than I ever did on the cover of a magazine or through the eyes of a man who wanted to possess me.

* * *

A kick in the ribs, then another.

'Wakey, wakey, *principessa*,' says a voice. Giorgio is standing above me, the tip of his monogrammed loafer poised for another kick. It lands in the pit of my stomach. 'Fletcher didn't check out. What the fuck?' I sit up and rub my bare arms for warmth. I've been wearing the red silk cocktail dress ever since the night Mario hosed me down and I watched as Clio was shot in Ajaccio.

'What do you mean?' I ask.

'She's MIA.'

'Oh.'

'Oh?'

'I don't know what happened to her. All I know is that she was one of the girls.' I search back through my patchy memory and try to remember what the circumstances were around Leana Fletcher, but can't immediately recall the details. She was American, a mixed-race girl from somewhere in the south, who was held for months as a sex slave in a villa in the hills of Portofino. I got her out, and arranged for a safe passage back to the States, funding rehab and the first year of her new life. I don't know more than that, and I tell Giorgio that.

'Liv,' he says, 'you're going to need to do better than that.'

'How—?'

'Oh, I know. I know everything. Do you like it when I call you that? Does it turn you on? I could never tell what turned you on, God knows I tried. Liv. *Life* in Norwegian, funny that. Ironic. Though presumably you wouldn't know. Or do you? Cute setup you had there, in Sandefjord, with your kid.'

'Can I see him?'

'Nope.'

'Please? I would do anything to see him. Giorgio, please.'

'Give me the rest. All of them.'

I nod. 'Yes.'

'And the complete breakdown of every single fucking transaction.'

'Yes.'

'I'll think about it. Though I don't think it would be in the boy's best interests to see his mother like this. He'll never forget it. You need to think about him. Perhaps better to retain the memory of a normal, loving mother than to be exposed to this new you: a washed-up, exposed whore falling to pieces at the end of her life. Does he really need to experience you at the very end? Ask yourself that. And if the answer is yes, then I'm sure we can work something out. If you really want to let the kid say goodbye.'

'I want to know what you are planning.'

'Nope. All you need to know is that this is a straight-up transaction. All of them, in exchange for the boy.'

'I'd need access to my files to give you more.'

'I'd imagine you're smart enough to have destroyed those. And we're still millions of euros short. Ten, in fact.'

'No,' I lie. We stare at each other. He takes a step forward, closing the gap between us and for a moment it is as though the past decade drops away. He cups my chin in his hand and gently rubs my bruised and swollen jawline with his thumb. I close my eyes, returning me to other caresses, to calendula oil and yarrow leaves pressed to childhood injuries by the gentlest of hands. There is a strength in growing up loved and cherished that never leaves you and I hope Adrian will carry that within him even if Giorgio gets away with my murder. I know I do. It feels good to know that despite everything, all the incremental moves away from that girl I once was and the family I was born into, despite being conditioned to believe that my beginnings were nothing at all, the feeling of being truly loved has been preserved and still retains the power to give me strength now, so many years later.

Giorgio moves his thumb from my jawline down to the center of my throat and presses it hard inwards. I draw back, gasping for breath, but he follows without releasing his vice-like grip.

'You've made me so angry,' he whispers, bringing his face very close to mine. 'So very, very angry.' He turns toward the door and motions to whomever is standing there in the shadows. The man with spiky blond hair steps forward, a hungry smile playing on his lips.

'Carl. I need you to loosen her up a little,' says Giorgio. 'You know what I mean? Take her down a couple of notches. Show her who's boss.' Carl nods eagerly. Suddenly he surges forward as though he's merely been waiting all these days for a green light from Giorgio to attack me, and perhaps he has. He grabs me by the neck, much harder than Giorgio did, and presses me up against the wall.

'Bitch,' he says. 'Bitch,' he repeats, as though it's the only word he knows. He glances around as if trying to get more direction from Giorgio. Giorgio has sat down on one of the chairs and is clutching a tumbler glass of whiskey, watching the scene unfold as if he is a spectator in a movie theater. He sloshes the globules of ice around and watches as Carl pushes me down into a corner, his face contorted and sneering; it's as if he's enjoying this so much he's gone into a kind of trance. He unleashes a loud growl, then shrugs his suit jacket off his comically broad shoulders.

'Camilla Asunción Gutierrez,' I shout. 'Iris Anton. Natalia Guchaeva. Emilia Bashinskaya.'

Giorgio sits up straighter, making notes on his phone. 'You'd better not be fucking with me,' he says.

'I'm not.'

'Time will tell. I'll get these checked out. Tomorrow you give me the rest. Good night,' he says. Then he adds, 'Knock yourself out, Carl. And her.' He winks at Carl, who's still standing above me, awaiting further command.

'No,' I say, my voice crystal clear and loud. It's as though something inside me is finally breaking free, refusing to be terrorized by this man for another moment. I will do whatever it takes, say whatever I can, to save not only my son, but myself too. Nobody else is going to. 'Don't do to your own son what was done to you.' Giorgio stops dead in his tracks.

'What did you say?'

'You heard me. I said, don't do to your son what was done to you.'

Giorgio comes back over to me and crouches down beside me, unable to hide the onslaught of emotions rushing through him.

'Don't,' he whispers, his face suddenly pale and tortured. He looks so much like Adrian in this moment that I could almost love him, if only for that reason. 'Just... don't.'

'Adrian is yours. Your son, Gio. Your only living relative. And I'm his mother. I know the hole that was left in your heart when Serafina died.' I will say anything at this point, anything to stay alive for my son, anything to not be left alone in this basement with Carl, even the truth. 'Adrian is a gift, the biggest gift either of us will ever receive. Let him love you back to life, I swear to God that he can. And let me love him too. Maybe we could even—'

'Shut up,' says Giorgio, but the aggression of earlier is gone from his voice. He's meek and struck quiet by shock now. The enormity of what I've said is dawning on him. He buries his head in his hands and rocks back and forth on his knees. 'How—' he begins, several times, never managing to complete a sentence from this repeated beginning.

'Did you not think that perhaps he could be?'

'No. You know damned well that I'm... injured. That there was damage.'

'I'm sure you can imagine that I've wished that he wasn't. More than anything. But he is. He's a miracle, Gio. *Our* miracle.'

For the first time since I've been here, Giorgio is visibly affected and uncertain. 'Are you sure?'

'Absolutely.'

'Is that why... Is it why you did what you—'

'Absolutely.'

Giorgio stands up, then sits back down, then stands up again. Tears glint in his eyes and for a moment I think he might burst into tears, but instead he mutters to himself intently, his eyes wild, as though he's arguing two sides of an argument equally passionately, trying to convince himself of what to believe. A sudden scream rings out and when he turns back around to face me, Giorgio is holding his right hand up, the remains of the crystal tumbler still held in its grip, blood gushing down his wrists from multiple punctures. Carl watches him, his mouth dropped open in a slack O. Giorgio opens his palm, the ruins of the tumbler dropping to the floor and smashing some more. Then he brings his hand to my face and smears it with blood before rushing from the room.

35

Adrian

When Adrian had finished speaking and signing, telling Gio everything he could think of about his and Mama's life in the house on the cliff, they had sat in silence for a long while. Finally, Gio had stood up and left the room without a word, and Adrian had assumed that he would return with Mama in tow. He'd agreed to let him see Mama, if only he told him everything he knew. But he didn't come back. The hours dragged on and the broccoli tree cast curious, elongated shadows onto the lawn before the sun disappeared behind the shoulder of the steep hill. At one point in the afternoon Adrian thought he heard the rhythmic chopping sound of the helicopter taking off or landing, but he couldn't be quite sure as a fierce wind was careening down the hillsides, slamming into the house and rattling the windowpanes. He heard the dogs barking, on and off. Otherwise, nothing happened.

The gray-haired lady brought lunch: tomato soup with crumbling balls of white cheese floating in it, strange but tasty. When she placed the tray down on the desk, Adrian could feel her eyes on him but he couldn't bear to meet her gaze; it would feel too awful to see the pity there. Later, she brought dinner – lasagna with shavings of fresh parmesan and Adrian was stunned to realize that it tasted almost exactly like Mama's recipe, his favorite. He waited and waited for the man to return, but he never did. Had he lied to him, saying he'd take Adrian to see Mama and on the helicopter if only he told the truth? Adrian doesn't understand lies; it doesn't make any sense at all that anyone would use words and energy to say things that aren't even true. He watches TV absentmindedly; he can't focus fully on anything other than the door and whether it's about to swing open, revealing his mama.

After a while, the old lady returns and collects the tray, but she's not alone; another lady, this one much younger and wearing a starched white apron and a little hat, trails behind her. She gives Adrian a gentle smile, but in her hand she holds a syringe. Adrian shakes his head as she approaches him, speaking slowly in a strange language, and Adrian wants to scream and hurl the desk toward her, even scramble from the window into the broccoli tree. In the end, he sits as still as a statue, paralyzed by fear, as the woman picks up his left arm, folds back his dirty sleeve, pinches his skin several times, then plunges the syringe into his vein; his blood runs fast and black into a little vial. Even after she's finished and secured a ball of cotton wool in the crook of his arm, Adrian remains in the same exact position, unable to move even an inch. It feels like hours before he's able to move his little finger, wriggling it back and forth like he's done since for as long as he can remember whenever he's been truly afraid or upset. When he tries to get up, his legs buckle and give way, and he slumps to the floor where he stays, apathetically staring at the cartoons running on a loop on the TV.

He falls asleep at last, waking in the middle of the night to cartoon voices and the flickering light of the TV. He gets up and draws until dawn lightens the sky: dogs and helicopters and the man with the ice-blue eyes and the lady who came and took blood from his arm.

**

Several days pass in the same way and Adrian is left in no doubt that the man has betrayed him. He is terrified to think that he might have placed Mama in even more danger by telling this man everything, how could he have been so stupid? Mama has always drummed into him that he must never, ever speak of her or his life in any detail to anyone, because 'they can only trust each other'. And now, he's failed her. On the morning of the third day, there is a knock on the door. A man he's never seen before enters the room. He has kind brown eyes like a dog and smiles at the sight of Adrian. He points to himself and says, 'I'm Claudio. Come with me, sir.' Claudio holds the door open for Adrian, who almost laughs out loud at the incredible strangeness of being called 'sir', like an adult in a movie. It's also incredibly strange to be called Claudio, thinks Adrian. Cloud-ee-oh! They head down the corridor in the same direction he walked with Gio that one time he was allowed out from the blue room. At the sweeping stairs, the man motions for Adrian to continue downstairs. Instead of heading all the way to the bottom floor where the grand piano stands in silence now, he steers Adrian down another corridor on the first floor. This space is much more beautiful than the unadorned, plain corridor that leads to the blue room. Works of art are placed on the walls with invisible fixings, making them look like they're hovering there. They're the kinds of paintings Adrian has only seen pictures of from museums. Beneath his feet is a very soft, very thick, pristine white carpet. The man opens a door about two thirds of the way down the corridor, leading into a huge space: three interconnected rooms overlooking the lawns and the lake.

'New room for you,' he says. Adrian sits down on a blue velvet chair; he feels as though he might pass out, and he can't help the tears rushing from his eyes, but this time he's not laughed at; instead, Claudio comes over to where he is sitting and very gently places a hand on his shoulder and hands him a tissue. After a while, he leaves the room and leaves the door wide open. Adrian peers at it and wonders if it's some kind of test, or perhaps Claudio doesn't know he's a prisoner? He takes a couple of steps toward it, his brain gathering speed and trying to come up with the best escape strategies, but just then, he hears a strange sound from the corridor. He retreats back to the velvet chair and draws his knees up to his chin, trying to look as though he's just been sitting there, admiring the lake that is glowing emerald today in brilliant winter sunshine.

Gio enters the room. He has a strange look on his face; he looks stricken, as though he might burst into tears. In his arms is something even stranger: a plump writhing puppy, battling to be placed down on the floor. Gio puts it down at Adrian's feet and the puppy flies at him, licking his hand

and yapping wildly. He picks it up and it is as though the puppy seamlessly slots into a hole in his heart.

'For you,' says Gio.

'Where Mama?' asks Adrian. 'You said I see Mama. You said.'

Gio nods. 'Soon. I promise.'

'What dog name?' asks Adrian.

'What do you want to call him?'

Adrian's eyes widen at the thought of naming the puppy. But his name is instantly clear to him. 'Hercules,' he whispers, the name coming out clearly on the first attempt. He'd never thought he could have a dog, Mama always said no. She said they're so much work, that they need walking all the time, that they bark in the night, and that, if they had a dog, they'd never be able to go anywhere. That sounded pretty stupid to Adrian because it's not like they ever go anywhere anyway, but he knew better than to argue with her. 'Thank you,' he says and looks up at the man, surprised to see that there are tears in Gio's eyes.

'We need to talk,' says Gio, gently stroking the top of Hercules' head. Adrian notices that his right hand is bandaged; perhaps Hercules bit him with his sharp puppy teeth. 'I'm sorry for what has happened to you. I really am.'

Adrian looks away; it's not like you can take a kid from his home and tie him up and shoot his father and fly him to your own house and lock him up away from his mama and then buy him a puppy and it's all okay.

'There's a lot you don't know.' Gio says everything slowly in English first once, then again, and this time, when Adrian shakes his head to show he didn't understand the last bit, Gio uses sign language. Adrian is stunned.

'What?' asks Adrian, palms open and moving back and forth.

'Adrian. You have the right to know this. I'm your father.'

Adrian is so stunned by Gio's words he is not only unable to speak, but to sign. After a long while, he shakes his head slightly, and mouths, 'No'.

Gio nods. 'It was a shock for me too. I didn't think it could be possible. And I thought... I thought you were dead.'

'Where Mama?' asks Adrian, releasing Hercules to the floor and standing up. 'You said. I take you to Mama, you said!'

'She's not your mama, Adrian. I'm so sorry. My wife died and that woman took you from me. When... when you were a baby. That's why all of this has happened. I've tried to find you for so long. To bring you home.'

'No,' whispers Adrian, walking slowly over to the long line of windows overlooking the lake. 'No.' Could it be true, that he was born here, that Gio was his father and that Mama was just a thief? No. There are things that you believe because you are told them, and then there are things you don't believe no matter what, because you know in your bones what the truth is. 'It's not true,' he signs, turning back around to face Gio. Gio has picked up Hercules and strokes him between the ears. There are tears in his eyes, and for the first time, Adrian realizes that his own eyes are exactly like Gio's, light blue like the winter sky. The feeling of a current running between them the first time they met was the sensation of looking into his own eyes.

'No,' he says again.

'Yes,' says Gio.

'I want Mama,' says Adrian.

'You only have me now, son.'

Adrian feels a violent wave of nausea gather and swell in his stomach and before he can even turn away, he spews vomit from where he stands, splattering Gio and the plush carpet and the little yellow dog. Then he passes out, slumping to the ground with a soft thud, and Gio places Hercules on the floor and scoops Adrian gently up in his arms. If Adrian hadn't been unconscious, he would have felt the tears dropping from Gio's eyes onto his face and into his hair; he would have felt him smooth his hair off his sweaty forehead; he would have heard him murmur, '*Mio figlio*'. And, '*Grazie a Dio*'.

Adrian is placed gently into a huge double bed with crisp white bedsheets adorned with the same gold crest he noticed on the helicopter's tail cone. Hercules settles obediently by the side of the bed. Gio calls the nurse, the same woman who came and took the blood sample for the DNA test, and she checks on Adrian's pulse and heart rate. Within a couple of minutes he recovers his consciousness but as soon as he opens his eyes he begins to whimper and says, 'No, no, no'.

* * *

In the night, he wakes screaming. Claudio comes with water. He taps something into his phone, his face ghoulishly lit up in the green glare from the screen, and moments later, Gio too arrives, wearing a navy bathrobe and slippers, rubbing sleep from his eyes. He sits by Adrian's bedside, stroking his sweaty brow and repeating the same strange words from earlier, '*Mio figlio, mio figlio*'. Adrian closes his eyes and drifts off to sleep again to the sound of Gio chuckling softly in the dark.

In the morning, Gio nudges him awake.

'Come on, Adrian,' he says. 'I said I'd take you for a ride. But first, take a bath.' Gio hands him a pile of clothing with labels still attached and leaves the room. Adrian has worn the same clothes since he left Sandefjord many, many days ago. It didn't occur to him to ask to wash. At home Mama always says, *Adrian, it's time for a shower*, and it's only now that Gio has mentioned it that Adrian realizes how long it has been. Claudio runs a hot bath with bubbles for him in the marble-and-gold bathroom adjoining his bedroom. He sinks into the bubbles, feeling his muscles loosen and relax, watched by Hercules, who sits panting on the bath mat, cocking his head and yapping whenever Adrian disappears beneath the water's surface. In the bath, he's able to think clearly. He remembers the man's words, how he said that Mama isn't his mama but a thief. He knows in his heart that this is a lie. He also knows that he must pretend to believe the man, and somehow make him allow him to see his mama. How else can he save her? And he has to save her; nobody else will. Adrian knows that he has to get smarter than he's ever had to be in his life so far.

After his bath, breakfast is served in his bedroom: scrambled eggs, boiled eggs, fried eggs, and a pile of crisp bacon rashers. Adrian glances around to see if anyone else will be eating with him – there is so much food, it could feed a family of six – but there is nobody there except Claudio, who is sitting discretely at a desk in the next room, typing on an iPad, glancing up and smiling at Adrian when he realizes he's being watched. Adrian is wearing his new clothes, and they feel stiff and strange against his skin. Adrian likes to wear very soft clothing, usually sweatpants and fleece hoodies, because he is more sensitive than other children to stimulation, and feels a visceral pain from things that most kids seem to tolerate, such as a slightly scratchy wool sweater or a label rubbing against his side. The clothes Gio brought are similar to what Adrian has noticed he himself might wear: a pink shirt with a navy embroidered horse above his heart, beige trousers and a navy V-neck vest that is the softest wool Adrian has ever touched. It's the first time he's worn pink in his life and he raises an eyebrow at himself in the mirror. He looks like a short Gio, and this makes him feel liquid and strange inside, as though someone has nuked his internal organs.

He's bad, Mama had said about his father when he asked. He understands now that Gio is telling the truth. But so was Mama.

36

Anastasia

She can't get past what happened, and the violence of the attack, though she pretends she does. She becomes good at acting, accustomed to behaving one way and feeling another. She knows she won't escape Giorgio; he decided long ago that he wanted her, and only her, and he'll never release her without a battle. She often thinks about how many millions of women, all over the world, are simultaneously going through the same as her; how many million tragic stories of control, manipulation, and violence are playing out.

Nothing changes after their tearful reunion once Giorgio realizes Anastasia knows his secret. The violence happens again, as these things almost always do. And again. Anastasia increasingly wants to go back to work and Giorgio grows increasingly insistent on her staying at home, whiling her days away behind the gates at Villa Serafina or behind the thick medieval stone walls at Palazzo di Arcimboldo. As time passes and Anastasia finds herself almost completely shut away from the world, she feels herself grow ever smaller and darker inside, like everything that was once good about her has simply faded away.

***

It's a beautiful day in early spring, only weeks to go before the wedding will take place in Umbria, and Anastasia drinks her coffee down on the jetty as usual, wrapped in a thick Loro Piana cashmere blanket. Giorgio is away; he's been gone all week, in Colombia on business. She hears the sound of a car arriving and the clang of the main gates swinging open and looks back up toward the house. It's strange; as far as she knows, they're not expecting anyone today. A figure, a man, comes walking down the path to the side of the house by the hedges, accompanied by Claudio. Anastasia squints, unable to tell with the sun glaring in her face, but as he approaches, she realizes with a jolt that it is Tom Kingsley.

'Anastasia,' he says, taking her hand and squeezing it warmly. She realizes she hasn't seen him in a long while, probably since the party at Michele Uragni's residence in Catania. She hasn't forgotten his kindness toward her after what happened in the Maldives. A memory flashes into her mind of that terrible morning, of standing there naked and bruised, Andrea Fiorentini's hollow laugh ridiculing her, and she closes her eyes for a long moment to make it go away and when she opens them again, Tom's warm gaze is still on her. She feels struck still and disoriented in his unexpected presence, as though it isn't possible that he could just come here to the house.

'Tom. Hi. I'm sorry, I wasn't expecting anyone. Giorgio

is away in Colombia. Did you have an appointment with him? He must have forgotten to let you know...'

Claudio hovers for a moment, just within earshot.

'Signorina, I hope it's okay I admitted Signor Kingsley. He asked to see you about a surprise for Giorgio...'

'It's fine.' Anastasia's heart is beating fast with the unexpected joy of receiving a visitor, and she realizes she's missed seeing Tom around. She asked Giorgio a while back whether he might perhaps invite Tom here to celebrate his investment in Tom's start-up, but Gio dismissed her, saying they'd celebrate out in Milan, no need for her to get involved. Deep down she knows it will always be like this, that she will be kept away from any semblance of real life, locked away in an opulent villa, while Gio is out there in the world, meeting people, working and socializing, but she wants to believe it could change. Vera always taught her that people really can change if you just love them enough.

'Would you be so kind as to set up a light lunch in the garden room?'

Claudio nods and heads back up toward the house. Anastasia briefly scans the grounds, but there is no sign of Ron or anyone else, and she realizes it's the first time she's been left alone with anyone other than someone who works for Giorgio.

They stand for a while down on the jetty, looking out across the water. Anastasia's heart beats noticeably hard in her chest, and she gets the strange feeling she'd sometimes feel when she was younger – that this is one of those moments when your life goes from one thing to another entirely, in a single instant, like that moment she turned around, feeling Silvia Nebbio's eyes on her as she swept the grounds at Ganina Yama.

'So. What can I do for you, Tom?' she asks, watching puddles of sunlight gather in the hollows of little wavelets on the lake.

'Look,' Tom says, voice low, glancing back up the vast, preened lawn toward the pink villa. 'I wasn't sure if coming here was a good idea but I knew Giorgio was away this week and I really wanted to speak with you.'

'Oh. I... Why? Claudio mentioned you were thinking of a surprise for Gio?'

'Anastasia. Look. I know we don't know each other very well. But the thing is, I've been feeling worried for you.'

Anastasia hesitates, then smiles. By now she's so used to being pleasant and mild-mannered, no matter how she really feels, having learned to be terrified of prompting one of Gio's rages if she slips up.

'The, uh, run-up to the wedding has been quite stressful,' she says, letting her eyes rest on the comforting stretch of deep-blue water ahead.

'I've noticed you're never in Milan anymore. Why not?'

'Well, it's not really like I have to work anymore,' Anastasia says, regurgitating Giorgio's words, but feeling a familiar, dull ache spread out in her stomach.

'But you want to, don't you?' asks Tom, softly.

Anastasia nods, her eyes pricking with tears.

'Hey,' he says, 'keep smiling. They're watching.'

She nods, smiles again, nods some more, pretends to laugh, trying to imagine the scene down by the jetty from the vantage point of one of the guards. How could she have thought nobody would be watching?

'I have an idea I really want to discuss with you. But it's dangerous. Can you come up with an excuse and meet me in Milan tomorrow evening?'

'I... Uh. It's hard. They watch me all the time.'

'He's away, though. Find a way. We can't talk here. Cameras and ears everywhere.' Tom drops his voice to a whisper as Claudio approaches them with a mellow smile on his face.

'Lunch is ready in the garden room,' he says.

They eat a beautifully presented carpaccio with caper berries harvested by Anastasia from the gardens at Anacapri and preserved in brine, the way Vera taught her. They speak of neutral things, like the upcoming wedding and the plans for summer, conscious of being watched by Claudio, who hovers at the periphery of the room under the pretext of polishing surfaces. Tom speaks loudly of plans to commission a special vase in Paris for Giorgio as a gift to celebrate his investment in his business. He leaves within minutes of finishing the meal, shaking Anastasia's hand formally before leaving. Anastasia watches him from the scullery window, waiting for the massive gates to swing open to let his shiny black Range Rover through. For the rest of the afternoon, a nervous energy flows through her at the thought of Tom's words, which she replays endlessly in her mind.

I have an idea. But it's dangerous.

37

Selma

It's late afternoon and growing dark. Selma left her original hotel within minutes of returning from Como with the intention of flying straight back to Oslo but after the shock of what Olav told her about Will Marlow being in jail for murder, she knew she'd have to stay longer. He didn't know more, only a brief mention in the *New York Times* from 2011, saying one of their former journalists, Will Marlow, was sentenced to life in prison in Italy for murder.

She found a new hotel on her phone, standing on a street corner, having already vacated the first hotel. She booked a large three-star tourist hotel near the train station, and walked there briskly, pushing her way through rush-hour crowds. *Find out more*, she messaged Olav, but now it's been over an hour since she's heard from him. She draws the blinds in the new, sparse hotel room, turns up the heating, and kicks off her shoes. She gets into bed beneath the duvet and opens her Mac. She tries a variety of searches to find out which prison Will Marlow is in, and it's a random combination of search words that finally brings results. She switches American 'jail' to 'prison' and adds 'Italian' and 'mafia' and 'Marlow', producing a hit from *Giornale di Sicilia*, Sicily's biggest newspaper, dated only five days ago. She copies it into Google Translate and reads the result with a mixture of shock and confusion, followed by a crystal-clear epiphany.

The search for the man who escaped Italy's highest-security prison, Pagliarelli, on Wednesday the 12th during a transfer to Catania's Bicocca prison, remains active and urgent, says Michele Uragni, head of Sicily's police force. The man has been confirmed as American citizen William Thomas Marlow, of Sonoma, California, a convicted murderer, considered extremely dangerous. Marlow confessed to the violent murder of Anastasia di Vincenzo in June 2010, and was sentenced to life in prison. Marlow is the third prisoner to escape Pagliarelli in the last two years, prompting questions around the efficacy of Sicily's prison management.

'Olav, it's me.'

'Selma, hi. I was just about to call you—'

'I've got something big. You know the man who was killed in Puttgarden who had a kid with him? They still haven't gotten a positive ID on him, I believe, but I'm pretty sure I know who he was.'

'Wait, what?'

'It's Will Marlow. Marlow escaped from prison in Sicily three days before Adrian and Liv disappeared, five days before he arrived in Puttgarten with Adrian in tow.

Un–fucking–believable! I actually don't know what exactly we're dealing with here. Can you get in touch with the police and bring them up to speed about this, I have to—'

'Selma, listen to me! I've been trying to tell you something. I've just heard from Terje Haakonsen and Oskar Olsen at Kripos that the man in Puttgarten is on life support at the UKE medical center in Hamburg. He isn't dead. And they've managed to secure CCTV footage of the child he was with, who has been positively identified as Adrian Carlsen by his teacher in Sandefjord. The police are all over this now, Interpol is about to release the images of the boy, the case is going to blow up big-time. Are you sure it's Marlow?'

'Yes. I just don't understand…'

'My guess is that Marlow has personal motives for seeking revenge against Liv Carlsen. He's probably killed her and was going to do the same to Adrian when he was intercepted.'

'But intercepted by whom? It's not like it was police who intercepted them and Marlow ended up shot. The kid's still missing.'

'Hmm, yes. Or maybe his escape was staged and he kidnapped Liv and Adrian to order for someone. Sounds like a dangerous guy. Who did he murder?'

'Anastasia di Vincenzo. Jesus Christ, must be Giorgio's wife.'

'What the hell?'

'Indeed. He said he'd never been married. Olav, can you find out about her?'

'On it.'

'This is seriously the weirdest story I have ever handled. I need to think. I'll call you back.'

'Okay.'

'Oh, and Olav? Can you find out from Kripos if Marlow has round-the-clock security at the hospital? If the news that he's alive is about to break, I imagine he's in pretty grave danger.'

'But it would seem Marlow is the bad guy here.'

'There's more to this. We need to figure out who Anastasia di Vincenzo was and how on earth Marlow is linked to both her and Liv Carlsen. I refuse to believe the guy's some random thug, he used to be a highly respectable journalist at the *New York Times*.'

'True. I just can't believe we haven't heard about this before. Wouldn't it have made headlines all over the place if an American journalist was convicted of murder in Italy?'

'Mmm. It's surprising. Or maybe not. Maybe it's an indication of something very sinister indeed. That whoever has dirty hands here is able to entirely control the narrative. Whatever it is, I'm convinced di Vincenzo's involved. The guy's a nutjob.'

'I'll get in touch with Kripos again now. And Selma, be careful. This is all very strange. Dangerous, I'm sure of it.'

'I will.'

'What are you doing next?'

'I'm going to Hamburg.'

38

Adrian

It's a clear and brilliant day when they approach Palermo, Adrian sitting on the jump seat in the cockpit, enraptured. If he didn't know it was January, he would have guessed it was the middle of summer. The two pilots smile and laugh with him, pointing out the various control panels, and though Adrian doesn't understand much of what they say in a mixture of Italian and English, he understands the functions of the various instruments. When he grows up and he's a pilot himself, he wants to fly a Gulfstream just like this one. He turns around and tells Giorgio this, using sign language. Giorgio is standing in the cockpit doorway, smiling indulgently at his son's excitement, reaching out to ruffle his hair. The plane banks and the captain speaks into his microphone.

'GDV zero nine zero, requesting four thousand feet at one eight zero,' he says. The coordinates are confirmed and entered into the autopilot and immediately, the plane banks again and begins to descend. Adrian catches sight of the runway in the distance, at the edge of the sea, framed by little green and red lights.

'Hey kid,' says the captain, a friendly older man with a thick gray mustache and big black sunglasses completely obscuring his eyes. 'Want to help me with the landing gear? Press here.' He indicates three buttons labeled 'L', 'R', and 'C'. Adrian glances back at Gio in disbelief, but Gio smiles and nods. Adrian reaches across and gingerly presses the buttons in turn, and they light up, first orange as the landing gear extends audibly from the hull, then green when they have slotted in place and are ready for touchdown.

'Time to buckle up,' says the captain. 'You can stay here if you like.' A flight attendant comes and helps Adrian with the three-point seat belt and places a headset on his head, and immediately the whoosh from the cockpit goes silent and he can hear the crackly voices from air traffic control and other planes in the airspace.

'Speedbird four four two cleared for takeoff on runway one. Ryanair three nine descending to three zero. GDV zero nine zero cleared for one five zero.' In spite of himself, and in spite of everything, Adrian can't help but smile.

* * *

Gio shows Adrian around his home in the city center, a strange place that looks like a big old stone castle with tiny windows high up from the outside, but from the inside is cozy and beautiful with art everywhere like at the other house. There's a huge roof terrace and they sit for a while in the gently warming sun, drinking Coke and watching planes coming in low over the city to land, Adrian cradling Hercules in his arms.

'We need to go back soon,' says Gio and Adrian thinks it was strange to go all this way just to have a Coke on the roof. 'Short trip, but I wanted to show you this place. You know, someday, all of this will be yours.' Gio's eyes fill with tears and he takes one of Adrian's hands in his own. Adrian feels acutely uncomfortable and wants to retract his hand but doesn't dare to, in case Gio gets angry. He has to avoid making him angry at any cost or he'll never see Mama again, he's sure of it. Adrian nods and makes himself smile at his father.

'I need to take care of a few things, then we'll head back to the airport.'

'Can I stay here?' Adrian asks, using signs, pointing up to the sky. 'To watch planes.'

'Sure. Fifteen minutes or so.'

When Gio has disappeared inside the house, Adrian crosses the vast terrace covering the entire roof of the palazzo with various seating areas, a bar, lots of potted olive trees and a section with sun loungers next to a very narrow water feature with overflowing edges; Adrian isn't quite sure if it's a plunge pool or a fountain. He stands at the far end of the roof, Hercules busy at his feet trying to catch some brown leaves dancing on the breeze. He looks down at people milling around down on street level, pushing past each other and laughing and talking in the narrow, shadowed channel between the palazzo and the building opposite. From his pocket he pulls a piece of paper he's folded into a small, thick square, and a pen. He unfolds the paper and smooths it down. He sits down on the warm, ochre floor tiles and writes 'Help' in big letters in the middle of the page. He adds 'Adrian Carlsen', then swiftly folds the paper into an expertly constructed DC3 Swallow, an old favorite, every last step internalized and easily remembered. When he's finished, he launches the plane and watches it glide, then lurch and spin, disappearing into the murky shadows far below, lost from sight.

***

It's getting dark when they arrive back at the pink house by helicopter, touching softly down on the white H painted on the lawn, the big mountains casting deep, pointed shadows across the surface of the lake. Inside the house, the pianist is playing and candles are burning from what seem like hundreds of candle holders, on walls, tables, and windowsills.

'Your company is here,' says Claudio, gesturing further into the house. Adrian can hear the sound of voices and women laughing, and thinks how strange it is that Gio can't hear them.

'I have a dinner tonight,' says Gio, placing his hand on Adrian's shoulder in the fatherly way that makes his skin crawl. 'It was fun to be with you today.'

Adrian forces himself to smile and nod.

'Claudio will help you upstairs.'

Claudio walks behind Adrian and busies himself with shutting the heavy velvet curtains and folding back the duvet on the bed while Adrian watches cartoons and has a snack of fruit and crackers. He hears the sound of the rotor blades shredding the air and gets up from the sofa at the foot of the bed and peers out the window. It's almost completely dark outside now, but he can see the blinking light of the helicopter as it rises vertically up from the lawn, then continues straight across the lake, heading south. Adrian glances quizzically at Claudio.

'Milano,' says Claudio. 'Restaurant.'

Adrian nods.

'*Buona notte*,' says the old man, and his smile is kind as he passes Adrian on his way to the door. Hercules is fast asleep at the foot of the bed, snoring softly, exhausted after the long day. Gio is away; this is Adrian's chance.

'Mama,' he says, using all his effort to expel the word. 'Please. Mama.'

Claudio turns around in the doorway, his expression sad and serious.

'Please,' says Adrian, his voice breaking as he bursts into tears. The old man shakes his head sadly and shuts the door. Adrian wants to run after him, screaming and crying, but he knows it won't work. Why did he think that he, a little boy who can barely even speak, would be able to rescue his mama from these terrible people? She'll be locked up somewhere far away, maybe another country even, or she's already dead. At the thought of his beautiful mama, dead, Adrian cries even harder, his sobs echoing around the huge room, as though there were lots of little boys there, crying. When he was little and needed to cry but couldn't manage it, he used to think of Mama dead, and then the tears would always come. She's all he has, but now that he doesn't have her anymore, he has nothing. He picks up the sleeping puppy and clutches him to his chest and that's how he falls asleep eventually, still shaking with sobs.

***

There's someone in the room when he wakes. Adrian can make out the outline of a man by the weak light of the moon which is spilling into the room through a slit in the curtain. He sits up fast, a frightened gasp emerging.

'Shhh,' says the man, pressing his index finger to his lips. Adrian recognizes him as Claudio. 'Come,' he says, motioning for Adrian to follow him. The old man has left the door open and they slip through it into the hallway which is still softly lit by live candles burning in gold candlesticks fastened to the wall between the paintings. At the end of the hallway, Claudio slides a panel aside, made to look like a normal section of the wall, to reveal a very small elevator behind it. He motions again to Adrian, pressing his finger to his lips. The elevator glides quietly down several floors with a series of soft clangs. They walk down a cold, unlit corridor with crude, gray-stone walls, using the torch on Claudio's phone to find the way. A door which is barely discernable from the wall into which it's been inserted is opened by unlocking a long series of locks and bolts. Claudio steps aside, allowing Adrian to enter the room, shining the torch onto an unmoving figure on the floor over by the window. Adrian approaches slowly; at first he can't be sure it isn't an animal, a big dog or a little horse, perhaps, it whimpers softly as it sleeps, its bony frame casting trembling shadows on the wall. But as he gets closer he catches sight of a red dress and long, matted black hair plastered to her skull and he realizes it's Mama.

39

Liv

I'm asleep when little hands pummel me awake. At first, I can't get my bearings; my mind is hazy and strangely blank as it is every time I come to from sleep or unconsciousness in this place. My captors blur into a single, menacing shape in my mind; black curls, cold blue eyes, thin pursed lips, a glint of an onyx tooth, tattooed wrists, monogrammed shoes, blond buzz cut, strong fists grabbing me. I can't tell one day from another; I can't remember when I last ate, or what. Every day when I wake it takes me several excruciating minutes before the reality of where I am dawns on me. But there's something I never forget, whose memory is crystal clear and constant in my mind. Adrian. And now my boy is here.

'Oh,' I hear myself saying. 'Oh.' And then tears, so many tears. He climbs onto me as though I were one of the ride-on crocodiles in the park at home in Sandefjord, clinging to me in a way he's never done before, and I breathe in the sweet, sweet scent of my only child, my beloved son, my little *vorobushek*.

After a long while he sits back up and runs his finger gently down the side of my face, unable to conceal his horror at the sight of me; I can only imagine what I might look like at this point.

'Are you okay, my love?' I ask out loud, drinking him in. He looks as okay as he could be considering the circumstances, but his eyes are anxious and his little fingers are rough from picking away at the skin around his fingernails. 'I've worried so much about you.' Adrian shoots a quick, alarmed glance in Claudio's direction; it's the first time he's heard me speak in front of another person. 'It's okay. He knows.'

'You lied to me,' he says, using his signs.

'I'm sorry,' I say.

'Gio says he's my father.'

I nod. 'It's true, baby. He is.'

'What about the American?'

I start crying again, to think that somehow, Adrian has found himself in the company of Will Marlow, and then Giorgio. 'Gio says you're not my mama. He says his wife died and you stole me.'

'No. It's not true. Think about what we've talked about so many times. How we know in our bodies what the truth is. You know you are mine, like I'm yours. Never forget it, *my little sparrow*,' I whisper in my mother tongue, our secret language. I tell him everything: that it had to be like this so that he could be safe. And yet, it wasn't enough. After a long while, Claudio is beckoning to Adrian to come, quick, and I reach for my boy and kiss his dry cheeks, hard, and then he's gone, the sound of his footsteps disappearing down the corridor the cruelest sound I've heard in all my life.

I give in to a wildness I've never known before, a desperation so deep and black I fear for my own life in its darkest moment. I cut the inside of my thigh with a glass shard, and blood gushes from me, mercifully; I have to release something of the despair I feel. I pummel the door with my fists until they grow raw. I cry and scream until my voice is reduced to a hoarse squawk. In the end, I sink to the floor in my usual spot beneath the window. I haven't been there long when I hear the sound of the numerous locks being unlocked and the door swings open.

It's Claudio again. He's brought a thick blanket and a woolen sweater. He helps me put it on, then wraps the blanket around my shoulders, I'm shaking so hard. He notices all the blood running down my left leg and a look of panic crosses his face. I glance at the bloody shard on the ground, glinting in the moonlight, and he follows my gaze.

'Oh, no, signorina,' he says. '*Aspetti.*' Wait. He rushes from the room, returning after a couple of minutes and very gently sets to work cleaning my wounds with hydrogen peroxide. I sit completely still; this is nothing compared to the pain I've already endured. I close my eyes and try to imagine they're my grandmother's hands on my skin, so warm and gentle, healing me with her touch.

'*Dio mio,*' Claudio mutters to himself. When he's satisfied the cuts are clean and I'm regaining some warmth, he gets up. 'I'm going to get you some proper food.'

'Where's Giorgio?'

'He's away, in Milan.'

Claudio brings boiled eggs, Parma ham, fennel salami, a

glorious mushroom and chestnut soup with hazelnuts. He squats down on his knees as I eat, watching me with a look of pity.

'Thank you for bringing Adrian.'

'I've been waiting for an opportunity. Mario and Carl have been around almost constantly since you arrived.'

'He's going to kill me, isn't he?' Claudio looks away from me and nods. 'You have to help me, Claudio. Please.'

'I don't think anyone can help you, signorina.'

40

Anastasia

Anastasia tells Claudio and Patrizia that she's heading into Milan to try to find a morning gift for Gio. 'A Russian tradition,' she adds. She calls a local taxi and pays the driver with cash she found downstairs in Gio's office. He always has cash lying around, on shelves, stuffed into pockets, in drawers; he won't notice a few hundred euros gone. She has a credit card she uses on the few occasions she's gone in to via Monteleone to buy whichever clothes or decorative items she wants, but she doesn't want to use it today; he'll see the charge and question her endlessly about where she'd been and with whom.

She gets out on the corner of piazza della Scala and calls Tom's mobile from a payphone outside the theater. He gives her an address and Anastasia hails another taxi, the deep thrill of deception and adventure rushing through her as she settles into the back seat and watches central Milan's iconic, beautiful streets creep past in slow-moving traffic.

The address Tom gave her is a restaurant in Gallaratese, a part of town she's never been to. She hurries from the taxi, drawing her coat around her against a chilly wind, ignoring the catcalls of a couple of men unloading furniture from a white van by the curbside. The restaurant is a no-frills trattoria on the ground floor of a modern apartment building, with white plastic chairs and a set menu scribbled on a chalkboard behind the bar. Anastasia is glad she chose one of the few fairly casual outfits she owns, dark jeans and a white merino wool V-neck sweater. Giorgio prefers her to be dressy, even when it's just the two of them at home. Tom is waiting for her over in the far corner, wearing a blue-and-green checked shirt and jeans.

'You made it,' he says, smiling, his ocean-blue eyes shining.

She nods, and smiles back at him, feeling emboldened just by being here.

'I can only imagine that was difficult,' says Tom. There is something about the kindness in his eyes, about the way he holds himself in such a trusting, open way, as though it has never occurred to him that something terrible could happen to him. Anastasia has heard it said about Americans, many times, by Gio and others in his circle, that they're gullible and overly trusting, and Anastasia thinks, looking at Tom, that that is a beautiful way to be.

'What is it you want to talk to me about?'

'Are you sure no one followed you here?'

'Yes.'

'I have been wanting to get in touch with you for a while. I'm not sure what you know about the business side of what Giorgio does or what his dealings with me are.'

'I know that he is investing in your company.'

'Yes. Yes, he is. Ten million euros. We're closing the deal in the next couple of weeks, hopefully. I've been here for almost a year now, working toward that investment, spending quite a bit of time with Giorgio and others in his inner circle. As you know, I've come to know him a little bit and we've established quite a strong rapport. I believe he trusts me.'

Anastasia nods.

'But here's the thing. And you can imagine the risk I'm taking telling you this. My name is not Tom Kingsley. I don't actually own CoreTech; it's just a cover. My name is Will Marlow and I'm a senior investigative journalist with the *New York Times*.'

Anastasia's mouth drops open. A very faint cry emerges. She grips the edge of the table, starts to stand up, but Will places his own large, warm hand over hers and implores her with his eyes to stay, so she does.

'No,' she whispers. 'He'll kill you. And me, just for speaking to you.'

'Anastasia, listen to me. I'm gonna take him down,' says Will, face serious, and he looks like an innocent boy. 'And I need you to help me.'

She can practically hear Vera's voice in her head, for the first time in a very long time. *This is the kind of person you should be spending your time with*, it says. Anastasia's eyes swim with tears. She realizes, looking at Will, how much she wants to help him do whatever it is he wants to do. And how much she wants to get away from Giorgio.

'When I first came to Italy, my plan was to infiltrate

Giorgio's inner circle and expose the corruption and all the shady business he's involved in, while passing himself off as some poster boy for marine preservation and deaf kids. Then I realized that it was all much worse than I thought, that he is seriously embroiled in trafficking, the drug trade, and prostitution, hiding behind the fairly reputable guise of an actual modeling agency. I've seen first-hand what happens to so many young girls who get sucked into Giorgio's toxic world. I've observed how he treats you like a prisoner. You don't have to live like this, Anastasia. I see you, I see that fire you've got, the strength you carry inside of you. You've got to let me help you.'

'We're getting married soon,' she says. 'If I don't go through with it, he'll kill me. I know he will.'

'So maybe go through with it and I'll set the plans in motion. It will help to have someone on the inside. I'm going to help these girls, Anastasia. And you. I'm going to get you out.'

'I just don't understand how.'

'Giorgio is about to pay ten million euros into CoreTech. The money will go into a holding company somewhere like Antigua, owned by another holding company in Cayman. And a third in Switzerland. Trust me, I know how these things work. How do you think Giorgio cleans all the money from the other aspects of GMA? We'll get you out of here to a safe place and use the money to get the girls rehabilitated and start them off on new lives. We'll fund education and help their families. In the meantime, you'll be my eyes and ears from the inside.'

Anastasia nods and tries to imagine what such a life might look life, a life in which she's free and safe, and finds that she cannot. What she finds so disturbing and difficult to accept is that she can't pinpoint the moment the relationship changed from something beautiful and safe to something the complete opposite. There were so many minor episodes of criticism and discontent, and an increasing level of control, so subtle at first that it was almost impossible to put a finger to the changes that were happening. And once the violence started, it became increasingly frequent. In the months since the initial episode at the photo shoot, after which Giorgio was sorry, so very sorry, confessing his childhood trauma after losing his mother and brother, he has broken Anastasia's elbow, pushed her down a flight of stairs in Anacapri, smashed her head against a stone wall, broken three of her fingers, punched her in the stomach full force, and throttled her on several occasions.

'Anastasia, will you help me? I promise you, I will help you in return.'

Will opens his jacket and from an inside pocket he pulls out a clear plastic bag. From it, he produces an iPhone and pushes it across the table to Anastasia. She nods.

'Only I have this number. Be careful.'

'Tom. Will. I… He'll kill me if he finds it.'

'So make sure he doesn't find it.' Anastasia swallows hard and nods.

* * *

That night, Anastasia gets out of bed when the moon is high in the sky and, though she's alone at Villa Serafina except for the staff who all live on the top floor, shuts herself in the padded cocoon of her walk-in closet. She switches the phone on in the dark and hides the glare from its screen with a silk scarf. A new message from Will flashes silently on the screen.

One more thing. I love you.

41

Selma

As soon as she begins researching the life and death of Anastasia di Vincenzo, née Nikitina, it seems impossible that she could have remained off Selma's radar for so long. She recognizes the tragic young woman's face from the thousands of hits produced on Google; she was a major international runway model at the time, and Selma recalls several of her campaigns, circulating when Selma herself was a teenager: Gucci, Bottega Veneta, and Louis Vuitton, among the most memorable. Born in Yekaterinburg, Russia, she came to Milan aged twenty-two after being scouted by Graziela Marco of GMA Models, and quickly rose in the ranks, gaining international fame and working in both Paris and London. And then it all went quiet. It would appear that Anastasia worked in the industry for around two years, then dropped off the face of the planet before ending up dead.

'Final call for Alitalia 773 to Hamburg boarding gate 20,' says a tinny voice and Selma glances up, realizing everybody else has disappeared from the waiting area and they are lining up on the jetway. She scans her boarding pass and joins them, still scrolling on her phone in the slow-moving line. After some creative searching, she manages to uncover an old mention in Italian gossip magazine *Gente*, dated April 2010. There's a picture of Anastasia, standing close together with Giorgio, both smiling widely, exposing perfect rows of very white teeth, like impossibly groomed dolls. '*Fidanzata*,' says the caption, helpfully translated by Google to 'fiancée'. Selma sinks into her window seat and fastens her seat belt, earmarking the article to translate when they land.

Anything? she writes to Olav, adding, *She was definitely engaged to di Vincenzo.*

Married! Di Vincenzo's a fucking liar, responds Olav almost instantly, attaching a screenshotted photograph from *OK Magazine* in May 2010 of a stunning Anastasia Nikitina in an exquisite wedding dress with a pearl-and-lace traditional Russian kokoshnik headpiece, posing alone underneath a stone arch lavishly decorated with white roses. Her face is serious and blank and she looks impossibly young for a bride. A month later she was dead, supposedly murdered at the hands of a *New York Times* journalist.

The plane begins to taxi and Selma puts the phone on flight mode, leaning her head against the gently vibrating plastic window. She closes her eyes and tries to bring each of the confusing strands of the case into some kind of coherent order. Two women, both linked to both Giorgio di Vincenzo and Will Marlow, one dead and the other most likely dead, her young son missing. Di Vincenzo lying about his marriage, Marlow shot multiple times and left for dead. None of it makes any sense. Selma has the sensation of looking straight at the answer without being able to compute it. She opens her eyes as the plane noisily lifts off the runway, a smudge of red at the horizon where the January sun has recently disappeared. She falls asleep as soon as she closes them again, lulled by the purr of the engines and the sheer exhaustion of the past week.

***

It's early evening when she arrives at the vast university medical center in Eppendorf, a short ten-minute taxi ride from the airport. The hospital has the air of busyness, though everything appears perfectly ordered and under control, with nurses walking calmly down long, white corridors and a few people sitting scattered around a large waiting room in the vestibule area, lazily flicking through magazines. Selma follows signs for *Intensivstation*, and when she gets there is stopped by locked double doors. She can make out a faint purplish light beyond the doors, and thinks of how surreal it is that Will Marlow is here, only meters away. She knows nothing about his state, whether or not he's conscious or considered likely to make it. There is an empty waiting area and a small, unmanned reception desk with a sign that reads 'Call for assistance'. Selma presses the button and after a long while, a man emerges from the double doors.

'*Ja?*' he says.

'Hi, my name is Selma, uh—'

'Can I help you?'

Selma pauses and struck by an intense moment of panic. What is she doing here? She's been so focused on grappling with the different threads of the Liv Carlsen case unspooling, and felt such a strong conviction that she needed to come here as soon as she realized that it was Will Marlow who had taken Adrian from Sandefjord and somehow gotten shot in Puttgarten, that it hasn't quite occurred to her what she would do or say in the moment she found herself standing here at the reception for the intensive care unit at Hamburg University Hospital.

'I...'

The nurse, whose name badge reads 'Ulli Metz', has an angular, pale face and kind, red-rimmed eyes, and he visibly softens at the sight of her, giving her a gentle, patient smile. Selma's probably not the first person to find herself struggling for words at the intensive care unit reception desk. 'William Marlow,' she says.

'Ah. Yes. *Der Amerikaner*. You must be his sister? Your father said more relatives would be arriving this afternoon.'

'How – how is he doing?'

'Well. Better than he was when he got here. As of last night, he's no longer critical, but we're keeping him in a coma for the time being. Let me go and tell your father you've arrived.' Selma opens her mouth to clarify and explain she's not Will's sister, not even a friend, but the nurse has already gone back through the double doors. Selma feels shaky and for a moment considers rushing back down the long white corridors and into the cool evening outside, but instead she takes a seat on a plastic bench next to the door. The nurse returns after a few minutes alongside a sprightly, white-haired man with a tanned, deeply lined face. He looks from the nurse to Selma and back again, a look of confusion and exhaustion on his face.

'Who are you?' he asks.

'Is this not—' begins Ulli.

'I'm sorry, Mr Marlow. I was wondering if I could possibly speak to you for just a few minutes.'

'I'm sorry. Who are you? Do you know my son?'

'Not exactly. But I am very committed to figuring out what's going on here and why Will's ended up here.'

'You a cop?'

'No. I work for a newspaper in Norway. I can guarantee you that our conversation would be entirely off record, Mr Marlow, and will not in any way be used or printed.' The older man sighs deeply and runs his hand through his hair.

'You know, I could use a coffee. And what's more, if you can get the real story of what happened to my son out there, I'm happy for you to run it all you want. Put it on the front page, I say.' Selma's heart picks up its pace as she leads Mr Marlow over to an area with a table and chairs, then gets them both a coffee from the machine. She knows there is more to this and will make sure the truth will be told.

'How is Will doing?' she asks gently, sitting across from Mr Marlow.

'He looks like ten kinds of hell but they're saying he's going to make it. I couldn't believe it when the call came. Just couldn't believe it. He was shot six times, but miraculously no major organs or arteries were damaged.'

'I'm so glad to hear that, Mr Marlow. What a terrible time for your family. Are you sure you are comfortable with talking me through what's happened, as you know and remember it?'

'Well, on Thursday last week we received a call from Sicilian police. They said Will had escaped on a transfer from

Palermo to Catania, and that it was clearly a professional job. He'd had helpers, they said. They wanted to know where we would think he'd go. Now, my son's been in jail for almost ten years for a murder he didn't commit. That changes your insides, you know? My wife and I have lobbied for him endlessly. We sold our house to cover legal fees. We fly out there twice a year but not recently, as my wife, Will's mom, is recovering from cancer treatment. That's why I'm here by myself. His sister Ginny is flying in from London; she'll be here tonight. Anyway. I told 'em I had no idea where he'd go if he really did escape, but that wasn't exactly true.'

'What do you mean?'

'He'd go to her.'

'To Liv? Liv Carlsen?'

Mr Marlow stares at Selma for a long moment, his eyes sorrowful. 'Who?'

'The woman who's missing from Norway. The mother of the little boy who was with Will. I assumed – I assumed they were lovers, or—'

'Oh, they were lovers, all right. Made Romeo and Juliet look like a happy ending.'

'I don't understand...'

'Will's escape has been orchestrated, most likely by di Vincenzo himself.'

'Mr Marlow, I'm really not following.'

'My son was framed for the murder of Anastasia di Vincenzo, Giorgio di Vincenzo's wife. He loved her, madly. I imagine he still does. He confessed to the crime, and got life in prison.'

'But why?'

'So she could be free.'

'Oh, my God. Anastasia and Liv. They're the same person. Jesus Christ!' Selma leaps from the seat, sending coffee splashing onto the plastic table, then sits back down again, trying to center herself amid an onslaught of thoughts. 'Wait, wait, wait, I don't get it. I just don't understand. So Anastasia faked her own death and went and lived in Sandefjord with her and Will's son, who was born, let me think—'

'Seven months later, except—'

'And she pretended to be deaf to cover up the fact that she didn't speak a word of Norwegian!'

'Only, the boy isn't Will's.'

'Wait, what?'

'We found out today. We didn't know about the boy at all. They were able to compare a DNA sample from Adrian found at the house in Norway to a blood sample from Will and have concluded there is no genetic link between them. We didn't know she was alive, he's never said a word about what really happened. But I guessed, years ago. Will would have fought his conviction with everything he's got, if it wasn't to save her.'

'Do you think he believed the boy to be his and found out he wasn't and… and hurt Liv, I mean, Anastasia as a result?'

'No. I'm certain he didn't know about the boy. And Will wouldn't hurt her, or anyone. Not ever. No way.'

'He might have changed after losing ten years of his life to prison.'

'I know my son, Selma. He'd never hurt her. My theory is that di Vincenzo somehow discovered that Anastasia is alive and figured that the way to track her down would be to get Will released from prison. Will went straight there and the rest you know.'

'Yes, but where is Anastasia?'

'My guess is, di Vincenzo beat him to her.'

'Jesus.' It all makes sense now. The old pictures of Liv that resemble the woman caught on CCTV at the farm, but not entirely, the pretend deafness, the fact that 'Liv' never contacted her own parents. 'But where is Liv Carlsen?'

'Dead, I'd imagine, judging by the kinds of people she got herself mixed up with.'

Selma pulls her phone out, scrolls through the images until she gets to the CCTV still from Kai Oserød's farm. She goes back and makes a comparison to the Google images of the young Anastasia Nikitina on the runway and the covers of magazines – it is, beyond doubt, the same person, with a small effort of disguise, her naturally sandy-blond hair has been straightened and dyed jet black, but that's the only real difference. Selma shows the screenshot to Mr Marlow and he nods sadly.

'Can't blame him for loving her, I guess. He always spoke so warmly of her.'

'Mr Marlow, I need to go. Thank you so much for your time. I promise you that I will do everything I can to get this story on the cover of every newspaper. And I shall pray for Will.'

'Thank you,' says Mr Marlow, standing up to solemnly shake Selma's hand while she gathers her stuff together. 'You know, until all this happened, I thought we lived in a time of free speech and independent media. But we don't. That asshole and his associates have bought half the media, and the police force too. You need to be careful with this. Very careful.'

'I will.'

'Di Vincenzo is the kind of guy who can only be taken down if he's outsmarted.' Mr Marlow nods and gives Selma a little wave, his face clouded by worry.

42

Anastasia

The darkest time in all her life, and the very brightest too. In the run-up to the wedding, Anastasia makes herself even more acquiescent than before, and goes to great lengths to remind Giorgio of Serafina in the way she dresses and in the way she moves, even in the way she consciously narrows her eyes when she smiles, learned from photographs. She drops any mention of returning to work, and begins to express joy in her existence as a kept woman behind golden bars. She does what Gio has asked her to do all along – go shopping, buy whatever she wants, make herself beautiful. When he returns home after one of his trips, she's on the chaise longue in the garden room, dressed head to toe in a current-season navy Chanel bouclé suit, hair carefully coiffed into a low chignon like the ones favored by Gio's mother, and he kneels down next to her, mesmerized, resting his head between her breasts, and she feels a surge of power return at the memory of earlier that afternoon, when she met with Will at a country house he rents near Puginate, north of the city, to make passionate love while Giorgio's plane circled high above on its approach into Orio al Serio.

Most afternoons they meet at the house, a yellow cottage with a faded trompe l'oeuil facade and an overgrown garden of brambles, if Anastasia can get away under the pretext of shopping or running wedding-related errands. After finally detangling herself from Will, still feeling his touch on her skin and the intensity of his kisses, she heads into the city and drops a few thousand cursory euros at Gucci or Loewe or Valentino before heading back to Villa Serafina. Giorgio, too, has been away a lot and doesn't seem to suspect anything; he seems distracted by the upcoming wedding and spends a lot of time in Umbria getting the estate ready.

* * *

The wedding itself passes in a blur, Anastasia feels she is having an out-of-body experience, and even as the day unfolds, she knows she'll retain little of it in memory. Seven hundred guests attend, from every corner of Europe and beyond. Anastasia only wanted one person there –Vera – but Vera doesn't come; she can't leave the plants, she says, but Anastasia knows she won't watch Anastasia tie herself to Giorgio. She wishes there was a way for her to speak freely to Vera, for them to sit side by side on the little deck like they used to, fingers intertwined, and she could tell her grandmother not to fear for her, that it is all actually different from how it looks – she's in love, deeply, beautifully, painfully in love with a man who honors her and that soon, soon, they will run away together and be free.

After, they go to St Barth's for two weeks and Anastasia

finds it impossible to stave off feelings of intense restlessness and longing for Will. She left the phone hidden in Como; it would simply have been too dangerous to bring it. She endures the way Gio rolls on top of her without preamble in the evenings, the sickly-sweet smell of tequila on his breath. She doesn't try to pretend that it's Will; it just wouldn't be possible to compare his gentleness, his playfulness, the way he has learned to adjust his touch to her, the way he holds her, to Gio's self-centered approach. If Gio senses the smallest hint of resistance when he places his hands on her body, he merely pushes past it, grabbing her harder, kissing her to silence her.

She endures long, unbroken days in Gio's company, staring out at the Caribbean, missing Will so much she wishes she could charge into the water and swim away from the man on the beach. One morning toward the end of the honeymoon, she looks up from the book she was reading to find Gio staring at her.

'You okay?' she asks, focusing on maintaining the mellow persona she's adopted in recent months that seems to somewhat appease him.

'Mmmm. You know, the *New York Times* just ran another piece about business in Italy, basically implying I'm some kind of crook.'

'Oh, honey, that's terrible.'

'Yes. Complete bullshit, of course. You know what Americans are like, though; they gobble stuff like that right up. Hopefully it won't sour things with Kingsley and CoreTech; we're about to close the deal.'

Anastasia's heart lurches at the mention of Will. 'Right.'

'What kills me, though, and keeps me up at night, is

where in the hell do these people get their information? Some of the stuff feels like it has to be coming from a source close to me. Somebody watching.'

'Watching?' Anastasia focuses on keeping calm, and not giving in to the rising sense of dread she feels inside at the topic of conversation. Does Gio suspect something? She tries to imagine what he would do to her if he knew what she had done, and calms herself down by envisioning a future far, far away from this man, living an authentic life with Will somewhere quiet, having a baby, perhaps, and helping others, girls like herself – survivors.

'Yes, watching.'

* * *

'Come here,' he whispers, in the dark.

'I'm already here,' she whispers back, tracing little shapes among the scattered wiry hairs on his chest.

'Come even closer.'

She laughs and rolls on top of Will, who buries his hands in her hair and nuzzles her neck, drawing the scent of her deep inside. 'I wouldn't be able to bear it if I had to spend another two weeks away from you,' he says. It's the first whole night they are able to spend together: Giorgio has gone to New York to appease his American connections after the disastrous piece in the *New York Times* implying ties to organized crime. Claudio and Patrizia believe Anastasia has traveled to a spa in the Swiss Alps for beauty treatments, and have promised Anastasia not to breathe a word to Gio, so she can surprise him with her rejuvenated appearance upon his return. What they actually believe, she doesn't know; but she is increasingly sensing that Patrizia and Claudio care about her and would likely protect her from Gio's tempers.

In the morning they drink white tea on the balcony and watch the sun rise above the fields, hands closely entwined.

'So. The money cleared last week and we're ready to go. Osorio is all set up in the city and we should get started with Fletcher and Carlsen in the next few days. She's going to need a lot of work to get clean,' says Will.

'Yes. I – look. We need to be very, very careful moving forward. He said something when we were in St Barth's. About feeling like he's being watched. Until we can get out of here and completely cover our tracks, we need to assume that he's suspicious.'

'I know. We're almost ready to go. Let's get Fletcher and Carlsen out, then set up a couple of the others before we disappear. Then we can do the rest from wherever we go.'

They spend hours talking about where their new life together will be built, dreaming out loud about the southwest of France, or inland from Valencia perhaps, or what about the Algarve? Will has more than enough to write a damning exposé of Giorgio and his closest associates, and he'll likely be arrested and incapacitated, unable to ever track them down. They'll set up home somewhere safe and beautiful and with the ten million euros, they'll be able to fund the rehabilitation of many of the young girls Giorgio procured for powerful men in Italy and beyond.

'Okay,' she says. But she's afraid.

* * *

Anastasia remembers Liv from when she first arrived in Milan; she was one of the ones who partied the most. There was something very sweet and innocent about her too. She'd wanted to make it so badly; Anastasia remembers thinking she would have done almost anything, but she listened to the wrong people and ended up doing the wrong things. Now she's addicted to heroin and has been living with one of Giorgio's business associates down in Calabria. He beat her, terrible stuff happened. Anastasia and Will manage to get her out under the pretext of booking her for a job, Anastasia posing as Graziela to make contact. They take her to a remote, rented cabin in the Dolomites to get her clean and take turns seeing to her over the course of two weeks. She reacts terribly in withdrawal, charging around and screaming at Will and Anastasia as if she is possessed. The plan is to send her back to Norway as soon as she's fit to travel. They've bought a little house in Sandefjord as a place for her to start her new life; Liv has expressed a desire for another chance somewhere by the sea, where she can keep a dog and retrain to be a teacher eventually.

That same week, Anastasia discovers her pregnancy. It should have been impossible, though she and Will are sneaking time together at any opportunity, taking bigger and bigger chances to evade Giorgio. She has a moment of intense happiness, believing the baby could be Will's, but deep down, she knows it just isn't. Anastasia goes to see a doctor, who confirms the pregnancy. She's already eleven weeks and realizes that the only time the baby could have been conceived was their wedding night, when Giorgio forced himself on her.

Anastasia doesn't know what to do, or to whom to turn. She worries Will won't want anything to do with her and she also knows Giorgio will hunt her down to the ends of the earth if he finds out she's carrying his baby. At the end of the week, he goes away again, to Palermo this time, so Anastasia is able to get away. Her mind is churning and she feels queasy and emotional that day as she drives back up to the remote valley in the Dolomites where they've hidden Liv, dreading another barrage of abuse from Liv as her body grows accustomed to sobriety. But when she gets there, she finds the cabin cold and dark. At first she thinks Liv has run away, unable to ride out the dreadful withdrawal symptoms for any longer. Anastasia walks slowly from one small room to the next, consumed with dread and anxiety, both over what has become of Liv, and her own situation. In the second room, between the bed and the wall, she finds Liv dead on the floor, having clearly rolled off the bed. It's clear she's taken a massive overdose and has been dead for several days, probably since Will had been to check on her earlier in the week. She must have snuck in the heroin even though she swore she wanted to get clean. Perhaps she did it to know there was a way out if she needed it; they'd never know.

She fishes her phone from her pocket to call Will, only to realize it's already ringing.

'Anastasia?' his voice asks, urgently. In the background, there is commotion, as though he were in a crowded space. She's crying so hard the words won't come. 'Anastasia, can you hear me? Where are you? I'm on my way to get you, we need to leave, now. I think he's onto us, Anastasia. I got home this afternoon, and my apartment had been ransacked. My laptop is gone, and—'

'Will—'

'I just can't think what's going on, it has to be connected.

I've felt eyes on me since the first piece ran. Are you totally sure Giorgio is still in New York? I've just sent the main piece to my editor. We seriously need to get out of here.'

'Will,' she says, again, louder this time. Her eyes rest on the warm, curved timber beams of the little cabin, careful not to stray in the direction of the grotesquely bloated dead woman by the window. 'Liv's dead. I got here, and she was dead.'

It's his idea. *Leave everything you own there. Your clothes. Passport. Take Liv's. Set fire to the place. Walk away. And I'll come get you, my love. We'll be together. Forever. It's all going to be okay.*

This is it – the way out. Another pivotal moment, one she knows she'll revisit in her mind as a turning point. She knows she could get away with passing herself off as Liv Carlsen with a few simple tweaks; people have commented on their similarity before and they'd once even done a shoot together for *Vogue* Serbia that played off on that likeness.

So Anastasia dresses in her clothes and leaves her own things behind in the cabin, then she sets it on fire and walks away; in fact she walks all the way to Austria. It wasn't as difficult as she might have imagined to get to Norway. No one was looking for Liv Carlsen at that point. She was suddenly a Norwegian citizen. She had a house to go to, and plenty of money, held in holding accounts across the globe. But Will never came. Will went to prison for murder and fraud, charges to which he pleaded guilty on all counts, so that she could be free.

43

Anastasia, now

It feels like a dream that my baby came here, that I held him and kissed his face. For a whole day, and long into the dark, cold night I listen out for any sign of him, but with the exception of the helicopter coming in at some point during the day, the silence is thick and loaded. I can't be entirely sure it even happened, that Claudio did that for me. There is a series of sounds as the metal bolts on the door are slid open. Giorgio is standing in the doorway, and I can see the bulky shape of Carl behind him.

'Hi there, *principessa*,' he says. I know the look in his eyes; he doesn't even attempt to cover up his fury, and I no longer have the leverage of Adrian being his son to use. I also have no more strength, nothing more to give. He's going to kill me whether I give him any more information or not. If I could trust him to save Adrian, I'd let him. I won't let him kill any more of the girls to save myself.

'End of the road for you, Anoushka. How does that

feel? You know, I thought we had a deal. You give me the information I want, and your son is safe.'

'Our son.'

'But still, you're stupid enough to play me. Camilla Asunción Gutierrez, Iris Anton, Natalia Guchaeva, Emilia Bashinskaya, Leana Fletcher, they're all gone. What the fuck, Anastasia? So you managed to warn them, or someone else did. Which one is it? Tell me how you did it.'

'On one condition.'

'Hah. A condition.' Giorgio laughs wildly, looking at Carl, who joins in, clearly without having understood a single word. 'Funny how the prisoner thinks she's the one calling the shots here. What do you want?'

'I want you to give me proof that my grandmother is alive and well and pass on a message to her.'

'Lucky for you, I've already thought of good old Vera. In fact, I sent someone out there to that godforsaken hellhole to check on your old babushka. She's doing great. Bent over her flowerbeds as usual. But that whole cute little peasant life of hers is easily ended with a single phone call and you know it.'

'I don't believe you.' But I do. Of course I do. Giorgio will stop at nothing to get what he wants; he never has. He pulls his phone out from his back pocket and scrolls for a long while until he finds what he's looking for. He bends down and turns the screen toward me. I'm looking at Vera walking up the wooden steps to the dacha's decking, a brilliant blue sky behind her. A clutch of earth-covered turnips dangle from her right fist. I burst into tears at the sight of her; I haven't seen her for ten years, and she looks exactly the same except for the lines on her face, which are deeper, and the way she now stoops a little, the top of her back having become rounded with all those long years tending the earth. The quality of the picture is so good I can make out the individual white hairs that have escaped from her usual twin braids emerging from a bright-orange winter kokoshnik. The person who took it must have gotten very, very close and I can't bear the thought of her standing there in the place she feels safest, unaware of a man taking her picture. 'Gio, please,' I whisper. 'You win. Please don't hurt her. And please don't hurt Adrian.'

'Tell me how you did it. I swear to God I will break every fucking bone in her body if you don't tell me how.'

'Will and I hid the money. In Zürich. Aruba. Cayman Islands. I learned how to trade it. I tripled it in two years on the stock market.'

'*You* traded it?'

'Yes.'

'Who would have thought it? I had you down as thick as shit. I assume Graziela helped you.'

'Graziela? No.' Less sinister than her boss, perhaps, but nevertheless a willing and knowing participant in Giorgio's businesses.

'In any case, she's done a runner.'

'Wait. What do you mean?'

'Graziela. She's disappeared. Oh, don't look so worried, I'll be sure to track her down soon enough. Well, I guess we're done here. Oh wait, since you've told me everything, I suppose I should too. After all, a deal is a deal.'

'What do you mean?'

'You must wonder about how I found you. The second thing I did after I realized you had fooled me and were alive was get your lover boy out of jail. Piece of cake, if you're Gio di Vincenzo. Hah.' Gio is pacing around and I can tell how much he is savoring these moments. 'Yes, it was pretty easy to figure out after your note to Osorio. Dumb bitch left it lying around like it was a fucking cookie recipe. "Tell M Lilia is safe."' He relays my note in a high-pitched, mimicky voice. 'Your thick-as-shit boyfriend did exactly what we thought he'd do, went straight to you like a bee to honey. We handed him a car and twenty thousand euros and a lovey-dovey note saying, "The Easter Lilia needs care". And bingo!'

'What was the first thing?'

'What?'

'What was the first thing you did after you realized I was alive? You said releasing Will was the second.' An increasing dread is flooding through me at the thought of what else Giorgio might have done. What if… Then, a terrible thought strikes me. There was something wrong with the picture he showed me of Vera. In it, she'd pulled turnips from the soil. The leaves on the trees at the edge of the forest behind her were orange and yellow. It was taken in autumn, and now it is January; Yekaterinburg will no doubt be buried beneath a thick layer of snow.

'The first thing I did was kill the old woman.'

'No!' I scream, a wild, bloodcurdling scream expelled from my deepest insides.

'I had to, Anoushka. Let's face it, I was a tad angry with you. And she always looked down her peasant nose at me. Now, if you'll excuse me, I have a lot to sort out here this morning—'

'No!' I scream again, scrambling to my feet and launching

myself at Giorgio, managing to grab hold of a handful of his slicked-back hair before Carl throws me against the stone wall. 'No,' I keep screaming, but Giorgio is moving toward the door, visibly shaken by my attack.

'Giorgio, please. Think about Adrian, he needs me...'

'*Giorgio, please. Think about Adrian,*' Giorgio mimics. 'Don't you think I think about my son? He's going to grow up here and he will never want for anything. I'll do everything I can to make him just like me.'

'He's nothing like you and he never will be.'

'We'll see. Oh, no. Actually you won't. Carl and I are taking you on a fun little trip this afternoon. To the Dolomites, a remote valley called val Travenanzes.'

'Gio—'

'Shut the hell up! I took you all over the world, didn't I, Anoushka? Well, I didn't take you there yet, so you shall have that to look forward to. I bet you're itching to get out of here. Wait, you've been before? Oh yes, silly me. And now you shall return. What a perfect little circle. In fact, it was you who recommended it to me. I went there, I fucking grieved for you. But you never thought about that, did you? Anyway, there are some lovely little wooden cabins up there. I bought one, in fact. So we're going to go there. I'm afraid I'll need to tie you up. Then I'll torch it.'

'Gio, please, I'm begging you, for Adrian's sake. Think about your own mother, and what happened to you. What it was like to live without her.'

'You're nothing like my mother. You're a whore. And the boy is better off without you.'

'You won't get away with it.'

'We both know I will.' Carl nods sagely, then he turns

toward the door and the sound of rapidly approaching footsteps. Gio follows his gaze, and then Mario is standing there, looking stressed and urgent, motioning for Gio and Carl to follow. I scream and cry, kicking wildly at the stone wall, I have nothing left to lose now, but I have so little energy I don't last long before I have to sit down. An echo of my desperate voice remains, but then I realize it isn't an echo at all, but someone else's voice, shouting so loudly its sound reaches me through the windowpane. I get back up, slowly; my legs are trembling violently and bile shoots into my mouth, making me gag, but I can see nobody outside. The voice is still shouting, and I slump back down, rocking myself back and forth, thinking about poor Vera's last moments, how she died because of me.

44

Selma

'You've got to be fucking kidding me. Not easily deterred, are you, *Thelma*?' Giorgio's voice is laced with sarcasm. He comes to the gate himself, Mario and Carl trailing behind.

The man standing in front of her only vaguely resembles the man she had lunch with a couple of long days ago. His light-blue shirt is disheveled and a long maroon streak that looks like blood is smeared down its front. His hair rises wildly from his scalp, as though someone has just yanked it. His eyes are narrow slits squinting in the winter sunlight and his lips are curled back in a furious sneer.

'What the hell are you doing here?'

'Can I come in, Mr Vincenzo?' shouts Selma through the gate.

'Get out of here. I'm calling the police.'

'They're already on the way.' Selma turns the phone she's holding in her hand around to show the men that she's recording on Instagram Live. 'Okay, everyone, these are the guys I've been telling you about. The guy in the middle, that's the prince, and those two are his braindead beefcakes—'

'What the hell are you doing?'

'I'm telling *Dagsposten*'s three hundred and fifty-seven thousand followers exactly what you're up to.'

'Look, I'm not sure what it is you're after, exactly, but why don't you come inside, and we can talk calmly about what you believe is going on here.'

'Where is Anastasia Nikitina and Adrian?' shouts Selma. 'What have you done to your wife?'

'What—' A desperate look crosses Giorgio's face, but he quickly recovers himself and smiles his slick, sickening smile. 'You're very mistaken, whatever your name is. Now, come on inside and we'll have a chat.'

'Our chat will be live, watched by thousands of people. In fact, it's going viral right now.'

The gate swings open. Selma steps inside.

'Okay guys, I'm going in. For those of you who just joined us, this is Villa Serafina, near Como, the home of Giorgio di Vincenzo, a man with established links to organized crimes and human trafficking. It has been revealed in recent days that Liv Carlsen, the woman who disappeared with her son from Sandefjord on January 14th, is actually Anastasia di Vincenzo, di Vincenzo's wife who was supposedly murdered in 2010 by American journalist Will Marlow. Marlow was framed, and it's all this man's work.'

Selma is led into the garden room adjoining the zebra-walled dining room and makes sure not to lose sight of the men for a moment, moving the camera between herself and her surroundings. There is no sign of anyone else in the house.

'Where is she, Giorgio?'

'I've told you. She's dead. She died in 2010. Burned to death by her lover boy. This is getting tiresome. I'm sure your fans have better things to do than watch you go off on a mad witch hunt, fabricating lies about respectable people.'

'Respectable people? Wow. Now, where is she? Why don't you give me a tour of this joint?' she stands back up and lets the camera roam the opulent room. Looking at the view count on the screen, she can see ninety-one thousand people watching, and steadily increasing. Giorgio gives Carl a nod and he lurches toward her, knocking the phone from her hand. Giorgio picks up the phone and shakes it.

'Oh no! I think you're losing reception here, *Thelma*. Thick stone walls here at the house. And time to leave. Mario here will show you to the door.' Giorgio switches off the phone and hurls it across the room, and Carl grabs Selma and throws her to the ground. She screams at the top of her lungs, but nobody can hear her now. Carl begins to throttle her, so hard she knows she won't survive even a minute, and Gio is standing over her, watching and nodding, his eyes icy and serpentine.

45

Adrian

At the sound of voices shouting, Adrian quickly gets up from where he was sitting drawing, big teardrops landing on the paper and blurring the pencil strokes. He's drawing his mama on the stone floor in the tiny, dirty red dress, her face bruised but still so beautiful, and in the middle of her chest, where her heart is, Adrian has drawn a little sparrow, its wings spread for flight. He runs out of his room, followed by Hercules, across the hallway to one of the guest suites overlooking the driveway, from where the voices are coming. He can see the tall wrought-iron gates from here and outside stands a woman, shouting. He watches as Giorgio emerges from the house, followed by Mario and Carl. The woman is shouting, and clearly filming Giorgio.

Suddenly, a hand touches his shoulder and Adrian spins around to see Claudio standing there, pressing a finger firmly to his lips, his big, brown eyes wide and serious. Together they slip into the elevator concealed behind the wall panel and as it drops down through Villa Serafina's levels, Adrian can hear the sound of his heart beating wildly.

They run down the corridor to the room where Mama has to sit in the cold, on the floor, and Claudio quickly unlocks the locks and slides the bolts open. Mama is lying on the floor. She's shaking and crying softly and Adrian runs to her, pulling her arm, but as he touches her, she cries out in pain and he recoils to realize how bony and fragile she is. Claudio stoops down and picks her up, helping her to her feet.

'Come quick,' he whispers.

'Vera,' she says, over and over, whispering it like a mantra. Adrian helps Claudio support his mama to the elevator and feels almost afraid of her; she's still muttering to herself and it's as though she's asleep and hasn't even noticed that Adrian has come to rescue her. They press themselves closely together in the elevator and Mama seems to come to, glancing around, a look of intense terror in her eyes. When her eyes rest on him, they soften as the elevator comes to a stop and she reaches out to touch his face so gently, as if she fears he'll disappear at her touch. In the moment before the doors soundlessly slide open, Claudio takes a gun from inside his jacket, shows it to Mama, and disables it with a soft click.

'Run,' he says, and Adrian and Mama rush down the long corridor as quickly as Mama can manage, Claudio following closely behind. It's strangely quiet now, the voices from outside having subsided. Suddenly they hear a thin, strangled cry from further inside the house and the sound of Giorgio chuckling. Adrian wants to scream and shout,

No, Mama, the door is that way, just run, but no words will come, not even a single sound.

Then Claudio is standing in front of Gio, who doesn't hear him approach. He doesn't hear the first gunshot, either, the one that strikes the blond man who is sitting on top of a lady on the floor, in the back of the head. Claudio waits for Gio to turn around, the gun trained straight at him, his finger steady on the trigger.

46

Selma

She comes to at the sound of the gunshots, and suddenly the pressure on her neck is released as Carl's heavy dead body slumps on top of her in a grotesque embrace. Someone shoves him off and she vaguely registers the second body, Giorgio's, on the floor next to her, blood pooling out around his head. A distinguished looking older man is standing above them, lowering the gun that fired the shots, a look of determination and defiance on his face. Behind him stands a woman with a gaunt, bloodied face, sobbing silently. The third man, Mario, is cowering and crying in a corner, covering his head with his tattooed, meaty arms and begging for mercy. The butler puts the gun away inside his jacket and the woman picks a little boy up from the floor and carries him carefully past the debris in the garden room, out onto the terrace, and on the air they hear the wail of sirens, drawing closer.

***

Two days later

She knocks at the door, then pushes it open. Anastasia is on the bed, sitting up, looking pale and tired, with dark bruises running across the side of her face and across her jaw line. The boy is there, curled into the crook of his mother's arm like a birdling in a nest. At the sight of Selma, her face breaks into a smile.

'How are you feeling?' asks Selma.

'I've been better.' They laugh.

'I just wanted to stop in and say hello. And thank you. I'm flying home to Norway this evening.'

'It's me who should thank you.'

'I guess you could say we saved each other. And ourselves. I take it you've heard about Will? Wonderful news.' Anastasia nods, and smiles. 'There is something I wanted to let you know. The other girls you helped, they're all fine. On learning what happened to Clio Amaury, Leana Fletcher realized she'd likely be next and went into hiding after alerting the others.' Anastasia nods, tears streaming down her face at the news and at the mention of Clio. 'It wasn't your fault, Anastasia.' She nods again. 'There are a few things I just don't understand. Would it be okay to ask you just a couple of questions?'

'Sure.'

'How did you manage to keep in touch with Will over the years?'

'I didn't, really. Except for a couple of messages that Tatiana Osorio was able to get to him. Tatiana pretended to still have a heroin addiction even though I helped her get clean. That way, she remained in touch with the men supplying the drugs and Giorgio apparently believed that she was some kind of double agent who worked for him. But I know she wasn't. He killed her when he realized I was alive and she'd been helping me from the inside.'

'Oh, my God,' says Selma, when Anastasia has finished talking. Her voice is hoarse and scratchy from the effort and she leans her head back on the pillow, briefly closing her eyes.

'Indeed. What about Graziela? Has she been found?'

'No, the police are still looking for her. They seem to believe she ran away when she realized I was investigating and it would all come crashing down. Probably hiding out in some palazzo somewhere.'

'Or maybe he's killed her. He was completely paranoid.'

'Yes. One more thing I don't understand. How come Gio never managed to find the other girls after you'd given their names? Who warned them?'

'Leana Fletcher did. She realized what was happening after both Tatiana and Clio ended up dead days after each other.'

'I see.' They fall silent for several long moments, then Selma continues.

'And were you in touch with Vera after what happened in the Dolomites?'

'No. I knew it would endanger her. But I sent her seeds for the gardens every year, always a different lotus flower, because I knew she would understand from its symbolism that it had come from me.'

'What does it symbolize?'

'Rebirth. Like the Easter Lily.'

'Lilia.'
'Yes.'

* * *

She walks through arrivals as though in a daze, image after image from the last few days in Italy playing on repeat in her mind. She's so consumed with her own thoughts that she doesn't realize who or what she is looking at even when she has to step aside to avoid crashing into it, full force.

'Hey,' says a voice. She looks up, into Olav's eyes. 'Welcome home, baby,' he says, pulling her close and Selma lets herself be held, clinging to him, and as she breathes in his familiar scent, the terrible images from Como finally let go and disappear in a blur into the far recesses of her mind. In this moment, her mind grows still, she's not escaping or imagining or worrying or creating or analyzing, she's just standing at Oslo Airport arrivals smiling at the man in front of her.

Epilogue

Anastasia, five months later

It's the first day of June, and when I wake, brilliant sunshine streams into the bedroom, unbroken by walls or ceilings or buildings opposite, pooling on the dark wooden floorboards.

The apartment on the Lower East Side was chosen for its dual-aspect windows that let so much light in, it's like being outside. I've had enough darkness. It's a cozy three-bedroom place, with thick rugs on the floor, some art we both love and chose together, and family pictures everywhere. We're high up, with views over the park and the city. Adrian goes to a wonderful school for neurodiverse children and every day when we pick him up, he rushes out from the gates with a big smile on his face. He launches himself into my arms, then high fives Daddy Will.

As Giorgio di Vincenzo's sole heirs at the time of his death, Adrian and I inherited the entire di Vincenzo estate, from Villa Serafina to Palazzo di Arcimboldo, to Villa Anastasia in Anacapri, as well as over a billion euros in art and assets, an inheritance that will be put to work to benefit and help others.

I went back to Koptyaki at Easter, taking Adrian and Will with me. We buried Vera like a little sparrow in earth that once held an emperor. We stayed at Krasotski Maga, our beloved dacha, sitting out on the deck in the moonlight, huddled beneath blankets, talking long into the night while Adrian slept on the bed in my bedroom inside. Huge swathes of Russian Easter lilies had crept from the earth, symbols of resurrection.

I went back to work, founding the Lilia Foundation, which supports and educates trafficking victims. The foundation operates out of Villa Serafina, which is being adapted to provide residential accommodation for up to forty girls and women who need refuge, rehabilitation, and resurrection.

I blink sleep from my eyes, and squint at the sun flooding the room. I inch closer to Will, breathing in the familiar scent of him, and draw lazy shapes on his chest with my fingertip, careful to avoid the tender dips in his skin where he was struck by bullets. Soon, the door to our bedroom will fly open and a beautiful little boy will burst into the room with his dog, laughing and signaling the beginning of the new day. But for now, all is quiet, and I slowly fill my lungs with air and smile to myself.

My name is Anastasia. This isn't the end; it's the beginning.

Acknowledgements

After She'd Gone is my fifth published novel and I enormously enjoyed writing it, but the writing of a book is only one part of the process, and it could not exist without the work, support and guidance of so many wonderful people.

A very big thank you to my agent extraordinaire, Laura Longrigg, none of this would have been possible without you and I'm so lucky to have you as my agent. A big thank you is due the whole team at MBA Literary Agents, and especially Tim Webb and Andrea Michell. Thank you to Louisa Pritchard for all your incredible work, I am very fortunate to be represented by you in the foreign territories.

To my fantastic editors at Head of Zeus, Madeleine O'Shea and Laura Palmer, *mille grazie*, *merci beaucoup*, *muchas gracias* for all your tireless work on *After She'd Gone*. Your insights and pitch-perfect instincts make a huge difference. Thank you also to the whole team at Head of Zeus, working with you is always a pleasure. A big thank you is also due to Louis Greenberg.

Thank you to my long-standing and much-appreciated writing group, how lucky we are to have each other. A special thank you to Jane Shemilt, for providing me with the most perfect cocoon to write a very unhealthy amount of words in a few days as *After She'd Gone* came together – it feels like the beautiful Oldbury and this book are intrinsically linked.

Thank you to Tricia Wastvedt, I know that you know how much I appreciate you and count my lucky stars for you, but I want to say it anyway.

To all my wonderful friends – you know who you are – I am very fortunate to be surrounded by such awesome people, especially during what have been interesting times, so thank you. A special thank you is due Laura Hadfield, whose friendship is a treasured priority.

To Lisa Lawrence, thank you for showing me instead of telling me.

Thank you to the Norwegian School of London and Wang Ung Sandefjord for the support and the fantastic care that enabled me to concentrate fully on this book.

I always mention the music a novel was written to, because for me it is a huge part of the process, and *After She'd Gone* came to be mostly to the sounds of Emma and Alessandra's 'Pezzo di Cuore', Laura Pausini's *Le Cose Che Vivi* and Antonello Venditti's *Alta Marea*.

A big thank you is also due to my family – my mother, Marianne, my sister, Emmanuelle, my children Oscar, Anastasia and Louison. You are my sanity, reason, motivation and providers of so much love.

About the Author

Alex Dahl is a half-American, half-Norwegian author. Born in Oslo, she studied Russian and German linguistics with international studies, then went on to complete an MA in creative writing at Bath Spa University and an MSc in business management at Bath University. A committed Francophile, Alex loves to travel, and has so far lived in Moscow, Paris, Stuttgart, Sandefjord, Switzerland, Bath and London. She is the author of four other thrillers including *The Boy at the Door*, which was shortlisted for the CWA Debut Dagger.

Rules for the girls' trip:

1) No kids

2) Out-of-office on

3) Keep the drinks flowing

4) DON'T TELL ANYONE WHAT WE'VE DONE

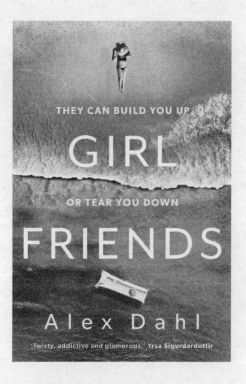

Don't miss the perfect beach read from highly acclaimed author Alex Dahl.

Coming July 2023